W9-BUK-687

HELLA

HELLA

DAVID GERROLD

DAW BOOKS, INC.
DONALD A. WOLLHEIM FOUNDER
1745 Broadway, New York, NY 10019
ELIZABETH R. WOLLHEIM
SHEILA E. GILBERT
PUBLISHERS
www.dawbooks.com

Jacket design by Leo Nickolls.

Interior Design by Fine Design

Edited by Betsy Wollheim.

DAW Book Collectors No. 1855.

Published by DAW Books, Inc.
1745 Broadway, New York, NY 10019.

First Printing, June 2020
1 2 3 4 5 6 7 8 9

DAW TRADEMARK REGISTERED
U.S. PAT. AND TM. OFF. AND FOREIGN COUNTRIES
—MARCA REGISTRADA
HECHO EN U.S.A.

PRINTED IN THE U.S.A.

FOR KARL AND UNA,

WITH LOVE.

I was in the shower.

I like the shower.

I like the way the water floats down.

Mom says it comes down faster on Earth, but I like it this way.

I close my eyes and feel it running down my skin and for a while I can forget the noise in my head.

It's not noise, not really. But sometimes it is.

My phone chirped.

It was Mom, so I had to answer.

I went voice-only so she wouldn't see where I was. She probably knew anyway. She says I spend too much time in the shower. But she doesn't understand why I need to feel it.

"Come home," she said.

"Why?"

"Jamie broke his leg playing soccer."

I didn't know what to say, so I asked, "Did it hurt?"

Mom said, "It's only a green-stick fracture. They're setting it now."

"So why do I have to come home?" I wanted to finish my shower.

"Because Captain Skyler is here."

"But why should I come home?"

But she had already rung off.

It didn't make sense to me. But there's a lot that people say that doesn't make sense to me. So I dried off. I don't like the hot air blasts, but they get me dry. I pulled on a blue longshirt and shorts and headed across the quad. The gym isn't that far from the summer pods.

Captain Skyler was sitting in the main room with Mom. They both looked serious. I can recognize that expression, even without the noise. They stood up when I came in. I still felt damp. It was the air. Hella's air is wet.

"Where's Jamie?" I asked.

"He's still in med bay. His dad is with him. Stand up straight." She turned to Skyler. "I told you. He's too small."

"Half a size, maybe."

"He's three months too young." Five Earth-months and ten Earth-days. But I didn't say that out loud.

Captain Skyler ignored her. He studied me. "You passed your field-readiness tests?"

"Yes, sir." Didn't he know that? Captain Skyler always knows everything. Sometimes I think he has the noise too. But he says he doesn't.

"You know how to operate the surveillance gear?"

"I know how to operate everything, sir." He should have known that too. So why was he asking me?

"Ride-along leaves 0700 tomorrow. Mission briefing is 0630. You'll be in tractor two with me."

I stared at him.

"Did you understand what I said?"

"Yes, sir."

Mom didn't look very happy about it. She must have been arguing with Captain Skyler before I came in. I think she must have lost the argument.

I should explain that. There's this rule on Hella. The way it works, everybody works. Even me.

Especially me.

Because I have the noise.

It's not noise, but I call it that. Because sometimes it feels like that.

Back on Earth, the way Mom tells it—I don't know this from my own experience, I was born on the twelfth voyage—but back on Earth there are too many people and not enough jobs. So every job has lots of people fighting for it.

But here on Hella, there are too many jobs and not enough people. So the rule is that as soon as you're old enough to hold a hammer, you're a carpenter. I don't know what a hammer is or what a carpenter does, but that's the rule. Jamie was eighteen Hella-months older than me, and he'd already done sixteen ride-alongs, four times as a driver.

What the rule means is that everybody has to learn as many different jobs as they can. I'm certified for Class-3 Child Care, Class-2 Farming, Class-2 Emotional Maturity (that's since the noise was installed), Class-3 Food Service, Class-3 History and Civics, Class-3 Data Management (that's the noise, of course), and Class-3 Health Maintenance.

That last one is mostly about keeping things clean, but it's the most important certification of all. You aren't allowed to advance in any other category beyond your current Health Maintenance Certification, so you always have to upgrade that one first. The rule is that if you don't take care of the colony, you can't expect the colony to take care of you.

There's a whole list of Certifications, nearly a hundred. Nobody has ever been certified in more than thirty items. I used to say that I was going to be the first, but Jamie says that the older you are the harder it gets.

Mom wasn't through arguing. "He doesn't have outer gear," she said.

"I can wear Jamie's," I said.

"It doesn't fit you."

"Yes, it does. I tried it on."

"When?"

"When Jamie ordered new. His old gear is too tight for him now. But it fits me."

"You're too small."

"No, I'm not."

"It'll be too loose. And the backpack will be too heavy."

"I'll be in the tractor. I'll be sitting. And if I'm in the tractor, I won't need the gear, will I?"

Hella is only a little dangerous. On a scale of one to ten, with ten being instantly fatal—like the surface of Luna, where I've never been, but I've read about it—Hella is only a three, which is equal to some parts of Earth. It's safe to go outside without protective gear if you stay out of the sun, if you keep your breathing steady and shallow, and if you don't drink any water you didn't bring with you.

That sounds scary, but it's a precaution. Humans haven't been on Hella long enough. We can vaccinate ourselves against all the things we know are out there and all the things we think are out there, but we can't protect ourselves against all the things that might be out there that we don't know. And there aren't a lot of volunteers to beta test new infections. So we have rules. Don't sniff the flowers. Don't eat anything. Don't let a bug fly into your mouth. Don't get scratched or bitten.

"There's only one way to settle this," said Captain Skyler. "Go try it on. Let's see if it fits."

Jamie's gear mostly fit me okay, except it was loose in the shoulders and baggy in the crotch, but Captain Skyler said if we tightened a couple straps it would be okay. The helmet needed a little adjustment too. And I had to wear the suit for fifteen minutes so it could calibrate all its bio sensors, because you have to establish a primary baseline for optimal survival, but the Captain was satisfied with the fit and that was the important thing.

Then after that, both the suit and I had to go through a routine decontamination. Decon works both ways. We don't want strange bugs coming in and we don't want any of our Earth bugs getting out. As curious as we are about the way that Terran biology will interact with Hella biology, we're still taking it slow and careful. We don't want to discover the hard way what happens when staphylococcus marries Hellacoccus. Nobody wants to be the asshole who betrays the First Hundred, even though they weren't really a hundred, only eighty-seven. They landed forty Hella-years ago. Fifteen more pilgrimages had followed the first one. We're not doing too badly, although we're nowhere near what all the initial projections had promised—because we're being meticulous and methodical. That was the mantra.

Anyway, I got scrubbed inside and out, so did the suit—it came back in a sealed bag, with a green tag that certified all its tools and appliances were working in high confidence. I wished I could have done it myself, but you have to be Class 9 to work on outer-gear, and I wouldn't be that for a long time yet. I wouldn't put the suit on again until just before boarding, and that would be in a decon chamber. The suit also came back programmed with my personal color codes, seven stripes making a gradient of blue. So it was officially mine now.

After dinner, I went to see Jamie. He was staying overnight in med bay so they could buzz his broken leg and make the bones heal faster. He looked annoyed. "This was stupid, huh?"

"What happened?"

"I took a bad fall."

"You don't fall."

"This time I did." There was something he wasn't saying, but he didn't want to talk about it. Maybe later.

I pointed at the splint, with all its little colored lights blinking red and yellow and green. "Doesn't that noise make it hard to sleep?"

"I can turn them off. I just like knowing that the buzzbox is doing its work."

"Does it hurt?"

"Nah. But Dad made a big fuss. He pissed off the staff. He wouldn't let the robots set it without a doctor supervising."

"He wants it done right."

Jamie made a face. "I don't need him to micromanage—"

"You're his only kid."

Jamie reached for my hand. I let him take it. I don't like being touched. Jamie is the only one I let. Not even Mom. He gave it a squeeze. "Hey, Squirt?"

"Yeah?"

"Do me a favor?"

"What?"

"It's your first ride-along. Don't get killed."

"I won't."

"They'll put you in a middle car. That's the safest place."

"I know."

"Don't talk too much. Don't say, 'Oh, wow. Look at that!' And you're going to want to. But whatever it is, they've already seen it lotsa times, so don't annoy them. Just do it the way you've been trained, and you'll be fine."

"Okay."

"And don't stress out. There's nothing for you to screw up. The monitors are recording everything, telemetry is total, and mission control will be sniffing every little fart anyway. You're redundant. This is just a test—to see if you can handle going outside. So it's not about the mission, it's about you. Don't screw it up."

"Okay. I won't."

"Does my gear fit you okay?"

"Well enough."

"Yeah, you look like a big wrinkly toad in it."

"Mom sent you a picture, didn't she?"

Jamie grinned. "Have fun. Watch out for booger-jacks."

I don't know why Jamie says that. There's no such thing as booger-jacks.

Hella Colony is almost forty years old. That's in Hella-years, of course. Over one hundred Earth-years old. Some people argue that we should count either from when the first robot probes touched down or from when the first humans landed. But the Hella calendar actually starts with the day the Charter was signed by the First Hundred. The Norteamericanos wanted that day to be May 5 or July 4. The French arrivals wanted July 14. The Brits wanted June 15 and the Chinese wanted October 1, but they'd settle for January 1. Unfortunately, the Hella-year is eighteen months and three days long, so the Earth calendar just doesn't work here.

Eventually, to make everybody equally unhappy, the First Hundred decided to start history with no cultural baggage left over from the past. They signed the Charter on Summer Solstice Day, which falls on the fifteenth of Darwin. All the months are named after great scientists, each representing a different field of study. I was born on the eleventh of Curie. Jamie was born on Mendel 22. Mom's birthday is the third of Turing. We go through the calendar twice, alternating years of male scientists and female scientists. The three days at the end of the year are always dedicated to someone who didn't score a whole month, a different person every year.

Some people are still arguing about which disciplines should have months and which people should be represented. Mom says that's a good thing. It keeps them from arguing over more important issues.

We have over 7,300 people in the colony, split half-and-half between immigrants and here-born. There have been sixteen pilgrimages from Earth. Approximately one every three years. Hella-years. A pilgrimage costs over nine billion caseys, so the funding corporations spread their investments across seven different livable planets. Hella is the most Earth-like so it's maybe the most promising. That's one reason why the expansion has been so slow and cautious.

There's another reason why the expansion has been so careful. Nobody knows what surprises might be waiting for us outside the fence. Nobody wants to be the first to find out. Impatience can be fatal. Too many people learned that the hard way. The best it gets you is your name engraved on the Big Black Wall. And there's a lot of empty space on that wall—so everything we do has to be meticulous and methodical. Help is a long ride away.

Hella wasn't supposed to be named Hella either, but that's what the First Hundred started calling it, and it stuck. There's an official name, but nobody uses it, not even on official documents. I looked it up. It's a silly name.

Hella is nine percent bigger than Earth, but it doesn't have as big an iron-nickel core, so it only has ninety-one percent of Earth's gravity. That means the magnetic field is weaker too, so it can't deflect as much radiation from the primary star. But because the Goldilocks zone is a lot farther out, about 250 million klicks, it sort of balances, and that's why Hella has an eighteen-month year. But the lesser gravity and the greater oxygen levels make it possible for everything to grow a lot bigger. Hella bigger. Even people.

So that's how it got its name.

Marley Layton is a Hella-year older than me. A smidge more than that. Her parents came out on the ninth voyage, mine came out on the tenth. Marley was born here. Mom popped me out two months before docking orbit. So Marley acts like she's better than me, like it counts extra being here-born. Except she's not truly here-born. She was grown in a bottle—one of the first bottle babies after the human wing of the nursery was opened. Pregnancy is supposed to be easier in lighter gravity, but I never heard anyone say it was easy, so that's why they imported the nursery.

Jamie says that Marley was grown in a bottle because none of her three moms wanted to carry her for 280 Earth-days. Like they knew ahead of time what she was going to grow into. But me, I think she's the way she is because her family always told her that she was special and made such a big thing of it that she believes it's really true, and that's why she acts the way she does, everywhere.

Marley is also a half-meter taller than me. Taller than everyone almost. She'd be bigger than that, except they finally turned off her growth hormone. Her primary dad calls her a "Hella Dolly." I guess that's supposed to be funny. That's something else I looked up. That's silly too.

When there's nobody around to see—except the cameras, which nobody looks at unless there's a reason—Marley bumps into me, hard. She hits and punches too. Mom knows I don't like her, but I don't think she knows why. She keeps telling me I have to be nice because her dad is a third-term administrator and we need him to be friendly to us. I don't understand, but Mom says it's important, so I try to keep out of Marley's way as much as I can.

Only thing is, Marley acts like privileges are inherited, not earned.

She has lousy scores in all the service domains, so even though she's six years old, Hella-years (that's sixteen Earth-years), she still hasn't gotten to go outside, not even a ride-along with her dad. And I guess she resents that. Everyone else her age is already pulling time.

So that's why Marley bumped into the table and accidentally-on-purpose dumped my dinner in my lap. "Oops," she said. "I'm sorry. I am *sooo* clumsy." She used that really snotty voice that meant she was anything but sorry. But she made a mistake. She did it in front of Mom. There's a lot of things Mom will put up with—but this wasn't one of them.

"Go clean up," she snapped at me, and then she had Marley by the arm, dragging her out of the cafeteria and off toward Admin. Marley wailed the whole way. "I didn't do anything—"

A shower and a clean longshirt later, I was back in the cafeteria line. This time I skipped the smashed potatoes and gravy. I wasn't really hungry anymore, but if I didn't eat I'd hear about it from both Mom and Captain Skyler.

Jubilee Pershing slid into the seat opposite me, clattering her tray onto the table. I don't hang out with Jubilee, she talks too much, but she seems to know everything about everyone, so she's interesting that way. "So while you were freshing—" she began. "Your Mom took Marley straight to the Councilor offices and registered an official complaint. Deliberate public assault. And they have to accept the complaint because there's a video record." She nodded toward the ceiling camera. "In fact, your mom—she's so cool, you are so lucky—demanded a search of all the video records to prove a pattern of assault against all the littl'uns."

I didn't say anything. I just took another bite and chewed slowly. This was a trick I learned from Mom. You're not supposed to talk with your mouth full, so if you take a bite and chew slowly, you have lots of time to think. I took a big bite.

Finally, I said, "Hm."

Then I took a drink of water. "That's going to be interesting." That was another trick I learned from Mom. Don't volunteer anything. Let the other person do all the talking. Most people can't stand silence, so they have to fill it up with their own words.

Jubilee liked talking anyway, so she didn't notice that I wasn't saying anything. She went on happily. "You know, they'll have to restrict her. They're certainly going to take her off the soccer team. First, she breaks your brother's leg, then she—oh, you didn't know about that? She was fouling him the whole game. She got thrown out finally, but not before she pushed him over a bench—"

"Marley broke his leg?" Jamie didn't tell me that. "Why?"

"I dunno. I guess she had an extra big bowl of grumpy-flakes this morning. I heard she wanted to go out on some big ride-along, but even her dad said no. She didn't have enough points and your brother had seniority anyway and—I guess she was angry about that. Jealous."

Oh. Now it made sense. I didn't say it aloud. If Jamie gets hurt, she's next in line. Except it didn't happen that way, I got chosen instead. Marley got mad, and I got a lapful of dinner. And Mom probably knew the whole story. Jamie's dad too. And certainly Captain Skyler. That's probably why he skipped over Marley in the first place.

I decided I wasn't hungry anymore. I put my sandwich down so I could think. The noise wasn't a lot of help. But I was getting better at figuring out these kinds of things.

This wasn't about the ride-along anymore. It was about me now. Whatever punishment the Councilors might give Marley, she would blame it on Jamie and me and Mom.

But it wasn't just us. Some people thought that Marley might be responsible for a lot of other bad behaviors. There had been vandalism and theft all summer long but always out of camera view so nobody could prove anything. But also, maybe if anyone actually knew anything, they might be more afraid of her dad than her.

Jubilee stopped talking long enough to drink her fruit juice. "You didn't hear this from me, but some people are already talking beyond restriction. They think Marley's going to end up an exile. She is *sooo* out of control."

"That would be very hard to do," I said. It's the kind of thing I say when I don't know what else to say. I wondered if I would vote to put her outside. Yes, I was upset about having to wash my dinner off my lap, but that wasn't bad enough for me to vote to put her outside. I knew what Jamie would say. He'd make a joke. It would be too dangerous—for Hella. Our local predators would get food poisoning.

Sometimes people say that there's another colony somewhere in the northwest, maybe in the jumble just beyond where we send our drones. Supposedly, they're people who went missing and are now living in caves. Supposedly they're eating local fish and fruits. Nobody knows if it's true, or if it is, nobody will say, but if someone is actually surviving outside, without any resources except their own brains, that would be important, wouldn't it? So I guess a lot of people want to believe it's possible, because they want to believe that human beings are essentially meaner and nastier than anything Hella can throw at us.

Jamie says the accounts of the exile colony are just another made-up story that people pretend to believe in—that one day humans will live safely and naturally on Hella. He says that a secret settlement doesn't make sense. If all of us at Summerland Station are working so hard to minimize cross-contamination, why would we turn anyone out into the Hellan ecology? And if they were being exiled from us, then why would they care about honoring our rules?

No, even if it's possible, it's still impossible. There's no way to survive outside any of the stations. There are way too many unknown things out there. Really *big* unknown things. The intelligence engines say that the life-expectancy of an unprotected human in the wild would be less than three days. Twelve if you could stay away from the local kill zones. But you'd still need food and water. There's not a lot of Hellan stuff that's been thoroughly tested and proven safe to eat. There's a lot of stuff we think might be, but we don't know yet. As fast as we can fab the necessary scanning equipment, we still don't have enough lab people to do all the testing. Not yet. Mom says it's something I could be good at. But the real job will take generations. There's just too much that we don't know.

0630.

I'd sat in on briefings before. It's part of the certification process. Every time a mission team goes out, the student teams parallel their operations on simulators. I'd sat in on mission games since I was four. Hella-years, of course. Or nearly eleven Earth-years.

I'd simulated so many missions, I already knew the agenda, and the noise knows everything too. Well, almost everything. Mom likes to say that the noise doesn't know what it doesn't know. That's its biggest flaw.

The briefings work like this.

First, context and purpose, so everybody knows why we're doing this. "This is strictly routine maintenance of our northern on-site surveillance. It's just a little look-see. But we are going out overnight because we're also looking to increase our observations of nocturnal activity on the plains. I could say that we're looking to clear up some anomalies, but everything on this planet is an anomaly. We just want to know what's moving around out there after dark."

Second, everybody reviews the route, so everybody knows where they're going. This morning, Captain Skyler said, "We're taking five trucks to monitor the migration. We'll have eight crew in the forward vehicle, nine crew in the middle, eight crew in the rear. We'll go northeast into the savannah as far as Big Bend, then north along the Dystopic River until we get to Flat Rock. We will not be climbing the rock. We'll turn west, all the way to Little Jumble and then follow the foothills south and then southeast home. It's a three-day ride, give or take half a day."

Third, everybody reviews the specifics, so everybody knows what they're individually doing. "We'll be releasing the new drones every two hours and planting seismic monitors at these sites—here, here, and here. Sniffers and weather stations—here and here and another two up here if possible. Replace or repair these two remotes which have gone offline. Your checklists have been downloaded to your vehicles."

And finally, safety instructions, because there are always safety instructions: "Nothing in this mission requires anyone to put themselves in harm's way. We will take no unnecessary risks. You're to avoid close contact with the herds and especially any of their outliers—those are the most dangerous. Over here, this red circle, Grumpy-Butt and his family are feeding off a land-whale. That should keep them happy for a week or two, but let's give them a wide berth anyway.

"We've got high confidence that our local predators are tagged and located, but as always we can't guarantee that there aren't a few hungry juveniles wandering through. They'll be following the migrations. Your monitors will warn you if you get within ten klicks of any of the locals, and the drones will be watching for tourists. As always, safety procedures take precedence over all other operations. Stop often, at least once a klick, and listen for thumps and sniff for trace. We'll have six lifters sitting hot on the pad. If anything with teeth even grunts in your direction, holler and all six will be airborne in thirty seconds. I know that a couple of you have been calling this a ride in the park. It isn't—it never is. And it never will be—at least, not in our lifetimes.

And those who think that way won't be riding out on any mission that I'm running. Any questions?" Captain Skyler stood next to the big display and waited.

Usually there aren't any questions. Captain Skyler always publishes the mission objectives and briefing books a day or two in advance, and everybody assigned would have the appropriate checklists on their tabs. But today, a hand went up. Lieutenant Bo-Say. "I'm not clear about one thing. Why are we going out so far? Wouldn't this be better in two operations? One close, one far?"

Captain Skyler nodded. "Ordinarily, yes. But time and cost analysis gives us a forty percent advantage. And we need to have all the monitors operational before the tenth of Curie. There's an important birthday coming up, right, Kyle?" He turned back to the screen, pointed at the map. "It's been a good year for the herds. Most of the calves survived. So we're looking at an aggravated situation when they get here. Not just the herds, but the predator packs as well. If we run this operation now, we can go to Lockdown three days early. It's about margin."

That was the way Captain Skyler always talked. He talked about plans and consequences and cost-effectiveness and investment of resources and always with one eye on the calendar. So I didn't understand why Lieutenant Bo-Say asked the question. Unless the question was about me and that's why he said what he did. Why were they taking me along on a three-day drive-around? Wouldn't it be better for my first ride-along to be a close perimeter check? Maybe the Captain was trying to make a point and the point wasn't about me. Maybe it was about . . . I don't know. He didn't need me, he could have left me at home. Maybe this was about making a point to Marley—or her dad. Jubilee said that Captain Skyler might be running for a councilor's chair next election. I need to pay more attention to those things. I'll be able to vote soon, not on everything, but some things. I have Class 3 Certifications in six domains, I only need one more Certification for my 5th birthday to be a Passage Ceremony, that's what Captain Skyler was hinting at.

Captain Skyler looked at his pad. "Suit up. We roll in fifteen."

Three concentric fences surround Summerland Station. After the Big Break-In—I remember it because it was just before my fourth birthday, and I never had a real birthday party—the Council ordered planning for a fourth fence, but it got slogged down in arguments about whether or not we should establish a second summer station instead. Shouldn't we decentralize? We're three years past the time-line. But whichever side of the argument was right, it didn't matter. We didn't have the resources to do either. Not enough people. Not enough machines. Not yet.

The fences are made from Atlas trees. That's what everybody calls them. The scientific name has too many syllables, but it mostly means the same thing: "Holy crap! Can a tree really grow that tall?"

On Hella, it can. A fully grown Atlas tree can be three thousand years old (Hella-years) and easily 150 meters high. There are even older and taller trees in some of the eastern reaches, but aside from the drones and robots and satellite scans, we haven't explored any-where near as much beyond our range as we'd like to. There's just too much planet.

At its base, an Atlas trunk is so thick you could carve out a house inside. A large house. How safe it would be with all that unsupported weight above, I don't know, but I wouldn't sleep comfortable. It can take more than a month to bring down an Atlas tree. A year is eigh-teen months, a month is thirty-six thirty-six-hour days. So that should give some idea how big a job it is. In the history of the colony, we've only done it twice. And probably never again. We still haven't used up all the wood from the first felling and most of the second felling is still in the forest. It's a formidable barrier all by itself. That was the original plan—to make a wall by putting sections of trunk all around the Summerland Station, but the logistics of carving a road and dragging the pieces were impossible. Well, not impossible, but ultimately impractical. It's another thing that isn't "cost-effective." We don't have the heavy machinery for the job. We'd have to fabricate two or three new fabricators just to print all the pieces we'd need. It's too ambitious. We had an easier solution.

An Atlas tree has the right size branches. We can send a crew up top and they can find exactly the size and length desired. We never take more than one or two from any tree. We don't know how much injury a tree can take, and we can't risk killing a whole slice of forest. We don't know what consequences there might be, probably none of them good.

Two scooters can pull a branch, but even a small branch can be as big as an Earth sequoia. You get enough of them, and you can build a pretty sturdy fence. You put up anchor-towers every thirty or forty meters, you stack your branches like crossbeams with enough space between them for a person to scramble through, but you couldn't if you wanted to, there are carbon-fiber nets on the fences to keep the smaller creatures out, and you send out scuttlebots to patrol the spaces between, checking for breaks or intrusions. It mostly works. And afterward, you tell yourself it seemed like a good idea at the time. Because anytime we forget, the planet is quick to remind us how the laws of physics work on a Hella scale.

It's not just that everything is bigger—it's that big moves differently than little. It's not about size, it's about mass. And if enough mass leans on a fence, you find out the hard way that you've got to have lateral shoring too. That's why the fences now have a triangular cross-section. And maybe this time they'll hold.

We still have to work to stop the littler creatures, the mice-like things and the lizard-like things. The scuttlebots help, but every so often we still have to shut everything down for a sterilization. We're still working on the problem.

Anyway. We rolled out early.

First we launched the drones, "the umbrella." As soon as they were up and confident, the trucks powered up. We exited through a gated tunnel. Like the fence itself, it's made of giant horizontally spaced logs. The three gates work like a kind of double airlock, so nothing unwanted can get in easily. But it takes time to get through them, because they're heavy and slow to move. And it takes a while to cycle five trucks through. We didn't always send this many trucks out a time, but this was a shakedown cruise for the newest one and practice for the seasonal migration when most of us would be moving to Winterland.

We rolled out past the final gate and down the slope and out toward the plain and the view opened up before me—and for a moment I felt very uncomfortable. I'd never been out here before, only in simulations. In the sims, I know I'm safe, no matter how scary the situation. But here, I suddenly felt naked and unprotected, as if just rolling out the gate would attract a dozen hungries.

But there's this thing I do. I go to the noise and it calms me down. It sends a signal back that everything is all right. That wouldn't be the best response to a dangerous situation, but it's the best response to irrational fear. That's what Mom says anyway.

Captain Skyler was down in the bridge. I was topside in an observation turret, but he must have been monitoring me on his display. He said, "You made it. You are now a candidate for Class 3," and that made everything all right. Now I could get my seventh.

Outside the truck, Hella looks empty. The biggest trucks are called Rollagons. The Rollagons have huge honeycomb tires, three times as tall as the tallest man on Hella and more than a man-length wide.

During migrations and storms they have chain tracks, and sometimes just because the Captain thinks it's a good idea. Like always.

We have two dozen at Summerland and another two dozen at Winterland, they convoy back and forth all year—except during storms. The Rollagons are tall, five or six stories, depending on how they're outfitted, and big enough that you could play tennis on the lifter deck on top. The bridge was just forward of the lifter deck and there were six turrets spaced around the edges, so everybody on shift always had a good view.

Tall summer stiffgrass surrounded us on all sides, making visibility across the plain an interesting challenge. It was like an ocean of rippling yellow. Captain Skyler said the stalks were high enough to hide an elephant—he'd seen elephants on Earth, I'd only seen pictures, but they're big. Not as big as Hella-critters, but still big. The grass was hardening, getting stiffer every day. If it weren't for the autumn fires and even our own regular burnoffs, Summerland Station would be lost inside a forest of things like bamboo.

Ahead, in the distance, scattered clusters of pink-trees waved in the wind. They stuck out of the yellow sea, towering thirty or forty meters high. The pink-trees are very thin, they don't have any low branches, only high ones with broad leaves of orange and red, sometimes shading all the way to deep purple, sometimes so dark they look black. But their long necks are mostly pink, so that's why they're called pink-trees.

They aren't really trees. Even though they're rooted, they're part animal, and instead of bark they have layers of pale skin, thin as paper, that peel away in long strips in molting season. They all grow from a common root system, so they only occur in thick clusters that we call families, but they're so very tall, and they have such broad leaves, that we called them trees anyway. Someday we'll figure out a better term for what they really are. Anyway, they wave gently whether there's wind or not.

The very tallest pink-trees in this family had leaves ten or more meters across, stark red with white veins outlining and highlighting them. Maybe they were the daddy-trees, that's what some people thought, but nobody was sure yet. It was the trees that huddled beneath them that had the darker foliage, all the way from red to purple, maybe those were the mommy-trees. But the very smallest trees at the edges of the cluster sparkled with leaves so pink and pale they were almost white. Right now we think that the colors reveal their separate genders—males and females, but nobody knows yet what the pale colors mean. Maybe those are the children? Nobody is sure. Life on Hella is on a different evolutionary path.

Past the pink-trees, we splashed across Little Stream and a little while after that Little Big Stream. We gave a wide berth to Deadly Hollow—long before the First Hundred landed, it had been a deep crater from a meteor strike, but now it was just a wide hole that filled up with water every rainy season and then turned into a dangerous mudhole when it dried out in the long summer.

Down inside, Deadly Hollow had a whole other ecosystem, shifting with the seasons. Raingrass, springblooms, mud-ivy, drygrass, and eventually autumn spracklies. Some of the scientists believed that these were different expressions of the same species, or maybe several symbiotic ones. Like I said, nobody knows. We just don't have enough people yet to study everything. There's just too much here.

A few klicks further and the savannah stretched away in a long slope down and then a longer slope up toward a horizon so far away that it doesn't make visual sense. Even the electronic range finders sometimes get confused. The land is an endless plain of yellow and pink. Even the slightest whisper of wind sends ripples of color shimmering across the land.

This far out on the plain, the clusters of trees and tree-things occur less frequently because this is a major part of the migration path. Either the tree-things don't want to be trampled or the ones that grew here all got eaten. We're not sure yet. Instead, the summer stiffgrass gets higher and thicker on the plain, maybe because it gets better fertilization from the way the herds stir up the earth, leaving a swampy wake of dung and urine behind them, so the grass gets thick enough to be a real problem for even the biggest vehicles. But we would have traveled slowly anyway.

Sometimes the ground is deceptive and a truck can sink halfway into soft dirt. So we go slow and test everything ahead. The lead vehicle always has a huge water-filled roller in front, flattening a path through the sea of yellow so the trucks behind can follow. Sometimes all the trucks have rollers and sometimes all the trucks are linked by strong chains in case one of them has to be pulled out of a hole or up a hill. Some people say this is an unnecessary precaution, that we've never had a single truck get stuck, but Captain Skyler just says, "Let's keep it that way." We can't afford to lose a Rollagon. Especially not this close to migration.

The bridge of the truck sticks out forward. It has a slanted window, so the bridge crew can look straight down at the ground in front of the vehicle. The bridge is wide enough to seat twenty people across, although usually there's only four in front. Just behind, there's a galley, sleeping bays, life-support services, and a complete communications deck. On each side of the Rollagon is a six-person airlock opening out to a big platform where all kinds of different equipment can be anchored, construction equipment, cranes, even heavy gauge weapons. The official designation is HellaCruiser and you can carry as many as sixty people on journey, if you have to. If they're friendly, you can carry even more. If you replace half the cargo bays with living quarters, like we do with migrations, you can carry a few hundred. And it's possible to triple or quadruple stack additional life support modules in case of emergency evacuation.

Just above the bridge are two lookout turrets with 360-degree coverage. The turrets can focus all kinds of sensors, but they also control industrial lasers, plasma beams, flamethrowers, railguns, and missile launchers, enough weaponry to fight a small war. Because that's how bad some of the predators can be. It doesn't happen very often, but after the first time, the First Hundred decided there wouldn't be a second time.

I rode in the port side turret, just above and behind Captain Skyler. It was a great view, more than six stories up—high enough that I could see distant furrows in the grass where previous vehicles had cut wide swaths and the grass still hadn't recovered. At least, I hoped those channels had been made by Rollagons. The grass recovers fast, so most lines begin to disappear within a few days, and these looked fairly recent. Whatever had cut those paths, I still wouldn't want to be down in that grass alone. Even a startled hopper can be dangerous. I would rather be up here, where it's safer.

The cabin is pressurized and filtered and temp-controlled, so I didn't need to wear my helmet or rebreather, and my suit could keep itself plugged in and charged and monitored. The displays in front of me echoed all the ones on the bridge, so I could see everything that Captain Skyler saw. In an emergency one person could control the entire vehicle from any turret. I was just thinking about that when Captain Skyler called up, "Yo, newboy? You want to drive?"

"Sir?"

"You want to drive?"

"Uh. Yes, sir."

"Take the controls then."

"Taking control." My display flashed green, and I reviewed all the controls in order: speed, terrain, location, orientation, path, and envi-

ronment both internal and external. We were already on
there really wasn't anything for me to do except watch
They were all green. Confidence was high.

The lead truck would automatically locate and steer
hidden obstacles. All we had to do was follow. Still, I was
sible for the vehicle and if I felt bold enough, I could even
autopilot and steered myself. I didn't feel that bold.

I could see my reflection in one of the screens in fron
smiling, something I don't do very often. Jamie would
though. I noticed it from the inside too. Not just a smil
the folks at home could see me now—then I realized th
they would be watching on the mission monitors an
simulators. Marley must be steaming. Not that it matt
thought. In addition to the Certification, this qualified r
grade of Field Service.

After a bit, I realized that Captain Skyler had don
pose. He was making a point. Not just to me, but to
well. Maybe Mom would explain when we got back.
have to listen to Jubilee's version.

The first half hour, there wasn't much for me to do
the monitors and the billowing grass, so Captain Skyl
checks and drills. It didn't matter that the ground cr
certified the cruisers. Every good commander does
checks. And sometimes drills.

I suppose that all the continual maintenance and
boring to anyone watching from behind the fence—a
realize how important it is to have everything green
highest confidence. Maybe in the story videos, adv
kicking in the front door, but in the real world you d
can to keep that door locked. Adventures don't always
ings. Jamie says that if people don't get hurt or die, it i

When we reached Big Nothing, Captain Skyler passed control to rgeant Jackle and acknowledged me with a simple, "Well done. You ln't drive us into a ditch." That was a weird kind of compliment. I ver had personal control of the vehicle, but I guess knowing when keep your hands to yourself is just as important as knowing en to get hands-on, so I took it as the right kind of compliment.

After another hour, the Captain put me on galley duty, and I made ndwiches and coffee for everyone. Mango slices and lettuce on eetbread. Greenradish mustard on the side in case anyone wanted ra tang. Fizzy limonade to drink. There were no complaints from one. It was the same menu we'd have had at Summerland Station. akfast at the caf is usually fruit and cereal. Lunch is salad and noo- s and assorted cooked veggies, and almost always a lot of rice and ns. Dinner is the heavy protein, tank-grown meat, potatoes, more and beans, and always more veggies. Sometimes lunch and din- are swapped, depending on the work load and the energy and diet uirements. Variety is still limited. We're not up to what Mom calls a Standard menu, but nobody's starving. We're installing new ks this year, so we're close to getting there. If we don't have another Break-In. It's all about work and patience and service. That's what m says. She says it almost every day. I think she says it to remind elf more than remind anyone else.

ome people don't like having to do service chores. They think it's eaning to wait on other people, but I like it. I'm not good at talking eople, so service gives me something to do. I'm a good listener, when people think I'm not listening or when they think I don't erstand, so I know stuff, a lot of stuff, sometimes a lot more than upposed to know. I know what a lot of people think about a lot of r people, and sometimes that can be really useful. That is, if I can e it out. Sometimes it takes a while, a week, a month, or maybe

even a year. And some stuff never makes sense. Not to me, anyway. Not even with the noise.

The noise is good for a lot of things, but there are some things it can't do.

The scenery changes fast on Hella. And there are a lot of things that require hands-on and eyes-on. We could send bots outside the fences, but we can't replace them as fast as we would lose them, so we have to keep our maps up-to-date.

There's this general feeling in the Hella Colony that we'll never conquer the planet if we hide behind the fences of Summerland Station. So we have to go out ourselves, smell the air and taste the world. We have to feel the dirt between our fingers. If we are ever going to make this planet ours, we have to give up our fear of it and get into a genuinely courageous relationship. That's what Captain Skyler says.

But that doesn't mean we have to be foolish about it. Captain Skyler doesn't take chances. After the Big Break-In, he set up a lot of very strict security procedures that everyone has to follow. While most of the records of his missions are publicly available, some are not. The reasons vary. Mom says it's because there's a lot of stuff that would be embarrassing or painful to others. So those files are locked for twenty years or more. You have to have special clearance to view them, and you have to promise not to tell what you've seen. Mom has had access to some of the stuff about the Big Break-In, because that's when my dad was killed. But she won't talk about it. Not to me anyway.

After lunch, Captain Skyler put me on weather watch. We had a mild storm front moving in from high in the northeast, but it was still a week away. If it got here at all. Probably not. It was too early for tornadoes anyway. But just the same, Hella could be unpredictable. Hellacious has a whole other meaning here.

We arrived at First Marker at 1430. We were now officially on the savannah. We paused for twenty minutes to calibrate, upload, download, synchronize, and all the other stuff you do at First Marker. It's also the first bathroom break. Not that you have to wait if you really have to go, it's just that there are procedures and rules about keeping every position crewed and green, so it's one more thing we have to manage. Timing. It's about timing.

There's also an experimental plot at First Marker. A few years ago, they cleared a couple of acres, burned it free of local life, then seeded it with various Terran species. Corn, tomatoes, potatoes, wheat, rye, barley, grapes, and even a few citrus trees. There are a dozen cameras and a couple of little-bots watching the plot, but from time to time, Ag Lab asks a team to bring back samples for testing. And tasting—after irradiation, of course. Mostly the Earth plants behave in the wild the same way they do in the greenhouses. They get taller. Outside though, the leaves get a lot bigger and so do the roots and fruits. Sometimes the leaves change color and even get narrower because the sunlight is so bright.

Jamie says the different spectrum of the primary has a weird effect on plants grown outside. The plants get different colors of light than they do in the greenhouses. And there are mutations too. We can't really keep up with all the raw data we're collecting. We just gather the information and send it back to Earth with every return voyage of the *Cascade.* Supposedly, they turn it over to the data-diddlers crowd-crunching, which is like crowd-sourcing only more so.

Everybody knows about the test plot, but it's one thing to see it on a big 3D wall and it's a whole other thing to see it in real life. So when Captain Skyler told me to suit up and grab a collecting kit, I got excited.

Outside! I jammed on my helmet and scrambled for the airlock. But when I slid down the ladder, I saw he wasn't wearing his helmet.

"Do you have all your vaccinations?"

"You know I do."

He thumped the top of my head and said, "Well, then take off the brain bucket. You need to smell this with your own nose."

Take off the helmet—?

He saw me hesitate. We weren't supposed to do that out here, were we?

"It's okay, Kyle. It's only air. You breathe it all the time. It's the same air we have at home."

I wasn't sure about that, but I trust Captain Skyler. So I unclipped the safety strap and lifted it slowly off my head—

The day was bright. Too bright. And hot! I blinked in the harsh sunlight, it seemed to give everything a sharp blue edge. It made my eyes water. "Ouch!"

"Yes. That's one reaction. When you're ready, open your eyes again. Take a deep breath. Tell me what you smell."

I sniffed. A little at first. Then a little more. "I'm not sure," I said. I inhaled again. "Something sweet. Is that the grass? Something else too." I looked up at him. "Does blue have a smell?"

"That's what air smells like when it doesn't come from a can. That's air so fresh it's never been breathed before. Not by anyone from Earth."

I started to take another deep breath, but he stopped me. "Uh-uh. You know better than that. You'll get dizzy. Slow shallow breaths. Remember? Or put on your rebreather."

I didn't want to, but it was probably safer. If I put on the rebreather I wouldn't have to worry about my oxygen levels, so this was probably another test to see if I would be reckless or careful.

Captain Skyler pointed me toward a row of tomato vines. "See how the leaves have frayed edges? Something's been chewing on them, tasting to see if they're any good. Collect a few leaves for the lab. But more important, look for droppings. They might look like little black raisins. Or even big black raisins. Anything you're not sure of, photograph and bag it. Oh, and grab a couple of the tomatoes too."

"They're not ripe yet—"

"Not for eating. For the lab."

"Yes, sir."

I went down the row, taking care where I stepped, photographing everything. Maybe if I found some interesting new species, they'd name it after me. There is no shortage of undiscovered plants and animals on Hella, so I collected samples of everything that looked unusual, which was pretty much everything.

After twenty minutes, Captain Skyler called me back. Despite the air conditioning in Jamie's suit—my suit now—I still felt sweaty.

"Find anything?" he asked.

I held up a box of collection vials. "Lotsa raisins."

He peered close. "Yeah, that looks like the same little munchers. Nothing new. But the lab will be interested to see if they're digesting Terran cellulose any better. This many generations in, we should start seeing some adaptation. Good job." He touched his com-set. "Everybody up. We roll in five."

Back in the trucks, we headed as straight across the plain as the terrain would allow. The grass was taller here and a lot stiffer. It crunched beneath the tires of the trucks. Here and there, we crossed furrows cut by things that were not Rollagons. We didn't see any animals. Not during the heat of the day. They'd be seeking their own shelter.

But Captain Skyler had us all watching out anyway, not just the scanner displays, but the eyeball view as well. Plus we had an umbrella of six drones, three orbiting close and three more circling at a distance. We stopped every ten or fifteen minutes to look and listen and sniff. Sometimes we got out of the truck to gather samples of dirt and grass. A few times we sank monitors into the ground. And whenever we crossed a furrow cut through the grass, two or three of us would get out and follow it in one direction and two or three would follow it in the other, all of us looking for footprints and droppings. This time we wore our helmets. I was "the mouse."

Let me explain that.

Everyone else wore battle helmets, which have integrated weapon displays. I did not. I wore a special helmet with two big parabolic receivers, mounted at ten and two o'clock positions. It also had a conical snout for sniffing the air. And it had two saucer-sized lenses for the primary eyes. The whole thing looked like a famous Earth mouse, so that was why they called whoever wore the helmet "the mouse."

But it's very practical.

The big eyes record everything in ultra-high resolution stereoscopy, other cameras spaced around the helmet pick up a 360-degree view, enough for a complete holographic recreation for mission control. They almost always watch in real time, sometimes in VR sets. The battle helmets do the same, but they don't have all the scientific sensors.

The interior display of the mouse compresses the spectrum so that the wearer sees a wider representation of frequencies—all the way from the darkest ultraviolet to the deepest infrared. The parabolic dishes are ultra-sensitive ears. They scan for all kinds of auditory signals, and they compress that spectrum as well. So the wearer can hear the ultra-high frequency shrieks of bat-things as well as the very low frequency subsonic rumbles produced by the saurs. It's possible to hear their footsteps from as far away as ten or fifteen kilometers, depending on the local geology. If you wait until you can feel the ground shaking, it's probably too late.

The conical rebreather on the front of the helmet adds enough carbon dioxide to every breath so that the wearer doesn't accidentally go hyper-toxic from too much oxygen, but more important it also sniffs the air for all kinds of particles—it's an electronic super-nose. The helmet integrates all this information and superimposes the augmented data onto the display. It even includes a visual representation of all the various smells and odors and scents it can recognize. It shows us which way the scents are blowing and that helps us know from which direction any carnivores are most likely to approach.

The odor overlay on the display can get very complex because there are so many different smells in the air. The plants and flowers give off pheromones to attract insects and even herbivores of all sizes. These usually show up as pale blue or violet. But the bigger herbivores, especially the saurs, they leave orange and yellow scent trails that can hang in the air for days and be carried hundreds of klicks downwind, so the predators always know where the herds are.

Before anyone can be trusted to go outside, they have to play a lot of simulations. Jamie told me I should think of each one as a puzzle. What problem do you have to solve? Even without the noise helping me—I wasn't allowed to use it anyway in the simulators—I could tell how fresh a scent was and which way the herd was headed. Knowing where the herds are is important if we want to avoid the things that follow and feed on them. There are a lot of those, from the very small to the very large. The large ones usually leave bright red swaths of stink floating in the air. A lot of times you don't need the display, you can smell it yourself.

Wearing the mouse helmet is supposed to be a special privilege. But the job of the mouse isn't.

I collected dung.

Or anything else that might have fallen off of or out of whatever made this particular channel in the grass.

Down on the ground, we were in an amber canyon with walls that waved and rustled. We were swimmers in a dusty yellow smell, and sometimes overpowered with the occasional stink of dung. If it was from a herbivore, the dung would have a grassy smell. If it was from a predator, it had a darker stink, sometimes so bad I could smell it in the helmet. Some of the piles of dung were as tall as Marley, and still moist though fortunately not steaming. That would have meant we were way too close to something dangerous.

It wasn't hard work. It was methodical. I'm good at methodical stuff, so I didn't mind. But other people do. They think it's a dirty job. I wondered if this was the reason Captain Skyler had brought me along, so nobody else would have to do it. But I'm a scientist. I think it's exciting. Most of science is gathering a lot of facts and looking for patterns

And it's not a dirty job. I would put the collection bag over my hand, grab a fistful of dung, then turn the bag inside out around the dung and slide the seal shut with my other hand. Usually, it was herbivore stuff, dryish lumps of stuff, mostly grass or even pink-tree skin, but on one of our stops we found a different kind of heap. It was dark and gooey. It had thick fragments of bone throughout. I tried not to think about where those pieces of bone had come from, but I knew that the lab techs back at the station were already getting excited in anticipation. I could hear their chatter in the noise.

We didn't stay on the ground too long in any one place. Fifteen or twenty minutes max. It was almost as if we were afraid that the grass would grow so tall around us we'd never get out. Some people say you can actually see the grass growing. You can certainly hear it, an endless whispering. Sometimes, you can almost make out the words. It sounds like, "What are these things? Who are these strangers?"

Jamie says that people go grass crazy sometimes. Not the teams, they're too well-trained. But sometimes it's someone who just arrived on Hella and who can't adjust. One day, they walk outside, climb over or under or through the fence, walk out into the stuff and disappear. It's the grass, the tall smothering stiffgrass. It always wins. Knock it down, it comes back. Burn it, it comes back. The grass is forever.

People who've never been out in the grass don't get it. I didn't understand what Jamie was talking about until I stood in the middle of a furrow, looking around at this very narrow world, a shadow valley with only a bright strip of sky above to remember there's a horizon somewhere. I didn't want to stumble into a gigantic footprint. It would be a fearsome reminder that something monstrous made this the topless tunnel. If I walked far enough I'd find it. And if I went the other way, following backward from the footprints, I'd be just as likely to find something even worse, something large and hungry creeping up the channel from behind.

But Captain Skyler says you have to get down on the ground to understand. After you know how hard it is for the Rollagons to push through the stiffgrass, then you can start to imagine how big and how powerful an animal would have to be to push through by itself. It's not that any individual stalk of grass is resistant. One at a time, they're just a little crunchy. But when you shove against the whole bulk of all that yellow straw, it builds up into a big stubborn mass. Sometimes the grass is so stiff and dry we have to put laser cutters on the lead vehicle, but even that's a problem because by the end of the summer the grass is so dry it catches fire. That's why we mostly use the big rollers to crush it, and the trucks travel single file.

One time, a team nearly did incinerate themselves until they could get upwind of the blaze, but that happened before I was born. That's when the water-filled rollers were added to the front of the Rollagons. Now if it happens, we can use the water in the rollers to put out any fire we might start. Except now we're a lot more careful. There's still so much to learn about Hella.

By 1800 the sun was at its peak, and the temperatures outside were rising uncomfortably. We stopped to release the second shift of drones and retrieve the first shift for detoxing. We couldn't risk them picking up Hellan microbes, and we try to minimize the risk of spreading our own. We know we can't, but we can't be careless either.

We were deep into the migration path now and in another week this would be one of the most dangerous places on the planet, the saurs were coming, thousands of them—but sometimes there were loners pushing ahead and we had to watch out for them. We'd planted over a hundred sensors this morning, drilling them deep into the ground at regular intervals. Maybe half of them would survive the ramming this terrain was about to experience, but we needed the monitoring.

The thing is—as dangerous as Hella can be, sometimes it's us, the invaders, who are even more dangerous. Jamie says we're the most dangerous species on the planet. Especially to each other. That's what happened on Earth and if we're not careful, it'll happen again here. Jamie didn't figure that out for himself. He was telling me what he overheard Captain Skyler say about Councilor Layton, Marley's dad. Mom doesn't like the Councilor for a different reason. She thinks he's a bad parent.

Captain Skyler ordered the trucks into a starfish shape, back ends touching, noses pointed outward. "Four hour nap," he ordered. "Three on watch in each truck." He pointed at me. "You take first watch port side. Wake Sergeant Orion in an hour. Call me if anything larger than a lizard farts."

I climbed up into the port side turret and settled myself in a huge comfortable observation couch, way too big for me. I had to adjust the back and foot rests. The display in front of me showed a 360-degree view, spread out in a horizontal strip with the rear view split at the edges. All the trucks were linked together, so the image was a correlated composite, high dynamic range, overlaid with augments and readouts. I could scan the horizon at various magnifications, and I could slide the image right or left across the display to look closer at any part of the surrounding terrain, but it all looked the same. Just a flat sea of rippling yellow waves. Nothing else was moving that I could see. Nothing was moving in the infra-red either. No heat signatures.

I did see a few hoppers perched on a nearby rise. They took turns, lifting themselves up, standing erect to look around, their long snouts pointing and sniffing. You can tell how old a hopper is by the color of its fur. The pups are brownish, the adults fade to yellow and eventually some color that isn't white or pink or anything else, but it is bright. Every few minutes, one or another would notice us. It would stiffen and stand tall on its hind legs. Its head crest puffing up tall, a warning I guess. Then all the hoppers would peer out into the distance, ears wide, noses wiggling. After a bit, the first one's crest would flatten, the ears would droop, and most of the others would drop back down and resume digging for whatever it was that hoppers dig for. Insects and grubs probably. If they could find a nest, the whole family would eat.

The hoppers were a good sign. Hoppers will leave the savannah long before the migration passes through, probably as soon as they feel the first ground-tremblings or hear the saurs' subsonic grumbles or maybe just smell the first smells. Or maybe something else. All of our different monitors showed the main bulk of the herd was still over a hundred klicks away, but in ten days or less, all this tall grass would be flattened to a sodden mess by hundreds of giant feet. Maybe thousands.

The herd would spend a day or two at the Big Muddy River drinking and wallowing, consuming and regurgitating, flushing their systems, cleaning themselves inside and out—and also widening the river channel even more. They'd drink up tens of thousands of gallons of sluggish brown water and piss half of it back into what would end up as a slowly rolling syrup. Downstream of the crossing, the water would reek for weeks.

Then, as they moved eastward again, they'd continue pissing and crapping, poisoning the present but fertilizing the future. They'd leave an ugly brown swath wide enough to be seen from space, and the plain would stink even more than the river, but the land would be rejuvenated and the winter grass would flourish for a few weeks until the ice storms swept down from the north.

But before the storms arrived, most everyone at Summerland would have evacuated south to Winterland, leaving only a maintenance team in place. Winterland Station was on the dry southern shore of the continent. It was cold and windy, but it wasn't buried under ten meters of snow on a good day and thirty on the worst.

I noticed a smudge of dust on the horizon. A cloud? Maybe. I zoomed in for a closer look. I couldn't tell. Too much haze in the air. I sent the nearest drone to loop around. From above, the view was just as vague. Haze or cloud or maybe something else? I frowned at the screen. Was this bigger than a lizard fart? I had to go deeper into the noise to find out.

I told the drone to swoop in lower, but not too low. All that dust didn't necessarily mean there was something underneath. It could have been a windspout, something that aspired to be a tornado when it grew up. I switched to infrared, maybe there was a heat signature. Not enough. Hard to tell at midday when everything was hot. Okay, one other thing to try—scan for a tag. Not every animal was chipped, we didn't have the resources, but we did track the biggest troublemakers. Finally, I asked the drone to show me any odor trails hanging in the air. It was unlikely, but sometimes you get lucky.

Better to be careful. I rang the Captain. "There's a dust cloud twelve klicks due west. Can't tell what it is from here and aerial surveillance is inconclusive. No confidence on the heat signature. No chip signal. Sniff test inconclusive."

"Copy that," he said. Then the link went silent while he double-checked my log. A moment later, he came back online. "Okay, you win the bonus. First sighting of a leviathan. Nicely done. Finish your watch and catch some Z's."

"Yes, sir. Thank you, sir."

I lay awake in my bunk for a while, waiting for sleep to come. The others on watch were a lot more experienced. Why didn't they spot the smudge of dust on the horizon? Or did they? Was this another test? But I didn't spot a leviathan, I only reported a smudge of dust that I couldn't confirm. So how did Skyler know it was a leviathan? Unless he already knew it was there and parked us in the path of it to see if I could spot it. Was this to make up for all the dung? Or maybe it was one more way to annoy Marley and her dad. And somewhere in there I fell asleep.

Two hours later, Lilla-Jack shook me awake. We were rolling again.

I wiped the sleep from my eyes with a damp cloth and joined the others on the bridge. We were heading west toward the dust smudge. Only it wasn't a smudge anymore. The displays showed it as a young leviathan male, plodding slowly and steadily forward, lifting one ponderous leg at a time. It swayed its body as it moved, swinging its great ribcage and belly from side to side to assist its heavy gait. Its enormous tail swung in weighty counterpoint. Even from this distance we could see how big it was, a huge mountain of walking meat.

Jamie says that calling a leviathan big is to stretch the word beyond its breaking point. Other words, like large and big and ginormous are also insufficient. A full-grown leviathan can mass a hundred times more than our biggest Rollagon. It's at least five times taller. Both the neck and the tail can be longer than a football field.

But this one wasn't one of the big ones. It was a juvenile male, exploring ahead of the rest of the herd. That's kinda risky. Sometimes there are small packs of predators moving ahead of the herds, waiting for them to arrive. They wouldn't hesitate to bring down a lone juvenile. Of course, then they'd be too satiated to attack the rest of the herd when it came through.

We'd argued about this in class. We were watching an old mission video and Marley Layton said it didn't make sense for a youngling to put itself at risk. If it was killed before mating, it couldn't pass on its genes.

"Well, think about it," said Mz. Kinnar, our biology instructor. There were nine of us in the class. The youngest was three Hella-years, the oldest wasn't yet five. "What are you assuming?"

"It's not an assumption," Marley said. "Evolution is about survival of the fittest. The strongest animals survive."

"Yes, that's the assumption."

"Huh?"

"Evolution isn't about the survival of individuals. It's about the survival of populations. It's about the species that can best adapt to changing conditions. It's about the success of the gene pool. So let's reframe the question. What's the evolutionary benefit of having an occasional outlier eaten by predators?"

I raised my hand. Mz. Kinnar pointed at me. "I know this one—I think. Let's say a pack of predators brings down a lone juvenile leviathan. That's enough meat that they can eat for a week or maybe even two. And when they're not eating, they'll be so stuffed and torpid they'll spend most of their time sleeping. That one animal will be enough meat to keep the pack from hunting for ten or twenty days. That's enough time for the rest of the migration to pass. By the time the pack of predators are hungry again, ready to track the herd, it's the sick and old at the rear of the migration who will be culled."

"Okay," said Mz. Kinnar. "So what's the evolutionary benefit to the herd?"

"The ones who get eaten—they're . . . I guess you could consider them necessary sacrifices. The predators are feeding on the animal they caught, they're not going after any of the mothers and calves in the rest of the herd. One dies so that many can live."

Mz. Kinnar nodded. "Thank you, Kyle."

"No. There's more." I took a deep breath. "The advantage to the rest of the herd is obvious. The mother that produced offspring with that behavior is now more likely to survive to produce more offspring with that same genetic expression. Males to be eaten, females to make more males in the future with that behavior."

"Yes," she said. But I don't think she was happy about my answer. She must have thought I got it from the noise. But I didn't. I got it from Jamie. He wanted me to learn things for myself, without the noise, so every night before bedtime we'd talk about all kinds of stuff, especially stuff that I would have to know for school.

"Thank you." I said thank you a lot. I wasn't always sure where it was appropriate, so I said it everywhere. Maybe that's why some people thought I was stupid. But I'm not. I'm just slower than other people. That's why I have the noise.

Then Mz. Kinnar said, "Thank your brother, too." So maybe she didn't think it was all the noise.

"That's not all of it," I said.

"But that's all we have time for today. We have to move on."

I don't like it when people tell me to stop before I'm finished. I have to tell the whole story. I think we need to know the whole story before we can understand any of it. But most people don't want to hear it. They think it's boring.

But I had to say it anyway. "It's like a contest. Every time a herd develops a new way to protect itself, the predators have to develop a new method of attack. And every time the predators come up with a new way of hunting, the herd has to develop a another defense. New behaviors are always being tested. If they work, then new behaviors have to develop on the other side. So whatever it looks like right now, maybe a hundred or a thousand generations from now, it could become something else. It's evolution. Nothing is ever really finished, it's all part of a much larger process. Everything is always being tested. Like us, here on Hella."

Mz. Kinnar thanked me again and this time we did move on.

That was one of the times when Marley punched me after class. Jamie said it was because my answer made her answer look stupid. So maybe it would be better for me to just be smart on my test papers and not raise my hand so much. The more you listen, he said, the more you hear what everybody else doesn't know.

Jamie understood stuff. I can know stuff, lots of stuff, but I don't understand things like Jamie does. That's the kind of smart you can't get from the noise. I asked Jamie once, "Why does Marley hate me so much?"

He said, "Because she's stupid."

"That doesn't make sense."

"Every time you show how good you are, she feels even more stupid. So she blames you for how she feels."

"That's stupid."

"That's what I said. She's stupid."

This was one I'd have to think about.

So when we saw this one juvenile exploring ahead of the herd, it reminded me again that I still didn't understand why Marley Layton was so mean.

I knew what the animal was doing. And why. He was an outlier. There were probably others, but we hadn't spotted them yet. If this one got as far as the Dystopic River, it would probably wait for the rest of the migration to arrive, along with any other juveniles who'd survived their explorations. According to our tracking displays, there were seven packs of predators ahead of the migration, two more than last year. And last year had been bloody enough.

But now we could see that this juvenile wasn't trekking alone. He was making the journey with a couple of buddies, one just a bit smaller and the other noticeably larger. Traveling together increased all their odds of survival. The smaller one was most at risk, unless it stayed between the other two.

"Want to see a leviathan up close?" The Captain looked at me.

"Is it safe?"

"Of course not. Want to look anyway?"

I considered it. Captain Skyler wasn't stupid. "Okay. Yes, please."

"Good answer." He touched his com-set. "One and three, orbit the target at a half klick. I'm going in closer. I want to tag these fellows." Another touch. "Lilla-Jack, you're upstairs on the cannon. Make your shots count."

It took the better part of an hour to close the remaining distance. The leviathans don't move fast, but they move steadily. With almost every step, one or another would lower its great shovel-shaped head and chew its way forward in great ponderous bites. Each of the beasts was cutting a swath wide enough to drive a Rollagon with room to spare—and these were only teenagers. A grandmother could leave a path wide enough for three or maybe even four trucks to travel side by side.

Even one of these animals would consume a dozen tons of vegetation every day. A single animal could strip a whole forest in a couple weeks. But there was another reason why they wouldn't stop, couldn't stop, why the whole herd circled through the southern realm of the continent in an endless migration: The trees would poison them if they didn't.

After about fifteen minutes of being munched on, the tree would respond with an increased production of tanninoids. The smell would be horrific and the beast would move on to a more appetizing tree. But it couldn't just move to the next tree over. The smell would alert every tree in the grove, every tree downwind. So the animals had to take a few bites, then move on to the next tree for the next couple of bites, then move on again, and again. The forests kept the herds moving.

The animals at the rear of the migration suffered the most, because by the time they got to the trees, the tanninoids were already building up. The sick and the slow became sicker and slower. And the predators would pick them off from behind. Captain Skyler thinks that the tanninoid reaction is one of the reasons we see juveniles pushing ahead. They want to get a fresh untainted lunch before the grammas arrive. I've seen that behavior at our own caf too, just by following Jamie.

At a half-klick, the forward and follow trucks unhooked their chains and split off to start a circular path around the slow moving mountains. We headed in closer. I climbed up to an empty turret to get a better view. Even from a half-klick away, the animals were scary-huge. It's one thing to know that Hella's lighter gravity and oxygen-rich atmosphere allow for everything to grow to enormous proportions, but until you can see an actual meat mountain in motion, up close and thundering, you can't really understand what it means.

Leviathans have huge flat feet that hit the ground with a great bone-shaking thump. Even a juvenile—each leg must weigh twenty or twenty-five tons. A leviathan moves only one foot at a time. The earth booms with every thundering step. That's why some people call them thunderfeet, but on a mission we have to use the scientific term—leviathan. This close, we could see the muscles straining, each leg shifting with audible moans and groans, all the way up to the shoulders, all the way up to the hips, and you could hear the animal's spine creaking in protest at its own horrendous weight. The ribcage was big enough to hold at least two of our trucks, and these were only younglings. The extended neck stretched out even longer than the animal's body and the tail was just as long at the other end, swinging ponderously back and forth.

Each animal's broad head moved from side to side, a counterbalance for the tail, but more than that, when you're made of that much pot roast, you have to pay attention to your surroundings, so the leviathans were watching out for each other.

But the thing I noticed most was the hide on these creatures. It was thick and flabby and wrinkly almost everywhere, but especially around the joints, the shoulders, the hips, the neck and tail—wherever the beast needed flexibility. Despite the dust and mud caked on the animal's body, it was still possible to see the dark tones beneath—gray, dark gray, shading to dark blue and even a hint of purple. But that was only the skin. The animals had a kind of moss growing on their backs and sides. It was patchy and uneven where the skin flexed and folded most, but it was thick across the back and sides and even down the flanks.

High up top, spread across each leviathan's broad back was a whole other ecology as well, a familiar contingent of slugs, leeches, and lawyerbugs, parasites of all kinds, and a good-sized flock of conductor birds to feed on all these passengers. The birds were the cleanup crew, the maintenance team, keeping their personal continent free of pests and vermin, lice and bloodsuckers. They looked like yellow crows, but with sharper beaks. They shrieked and gossiped, flapped their wings, and threatened any trespasser that violated the leviathan's airspace. But on closer observation, it was evident that the birds were serving another purpose too; there were always a few circling above, protecting their mobile island by keeping a high watch for predators.

Of course, this entire organic circus had its own distinctive smell. You didn't need the augmented display to know it was there. It was a brown earthy scent, a musky dirty smell, a sweaty animal smell. Members of the First Hundred said it reminded them of cows, a whole herd of cows, an endless herd of cows, an inescapable pungent herd of cows. It wasn't offensive, it was just strong and inescapable.

All three of the animals grumbled as we rolled closer, a low deep-throated complaint that was more earthquake than sound. We were in no danger, the beasts were too large and too slow. Even if one of them were to charge, we could easily outrun it. And if we were too close, and it looked like it was going to rear up, we'd see its head lowering and its muscles tensing in plenty of time to retreat. A leviathan would more likely use either its long neck or its tail as a weapon, swinging one or the other around with more than enough force to overturn a Rollagon. Back at Summerland, people had a lot of different names for the leviathans. Some people called them longnecks, other people called them other things, but out on the drive-around, we only called them leviathans. Even these younglings would be dangerous. But the Captain had no intention of getting close enough to test their tempers.

Lilla-Jack sat in the higher central turret. I watched as she loaded a tagging dart into the railgun. She could easily have hit her target from a half-klick away, but the homefront always preferred as close a view as possible. We approached the animal slowly and matched its pace about a hundred meters off its right flank. Lilla-Jack's red-laser painted a bright circle, split with cross-hairs, high on the shoulder of the largest creature.

"I have a lock," she reported.

"Anytime," said the Captain.

Lilla-Jack squeezed the trigger. The railgun fired with a soft *thunk.* The leviathan's shoulder twitched involuntarily as the needle dart went in. Other than that, the mountain of meat never even noticed it had been punctured.

"Stand by," the Captain said. I could hear quick typing on his keyboard. "All right, we've got a signal. Lilla-Jack, you may have the honor of naming this fellow."

Lilla-Jack considered it. "He's nice and dark. How about Blue Boy?"

"Blue Boy it is." Captain Skyler typed it into the record. "What do you think? Shall we circle around and tag the fellow on the other side?"

"It wouldn't hurt."

"Mission Control says go." Captain Skyler wheeled the truck around to the left to make a wide U-turn. We headed rearward for what seemed like a much longer time than it really was, but it was necessary so we could circle the slowly moving animals from behind. We had to keep out of the range of their tails. Even the spike at the end could be dangerous. If one of those animals swung its incredibly long tail, the tip would crack the speed of sound just like the snapping of a whip and could slice or puncture even the best-armored vehicle.

When we finally did turn to come around behind the beasts, the birds on all three of the animals started clattering loudly and frantically. They swarmed up into the air in a sudden bright cloud of fluttering wings.

"Okay, what's that about?" the co-pilot asked. Halloran was tall and lanky, with a shiny-shaven head. This was the first time he'd spoken since we'd rolled out. Behind his back, his nickname was "The Silence." If he knew that, he never said.

I whirled around in my turret to look. What had startled the birds? And then all the alarms went off at the same time—and there were voices shouting in my headset too.

"Bogies at the six!"

I looked to my left. Just coming up over the top of the rise to the west—a pack of six bigmouths. All sizes. A family. A very lean and hungry family of carnosaurs. How had we missed them? They were moving thirty klicks per hour. And we were headed directly between them and their prey.

The truck lurched as Captain Skyler accelerated. We could outrun the pack on the straightaway, they didn't have the endurance of a Rollagon, but we were on an intercept course, and the real danger here was that the bigmouths would see the vehicle as a more attractive target than the leviathans. "Cannons, find your targets, but don't fire unless I give the order." That last part was unnecessary. The Captain was the only one who could arm the weapons.

Carnosaurs aren't as big as leviathans, but they're big enough. Each one is twice as tall and twice as long as a Rollagon. Across their backs, they have coarse fur that sprouts into bright feather-like growths, but beneath that, especially on the lower sides and belly, they have rough, almost-scaly skin. They're leaner and faster than leviathans, but it takes a whole pack of them to bring one down. Carnosaurs are faster than leviathans—but by human standards, they seemed to be moving in slow motion. It was an illusion created by the contradictions of distance and dimension. The brain doesn't do size well—it insists that nothing could be that big, so obviously it has to be close. But because it isn't, even when it's moving fast, it still looks slow. There was a whole big discussion about this one time, right after the Big Break-In, because so many people said they couldn't understand why we hadn't been able to do more. After all, the creatures hadn't been moving that fast, had they?

Um, yes, they had. It's all about physics. The larger the animal, the more mass it has to balance, the more inertia it has to overcome, the more momentum it has when it finally starts moving, and how much that momentum acts on its ability to stop or change direction—but just off our port side, we had plenty of evidence that the long strides of the carnosaurs more than made up for the challenges of their size. One of the newer colonists once said that she saw them as two-legged lions with big jaws attacking giant land-whales.

The leviathans were grunting now. They knew they were being

tracked. They weren't running, leviathans don't run, but they were moving with intention. At best, the leviathans could manage maybe ten klicks an hour, maybe a little more if they were headed downhill.

Eventually the carnosaurs would catch up to them, probably in the next five or ten minutes. The carnosaurs were probably running for the smallest animal. If they could get it by the neck, they could pull it down and suffocate it. Or if they could leap up onto its back, they could dig at its skin with their two-meter claws. If they could inflict significant blood loss, the animal would collapse within hours.

We didn't know what prey the carnosaurs had locked onto—us or one of the leviathans. Even at this distance, we already had laser-targets painted on four of the six advancing predators, the four largest. We could take them down if we had to—if they started toward any of the Rollagons, but we had a longstanding policy not to interfere with local animal behavior if we could avoid it. We simply didn't want to risk triggering any kind of ecological tipping point. But we also had an it's us-or-them rule too.

Somebody switched off the alarms and now I could hear Captain Skyler calling out, "Hold your fire. Everybody hold. It looks like they're going after Blue Boy."

"Crap," said Lilla-Jack.

"That little bigmouth at the back. It's not certain what it's doing. Lilla, paint it please."

One of the red targeting circles shifted to the young predator's breastbone and Lilla-Jack reported, "Locked."

"I'm taking control of the cannons," the Captain called. "Lilla, you're the secondary." In case anything happened to him. "Halloran, you're third."

"Ya, boss."

"Where'd they come from?" I asked.

"Shut up. We'll worry about that later." That was Lilla-Jack.

The ground was thundering now. The whole truck was shaking. We were between the retreating leviathans and the pursuing carnosaurs, but the Captain was pushing the truck as fast as it could go through the heavy grass. If the carnosaurs didn't change course, they'd pass only a hundred meters behind us. Too close for comfort, they could change both their minds and their direction without much warning—but now I could see that the other two vehicles also had their cannons locked on the predators. A single command could take down the whole pack. But if they were right on top of us, we would probably experience what some people call collateral damage, that place where people say, "Oh, crap!" And the "Oh, crap!" zone was rushing toward all of us awfully fast.

Horrendous bright screeching suddenly filled the air. Blasts of awful stink as well. At first I thought we'd been attacked, then I realized that Captain Skyler had done it. Sonic blasts of warning screams. Synthesized fear pheromones. Randomly triggered ultra-bright dazzler flashes. And even a few flash-bangs too.

The pack of carnosaurs skidded, one of the forward ones stumbled, the one behind it crashed into its rear, a third one sideswiped and veered off, but it was enough to unbalance the first two and they went down in a gigantic bone-crunching avalanche. A landslide of hellacious hunger, screeching and roaring and hissing.

The remaining carnosaurs staggered in bewilderment. The two on the ground thrashed in confusion. One of them kept trying to stand, but its leg was twisted in an impossible direction. The other just spasmed and convulsed. The laws of physics again. Things that big tend to go splat when they fall down. Especially on Hella.

Captain Skyler brought the truck to a stop and we watched as the rest of the drama played out. To the east, the leviathans were steadily putting more distance between themselves and the danger they had just escaped. The four uninjured carnosaurs circled their injured colleagues curiously, cocking their heads, staring, considering. The two on the ground grunted and hissed desperate warnings. The four on their feet hissed back.

"This is going to get ugly," said Lilla-Jack.

"If you're a bigmouth, meat is meat," Captain Skyler said.

It didn't take the four circling carnosaurs long to figure that out. Perhaps it was hardwired into their brains—if it's not standing up, it's lunch. If it's an injured buddy, it's still lunch. Why wait till it's carrion?

We watched in silence for a while. There was nothing much to say—and most of us had learned a long time ago not to say anything when a camera was running. Having a dramatic video punctuated by astonished cries of, "Oh my god, look at that!" did not add to the impact of the recording, it only provided hours of future embarrassment for the person who said it.

The Captain put up a handful of little drones, skyballs, to circle the carnosaurs. Nobody had ever dissected one—for obvious reasons, think about it—so these videos would provide additional scans for our growing library of digital reconstructions.

The two larger carnosaurs were feeding high on the flanks of their fallen comrades—each one ripping away huge chunks of heavy musculature, then jerking its head to throw it to the back of the throat, where they gulped it down in one horrible swallow. I wondered that they didn't choke themselves. The two smaller animals grunted and growled as they peeled back a huge strip of belly skin, revealing thick layers of blubbery fat. They thrust their snouts in, jerking their heads back and forth, gobbling and growling in hunger.

Lilla-Jack was already adding her observations to the log. "The cannibalism is understandable. It's fresh meat. But it's disturbing to think that these carnosaurs might be eating their own parents or children alive. It's not a good argument for having children."

The four survivors continued to tear chunks of bleeding flesh from the two fallen animals. After a bit, the fallen stopped writhing, and then after another bit, they stopped breathing. But their arched necks and staring eyes still looked agonized. Then, for another while, there was nothing but growling and ripping and gulping. And then finally, the fallen carnosaurs stopped being recognizable as animals and were just pulled-apart jumbles of meat and bones.

There was enough here for several days of good eating and the surviving carnosaurs could go another two week or two before they became really hungry again. By then, the rest of the herd would have arrived, but with two less bigmouths to help, bringing down a leviathan would be difficult. Problematic, as the Captain might say.

We left the skyballs circling to finish the surveillance. Operators back at Mission Control would focus on whatever they still wanted to see. Captain Skyler wanted to catch up to the leviathans again. It would be useful to tag the other two and monitor their behavior, especially long-term. So we turned east and chugged along through the swath they had cut through the grass. The other two trucks rejoined us and we actually made pretty good time. The leviathans were still visible in the eastern distance and it wasn't likely that they'd get to Dystopic River before sunset. But even if they did they'd still have to wait till morning to cross, so we had more than enough time to catch up to them.

Captain Skyler did have us stop a few times to plant a few more monitors and pick up samples of the leviathan droppings—still my job. The leviathan poop wasn't as wet and stinky as the droppings of the carnosaurs. Instead, it came out like giant pellets, all greenish-brown and a little bit moist. They were thick balls of rolled up straw with a distinctly grassy animal smell. You could make bricks out of them. If ancient history was any guide, you could probably even use them all dried out as fuel for a campfire.

We caught up with the leviathans at 2430. The sun was lowering behind us and our long shadow reached ahead across the whispering waves of grass. This was how the carnosaurs tracked their prey, following the furrows that the big beasts left behind, so the rear vehicle was always on the lookout for anything else that might be coming up behind us. Aerial surveillance didn't show anything, but aerial surveillance had missed our pack of carnosaurs. Captain Skyler got into an hour-long argument with Mission Control about that.

The best guess was that the bigmouths had been sheltering under a thick copse of warping willows. There's a series of gullies beyond the western rise. A spattering of streams nourishes a mini-jungle of forest and ferns, cooling everything under its canopy. I said, "Maybe the carnosaurs had been having their midday rest when the noise of our trucks disturbed them."

"Gosh," said Lilla-Jack, sarcastically. "And the noise of big thunderfoot and his two buddies had nothing to do with it?"

Captain Skyler made a hushing gesture. "We'll study the records ourselves when we get back. Someone on the oversight committee suggested it as a possibility. It's under advisement."

"Yeah, someone. Some councilor's flunky, looking to score points. We didn't break protocol."

"Shh," said the Captain, and that was the end of it.

The leviathans had stopped at a shallow pond. Slowly and ponderously, they dug at the mud with their gigantic front feet, then they'd back away and lower their great heads into the brown sludge, scraping even deeper. This late in summer, there wasn't enough water to make a real wallow, but they could certainly find enough to wet their whistles—and they had very large whistles.

The herd that followed would dig this pond even deeper. After a few more migrations, this might become a major water hole, not just for the leviathans, but for all the other creatures in this domain. When the water hole was deep enough it would become permanent. And then ferns and bushes and even trees might start to grow. Whether or not they could survive being in the path of the migration—that was unlikely.

Lilla-Jack heated vegetable stew for first supper. We ate in silence, each of us turning over our own thoughts on various matters. Myself, I realized I was having an actual *adventure*. I'd seen more on my first outing than most people saw in a dozen. Jamie would be proud of me. Marley would be really jealous. That would have made me smile if it didn't also worry me. Marley was already angry enough. And I wondered again if it was true, what Jubilee had said. Had Marley broken Jamie's leg on purpose? Or had that happened by accident? Either way, I could expect more trouble from her in the future.

After dinner, Captain Skyler invited me to join them on the bridge. I didn't know if this was a privilege or an honor, or if he was still training me. But I was glad to go.

I hadn't finished fastening my seat belt when the radio started blaring.

At first, I thought it was noise. Then I recognized it as music. Enthusiastic but clumsy. Something from old Earth, something religious maybe? Like a joyous march into the kingdom of heaven? Something triumphant. I'd never paid enough attention. I could ask the noise.

"What the hell?" said Lilla-Jack.

Captain Skyler flipped a switch on his panel. "Mission Control, what is that?"

"It's Beethoven. Beethoven's Ninth. Fourth movement." There was an excited edge to the reply.

"Yes. I recognized that much," said the Captain. "It's kind of thin. Almost amateur. Why are you playing it?"

"We're not playing it. That's an incoming signal. We're relaying it. It's the *Cascade*! She's arrived! The Seventeenth Pilgrimage is here!"

"Say what? Say again!"

"Starship *Cascade* has dropped out of hyperstate."

"How far out?"

"That's the bad news. She's on the far side of the system. This signal is more than two hours old. They're a long way out and headed in the wrong direction, but they're probably already correcting. We sent an immediate acknowledgment, and they should have it by 2630. They're already transmitting their final manifests, and it looks very good. Lots of seeds and equipment. And twelve hundred new colonists."

"Hm." Captain Skyler didn't have to say it aloud. Twelve hundred new problems. "Do we have an ETA to orbit?"

"Hard to say. We're still processing. Apparently they had some trouble on the first leg. Nothing they couldn't handle, but it affected the accuracy of their astrogation. She overshot the primary by a few billion, and she's got a lot of delta-vee to burn off. At least three months. And then at least another two months to come around the star and match orbit. It's a bigger slice than they expected."

"So they're not going to be here until the middle of winter."

"That's what it looks like."

Captain Skyler nodded. "Not good."

I didn't need the noise to understand. Hella storms are hellastorms. It's not safe to land anything when the winds are hitting hurricane velocity. It would be safest for the new arrivals to wait in orbit until spring. Probably six months until the weather settled. Add it all up, after three months in transit to arrive at orbit, they might spend more time waiting upside than the actual length of their hyperstate voyage.

But that could be good news, too.

It's all about logistics. That was the noise talking again. We didn't have accommodations for twelve hundred more people.

But the *Cascade* hadn't been expected until spring. The ship was nine months early. That was interesting by itself. Had somebody invented a faster way to travel hyperstate?

Winterland was budgeted for the expansion, but digging out the new caves hadn't started yet. And Summerland expansion—well, that wouldn't be a problem. We knew how to do that. The newbies could land on Convenient Meadow; their life-pods were designed to convert into homes and stuff, and we could truck them in and stack them into towns. The maintenance facilities would be dug in deep for the long-term. That's what previous immigrations had done. It was a good plan, but every new arrival was a major upheaval for everyone. So a five-month delay before landing people and their supplies, would give us more time to adjust the plans.

Even better, it would give us five months to open up channels and get to know the new people before they actually landed. It would give us five months to teach them the ways of Hella and give them a better chance of surviving without a leash.

Newcomers don't always understand. This planet has killed a lot of colonists in the last thirty years. And only six of those deaths were caused by saurs. Twenty-nine were caused by infection. The rest were caused by stupidity. We have anti-stupid classes every week, with almost-daily reminders from those who'd survived. Captain Skyler said it best: "The worst kind of stupidity is overconfidence—thinking that you already know."

A new voice now. "Good evening, Captain Skyler. They're already asking how soon they can start landing after achieving orbit. They want to start prepping." The screen lit up to show Lawrence Leibowitz, Madam Coordinator's deputy. He must have been in the executive offices, the wall behind him was blue, but he was still buttoning his shirt and his hair hadn't been combed.

Skyler replied, "Morning, Larry We've been through this before. We can let them bring down an advance team, but we're not going to risk any landings in high weather. Tell the Coordinator that I'll see her as soon as we get back. It'll be sometime tomorrow night. Twelve hundred is going to require a lot of planning and prep. Otherwise people are going to die from an overdose of stupid. Tell her she needs to call a meeting of the Landing Committee as soon as we can get everyone in the same room. You got all that?"

"Copy that. And uh, I don't have to tell her. She's standing right beside me."

Madam Coordinator stepped into the picture.

"Ah," said the Captain. "Good evening, Madam Coordinator."

"Captain Skyler. Quite an afternoon you had. Very exciting."

"More than I planned for."

"Obviously. These things are never planned, are they?"

"There was never any danger."

"We've both heard that one before. What's that thing you say to the younglings? Perhaps you could remind me—the one about how everyone is entitled to one fatal mistake?"

Skyler nodded to the camera. "Point taken."

"Thank you. I know how strictly you run your teams. But I've been taking calls all day about the issue of proximity. And you do have a child aboard."

"Not a child, Madam Coordinator. A fully trained intern. And I should add, this intern has done an excellent job in every capacity."

"That's good to hear, but the question was raised, and I am informing you that there are some who are concerned about the endangerment of children."

"I'll be happy to address that with anyone who wants. As soon as I get back."

"I've already set up the meeting," she replied calmly. "But there's something else I want to talk to you about. We have a second decision to consider. This could be the last voyage of the *Cascade*."

"Ma'am?"

"Things are bad on Earth. Very bad. The *Cascade* barely got out.

We don't have the full story yet. The transmissions they received on the way out were fragmentary. Look—ordinarily, I'd want to put a lid on this until we could figure out how best to break the news, but there's no point. Too many people already know. It's better to just tell the truth than let rumors run wild."

"I agree."

"I want you back tonight. Let Halloran complete the mission. He's overdue for certification anyway. Oh, and bring the intern back with you. I think he's had enough experience for a first time."

"Yes, ma'am."

They exchanged a few more words and then the Coordinator signed off. Captain Skyler turned to me and said, "You heard the boss. Get your gear."

I'd never ridden a lifter before. Well, not awake. Mom says we rode one when I was little, but I slept the whole way.

Flying is interesting. All those big fans are whisper silent, so it's like gliding through the air. The technical appellation is "transport," a large lightweight disk, surrounded by impellor plates, easy to lift, hard to knock down. The biggest cargo transports even have helium pods to offset their weight.

We had a lifter attached to the roof of the Rollagon. A covered access ramp came up from the deck and attached to the hatch so we didn't have to suit up. Even before the door was sealed, Captain Skyler was buckling himself into the pilot seat. He pointed me to the copilot's place. "Might as well give you the whole show."

As soon as the last panel flashed green, he unclamped from the deck and we whirred up into the darkening sky. We rode high and fast, the ground sliding away beneath us. Long shadows pointed eastward across the yellow grass. Outcrops and trees and, once, a lone leviathan, another outlier from the herd. The furrow behind it looked like a crease in the ground. In the west, the sun hovered just above the horizon, its slow descent temporarily halted by our altitude.

After a bit more, Summerland Station popped up ahead of us, already lit up like a holiday. We dropped down to the landing pad and settled as silently as a lifter can. Madam Coordinator and Councilor Layton waited just under the local canopy. They didn't look happy. Captain Skyler approached them, helmet in hand. Not knowing what else to do, I followed—until he told me to wait by the lifter. He said he'd walk me home because he had to talk to my mom.

Maybe he forgot, at least I think he forgot, but the communicator in his helmet was still on. So I could hear everything the Coordinator and the Councilor said to him. Madam Coordinator was mostly concerned with logistics—mostly the coming migration and the preparations for twelve hundred new bodies. The rumors about the *Cascade* and Earth were complications, but the logistics were still the same. Councilor Layton kept interrupting with assertions about how all this was going to affect the next election, how today's little adventure wasn't going to help Captain Skyler's chances if he still planned to stand for a seat on the Council, and oh, by the way, that business with the intern—and that's when I started paying real attention. "What was all that about?" he said. "You should have taken Marley, not that fraggy little droop. No brain-chip is going to make him a whole person. You're only pumping up the freak so you can get into his mother's bed—"

I don't get angry very much and I don't always understand why other people do, but sometimes I get this hot rush of feeling that everybody calls anger, and that's what happened then.

I ran over shouting. "I am not a freak!" I shouted at him. "I have a syndrome. That's all. And I have a compensator chip. That's what makes me so good at everything. My chip makes me smarter than just about everybody. I can do better and faster research. And I don't make stupid mistakes—" Captain Skyler touched my shoulder gently, but I shook him off, I wasn't through. "I'm qualified. Marley's not. And if you can't see that, then you're the mental cripple, not me!"

Madam Coordinator interrupted then. "Kyle, that's enough." So I stopped. Because she was the Coordinator. She was the law.

It was only after Captain Skyler led me away that I realized that every word I had said had been broadcast out through his open com-link. His conversation first, then mine. Everybody who been listening had heard every word. That couldn't have been an accident. Captain Skyler never did anything by accident. But he was real good at making things look like they just happened by accident, or coincidence. Like arriving just in time between three leviathans and a pack of carnosaurs. Something to think about.

We stopped halfway across the quad. He held up a hand for silence, then turned off his helmet. "Kyle. About what you said to Councilor Layton—"

"Do I have to apologize?"

"No, you don't. You were right. But . . . please don't do it again. Okay?"

"Um. Okay. But he shouldn't have said those things about me."

"No, he shouldn't, but . . ." Captain Skyler paused. "He wasn't talking about you. He was talking about everything he doesn't understand. Everything he's afraid of."

"It sounded like he was talking about me."

"Yes, but that's because he's stupid. Like Marley. Okay?"

"I have to think about this. I'll have to talk it over with Jamie."

"That's a good idea, yes."

Mom was waiting at the door when we arrived. She hugged me tight, then sent me off to clean up and go see Jamie. Jamie had watched the entire mission and wanted to hear all about the leviathans and the carnosaurs. He'd never seen a kill that close.

The Rollagons have showers, but it's not the same as home. A thirty-second shpritz isn't as much fun as a ten-minute lather. And besides, there's a lot more you can do in ten minutes than you can do in thirty seconds. Jamie caught me in the shower once, but before he could say anything, I said, "It's my penis and I'll wash it whatever way I want to." After that, the shower was a private joke between us. "Are you going to wash fast or slow?" "Whichever way I want to."

I dried off in the air-blaster, wrapped a robe around me, and went to see Jamie, but he was asleep. I started back to my room, but Mom and the Captain sounded like they were arguing about something, so I waited behind the door and listened.

"—and no, I was not *using* him. Testing him, yes. But more than that. Showing you what he's capable of. Showing everyone. You heard him, he said it better than anyone, he writes the best documentation of anybody on Hella. Okay, yes, sometimes it looks like he goes into much too much detail, but if you go back even a month, a year, you've got real history recorded there, all the information you need and a lot more that you didn't realize you needed. He puts things in context."

"We have the video records," Mom said. "We don't need to have him doing busywork, writing all those reports—"

"He likes doing it. And the video records don't give context. They don't explain what's going on—the logic of the moment, the relationships, the deep understanding. That's what he's good at. He sees things that the rest of us overlook because we think it's so obvious it doesn't need to be said. Sometimes we're the cripples."

I could tell the Captain was pacing by the way he spoke. "We forget how much of our job is training the next guy in line, the one who's going to take over when we move on. Your son can write the manuals for every job he's ever done, because he's so good at explaining every specific detail. Anybody in this goddamn colony who doesn't recognize his value is the real jerk. You're not going to be there every time some malicious little bitch dumps a lunch tray on him. It's the only way to make this colony respect him as a fully functioning person."

"Cord—" she began, but then stopped herself that way that she does when she's rethinking what she's about to say. "I know you think you're doing right, but what if you're wrong? What if he can't handle it. You know how he gets when he hits the wall—"

There was silence for a moment, then Captain Skyler spoke in a much lower, much softer voice. I had to strain to hear. Fortunately, the noise is good at clarifying. "Sweetheart, listen to me. He's going through puberty. Frustration is normal. Learning to deal with it is normal. Look at me. He's almost a man. You have to think about his future. That's why this has to be done now. Before it's too late."

She hesitated. "Yes, I know. I understand. But he really pissed off Councilor Layton. You know how he'll use that. And if the Self-Sufficiency Resolution passes—"

"It won't. At least, I think it won't. It's insane. But if it does, I want Kyle to have *a priori* status."

It took me a minute to figure it out, what they weren't saying. Marley's dad, Councilor Layton, wanted to create a law that everybody in the colony had to be self-sufficient. No freeloaders. No dead weight. He said that collectivism destroyed economies because it destroyed incentive. It kinda made sense—why should the people who work have to support lazy people who didn't want to work? But as soon as you started thinking about how it might work for real, it didn't make any sense at all.

Because what about people who are sick or injured? How do you decide what constitutes self-sufficiency anyway? What about someone so badly injured in the Big Break-In they're unable to work now? Or what about the people who helped build the colony in the first place, but now they're too old to work? Like the First Hundred? Aren't they entitled to live? Or do we have to push them out the gate and leave them to die? How would this rule make us a better people?

There's a book about politics we studied in school. It's all about how to run a government. It says that the most important question to ask before you introduce any new law is this: What problem will this law will solve? Who does it make life better for? If it doesn't help everyone, it's a bad law.

Mom says that a lot of politics isn't about what you see. It's about what you don't see. I guess she's right, because I don't see the sense in any of this. Everybody I know works at least twenty-six hours a day, usually more. Is there anybody who isn't exhausted by second supper? So what's the point of Councilor Layton's proposal? What does it accomplish? And why was the Captain talking to Mom this way?

And one more thing. Did he just call my mother "sweetheart"?

Later, when Jamie woke up, I sat on the foot of his bed, cross-legged, and we shared avocado-bacon sandwiches. We didn't have bacon often, the tanks weren't producing enough of it yet for it to be anything but a luxury, but I wanted to do something nice for Jamie because I knew he felt bad about not being able to go on the mission. But Jamie shook that off and said we should celebrate my first ride-along and my first time as a driver, even though I hadn't done any actual driving, just watching.

I told him about what Councilor Layton said, and how angry I got and what I said to him. Jamie said that the recording was already online. Emily-Faith had sent him a copy.

"Did I do wrong?"

"Well, there's wrong and there's politics. What you said wasn't wrong, but it wasn't politic."

"Is that like nuance?"

"Uh, yeah. Kinda."

I don't listen the same way other people do—I listen literally. I hear the words. But Jamie says I don't hear nuance—what's under the words, where people are coming from and where they're trying to go. He says that probably makes life simpler for me in some ways, but harder in others. He says I shouldn't worry about it. "You're smarter than any ten of them put together and that makes you worth twenty of them. Just be good at what you do, Kyle, that's all that matters."

But that's why some people think I don't have emotions. They're wrong. I do have emotions. But most people don't understand what emotions really are. Or maybe they just don't think about what they're experiencing. Emotions are physical reactions. All emotions are variations on Yipes or Goody. This is because the mammalian nervous system evolved concurrent with the internal organs. So emotions are experienced physically. Fear is in the gut—it's a fight or flight thing. Anger is in the heart and chest, a surge of adrenaline. Happiness is a flood of endorphins.

I have emotions. Yipes and Goodies. I have the same physical reactions as everyone else. I just don't express them the same way. That's because of my chip. It modulates. It moderates. It does something. It's supposed to keep me rational—which is the polite way of saying that it's there to modify my behavior. I don't know. I do know I have a lot less Yipe in my life now and a lot more Goody, so that's something.

Because I don't react the way they think I should, some people think I don't understand their feelings. But I do. I just don't understand them like they do. Mom and Jamie are good at it, so I use them as role models for how to behave, when I can remember to do it. I ask myself, "What would Mom say? What would Jamie say?" And sometimes, I even ask, "What would the Captain say?" I don't always get it right, but I'm doing better than I used to. It's called nuance. I'm working on it.

Anyway.

Jamie and I sat and ate our sandwiches and talked about all the things we talk about. I like being with Jamie. Jamie is the very best kind of brother. He always has time to listen. Jamie says he's fascinated by how my mind works. He says I'm like a little machine that's learning how to be human. He says the way I think is special. The way he says it, it's a good thing.

Jamie was the first to figure out that I was different. When I was little, I'd stand in my playpen and watch everyone. Jamie would turn to me and wave and say hi and make faces. Jamie says that most babies smile and laugh when you wave at them or say their name, but I wouldn't smile, I wouldn't laugh. So Jamie told Mom, "There's something different about our baby." Not wrong. *Different.* That's how I know Jamie loves me. He knows it's okay to be different.

I asked Jamie about the things I'd overheard Mom and the Captain talking about, and he looked sad. I think it was sadness, but he could have been frowning too. He took a long time before he answered. He said, "Well, it's complicated."

"I'm not stupid."

"I know that. You have a special kind of smart." He reached as far as he could without bending his leg and patted me on the knee. Jamie is the only one who can touch me. I won't let anyone else.

I asked, "So do you understand what they were talking about? Is this about the *Cascade*? Does Marley's dad think the new colonists aren't coming here to work?"

Jamie shrugged. He said, "Okay, I'll try to explain. Only first you have to tell me something. What did you notice today? Did you notice anything interesting about dinosaur poop?"

I shrugged back. "The carnivores' poop is wet and stinky. The herbivores' poop is dry and full of grass."

"Yeah, the herbivores don't digest cellulose very well. Even though they have all kinds of bacteria in their gut to help them, they still poop a lot of fiber."

"So what does that have to do with Mom and the Captain? And everything they were talking about?"

"Well, it's like all that poop. It's mostly crap and there's a lot of different things in it holding all that crap together."

We both laughed. Any joke with crap in it is a good one.

"Okay, it's not about self-sufficiency, kiddo. That's just one little piece of a much bigger pile of crap. There are a lot of other ugly pieces in that pile too. There's a Genetic Protection Resolution. That one's about not letting certain reproductive combinations into the colony's very limited gene pool. Strictly enforced genetic management so we don't get congenital birth defects. Like dwarfism and cleft palate and Down syndrome, for example."

"And people like me?"

Jamie didn't hesitate. "Uh-huh. That's in there too. There's a whole list of things. That's one of them."

"So how would that work? What does 'strictly enforced' mean?"

"Sterilization, probably. Abortion, certainly."

"Abortion?" I didn't know the word. I had to look for it in the noise. It was very complicated. It took me a minute to figure it out. "So . . . if they had their way, I wouldn't have been born? Mom wouldn't have been allowed?"

"Yeah, you wouldn't have been born. They'd have stopped you."

"But that's not fair! I'm good, Jamie. Aren't I? Aren't I?"

Jamie looked worried. I think it was a worried look. Maybe it was an angry look. I wasn't sure.

"Kyle," he said. "You're my best friend in the whole world. I love you. Mom loves you. And I wouldn't want you to be any other way than you are, because you make me smile."

"Well, then why—why?"

"They say it's for the good of the colony's genetic heritage. It's part of their whole 'Mission to the Future' plan." He put his hand on my knee again, this time he left it there. "But I don't think you need to worry about it yet. It has to pass two separate votes. This year and next. If the Captain can delay the referendum until after the colonists from the *Cascade* download . . . well, I think he hopes that they'll bring a sufficient margin of votes to guarantee a defeat. Nobody knows."

"But what if it passes? What if it becomes a rule? Then what? They'll want to sterilize me, won't they?"

"I don't know, Kyle. But I don't think you should worry about it right now. I mean—it hasn't even been put on the ballot yet. Nobody's moved to bring it to a vote."

"But they could! Marley would do it. She hates me. I know what sterilization is. I'm not going to have an operation. I'm not. Nobody's going to change me unless I want to change. I'll go live with the exiles if I have to."

"Nobody's going to change you. And there aren't any exiles, that's just a fairy story."

"Then I'll go live with the fairies."

Jamie smiled his crooked smile. He squeezed my knee. "I'll tell you what. If anything like that happens, we'll both go. I'm sure Auntie Uncle and his red-haired boyfriend will make room for us. We'll just have to find them, right? But I don't think we'll have to worry about that for now. And not for a long while."

"Okay," I said. If Jamie said something was all right, then everything was all right. He never lied. "Oh. I just remembered something."

"What?"

"Captain Skyler. He called Mom 'sweetheart.'"

"He did?"

"Uh-huh. I heard it myself."

"Wow." Jamie's mouth made a perfect little O.

"What did he mean by that?"

"It means . . ." Jamie said quietly, " . . . that he cares for her. A lot."

"Is he going to marry her? Would that make him our dad?"

"I don't know, kiddo. How about we keep this to ourselves for a while and give Mom a chance to make up her own mind? Okay? Stinky promise?" He licked his middle finger and held it out.

"Okay. Stinky promise." I licked my finger too and hooked it with his.

The next day, after first work shift, there was a meeting of the Personnel Management Committee. Marley and her dad were there. Mom and I were there, and Jamie hobbled in on crutches. A few other parents sat in the back. Mom had submitted video records of Marley's bullying, and the three-member committee had reviewed them all.

I turned on the noise so I could understand faster.

The head of the committee was one of the First Hundred. Commander Moses Yalel Nazzir, co-pilot of the first landing. He was seventy years old. Hella-years. He was thin and brown and shiny and he had a fluffy halo of silvery hair. He was everybody's honorary grampa. But today, he didn't look happy. Neither did the two other committee members. Lady Pershing was brushing imaginary crumbs off her shelf-like bosom with an annoyed frown, and Doctor Gomez's famous smile had vanished beneath his bushy mustache.

"We have a lot on the agenda today," Commander Nazzir began. "And I know that many of you are impatient to be heard." He took a breath. "But before we can get into any of that, there's this other matter that has come up that we have to handle first." He glanced at me, then looked sternly to Marley and her dad. "You wanted this fast-tracked? All right, your request is granted. But I don't think you're going to like where this track goes."

He picked up his pad and tapped at its display until he found the page he wanted. He studied it for a long moment. I was sure he already knew what was on it and was hesitating on purpose. I don't know why people do that. Maybe it's because they don't want to do whatever it is they have to do anyway. I don't know.

"So," he finally said. "Let me preface this with a little bit of context. This isn't about guilt or innocence, because this isn't a trial. So the usual courtroom procedures can be dispensed with. We're going to treat this as a breach of appropriate conduct. A serious breach. Are there any objections?"

I looked to Mom, but she just leaned in and whispered, "Shh."

Commander Nazzir said, "All right. If there are no objections, we're going to go directly to our judgment in this matter. I and the other members of the Personnel Committee are very troubled by what we see in these records." Now he looked directly at Marley. "This represents a very ugly pattern of behavior. It suggests that either you're very stupid or you just don't care. And if you just don't care, then you really are stupid. No, do not speak. We are not interested in what you have to say. There is no mitigation possible here."

The Councilor stood up. "Sir, I object—"

"You may object all you want, Councilor Layton, but I am doing you and your daughter a favor. Any attempt to justify or excuse or rationalize or explain away the pattern of behavior in these records could very well work against you. It would show up as an attempt to evade responsibility. Is it your intention to prejudice this committee even further?"

The Councilor sat down.

Commander Nazzir focused on Marley now. His voice was low, but intense. "Mz. Layton. Personally, I am appalled. What you have been doing, young woman, is disrespectful to others. That you have gotten away with it for so long is even more appalling. You have abused those who would be your teammates. Such behavior is counterproductive and hurts the well-being of the colony. To be blunt, it is unacceptable for any member of this community to act with such deliberate intention to cause harm to others. And no, the position of your parent on the Council does not grant you any degree of immunity from the consequences of your behavior. If anything, your abuse of such presumed privilege demands even graver consequences."

He turned away from her then and spoke to the rest of the room in his official voice. "It is the decision of this committee that Marley Layton will perform five hundred hours of community service. Until this service is completed, Marley Layton will not be allowed to participate in any group activities. Marley Layton will be denied use of all public meeting places, including the pool, the gym, the theater, the cafeteria, the quad, the playing fields, and the open market. In addition, Marley Layton will at all times keep a distance of fifty meters from the following people . . . ." He started with me and my brother and my mom, then went on to list a half-dozen other families.

Commander Nazzir finished the list, then turned back to Marley and said, "In addition to this, you will be denied all opportunities for advancement and certification until such time as the Personnel Committee reviews your behavior again. You will report to a Management Officer twice a day—or more if they require. Do you have any questions?"

Marley shook her head.

"It is the further decision of this committee that you and all of your live-in parents will be required to complete one hundred hours of family counseling. It is apparent that there are serious issues at play here—issues between you and your father that perhaps may be at the root of your behavior. These issues must be resolved. No other petition from either you or your parents will be heard by this committee or any other management group until the completion of your assigned counseling."

Marley muttered something, a little too loudly. "All this because I dumped a cafeteria tray on a stupid retard—?"

"No!" Commander Nazzir slammed his hand down hard on the table. It sounded like an explosion. "No! This is not about any single action. It is about the total pattern of your behavior. This is not the first complaint about you that has been brought to this committee. More than once, your father requested a second chance for you and promised to bring your behavior under control. Out of respect for your father, out of a belief that such matters are best handled in a family environment, we deferred any public action. Obviously, that hasn't worked. We can no longer overlook your antisocial behaviors. One more word out of you, and this committee is prepared to double the terms of your reparation."

The Commander looked to the Councilor. "Do you have anything you wish to say?"

The Councilor shook his head.

"That's very wise of you. You made promises to us that were not kept. We hold you equally accountable for your daughter's behavior. But we also recognize that she is of an age that we used to call 'teenager'—" He interrupted himself, shaking his head and remarked to the woman sitting next to him, "We really are going to have to find some other terminology that matches the Hellan calendar." Then he turned back to the room. "We recognize young people of such an age can be unruly, uncontrollable, even rebellious. But while there may be appropriate avenues for such behavior in other societies, unfortunately we do not have the same margin here. This kind of behavior represents a potential for serious and unforgivable damage to the morale of the colony." He peered over the top of his spectacles. "We all know, Councilor Layton, that you have made the long-term health of this colony your own personal mission. I recommend that you put your own house in order before you proceed with any other agenda.

All right, we're now going to take a fifteen-minute recess and then we'll hear the certification petitions—"

As I stood up, I glanced to the back of the room. Captain Skyler waited there. I didn't know how long he had been standing, but he must have been there for a while. As the Councilor and his daughter strode out, they both gave him an angry look. Beside me, Jamie laughed—a little too loudly. "Captain Skyler wins this round."

"Huh?"

Mom said, "You heard the Commander. Mr. Layton can't call for a vote on any of his resolutions until Marley completes her community service. Five hundred hours? She'll be out of circuit for a year. Maybe longer. The way she acts—she'll pull another five hundred hours of penalties. Maybe I should start a betting pool. Either way, the *Cascade* will have downloaded her colonists long before then, and the whole political spectrum will have rearranged itself."

"As long as she leaves me alone, that's all I care about. I'm hungry. Can we go to the caf?"

"Not yet," said Mom. "There's another piece of business. Captain Skyler wants us here."

"Okay." I sat back down.

When the committee reconvened, the mood was a lot more relaxed. Commander Nazzir looked at Captain Skyler. "Captain, we appreciate your taking the time to make a personal appearance. We know you have a very busy schedule—even more complicated now with the impending arrival of the *Cascade.* I see that your petition addresses one part of that, so we'd like to hear from you now."

"Thank you, Commander. I genuinely appreciate your making time for me in today's agenda. I think you'll find this useful."

"It's our privilege to have you here, Captain. Please proceed."

"Thank you. The petition in front of you asks that you add Kyle Martin to the *Cascade* Liaison Team."

"Huh?" I said. "Me?"

"Shh," said Jamie, tapping my knee. He was grinning broadly.

Captain Skyler continued. "The petition is quite thorough, but I want to add my personal endorsement. Young Mr. Martin has an extraordinary ability to observe and report and share what he has seen. That was why I added him to my most recent drive-around, because with his fresh eyes, I believed he would be the one most likely to discover something that the rest of us might overlook."

He glanced at Mom and me, flashed us a smile, then turned forward again. "Very shortly, we will have twelve hundred new colonists, the largest pilgrimage ever. Bringing them up to speed, training them, assimilating them into our culture, and also recognizing the unique values that they will bring and contribute—we'll need to give them as much hands-on information as possible to prepare them for the challenges of this world. Young Mr. Martin has an amazing focus of attention and would be an enormous asset, perfect for this task. I've known him for years, watched him grow, and I've had the privilege of having him on a mission team. He's certainly qualified, and I recommend whatever certifications you deem appropriate."

"Thank you, Captain. Is there anyone else who'd like to speak to this petition?"

Mom looked like she wanted to say something, but she just shook her head once.

"Is there anyone who opposes this petition and would like to speak against it?"

Captain Skyler turned around and studied the room. Councilor Layton had already left, and if there was anyone else who might challenge the Captain, they kept their hands in their laps.

"All right, thank you, Captain. We will take this under consideration. We'll want to interview the candidate, of course, but we should be able to make a decision before our next meeting. Thank you for your insights. Now, in the matter of . . . ."

That night, Captain Skyler came to second supper, the last big meal of the day. We ate at home instead of the cafeteria. Jamie and I looked at each other like we expected something important to happen, like there was something maybe he and Mom wanted to tell us, but neither of them said anything, so we just enjoyed our omelets. Mom had a new recipe she wanted to try out, this time using mushrooms and onions and Hella-peppers, which were sweet more than spicy, something that surprised everyone, especially the biologists who insisted that sugar-rich fruits shouldn't have evolved here yet, but they were making the mistake of assuming that Hellan evolution had to parallel Earth's, which it hadn't and wouldn't and couldn't and shouldn't, for more reasons than anyone could list in a single conversation.

We nattered about the events of the morning for a while. Mom was satisfied it had all worked out so well, to which Captain Skyler replied that we shouldn't ever get over-confident. The Layton family was known for holding grudges. But he wouldn't say anything more about that. "We'll cross that bridge when we get to it." Instead, he talked about my upcoming interview with the committee. It hadn't been scheduled yet, but he wanted to start coaching me right away on what to say and what not to say. It was that important.

We were halfway through dessert when the door chimed. I got up to answer it. Councilor Layton and one of his wives, the big one, stood there. "Hello, Kyle," he said. "I'd like to speak to Captain Skyler. The locater says he's here."

"What is it, Councilor?" The Captain had come up behind me. Mom was behind him.

"May we come in?"

The Captain looked to Mom. She nodded. The Captain stepped aside to admit them.

Mom said, "Would you like some tea?" To me, she said, "Kyle, clear the table."

"But I haven't finished my pudding—"

"Please—" Councilor Layton interrupted. "Don't go to any trouble on our behalf."

"No," said Mom. "I insist. You are guests in my home. Come in, sit down. I'll put up the kettle. Kyle, finish your pudding in the kitchen. Jamie, can you help Kyle?"

I was frustrated. This wasn't right. I wanted to finish my pudding. I could feel the upset building inside me, but Jamie put his hand on my shoulder and whispered, "You can have the rest of mine too if you don't say anything else."

Deal.

The Councilor and his wife sat on the couch in uncomfortable silence while everybody else bustled around. Captain Skyler sat down opposite them. Mom made tea, Jamie filled a plate with biscuits, I loaded the dishwasher. Eventually, everything was sorted out. I put the unfinished pudding in the fridge for later, and we all adjourned to the dining room table. I figured this visit must be important, so I turned on the noise. And if I still couldn't figure it out, Jamie would explain it to me later.

"This afternoon," Councilor Layton began. "I went to a caucus meeting. I sat with the people who supported my election to the Council. I offered them my resignation. They refused to accept it. They told me that they have complete confidence in my ability to continue representing them."

"So what does that have to do with us?" asked Mom.

"Simply this. I'm here as your neighbor, as your colleague. And in my capacity as a member of the Council, I'm here to apologize." He looked around at all of us with a sad expression. "I'm here to apologize to Jamie and to Kyle first. I had no idea Marley had behaved so badly to you. I only had a chance to review all the videos this afternoon, and I was very upset at what I saw. You did not deserve such treatment."

To Mom, he said, "And I owe you an even greater apology for not recognizing the seriousness of this issue sooner. I know that you have tried to bring it to my attention more than once and I dismissed it as merely an overprotective reaction to the schoolyard arguments of children. That was wrong of me. I promise you I will never dismiss your concerns so cavalierly in the future. You will have access to my office whenever you need it."

He turned to Captain Skyler. "We've had our differences in the past, and I expect that we will have differences again in the future. But that does not justify either of us behaving disrespectfully. You should know that I admire and honor your service to the colony, and I hope there will be times when we can find common cause for partnership."

Beside him, his wife—the one we called Bruinhilda, because she looks like a big fat bear, but never where she could hear—nodded a stern agreement.

I didn't know what to say. Jamie didn't respond either. I couldn't tell what Captain Skyler was thinking. Finally, Mom spoke up. She said, "Thank you, Councilor. This whole situation must be very difficult for you. I appreciate that you thought it important enough to apologize in person. May I pour you some tea?" There was something about Mom's voice, the way she offered to pour the tea. A wise man would have hesitated before drinking it.

Once the tea was poured all around, she sat back in her chair and said. "There is something I tell my children. I'm sure you have probably heard it yourself many times, but it's worth repeating here. 'Sorry' is not an eraser. It does not magically make everything all right. One of my sons has a broken leg, the other has been ridiculed and embarrassed repeatedly in front of his peers. A broken leg is part of growing up. It will heal and Jamie will be on the soccer field again before the season is over. But as for Kyle. Well, you said some very ugly things about him. You said them where he could hear, as if he had no right to his feelings. I say it bluntly, that hurt is not going to go away quite so easily."

Councilor Layton nodded. "I understand."

"No, you don't. Please let me finish. I have no power or authority to compel you to do anything. I can only request. But I do hope that with your apology, you will also bring a sense of obligation to make some form of reparation to my son."

The Councilor hesitated. "I would certainly consider any request you might make . . ." He trailed off uncertainly.

"Thank you. This morning, we put a petition before the Personnel Committee, asking them to appoint Kyle to the *Cascade* Liaison Team. Perhaps you would consider endorsing that petition?"

Councilor Layton looked at his wife. She gave an almost imperceptible nod. He looked back at Mom. "I know about the petition, I haven't seen it yet. I'll have to review it before I can make any commitment. Of course, you understand that as an elected representative everything I do must be weighed against its value to the colony."

"The value to the colony is obvious here, Councilor. And your endorsement would carry a lot of weight in front of the committee. And it goes without saying that it would go a long way toward making things better for both of our families. It would ease tensions all around. And we all want that."

"Your points are well taken, Mz. Martin. I promise you that I will review this with . . . with my staff to make sure there will be no unintended consequences. If everything is in order, as I'm sure it must be—the Captain having helped write the petition—then it would certainly be appropriate for me to lend my support and, as you say, it would make things better for all of us." He took a sip of tea. "This is very good tea, thank you."

Mom closed the door behind them, turned around and looked at the Captain. "Well that was unexpected. And very generous. Why are you frowning?"

Captain Skyler looked unhappy. "I'm frowning because if my face showed what I was really thinking, it would explode. Those people have just shown themselves to be so much more vicious and vindictive than I ever allowed myself to believe, I feel like vomiting. And I'm even more upset with myself for being vicious and vindictive enough to recognize what they're up to."

"You didn't say a word the whole visit—"

"Because the whole time, I had to keep reminding myself that yes, I am descended from killer apes, but no, today I am not going to kill. Be grateful that I have that much self-control."

"Okay," said Mom. She folded her arms. "Explain it to me."

"He played you," said Captain Skyler. "Oh, he made all the right noises of apology and all the official-sounding noises about having to review the petition, blah blah blah, because that's what a politician is supposed to say, that he's going to give it careful consideration and all the rest of the blah blah blah that makes him look good before he says no, I don't think so."

Captain Skyler looked at me, looked at Jamie. Even I could see that he didn't want to say the rest. Not in front of us. He took Mom's hands, drew her close. "Sweetheart, you are very important to me. So are your sons. If I'm more protective than I should be, then I'm sorry. You are a marvelous scientist. You are one of the most dedicated human beings I have ever known. And you're brilliant. And—"

He didn't get to say the rest. Mom stopped him with two fingers placed gently against his mouth, "Yes, I know. I'm the smartest woman on the planet. So what? What is it you don't want to say."

"All right," said Skyler. "Let's have the talk. Everybody sit down. Jamie, watch your leg. And put away that damn tea. This deserves coffee."

While we waited for the coffee to brew, the Captain explained. "I was watching—what do you kids call her?—Bruinhilda. How appropriate. Did you notice that her lips never moved the whole time Layton was talking? And both her hands remained quietly folded in her lap. He even spoke while she drank tea. I've never see a ventriloquist that good. She's very good."

Mom's eyes widened.

"That's right. Layton is not allowed off the leash. He's never had a thought of his own. Everything he says, everything he does, it's decided beforehand by the troika of witches that run that family. I've suspected it for a long time, ever since they fabbed that big black cauldron—but I didn't know for sure until today." He stopped himself. "All right, maybe I exaggerate. Maybe he can still take a piss without someone else having to hold his . . . uh, hand, but this—"

"This what? I'm sorry, Cord, I really don't understand."

"All right, all right." He slowed down. He stopped himself. He took a breath. "You want to know why Marley acts the way she does—especially toward Kyle? She learned it at home. She's just imitating the behavior she sees from her mothers. That's why there's no discipline there. They approve of her behavior."

Abruptly, he turned to me. "Kyle, I love you—like you're my own son, do you know that?"

I nodded, a little confused.

"So this is very hard for me to say, but I think you're old enough to understand. And I think it's important for you to hear."

"Okay . . ."

He swallowed hard. "You know, you're not easy to like."

"I know that."

"You don't have a lot of people who understand you. So you don't have a lot of friends. It's hard work being your friend."

"I know. Because I'm different."

"Yes. And it's a good difference. Your Mom knows that. Jamie knows that. I know it. Lilla-Jack knows it. A lot of other people know it too. But not everybody. And you need to know what you're up against." He turned to Mom. "Councilor Layton will endorse your petition. They want Kyle on the Liaison Team." He turned back to me. "They don't understand you. They think there's something wrong with you. So they think you'll fail. They want you to fail. They expect you to alienate the new colonists."

"Oh, Cord, he won't do that."

"He can't help himself, Dora. It's not his fault, it's the way he is. Kyle is Kyle. People put up with him, but that doesn't mean they like him. He makes people uncomfortable, the meticulous way he speaks, the way he focuses on the details that bore the shit out of most people, the way he . . . everything. I had a fight with my own team, just getting him on my drive-around." Back to me again. "Kyle, you need to know this. You need to know what's at stake. If you don't want to be on the Liaison team—"

"But I do!"

Jamie looked angry now. "He'll do great!"

Captain Skyler said, "I'm sure he will. But you all need to know this. They want to use Kyle as their primary argument to pass the Genetic Purity Resolution. They don't care if they have to wait an extra year or two, they're thinking long-term control over the whole colony and they'll use whatever tactic they think will work for them."

Mom's expression got hard. Jamie put a hand on my shoulder. I didn't know what to think. This was the Captain.

"Cord—I think this conversation is over."

"Dora, listen to me. Remember that old saying? 'The truth will set you free, but first it's gonna piss you off.' I didn't say any of this to hurt you. Certainly not Kyle."

Mom was standing. "No, Cord, of course not. But you're overthinking this to the point of paranoia. And the one thing I know about paranoia is that it's infectious. I think you should go now. Kyle didn't need to hear you say those things. And I'm appalled to know that you think them. No, just go. Just go now. Don't say anything else."

The door whooshed shut behind the Captain, and we were alone. Mom ran to her room, crying. Jamie and I looked at each other. He put his arm around my shoulder and pulled me close. He must have needed that hug, so I let him.

We never did get to the coffee.

The next couple of days were confusing. And hard for all of us. Lilla-Jack came by to coach me on what to say for my interview, so we knew that Captain Skyler still cared, but as far as I could tell, he and Mom still weren't talking.

The interview wasn't as hard as I expected it to be. Councilor Layton's letter was read into the record, along with recommendations from Captain Skyler, Lilla-Jack, Commander Halloran, and several other friends of the Captain. For a bunch of people who didn't like me all that much, they sure didn't sound like it in their letters.

The committee asked me how I would deal with the new colonists and their questions. I said I knew I wasn't very good with what other people call emotional subtext, but that shouldn't matter in this circumstance because mostly my communications would be about facts and details and explanations, not social integration. But just in case, the team captain would be reviewing all my interactions anyway, wouldn't she? So she'll be there to help out with anything I don't understand.

The committee asked a lot of questions. They knew I used the noise for research of all kinds and they asked if I would use it in my work. I said yes and explained how. They seemed satisfied with that answer, all my answers, that I knew what the job was and that I was qualified to handle it. So they approved the petition two days later. With conditions. I would be on a six-week probationary period. If the team leader found my work satisfactory, my status would be for the duration. If I completed all five months on the Liaison Team, I would be eligible for Certification as an Information Specialist. It was a new category. Jamie said they were going to create it just for me—if I didn't screw up.

So all I had to do was what I wanted to do anyway. And if I did, then everything would work out all right. And if that happened, then Mom was right about Captain Skyler, and he was wrong about the Laytons, but if Mom was right and Captain Skyler was wrong, then she was the real loser, because she'd be losing Captain Skyler. But Mom didn't want to be wrong. Because if she was wrong, then Captain Skyler would be right about all those things he'd said about me.

I know I'm not normal. Normal is a delusion. There's no such thing as normal, there's only ordinary. And I'm not ordinary either. I am what I am and it's fine with me, so why can't it be fine with everybody else?

I like being me. It's fun to know things.

I thought about the best way to be an Information Specialist. Nobody in the colony had ever been an Information Specialist before. Everybody always just shared their expertise. So I had to invent the job.

I don't like being videoed. I'm not very good at it. Most of the time I talk in a monotone, and I know that's boring to other people. So just turning on the camera and talking about what I know was probably not a good idea. But just to be sure, I asked Jamie about it, and he agreed that some people might see me as a boring little know-it-all, his words not mine. So we talked about the best way to do what I was good at, and in the end, I wrote out a detailed game plan and gave it to the Liaison Team leader, Mz. Campobello.

I told Mz. Campobello that I would write detailed reports on whatever aspects of Hella she thought the new colonists would need to know. Then I would edit a short video to illustrate the most important points of the report, using clips from available records. That way, those who needed all the details would have the detailed reports, and the rest of the colonists could just see the most important points illustrated. Mz. Campobello liked that idea. She said I should sign my name to every report and put it at the end of every video, so the new colonists would know who to thank when they arrived. That was very kind of her.

Mom and Jamie reviewed my first efforts and made a few suggestions, but after a while they saw I was getting the hang of it, and then they were both so busy with their own responsibilities that I was pretty much on my own. Except once in a while, I'd get a note from Lilla-Jack or Captain Skyler, suggesting this or that or the other thing too. So I knew they were reviewing my work too whenever they had a chance.

We sent off the first batch of reports and videos as soon as they were approved. We knew the colonists would be most interested in the saurs, so I made the first upload about the drive-around with Captain Skyler because that let me show the sea of grass and the furrows cut through it and finally the leviathans and the carnosaurs. I showed them all the most interesting details like the huge piles of dung, the thundering footsteps, the wrinkly skin, and the enormous muscles under the skin, and then all the different lichens and moss and bugs and parasites and birds that made their living on the saurs' backs. I called them walking ecosystems, which I thought was a good way to explain how everything was connected to everything else. It still took two hours for transmissions to reach the *Cascade,* so I didn't expect to receive immediate responses.

But all of that was only when I wasn't working on preparations for Lockdown. Everybody works at getting ready for Lockdown. The biggest leviathan herd of the Hellan year was rumbling toward us, like a monstrous grumbling tsunami of flesh. It wasn't one herd—it was fifty or sixty separate herds, some as large as a hundred individuals, all coming through the grassy plains on our north.

For most of the year, the different herds travel apart from one another—they have to, there wouldn't be enough foliage to feed all of them if they tried to travel together. But once a year, to get through the narrowest part of the migratory circle, they all converge on this single bottleneck. By the time it got to our neighborhood, the migration would number *thousands* of lumbering leviathans.

Before they moved on again, there would be a lot of very noisy, earth-shaking mating duels, followed by the ponderously slow mating frenzy of the victors. Then, just as quickly, they'd break up into new herds of varying sizes. The calves would follow their mothers of course, but the rest would just as likely follow whatever group was in front of them. The leviathans weren't very smart.

Behind them, they would leave a devastated landscape, churned up and stamped flat, swampy with their shit and piss, stinking like a vast latrine and ready for the winter storms. By spring, the land would be ripe again and all the waiting seeds would be eager to reach for the sun.

This particular coincidence of geography and migration made this part of the savannah uniquely fertile. It also guaranteed that there was a lot of interbreeding among the various herds, but it also put a lot of calves at risk because of the duels and subsequent mating encounters. Plus, when the migration bottled up like this, it became a target for dozens of packs of predators—and *their* mating duels too. For a week or longer, the savannah would be very noisy and very dangerous. We usually kept a swarm of drones overhead. Every year we learned something new about these creatures.

Summerland Station isn't in the direct path of the migration—we're twenty klicks south—but sometimes the southern edge of the migration comes a little too close, and we see occasional outliers near the lookout towers. Sometimes, even the test plot at First Marker gets trampled. The Big Break-In happened because a sudden summer storm pushed the migration farther south than usual. Our fences are pretty strong, designed to take a direct hit from a determined humongosaur, but after a few hundred times of being sideswiped and bumped by thirty or forty tons of clumsiness on giant flat feet, even the strongest wall is going to groan.

Some people think that it was a mistake to put Summerland Station so close to the path of the migration. The First Hundred knew about the migration for years before they moved out of Winterland. Summerland had been one of several outposts. It was close to six different ecological zones, so it was a good place for convenient studies of Hellan plants and animals. It was the closest site to the path of the herds and was a great place to study their behavior.

But if you read the historical records, you know that nobody woke up one day and said, "Hey, let's expand Summerland Station into a whole town." No, it just grew like this over time, because it was convenient, because so many people wanted a chance to see the saurs up close, and because it had some of the best weather of the year for outdoor crops.

After the Big Break-In, a lot of people wanted to locate Summerland farther south, but the colony didn't have the resources to move, and we had too much invested in this location. So instead, we built a bigger fence, instituted a whole new set of safety procedures, and hoped it would be enough. Up to the Big Break-In, it had been, but there were a lot of people—including Captain Skyler—who thought it was only a matter of time until the next big summer storm and the station found itself directly in the path of the entire herd, instead of being brushed only by its southern flank.

This year we should be okay. That little dust storm I'd noted on the drive-around had grown to a bigger storm, headed south, but so far it didn't represent a threat. Not a big one. Captain Skyler's convenient test of the dazzler system on our drive-around suggested that we might be able to annoy the herd a little, maybe distract it, maybe even nudge the outliers a little. Some years the outer fence got bumped, some years it didn't. It was too early to predict this year.

So my second report was about the migration and how we have to manage our defenses. It takes almost two weeks for the whole herd to pass by, and it's a very tense time because the herd could get spooked by the slightest thing—by lightning, by predators, by a change in the weather, or even by one of their octogenarians stumbling and falling. It wasn't likely they would stampede in our direction, but we kept the trucks and lifters ready for immediate evacuation the whole time.

Everybody knows the dangers. We even have a doomsday plan—install a field of landmines just beyond the outer perimeter. It would take less than a day to put the devices in place. There's a special ops team that preps the armaments every year, starting a month before the migration is due. The idea is that if we can stop the first animals in the stampede, the rest will turn back—or at worst, stampede themselves into a large impassible barrier of dead bodies and hungry predators feeding on them. We've never tested it, we've never had the need to, but that's why it's called a doomsday plan—because if it doesn't work, there will be nothing left of Summerland Station. After the migration passes, we do all our necessary repairs and then begin the winter Lockdown and evacuation.

We had drones and skyballs all over everywhere now, even a few scooters and lifters. But even those things could spook the herd, so we tried to keep them high and distant. But it's migration season, and we have to pay attention to everything. Yes, the saurs are magnificent, and I think everybody likes to watch them, but mostly we pay such close attention because we might have to get out of their way in a hurry.

We were seeing a lot more outliers this year. A few of the animals had already been picked off by carnosaurs. Once the carnosaurs had a kill, they would be too busy feeding to care about any subsequent outliers. But the skyballs and drones showed that the herds were spread out a lot more than we usually saw, so maybe that was the reason we were seeing so many smaller groups. But as long as none of them came within ten klicks of Summerland, we stayed at condition yellow—high alert, but no immediate threat.

Over dinner one night, Mom said that the census of the herds was showing a lot more calves. It had been going on for two or three years now. It might be an anomaly, but people on the science team think it's part of a longer cycle, that the total population of leviathans rises and falls over a period of many years in response to a matching cycle in the vegetation. When the population of leviathans rises, the Atlas trees develop increasing tanninoid production. Does that slow down fertility among young females? A few years later, when the population levels drop enough, so do the trees' defenses. Mom says that's a likely explanation, but there could be other interactions as well that we still don't know about. I put that into a sidebar report. Something extra to think about.

And there was that other cycle too—the back and forth between the leviathans and the carnosaurs. More calves this year meant more outliers next year and more outliers meant more meals for more carnosaurs, plus the normal culling of sick and elderly, so the carnosaurs would be able to increase their own reproduction rate and that would put another kind of pressure on the herds. So if enough of the herds died, or even had a population crash—we hadn't seen one yet, but it wasn't impossible—a die-off would mean a corresponding die-off for the carnosaurs, and that would create a growth opportunity for the forests. Then the herds could flourish again and the cycle would start all over. Jamie says the cycles are a way of maintaining ecological balance. We have a lot of historical records, but the cycles seem to be longer than a single lifetime, so we still don't have a complete pattern, just a lot of simulations and guesstimates.

Migration time is kind of like an extended holiday. Everything stops while we wait to see if the passing saurs are going to come too close. Most of the time, we never see them, not even from the towers. At their closest, they're still ten or twenty klicks away. Occasionally, one or two outliers will cross the open spaces near the outer perimeter and everybody will rush to the fences or the lookout posts to watch.

But most of the time, it's just an excuse for an end-of-season party. The cafeteria serves dino-shaped cakes and some folks dress up in dino costumes or wear dino-hats. It's all very silly and fun. The Summerland Band plays monster music and everybody dances the dino dance. The only thing we don't do is set off fireworks or shine lasers into the sky. That might be something that could spook the herd and nobody wants to find that out the hard way.

And five Hella months after migration time, there are always a few babies born, sometimes more than a dozen. So that's another holiday—Baby Season. There are over three hundred people in the colony all with the same birthday, or within one or two days of each other. So we have birthday season five months after migration season. Hella months. Some people speculate that if we were to keep that up for a few hundred years that eventually humans would evolve a yearly mating cycle too.

That was another sidebar report. It would be good for the new colonists to share the migration holiday, even vicariously. Mom said that it would help them understand the cycles of life on Hella, not just the saurs, but the human calendar too.

I was getting pretty good. I could write out a whole report in the morning, finishing before midday nap, then put together a video summary before second dinner. If I turned it in early enough, Mz. Campobello would have notes for me the following morning. Sometimes though, she would just approve my work as is and upload it straight to the *Cascade.*

For the longest time, I didn't get any response at all from the starship about any of my reports. They were too busy figuring out orbits and trajectories and their eventual download schedules. Plus they had to work out what crops to plant in their own starship farms, so they could sustain themselves for those extra few months in space. But they did send us a lot of music from the Dingillian Interstellar Orchestra and also biographies of the entire contingent of colonists so we could start planning how best to assimilate their population into ours.

We plugged their social network into ours and every night, our people would scour through their biographies, looking to see who was hot and who was not, who was weird and who was interesting. We assumed they were doing the same with our bios. By the time they actually started dropping pods in the spring, a lot of people would be good friends.

I knew that I would be happy if I could find a friend like myself.

And then, finally, the saurs arrived. The entire herd. A little closer than we liked, but not so close that we were unpacking the landmines. Despite the distance, several klicks, we could hear them very well. They were a distant chorus, very faint and far away, like something just below the edge of the horizon. Something spooky and disturbing. It went on all day and all night. They moaned and grumbled and growled in such low frequencies that we felt them as much as we heard them. The ground vibrated with a relentless rumble, like an unsettling earthquake that wouldn't stop.

We smelled them too. Even before the morning dew evaporated, the grassy, sweaty, beefy miasma came rolling in—a great stinky cloud, like a silent-but-deadly fart from some giant sky-god. People wrinkled their noses and waved their hands in front of their faces, but they smiled too because after all the annoyances, it was funny.

Migration time is my favorite holiday. It's one of the biggest. We hang colored banners and flags above the quad and paint our faces with green and yellow stripes. I made a video and uploaded it to the *Cascade*, so they'd know how we celebrate.

On the third day, several outliers crossed the fields just beyond the outer perimeter, and one of them even sideswiped the outer fence, a slow grinding movement. The fence groaned and creaked, but it held and everybody breathed a great sigh of relief and said things like "whew" and "good job." Sensors showed that despite their overall flexibility, a couple of the outer mid-logs had cracked under the assault and would have to be replaced, but the total integrity of the fence remained high. We had extra logs laid out over the warehouse trench, so a crew would get out there tonight, working under the lights to repair the damage. The cracked logs wouldn't be wasted, we'd use the lumber elsewhere.

Later in the day, when three more animals came wandering through, Captain Skyler drove out and tried his "Go Away" system on the beasts, all the lights and sounds and smells, but while it had startled the carnosaurs, the leviathans were a lot less responsive to the flashes and noise and stinks. They grunted. They moaned a little louder than usual. One of them made as if to rear back, then decided that was too much effort. Instead, it just "trotted" away. How do you know a leviathan is trotting? Instead of going *boom boom boom*, it goes *boom boom boom!* Old joke, but still true.

Several teams on scooters waited at the gate. Every so often one team or another rode out to tag the passing animals. It was a routine operation, but everybody watched just in case it wasn't routine. It was our own Hella-rodeo, an exciting competition between the teams. We all cheered every time a dart was fired and cheered again when the signal came in green. Once, before I was born—but everybody still talks about it—two outliers actually mated just on the other side of the fence. Everybody with a camera took videos. All of that, plus the official recordings, were some of the most viewed files in the library. Look it up under, "So that's how they do it!"

That night, after second supper, Captain Skyler came to see Mom. They hadn't spoken since the evening of the big argument and things had gotten very tense, so Jamie went to stay with his dad, which made his dad happy. Jamie asked me if I would be okay and I said yes I would, he should go be with his dad for a while. Mostly I hid out in my room, writing reports.

Some people can dictate easily. I think better when I type. I can type very fast, sometimes even faster than I can think of what to type. Sometimes I have to stop and think about what to say next. That's what I was doing when the door chimed.

"I'll get it," Mom called. I heard her say, "Cord," as if she meant "turd." And then she said, "Come in." I tried to hear what they said next, but they were talking very softly, so I dug out the toy mouse ears Mom gave me when Jamie did his first ride-along, so I could feel part of the mission too. I put them on and turned the volume up. I'm not supposed to do that, it's impolite, but that's what everybody does with outside-ears anyway. I still had to strain to listen.

"I came to apologize."

"That's not necessary. You said what you said. You can't take it back."

"I'm sorry I hurt you. You know how I feel about you. You know how I feel about the boys. I'm trying to protect you. You're so busy in your laboratory that sometimes you don't see what else is going on. This place—it's gotten big enough to have real politics. The worst kind. Selfish. And selfish people—they don't care who they hurt. I don't want you getting hurt. And I don't want the boys getting hurt—"

"Cord," she said. "Shut up."

"If it's over between us, just say so—"

"Cord! Shut up and listen." There was a loud silence while the Captain shut up. Then Mom said, "I'm pregnant."

And then they didn't say anything else for a long while, but it sounded like Mom was crying.

Most pregnancies are planned. You do all the tests, all the genetic mapping, and if you're satisfied with the result, you reserve a bottle, you wait five Hella-months, and you have a baby. But sometimes, people get pregnant by surprise. Sometimes the pills don't work the way they're supposed to. It happens. And sometimes, people actually decide to have a baby the old-fashioned way. I don't know why. It looks messy and painful and ugly to me. But that's another of those things I don't understand.

Mom is old-fashioned about babies. Maybe it's because she was born male, but changed so she could experience her own pregnancy with Jamie, and then with me. I asked her why she never changed back and she said she was having more fun this way, but she said I should make up my own mind. Mom says it's a good thing for people to know both sides. It makes people happier. It also makes them better partners, but she didn't explain that, she said I'd understand it better when I got older. Sometimes I wonder how old I will have to be to understand everything. But I think she meant that people who've been both male and female usually have better sex. That's what the noise said.

Mom says that all the genetic testing and bottle-growing will likely have an evolutionary effect over time, and she's not sure that's a good thing. What if we're throwing away genes we need and don't know yet why we need them? Mom says that the worst kind of ignorance is that we don't know what it is that we don't know. But that's why Mom thinks babies should be homegrown, not bottle-grown, because as good as the bottle-babies are, there's a whole different mother-child relationship in an old-fashioned pregnancy. Mom has very strong feelings about babies.

I don't even understand why anyone wants to have children in the first place. I certainly don't. They're loud and messy and they usually smell funny. And they're kinda stupid about everything. But if Mom was going to have a baby, then I was going to be a big brother. Like Jamie. So that meant I'd have to be the best big brother possible. Like Jamie.

I thought about that for a bit, then after I was through thinking, I came out of my room. Mom and Captain Skyler were sitting quietly on the couch, holding hands. Mom's eyes were red.

"Kyle," she began. "We have something to tell you—"

"I know," I said. "And I can help. I'm Class 3 on child care, and I can get certified Class 4 in time to help."

Mom and the Captain looked at each other, smiled, then looked back to me. "No, that's not what we want to tell you. We've decided to get married."

"Oh. Okay. But I still want to help with the baby, okay?"

The next day, there were even more outliers passing through the outer fields. The overnight team had laid extra layers of logs on the outermost fences, and that would be enough for a normal season, but this season wasn't normal anymore. We were seeing a lot more leviathans than at any time since the Big Break-In, and people were starting to get concerned. As strong as the fences were, they wouldn't stop an entire migration.

After the Big Break-In, the Council had declared an X-Prize for whoever came up with the best defense system. The X-Prize would be a private suite at Winterland. A lot of people suggested a lot of ideas, some of them impractical, like digging a big moat around the station, and some of them were just impossible, like spraying the whole perimeter with carnosaur urine. Carnosaur urine would work, but the bigger problem would be collecting it. No thanks. We could synthesize the key odor ingredients but anyone who's smelled carnosaur urine would know they wouldn't want to live inside a great big circle of the smell.

One of the behavioral researchers suggested that we could mount super-brights on top of the fences to display rapid blinking, hyper-ugly, dazzler patterns, like Captain Skyler's Go-Away lights out in the field, only more intense. A lot of people thought that might work, and the Council agreed, so the engineering team fabbed an array of multiple displays, each one brighter than the sun, designed to flash all kinds of disturbing colors directly at the animals. From inside the station, all those lights would certainly add to the party atmosphere of migration time, but on the outside—if having dazzlers flashing before your eyes annoyed the creatures as much as it annoyed humans, it would be one of the most efficient solutions possible.

Some people also wanted to add high-pitched screeches, or low-frequency booming to the displays, but the Council put those suggestions on hold, because we still didn't know if the lights would deter or spook the herd. We'd know better after an actual test.

I made videos for the colonists on the *Cascade.* One of the best had lots of closeups of their heavy feet pummeling the ground, raising clouds of dust and small insects, showing why the leviathans are called thunderfeet. Some people like the way they make the ground shake as they lumber along. They think it's fun. I don't. It's hard to sleep with the ground booming.

By mid-morning, there were half a dozen thunderfeet plodding heavily through the outer fields and Madam Coordinator gave the go-ahead to turn on the dazzlers. From inside the fence, it looked as if the whole world outside had gotten brighter, more colorful and even a little flickery, a whole lot more unreal-looking, like something in a fantasy movie. It was almost too bright to look at. Most interesting, the leviathans shone with new colors, as if they had all turned into an HDR video.

From their side, it should have been painful. It should have disoriented them—but it didn't. The leviathans have thick eyelids that they close against the big dust storms that scour the dry regions. They closed their eyes now and kept blindly on, waving their great shovel-shaped heads back and forth, following their noses and paying no attention at all to the dazzler lights. No X-Prize there. Carnosaurs, maybe. Leviathans, no joy.

But we still had our fences, strengthened by the overnight crews, so as much as we were all disappointed, we weren't anxious. Jamie and I went to the outer fence and peered through the spaces between the log rails. We watched the monsters shamble east, each ponderous footstep rumbling through the ground, a feeling more than a sound. Jamie called it the kettledrums of the underworld. The dust was vibrating and leaping with every thump. Tiny creatures scurried back and forth, unsettled by the trembling.

At sunset, the migration slowed. All the different things we called them—leviathans, thunderfeet, longnecks, shovelmouths, Hellathings, and dammitalready—had mostly settled down for the night, huddling together in groups to preserve their body heat against the cold wind. The night winds hadn't gotten dangerous yet, but they were starting to get uncomfortable. Already some people were beginning their preparations for winter. Mom was shutting down the parts of her lab that wouldn't be moving to Winterland. Other people were loading the trucks with important equipment and as much produce from the summer harvest as we could carry.

The rule was to always have enough food stored at Winterland for at least three years of famine. Even though we had sufficient grow-tanks at both stations now, nobody wanted to risk a repeat of the Great Winter Famine of the Ninth Year. The colony had been caught by surprise then. Never again.

After sunset, the cafeteria always serves first dinner and a few hours later, second dinner. It's not a major meal for most people, but a lot of teams are still out when first dinner is served, so second dinner is just as big. During migration week, both dinners are heavily attended because a lot of young people stay up late to party.

After I finished uploading the day's video, I found Jamie at our regular table, sitting with friends. Sometimes Jamie gives me a signal to sit somewhere else, but not tonight. Jamie explained it to me once. Sometimes he wants to have a private conversation with a girl or with a buddy, and a third person—any person—would make that difficult or impossible. He said it was just like sometimes how I like to be alone in the shower. When he explained it that way, I sort of understood, so I don't mind too much when he gives me the signal. But this time he waved when he saw me and called me over to join them.

Emily-Faith sat next to Jamie. She was his sometime-girlfriend-but-not-quite. Jubilee and Malik and Farron were there too. They looked very happy. They were laughing very loudly.

"What's so funny?" I asked, putting my tray down on the table.

Jamie helped himself to some of my fries. "Marley Layton is funny."

"I don't understand." There were a lot of jokes I didn't understand. Jamie always did his best to explain them to me.

"Marley has been sent to Bitch Canyon to do her community service."

"Oh."

"That's the joke. It's so appropriate."

Farron said, "It's not like they don't already have enough bitches there. Why do they need one more?"

"Oh. I get it. I guess."

Farron patted the table next to my hand, her way of almost touching me. She said, "Kyle, you are so cute." She turned to Jamie. "You know, one day, I am going to pop his cherry."

"Good luck with that," said Jamie. "First you'll have to find it."

It took me a few seconds to figure out what they meant. I had to visit the noise. When I did get it, I frowned slightly. Or maybe I blushed. Or maybe I did both at the same time. I opened my mouth, then I closed it again. The last time I said what I thought about sex, that it's kind of icky, everybody laughed. Jamie said, "Someday you'll feel different. You're weird, little brother, BUT not that weird." Jamie is the only person who can say things like that to me because I know he means well and those are friendly jokes, not mean ones.

Bitch Canyon is nearly a thousand klicks west. It's a deep chasm that started as an earthquake fault and ended up with a rapid river carving a series of deep gullies through layers of shale and sandstone. The walls of the canyons are pitted with countless caves, each one with its own personal ecology of things that look like insects or reptiles, and even a few things that might one day be mammals. There are creatures that look like spiders and crabs and centipedes and scorpions and lizards and snakes and scuttlebugs and rats and birds, all sizes, but aren't really any of those things—just things that took advantage of a convenient evolutionary path.

The outpost there is a year-round station. Less than thirty people live there. Their job is to study a very weird ecological phenomenon, an isolated population of creatures that look like they're going to evolve into flying mammals. Kind of like bats, only bigger. And meaner. But they haven't quite mastered homeostasis yet, so they're still limited to a region where the weather is mostly uniform. They're almost all females. A female can give birth to only one pup a year. If it's a male, she might reject it or even kill it. Only a third of all male pups survive to reproduce. I read that in the reports.

Mom says that this behavior should produce females who are hormonally or genetically designed to produce more female pups than males. Already, the local population produces six female pups for every four males, and the best projection has it that sometime within the next thousand generations, that ratio could rise to 7:3. At some point, that would favor the parent that produces male cubs, because a single male could distribute its genes to many females in a single mating season. We don't know yet because the ratio of females has been rising for as long as we've been monitoring the populations.

Mom says it's difficult work, trapping, tagging, measuring, sexing, dissecting, and evaluating. It requires a lot of patience. Marley Layton will probably hate it. But Mom says it's important because it's a remarkable evolutionary laboratory. We've never had the chance to observe anything like this before, and it's important that we do, because Hella isn't Earth, it isn't even Earth-like. As the geologists tell us, don't take anything for granite. Jamie had to explain that one to me, too. And other people think *I'm* weird.

Jubilee said, "What if Marley has a natural affinity for all those little bitches? Maybe she'll discover why they eat their children."

"It's too bad Marley's mom didn't feel the same way," Malik said. Everybody laughed.

Jamie looked across the table at me, he could see my expression was pinching up.

"Guys?" he said. "We gotta change the subject. Kyle doesn't like ugly talk like this. Even when it's aimed at someone who deserves it."

"You're right," said Malik. "Sorry, Kyle."

I said thank you back to him. Most of Jamie's friends understand how I feel, but sometimes they forget. Jamie says they're good people and that they like me, so it's all right for me to like them.

I turned back to Jamie. "When are you coming back home?"

"Is Mom still mad?"

"I don't think so." I looked at his friends, then back to him. I didn't know if it was all right to say anything in front of them. "She said she was going to call you and talk to you if you didn't come back tonight."

"Is it important?"

I didn't know how to answer that question. Different people have different interpretations of the word "important." Some people mean important-to-the-colony, some people mean important-to-me, some people mean important-to-you. Some people mean important even when it isn't important to anyone. "I think it's important to Mom."

"Oh," he said. "One of those kinds of talks."

"No. This is not one of those kinds of talks. It's something else."

Jamie looked around at his friends, then back to me. "Okay. Do you want to tell me privately?"

"It can wait," I said. I bent to my soup.

Jamie grabbed his crutches and levered himself to his feet. He nodded toward the side of the cafeteria and hobbled away from the table. I followed him off to the west wall where no one could hear us. He anchored himself and leaned toward me. "Kyle. Tell me. Did she find out?"

"Huh? What are you talking about?"

"You can tell me. Did she find out?"

"Find out what?"

"I'm not going to Winterland."

"Huh? You're not? Where are you going instead?"

"Nowhere. I'm staying here at Summerland Station with the maintenance crew. So is Emily-Faith."

"But who decided that? You didn't tell me."

"I haven't told anyone. You're the first. My dad arranged it this morning."

"Without talking to Mom?"

"I'm almost six years old! That's old enough for me to make my own decisions. Dad agreed. I thought you'd be happy for me."

"I guess I am. I mean, but I thought we were going to be together at Winterland."

I'm not very good at eye contact, especially when I get surprised or confused, I look away, so Jamie had to turn me to face him. "Kyle, please don't be upset. I was going to tell you tonight, even before I told Mom. Except you said that Mom wants to talk to me. How did she find out?"

"She didn't. I mean, I don't think she did. That's not why she wants to talk to you. She's having a baby. We're going to be big brothers, both of us. Oh—and she's marrying Captain Skyler too."

"Oh, that's no surprise. I knew they were going to get married. That was obvious weeks ago. But a baby? What is she thinking?"

"Um. It's already started. I don't think you can change your mind after you've started, can you?"

"Uh—" Now Jamie's expression got really bad. "Um. Yeah, actually. Sometimes you can. But—it would have to be really serious. I'll explain it later, kiddo. Or you can look it up for yourself. Argh. This complicates everything." He turned away, turned back to me, turned away again, in that little dance of frustration he does sometimes when he isn't sure what to say or where to go or what happens next.

"Jamie! What about me? What am I going to do all winter without you?"

That stopped him. He faced me. He put his hands on my shoulders. I shook them off. I didn't want him touching me now.

"Kyle," he said. "You're my brother. You're always going to be my brother. We'll see each other every day, we'll talk to each other just like now. Only it'll be—you know, on the phone."

"It's not the same. It won't be the same."

"Kyle, you're almost five years old." On Earth, that would be thirteen and a third. The noise automatically gives me that calculation. "You have a job. You're going places. You've already had your first outing. All you need is a little practice being on your own, and you'll be fine."

"No, I won't."

"Sure you will."

"Jamie, you're the only real friend I have in the whole world. And now you're leaving me. You're not going to be there when I need you. That's not fair. It just isn't." I could feel an upset building up inside.

"Kyle? It's a very big opportunity for me. I can get credentialed. Do you want me to turn it down?"

I wanted to say yes, please turn it down, I wanted to yell at him, I wanted to throw something at the wall and stamp out of the cafeteria. But I didn't have anything to throw and even if I did, I knew I shouldn't do any of those things. Instead, I made myself count my breaths. I could have used the noise, but I didn't. Instead, I counted and counted and breathed as slowly as I could. Jamie never took his eyes off me the whole time, and I think maybe that's how I was able to bring myself back. As mad as I was at him I still didn't want to disappoint him.

At last I looked at him, straight on, and I said, "Jamie, you're always teaching me how to be careful, how to watch what I say so I won't be selfish. This is one of those times, isn't it? I have to do what's best, yes? Not what I want, but what you want?"

"Kyle, that's right. This is one of those times. And I'm proud of you for recognizing it. See? That proves you're ready to be on your own."

He was right, but it didn't change anything. I wanted to cry. And I hadn't done that since my dad died.

I'm not allowed to act out anymore. Jamie says I have to find something else to do instead. He calls it "sublimation." I don't see anything sublime about it at all, but Jamie says that's a different word even though it looks like it comes from the same root.

So I went home and took a shower and washed myself for a long time, then I put on a soft longshirt and nothing else, closed the door to my room, and started editing a longer video about the leviathans and their annual migration. It was something to do, so I wouldn't have to think about things I didn't want to think about.

Jamie knows I don't like being touched. It's even more than that. I don't even like wearing clothes, it's like being in a portable cage. Most of the work clothes we have to wear feel too rough, and when I have to tighten the belts and the straps and wear all the necessary tools and survival kits, I feel confined. So when I'm alone, I wear a kilt or a longshirt and nothing else. When I was little, Marley teased me that I was "girlish," which didn't make sense at all to me, because I stopped being a girl before I was three, when I wanted to be a boy like Jamie. Besides, Marley was tall and burly and only wore workshoes and jumpsuits. If I wore a heavy jumpsuit like her, would that be "girlish?" And why was "girlish" an insult anyway? I told Marley she was stupid and she punched me.

Mom says it's all right to wear whatever makes you happy, that's why we have lots of dress-up holidays all year long. But the fabbers and weavers and cutting machines and sewing bots are always so busy with other things that we really don't spend a lot of time on costumes. Mostly it's face-painting and silly hats and the occasional old robe pulled out of storage and repurposed. Migration time, everyone wears something silly. It's a tradition that started with the Big Break-In when everyone had to evacuate in whatever they were wearing. So now we wear whatever.

It's the mid-party that gets the most attention because it's the halfway point, at least we hope it's the halfway point. Everyone says that if nothing bad has happened by the halfway, nothing bad is going to happen at all because more than half the herd has passed.

But that's not really true, because after most of the migration passes, there's another few days of prowling bigmouths trailing the slower members of the herd, so people have to stay close to the station and concentrate on preparations for our own migration. Sometimes the carnosaurs will gnaw at the outer fence or even throw themselves at it. We think they're trying to get at our cows. So if anything really bad is going to happen, that's the most dangerous time.

We have a lot of videos of the Big Break-In. I love watching them, because they're some of the best close-ups we have of leviathan calves. Most of the time we can't get close to them, the moms are very protective. The Big Break-In started with a crush of leviathans bringing down a whole section of outer fence. Three of them were so badly injured in the stumble that they couldn't get up again. And two of them had calves who stayed with them, moaning pitifully. It's really sad, because the bigmouths moved in that night and killed the calves first. The moms could only watch and screech.

The Council voted to euthanize the injured leviathans, they were calling them thunderfeet in the video, I think that's where that name got started. That was merciful, but then they started talking about taking down the carnosaurs too until someone pointed out that if they did that, the pile of meat would just get bigger and attract even more predators, so they had to "let nature take its course" which mostly translated out to "do nothing," watch and wait.

According to the records, some people, my dad included, wanted to torch the carcasses. All of the saurs are afraid of fire. But the Council didn't want to spare the fuel and some of the scientists wanted to gather samples of leviathan meat. Some of the others just wanted to watch the carnosaurs eat, because they thought it might be important to know. But some people, I think Mom was one of them, said they just wanted a close-up seat for the gore-fest.

A special emergency team had to stay at Summerland to repair the broken fences. It took most of the Winter. Everybody else had to evacuate. It wasn't until after we got settled in at Winterland Station that Mom told me that my dad wouldn't be joining us. I was very young, not even two. All the youngest and their moms had been evacuated first. We were lifted out, Mom said I slept the whole way, they might have sedated me, Jamie said I could be difficult, but that was before I got the noise, but anyway Mom didn't know how to tell me what had really happened to my dad and how I might react, so she just said that he couldn't come with us. Of course, I didn't believe her, I wanted to walk all the way back to Summerland because I knew she was lying to me, but she wasn't. If it wasn't for Jamie staying with me all the time, I don't know what I would have done. He says it was hard because he knew what Mom wasn't telling me, but that's when Jamie and I started being friends.

I put as much of this as I could into my own videos. If you just access the raw video, there's a lot of boring stuff, animals just plodding along or munching grass or standing around not doing anything at all. What I like to do is focus in on all the little details, the way the skin wrinkles when a leviathan shifts its weight just before it lifts a huge foot, the way the ground quakes when that same foot comes down again, the way the dust leaps up around every booming thump, the way the huge tail lifts when the leviathan starts dropping its big manure-bombs, all the little insect-things that come scurrying out of the dirt attracted by the droppings, all the creatures that live on the backs and sides of the giant beasts.

I especially like to show how the great shovelmouths work—that's another thing we call them. You have to see them eat to understand.

Grass doesn't have a lot of nutritional value in it, so the leviathans have to gather in as much as possible with every bite, that's why they have such wide faces. They're not very neat eaters either, they pull up great clumps, but as much falls back to the ground as they gather in. They chew and chew and chew. They also pick up gravel from the gravel beds, because the grinding of the stones in their guts helps break up the stiff grass so the bacteria in their intestines can convert the cellulose to glucose. Wherever you find a pile of time-rounded stones, you've found a place where a leviathan died. A lot of times, carrion-eaters drag the bones away, but not the belly stones.

The migration goes in a great clockwise circle, although for a couple years it was a lopsided hourglass shape because a series of crushing storms pushed the migration in on itself. I wonder if the migration is clockwise because of the direction the planet rotates, like the way water circles the drain in the northern hemisphere, or is it just the way the animals have evolved to make the most of the availability of food across the changing seasons. And how much of it is the weather? Someday we'll get around to modeling all the different factors, but Jamie says we still don't know what all the different factors are.

There's a place on the southwest end of the migration, even farther south than Winterland Station, where the spring floods make for some very dangerous river crossings. The water rushes fast, the river is deep, the footing is slippery, and the crocosaurs come rushing in to attack the leviathans. When the rivers shrink to streams during the driest part of the summer, there are bones everywhere, and layers and layers of rounded stones, thousands of years of belly stones. Some of the explorers call it "bellystone park." I think that's supposed to be a joke, but I don't get it. It must be an Earth-joke. We seem to have a lot of those. I put that into the video because if it was an Earth-joke, the new colonists would probably get it. Maybe one of them would explain it to me, but Jamie says when you explain a joke, it stops being funny.

According to the clock, I worked twelve hours and missed a few meals. It wasn't until Jamie hobbled in that I realized how long I'd been working. "Come on, Kyle. I checked. You've missed three suppers." I didn't want to go, but he wouldn't take no for an answer. I followed him back to the caf where Mom and Captain Skyler and Emily-Faith were all chattering happily over late night pie and coffee. Apparently, I had missed a lot of conversations.

I got myself a cheese and mango sandwich and a couple of hard-boiled eggs and a bowl of fruit salad and a limonade fizzy. I'd go back for pie and coffee later, if I still had room. I sat down at the end of the table without saying anything. Everybody said hello, and I grunted hello back.

"Hey, Kyle," Captain Skyler said. "I see you got a lot of good work done. Very nice job today."

"Thank you," I said, without looking up from my sandwich.

"Listen, Kyle—" He moved his chair around so he was closer to me. "I want to tell you something. It's all right if you don't ever want to call me dad. You can keep calling me Captain if you want. But I'd like to know if it's all right for me to call you son?"

"I don't care."

Mom and the Captain looked at each other. Then both looked back at me. "Are you unhappy about something?"

"No. Yes. Jamie's not coming with us. I'm going to be all alone."

"No, you won't, you have lots of friends—" Mom started to argue, but Captain Skyler put a hand over hers to stop her. Amazing—it worked.

He turned back to me. "Yes, Kyle, you will be alone. More alone than ever before. Because that's part of growing up. That's what it means to be a grownup, being able to be on your own. But your mom will be there. And I will too. So you won't always be alone."

"It won't be the same," I said. Then I took a big bite of my sandwich so I wouldn't have to say anything else.

"Well . . ." The Captain said gently, "I don't think you have any choice in the matter, Kyle. No, wait, that's wrong. You do have a choice. You can grow up—or you can just grow older without growing up. Like Marley Layton. Do you want to be like Marley?"

"No." I muttered it into my sandwich.

"I didn't think so. Kyle, you're very smart. You're one of the smartest people in the colony. You're even smarter than you think you are."

"So what?" I took another bite.

"So this." He slid a memory card across the table.

"What's this?" I said it with my mouth full.

"It's a whole bunch of messages from people on the *Cascade*, thanking you for all the videos."

"Really?" I looked at the card in front of me.

"Really. And they want you to make more. They've got all kinds of questions about all the things that live in the savannah. They want to know about the crow-birds, the hoppers, everything—the swimmers, the flyers, the crawlers, the mud-bugs, the night-grumblers, everything. They want you to make more videos."

"Really?"

"Yes, really!" That was Jamie. "See? You're already making new friends."

"But you're my best friend. And I'm going to miss you."

"You're my best friend too, Kyle. And I'm going to miss you a whole lot. More than you know."

"Really?"

"Yes, you numble-butt! Really!"

"Am not a numble-butt! What's a numble-butt?"

"You are."

"Jamie! I don't want to lose you—" The words came out before I could stop them. "My dad got killed staying at Summerland!"

"Oh," he said. "Oh. Now I understand." He came over and sat

beside me on the bench. He put his arm around my shoulder. I let him. He leaned in and whispered into my ear. "I'll be careful. I promise. I'll be super-careful."

"My dad was super-careful."

"Uh-huh. And you're scared that you'll lose me. That you'll be alone."

I nodded.

"Hey, don't you know how hard this is going to be on me, not having you around? You're my best friend."

"Um." That's one of the things about my syndrome. I don't think about other people enough.

Jamie said, "Kyle, I don't have to tell you how big an opportunity this is. Maintenance engineers are some of the most important jobs on Hella. They make things work. They build things. They design things. They run the fabbers. I almost didn't apply, because I didn't want to leave you, but—" He looked across to Emily-Faith, then back to me. "—but Emily-Faith said that you needed to find out that you could do things without me. You're growing up, Kyle. You're turning into a really interesting person. I am so proud of you. Part of me wants to stay and see what you're going to do next. And part of me wants to know what you can do on your own. But just like you have to figure out what's next for you, I have to figure out what's next for me. Otherwise we both stay stuck. So here we are and I'm already so unhappy I can't even think right." He stopped then, out of breath.

"Oh," I said. "But we'll still be able to talk to each other, Jamie. Every day. You won't have to worry. I'll be all right, I know that. I'm just going to miss sharing sandwiches with you and sitting on your bed and talking over the whole day with you."

"Yeah, I'm going to miss that too."

"I'll be all right," I said. "Really."

Emily-Faith looked at Jamie. "See? I told you."

The memory card was filled with messages from a lot of people on the *Cascade.* It took me several days, but I read all of them, each and every one. There were a lot, but I answered all of the questions that I could. Each time I opened a note, I also looked at the biography of the sender. A lot of the notes were from people who planned to research the plants and animals of Hella, but a lot more were from people my age.

A girl named J'mee Cheifitz wrote that she loved all kinds of animals. She hoped that we had dogs. I told her that we do have some dogs working lookout, but we don't have any dogs for pets yet. But we have stem cells in cryo, so maybe someday.

A boy named Trent had lost his father on the voyage. He still had his mother though, a little brother named Jason and a littler sister named Willa. He asked a lot of questions, mostly about the kinds of trees and plants and flowers that grew on Hella.

I also heard from Gary Andraza, Chris Pavek, and Milla Nomor. Milla wanted to know about recipes and cooking and painting. Chris wanted to know more about the drive-arounds, he wanted to explore Hella. Gary wanted to know everything.

And then there was Charles, he was the one who had organized the band that played the music that they broadcast to us when they popped out of hyperstate. Charles was my age, almost five Hella-years. He had an older brother who was married to his boy friend, and a younger brother too. He asked if we had people in the colony who played instruments. Did we have a band or an orchestra? I told him that I knew several people who played instruments, and they played as a band for holidays. I promised to introduce him to them.

They all asked about the leviathans, of course. Then I surprised them by telling them that the leviathans weren't the biggest animals on Hella. The humongosaurs were almost twice the size of leviathans. But they didn't form gigantic herds. The land couldn't support such an ambulatory biomass. The largest humongosaur family we'd ever tracked had only fifteen members, mostly moms and calves. But if a group ever got larger than that, it would have to split into two families. We'd seen that happen twice already.

Occasionally, we saw a few humongosaur families traveling with the leviathan migration, but for the most part they had a different path across the continent, because they could eat higher up on the trees. But as curious as we were about the humongosaurs, the leviathans were of much greater interest.

The more we learned, the more we realized that the leviathan migration was one of the engines that drove the entire life cycle of the continent. They were the keystone species. They churned through every ecological zone—digging water holes, fertilizing, stamping the grass flat and giving other plants a chance to grow, providing vectors for all the creatures that lived on them and off them, feeding predator families with their sick and elderly, carving passes through difficult terrain, and probably a whole bunch more things we hadn't seen or realized yet.

There were other people my age on the *Cascade* too. Mom encouraged me to write back to all of them because you never know which ones will end up as best friends. Sometimes we sent video messages too, but I don't like video messages. It takes too long for people to get to the point. I can read faster than I can listen. And I don't like sending video messages because sometimes people react weird. Because some people think I talk funny. Not normal.

But in one message, Milla was all breathless and excited. She had heard it from Charles who had heard it from someone named Harlie that the *Cascade* was not going back to Earth for any more pilgrimages. More than half the crew had voted to stay here on Hella, at least for a while, until they figured out if it was safe to return. They were going to send a remote probe first. Because Earth wasn't Earth anymore. The polycrisis had settled that.

Apparently, they talked about it a lot and finally decided that there wasn't much the *Cascade* could do to help the people on Earth except maybe evacuate another fifteen hundred. And that was problematic too. It would depend on being able to find people who would be good for the colony and load the right kinds of supplies and equipment to sustain the voyage and bring enough useful payload back to the colony to make the voyage worthwhile. Without a functioning authority, none of that would be possible. Milla said that just getting away from Luna for this trip had been a little "hairy-scary."

I shared Milla's message with Mom and the Captain, and they confirmed it. Instead of twelve hundred new colonists, we would have to prepare for more than fourteen hundred. The crew of the *Cascade* was committed to keeping the ship star-worthy, but they were still arguing about when it would be safe to attempt a return to Earth. Maybe not for a long time. So right now, the plan was that they would stay for at least a year and help us with our summer crops and whatever else they could do to give the colony more resilience. At the end of the year, the remote probe should have returned, and then they could decide what to do next.

The more immediate problem was here on Hella.

Councilor Layton and some of the other Council members introduced a resolution to reassess the download schedule, perhaps delaying the bulk of the landings, or bringing them down only a small number at a time.

A lot of people looked puzzled by that, so Councilor Layton explained that we were always adjusting plans and schedules according to circumstances, mostly weather, but also resources, maybe we needed to be more cautious before we overextended the colony's resources. It's all about logistics. We can't risk overextending ourselves. Not right now. There's too many of them. We don't have the space for them. It'll put a huge strain on our resources. This planet is dangerous. If they don't learn how to survive, they'll put us all in danger. It'll be chaotic. People will die.

A lot of hands went up, people had questions or comments. But Councilor Layton held up a hand for people to wait while he took a drink of water from the glass in front of him. When he continued, he said, "Yes, we have to be fair. I recognize that many of them will have valuable skills, but we've all looked over the rosters and not all of them do. There's a lot of families, a lot of children. We need to manage the arrival process so it works for everyone."

It almost made sense, but I could see the other Councilors frowning, making notes, checking their tablets, looking up data, even running simulations.

Apparently, Councilor Layton had been planning this for a while, because all of a sudden, there were people standing up to agree with him. One by one, they added their own arguments. They said that adding so many new people to the colony would push us to the limit. That was true. We'd lose our resiliency. That was possible. And if they weren't the right kind of people, why should we let them land and be a drain on our economy?

That's when the conversation got all weird and red-faced.

The next person up was Torg Sumpton, one of the outland mechanics who only came back to the station to resupply. I don't think anyone knew him very well, but he always had something to say about everything. "These people, they're all rich-bitches, aren't they? Poor people don't buy starship tickets. No, they don't. These are the people who screwed up Earth and then ran away. They'll do the same here. We can't trust them. We shouldn't allow any of them to land. Only some of them. The right ones. The rest should stay on the *Cascade.*

Let the *Cascade* be a self-sufficient space station. They can observe Hella from orbit. And if the crew decides to go back to Earth, they could take all those unwanted people back with them."

He had a lot more to say, but he didn't get a chance to finish, because so many people were shouting at him.

When Madam Coordinator finally restored order—well, it was a kind of order, but a lot of people were still talking—Captain Skyler stood up. He had a lot to say too, most of it angry. I'd never seen him so furious. He wasn't the only one either. A lot of people stood up in opposition, but Captain Skyler was the first to speak.

"We're all immigrants here," he said. "Every single one of us. And we all came here for the same reason, to build a new world and have a better life for ourselves and our children. All those people on the *Cascade*—they're us. They came here with the same dreams—so what kind of people would we be if we said, 'no, you can't share the dream'? And let me get specific here—those people, those colonists, everyone on the *Cascade*—they're an important resource, a necessary one—and not just for the work they can do, but also for the cultural heritages they represent. And one more thing. Our gene pool is still too small. This colony is going to need them more than they need us. This kind of talk is shameful. It's bigotry. It's wrong. It's disgusting."

He was right, but as Jamie explained later, getting angry like that only made the problem worse. The shouting started again and finally Madam Coordinator abruptly rang the final bell, got up and walked out. The meeting ended without resolving anything.

Jamie said to me, "There's gonna be a lot of talk, a lot of negotiating, before the next meeting—"

"But we'll all be on the way south by then—"

"That's right. So the next meeting will be at Winterland, with a whole different group of people in the room."

It was upsetting to see how many people we thought were friends were suddenly arguing for selfishness. But it was also good to see how many people were arguing for community.

On the way out, one of Councilor Layton's wives grabbed my arm, it was Bruinhilda—I yelped and tried to jerk away. She leaned in at me and shouted in my face, telling me I had to erase all my videos. "Don't you dare upload any of this meeting." Jamie started to protest, and Captain Skyler stepped up too—but it was Mom who got there first. "Take your goddamn hands off my son!" I don't think I'd ever heard Mom that loud. I think she had a lot more to say, but Jamie dragged me out of the room before I could hear it.

I said, "I wasn't going to upload any of that anyway. That's all supposed to be official stuff."

Jamie said, "Don't worry about it. But save the video."

Later on, I heard that Mom had said a lot of angry things to Bruinhilda, and a lot of people heard her. Then Bruinhilda said some nasty things back. And then a lot of people said a lot of things back and forth. But none of it got recorded, not that I ever saw, so I only heard about it from Jubilee, who embellished the whole story with her own commentary.

We still had to prepare for Lockdown and evacuation to Winterland, and the *Cascade* wouldn't be arriving in orbit for another two months, maybe more, so whatever decisions might eventually be decided, they couldn't be made until the Spring winds died down and that was a long way away. But now that Councilor Layton had made it into a discussion, a lot of friendships were being tested.

And then, despite everything or maybe because of it, Mom and Captain Skyler decided to hold their wedding on the last day before the winter evacuation departed. That way we could combine the two celebrations into one. Mom and I would travel in the first convoy. Captain Skyler would follow in the last. But there was still a lot of work to do before we could leave.

On the last morning of the migration, a very old thunderfoot came stumbling through the outer fields. She was huge, a matriarch, one of the biggest we'd ever seen, and we'd been waiting specifically for her. She was tagged, she had a number, but everybody called her White Foot because she had some kind of pale fur growing on one of her back feet, probably a symbiote or a parasite of some kind. Nobody had ever gotten close enough to take a sample.

White Foot was a favorite, the colony had been tracking her from the beginning. No one knew how old she was; she was already a senior when the First Hundred started monitoring the migrations. She was one of the first ones tagged. But now she was injured, lame in her right front foot. That was why she hadn't kept up. Her gait was lopsided and slow—so slow that it looked like she was walking in place. She grunted in pain every time she had to put weight on her injured foot.

She was in bad shape. Worse than that, a pack of six hungry bigmouths were following her, hissing and stalking. There were three adults of varying sizes and three half-sized juveniles. Captain Skyler identified them as CP-039, the Sackville Bagginses—they'd been tagged six years ago when they split off from a larger pack, but they'd never quite stabilized. They got their name because they were an unruly and undisciplined bunch. Last year, they'd lost two males in a mating duel and they were under-strength. So finding an injured leviathan was a bit of good luck for them. If they could bring her down.

Either they were waiting to see if she would collapse on her own, or they were waiting for the right moment to attack. The Captain said they could afford to be patient. Either way, they were going to get the meal of a lifetime.

All of the scientists went up onto the catwalks to watch. They were very excited too, this would be a wonderful opportunity to see how the bigmouths worked as a team. But a lot of the moms were not happy, so all the younger children were hustled off to the bunkers as soon as the carnosaurs appeared. Mom almost sent me off too, but I argued that I needed to make videos. Mom only agreed when Captain Skyler promised to keep me safe.

If the bigmouths brought their prey down on our front porch, they'd be feeding for a month or longer. It would be quite a show. And quite a stink as well. And when they finally wandered off in search of more meat, the smaller carrion-eaters would take over. That would be even more dangerous, because the various vulture-things and other little bird-things might decide to fly down and take a snack from the quad. The whole event would be interesting and dangerous and ugly and gruesome. And next spring we'd have our own little bellystone park right outside our front gate.

The colonists on the *Cascade* were also watching the spectacle. They were linked to our satellites now and could see the whole gigantic scale of the migration. They could even see how close the animals were to approaching Summerland Station. Some of them even posted how concerned they were and wondered if it was safe. That made a lot of people down here laugh. We'd been living with that question for forty Hella-years.

But then White Foot arrived at our perimeter, the grand old thunderfoot matriarch, and when I uploaded videos of her from past migrations, including her with her calves, a lot of them started caring about her like we did, and they asked for even more videos. Captain Skyler told me to go ahead and give them a good view of everything, but to make sure to include all the ripping and tearing and bleeding—all the goriest details. When I asked why, he said he wanted to impress upon the new colonists how dangerous Hella could be. If we scared them enough now, we might not have to dig as many graves later on.

Captain Skyler got permission from Madam Coordinator to send out as many scuttle-bots as we could spare, as well as extra skyballs. He mostly wanted the scuttle-bots because their low perspectives would give a better sense of the size of the animals than an aerial view. The scarier the better, he said.

Right after midday, a bunch of us went to the outer fence to get a closer look. I went with Jamie and his friends, but the bigmouths were getting so agitated, pacing around her, nipping at her flanks, screeching and growling, I started to get scared. What if they attacked the fence? Jamie said not to worry, the fence was strong enough to hold, but I worried just the same. The bigmouths are big. They have teeth twice as long as a man. They could swallow a person whole, just for a snack. I pointed the remote cameras at the drooling mouths of the carnosaurs, at their big dreadful eyes, at their snorting nostrils. Other cameras I pointed at White Foot's head. Did she look frightened? Do saurs have expressions? Some people say they do. I can't tell. But she was agitated. She waved her tail back and forth. She swung her long neck from side to side.

The bigmouths kept their distance. Even slow and injured, the grand old lady's thirty-ton tail could still be fatal to any unwary bigmouth that made the mistake of getting in range. The bigmouths didn't roar, they didn't need to, this wasn't a mating duel. Mostly the only time carnosaurs roar is in mating duels, but this was lunch, not a dance. Sometimes they hissed at each other, usually when two of them accidentally bumped or merely got close enough to bump. Carnosaurs don't want to be vulnerable, and we already had video of what happens when two of them collide at speed and get knocked over.

White Foot moaned and rumbled in response, her own deep warning growl. The carnosaurs rumbled and growled back. All of them together, it was loud and scary. The carnosaurs stamped impatiently, shaking the ground—not as much as a thunderfoot, but there were six of them and the adults were big enough to make their own little tremors. The whole thing went on for a long time. The old lady leviathan just kept pushing herself forward and the carnosaurs kept circling around her, hissing and grunting and growling. They stopped frequently, turning their heads from side to side, watching and calculating, waiting for that one moment of weakness, that perfect opportunity to attack. They must have been harrying the old matriarch for a long time. It was easier for them to exhaust her than risk death or injury in a premature attack.

That was another whole set of videos I sent up to the *Cascade.* The death rate for carnosaurs is astonishingly high. They were often injured and sometimes killed just in the process of bringing down a meal. That much meat flinging itself around—force equals mass times acceleration. Hella is a bitch. The lighter gravity lets the animals hurl themselves with even more energy. You can hear the bones crack and crunch in some of the recordings. We have forty-five years of close-up recordings. Forty-five years of colossal carnage.

And then it happened. White Foot stumbled. Not badly, but her right foreleg gave way at the knee and even though she caught herself before she collapsed forward, it threw her off balance. Her long neck swerved and her head scraped the ground, throwing up a great cloud of dust. It glittered in the bright blue sunlight.

One of the carnosaurs had been worrying her flank, snapping and making abortive biting movements. Now, he leapt up her side, scrambling with his hindclaws, carving deep gouges into her skin as he scrabbled for purchase, tail lashing wildly, finally screeching onto her back. Despite her boney ruffles, her grassy crust, he managed to get his jaws locked onto the side of her neck, and even when his hindclaws lost their grip, he hung precariously for a moment as she endeavored to swing him off. But all he needed to do was drag her head down low enough for the other bigmouths to leap, and that was enough, they were on her immediately, grabbing and holding and pulling her neck down even further.

Her front legs buckled, a moment later her hind legs collapsed. Her tail still thrashed, but the last two carnosaurs leapt aside and charged for the vulnerable spot on her neck just behind her head. They both grabbed on and held, almost frozen. Now, the whole pack was choking off her long vulnerable windpipe. It was a terrible tableau, silent except for the great shuddering tail of the leviathan. It went on and on for the longest time, the grand old lady wasn't dying easy. Some of the people watching cried out in horror, some of the men muttered curses, some of the women wept. At last the giant tail shuddered and lay still, the great rise and fall of breath slowed and slowed and eventually stopped. The leviathan was dead.

The carnosaurs held their bites a while longer, then one by one, they released. They stood for a moment, catching their own breaths, then cocked their heads, stared, and circled the mountain of flesh as if deciding where to start—and who would take the first bite. The leader of the family, the largest, grunted and rumbled, lowered his head to sniff, then raised it again to poke the motionless flank. Finally, almost tentatively, he pushed his snout forward and then began to rip a great slab of flesh from her belly. It made a terrible tearing sound as it came away. Then another bigmouth leapt in and began ripping. The third one followed, and finally the half-sized juveniles. A wash of dark syrupy blood spilled down into the dirt. Soon it would be a huge stinking swamp of blood and mud.

The carnosaurs tore at White Foot's body. Soon, they'd be up on her flanks as well, ripping and gulping and making loud wet swallowing sounds. They'd feed long into the night, gorging themselves into insensibility. But their rest periods would be brief. They had to fill their bellies as fast as they could, before other hungry carnosaurs came roaring in to share the feast, so no matter how late it got there would always be one or two working at the carcass, growling and grunting deep in their throats, warning all other predators and carrion-eaters to keep their distance.

Dinner in the caf that night was subdued. A lot of people were unnerved by what they had seen close up. Despite years of recordings, despite all the colony's experience observing the saurs, having a leviathan brought down just outside the perimeter fence unsettled a lot of people. Even under the canopy, even in the main rooms, we could still hear the wet ripping noises outside, the deep gulping sounds, the occasional grunt and growl. It was difficult to eat anything, even a salad, with all the terrible grinding noise so close.

I left the cameras to record and went back to our pod, back to my room. I put on my headphones and edited videos until midnight. I had worked out a whole system. First I'd find a fact. Then I'd find all the facts around it. Like this: "When a full-grown leviathan takes a step, its foot hits the ground with thirty tons of force." I'd put that fact on a slide, just simple white text, Helvetica font, on a black background. Then I'd go to a really good close-up of a leviathan foot hitting the ground, showing the little cloud of dust jumping up into the air around it, lifting again, leaving a truck-sized crater in the dirt. I'd show a front foot, a back foot, over and over, I'd show big feet and little feet, matriarchs and calves. A full minute or more. Sometimes two or three minutes. Then I'd go to the next slide. "When a herd passes through an area, they flatten the grass." And I'd show that. "When the leviathans urinate, they leave a swamp behind." And I'd show the soggy muddy furrows. "Leviathan dung feeds the savannah." And I'd show all the little creatures that swarm around the droppings. "When a herd arrives at a water hole, they dig it deeper. They carve a lake." On that one, I showed an aerial map of how many lakes existed on the migration path. Then, "Many creatures live on the backs of the leviathans."

And so on. Until I reached the final point. "The leviathans are a walking ecosystem."

It was a good way to work, because everything explained itself. All I had to do was take all the facts I knew about anything and list them carefully. Then I'd search for video records that demonstrate the fact and edit them in, closer to wider or wider to closer, depending on the fact I wanted to illustrate.

I'd try to find a rhythm in the records. If I couldn't find one, I'd figure out what rhythm I thought was best. Then I'd look for a piece of music that matched the rhythm. The display would list them all, and I could sort them for mood. The biggest creatures got the most ponderous and important music. Smaller creatures got lighter happier music. Some of my videos were as short as thirty seconds; the longest I'd ever made was almost ten minutes long. I didn't like sitting through a long show myself, so I kept them as short as possible.

I had made videos of the leviathans, and the carnosaurs, then the hoppers and the ground-monkeys, and the things at Bitch Canyon too, then the lesser-mouths, the crow-birds, the humongosaurs, the crocosaurs, the scuttle-bugs, the grinders, the grumpies, and the slow-walking night fungi. I'd already edited and uploaded most of those. But now I wanted to go back to the leviathans and the carnosaurs, only different this time. I wanted to show the families, all the leviathans we had tagged and named and tracked, the calves, the moms, the juveniles, the matriarchs, the octogenarians, all the ones we knew.

Then the carnosaurs. I showed how big they were, how hungry—how many tons of meat they needed to eat in a week, how they birthed their young, how they attacked and killed. How many times they'd attacked the fences and the damage they'd done. And then I showed who had been hurt and who had been killed and not just the humans—everybody already knew that—but the thunderfeet we'd been watching for most of the last fifty years and had come to think of as friendly mountains.

I hardly ever see the clock tick over to 0:00, but tonight I didn't want to go to bed. Exhaustion finally caught up with me at 02:30. Mom has this very soft longshirt she brought all the way from Earth. When I was little, when I cried so much I couldn't be comforted, she'd wrap me in it and I'd fall asleep. The softness always felt so nice I felt safe. Eventually, she put it in my bottom drawer for me, and ever after that, whenever I had a very bad day, I'd put it on and feel safe again. I hadn't worn it in more than a year, but I put it on now, crawled into bed, and fell asleep in minutes.

I woke up at dawn, feeling very strange. The carnosaurs were still eating, I could hear the grunting and all the other horrible noises, and I could feel the thumping coming through the floor. Still wearing Mom's longshirt, I wandered into the kitchen where the screens were still showing the scene outside the fence. The lights had been kept on all night, and the carnosaurs had carved a good-sized wedge into the belly of the dead leviathan. Great strips of flesh had been pulled away from her flanks, but she was still recognizable as the grand old lady. They would be at her for days.

Captain Skyler looked at me oddly when he saw me in Mom's longshirt, but he didn't say anything about it. "There's coffee."

"Okay," I mumbled. I poured a cup. It was hot and bitter. I went looking for milk.

"You were up late," he said. "I looked at your videos. They are very good."

I grunted something that was supposed to be thanks.

"Hey, Kyle. Are you okay?"

I shook my head.

"Want to talk about it?"

"No."

"Okay." He pushed a plate of toast toward me.

I took a slice. I buttered it slowly. I took a bite.

Finally. "They killed White Foot."

"Yeah."

"She was my favorite."

"She was everybody's favorite."

"I wish we could have saved her."

"I do too."

"Then why didn't you?"

"If we were to kill the bigmouths every time a favorite leviathan was in danger, then pretty soon there wouldn't be enough bigmouths, and there would be too many thunderfeet, and there wouldn't be enough food for all of them. The calves would starve first, then the old ones. Then a lot of the breeding stock. It's called a population crash. The bigmouths are a necessary part of the Hella cycle. They keep the leviathans from overbreeding."

"I know that. But couldn't we have saved White Foot?"

"And if we'd saved White Foot this time, then what? Next time, someone else would demand that we save Little Face. And then after that, Big Stinky or Grumpy Butt or whichever." He slid his chair closer to mine and spoke softly. "It was her time, Kyle. This is how leviathans die. Most of them anyway. White Foot had a good life, she had a lot of healthy calves. And her death serves a purpose too. The carnosaurs will be working at her for a long time, they won't be chasing the herd, and by the time they're hungry again, most of the herd will be too far away for them to catch up. By dying here, White Foot keeps them here. So this is one last way for her to protect the lives of her daughters and her granddaughters—so they can have more calves of their own. Even in death, White Foot helps her family."

"I don't like it."

"I don't think anybody does. The best we can do is . . ." He shook his head.

"What?"

". . . appreciate the horrible design of it." He added, "It's how life works. Everything feeds on everything else. Except for the very smallest and lowest of all organisms, the ones that feed on light and rust. Everything alive survives by eating other living things. Everything becomes food for something else. White Foot was beautiful in her time, and we're all going to miss her. I'm so glad we have so many wonderful pictures of her. But it was her time to pay her debt forward to the next generation, and as difficult as it is to say goodbye—it's a part of life."

He waited to see if I was going to understand. Eventually, because I didn't say anything, because I was still thinking about it, he got up and poured himself more coffee. He put the pot down and looked at me seriously. "Kyle, it's this simple. Life is about saying goodbye. The older you get, the more goodbyes you have to say. It doesn't get easier. If anything, it gets harder."

I took a bite of my toast and chewed silently, so I wouldn't have to say anything.

"But, maybe . . ." he started to say.

"What?"

"Maybe every time you have to say goodbye, it's another chance to say hello to someone new."

I looked at him skeptically.

He laughed. "Okay, there's no fooling you. But it does sound good, doesn't it?"

I shook my head. "No. It doesn't. It sounds stupid."

"Well, then, let's pretend I didn't say anything at all. You look pretty in your nightgown. Are you thinking about changing back?"

"No. It's just more comfortable."

"It must be or you wouldn't wear it. You used to wear it all the time when you were little, even around the quad. But you might want to put on a heavier longshirt if you want to come up to the lookouts with me. It's starting to get windy."

Jamie told me once that back on Earth there was—or is, I don't know if they're still there—a group of people called Arabs. They lived in a very hot climate, and their longshirts were called robes. When humans first landed on Hella, they wore sealed suits at first, then lighter bio-hazard suits, then later on, just bio-conditioned suits. But all those had to be custom fitted, which was time-consuming. If you had to go outside for anything at all, it could take as long as twenty or thirty minutes to suit up.

Robes were easier. You only needed three or four different sizes and whoever needed to go out could just pull on a robe, and a hood if necessary, and go. The thermal controls and bio-monitors could be woven into a robe a lot easier than a shirt and pants or a jumpsuit. Plus all the other sensors and scanners and gear as well. After a while, as the First Hundred figured out what was safe and what wasn't, robes became longshirts. And after that, they just became convenient. Longshirts were available in ankle-length, knee-length, and thigh-length, whatever you want. You could wear shorts with them or not, depending on how you felt or what you had to do. Lots of people still wore pants and jumpsuits and worksuits of all kinds, but the longshirt is a permanent part of Hella's culture. It's traditional, like skirts and sarongs and hats shaped like a wedge of cheese. I should make a video about Hella cheese, sometime.

The colony isn't totally isolated from Hellan ecology. We try to maintain what we call "a cautious isolation" while we figure out what's safe for us to be exposed to. And vice versa. We're an invasive species. No, we're an invasive ecology. Everything we brought with us, from the tiniest microbes all the way up to ourselves and our animals, is alien and dangerous. I never thought of us that way, but Mom says we're an invasive presence of enormous magnitude, so we have to watch what we introduce into any Hellan ecosystem or we could trigger a massive bio-collapse.

On the other side of that argument, some people say that it's specifically because we are an invasive presence that we should introduce the Earth species that are most useful to us and let the Hellan ecology adapt or die. We're going to be here forever, we might as well get on with the business of terraforming the planet.

But if we do that, we lose Hella and everything that makes it special. It's very confusing.

One of the things that people learned back on Earth about ecology and evolution—and they had to learn it the hard way—is that not only is everything connected to everything else, it's always in a state of flux. Everything cycles, everything adjusts, everything rearranges itself, there is no steady state, there is only change. Invasive species are not the exception, they're the norm.

But even if we were to introduce Earth bees and bunnies and whatevers, we don't know what will happen to them when they start reproducing in Hellan gravity and under the Hellan sun. Will they get bigger? Certainly. We know that from our sealed greenhouses. But what other adaptations or mutations will we see out in the wild? When they interact with Hellan life forms, what else will they become? And how will Hellan life forms respond? Whatever we start, it's not going to be undoable, so nobody wants to start anything at all. It'll be like the prickly pears in Australia. And rabbits. And cane toads. Those are the obvious ones. But there's a lot more examples too. Africanized bees and lionfish and Burmese pythons. It's a long list.

We know that there's already been some crossover events. Some Hellan bugs have taken up residence in the quad and we've been watching them carefully for a long time, there are mini-bots everywhere, not just cleaning, but analyzing too. We think that some of our bacteria may be responsible for a rash of deaths among the ground-monkeys. Those things aren't quite primates, but one winter several nearby colonies died out almost overnight. The samples we gathered suggested a staph-like infection. So did somebody sneeze in the wrong place? Did an opportunistic virus find a new vector? Did it kill those colonies so quickly it didn't have a chance to spread? If so, we were lucky. The ground-monkeys were lucky. But whatever it was, did it die out, or is it lying dormant somewhere? How long till a new family of ground-monkeys settles here and gets exposed? We don't know. We did go in and irradiate the suspect areas and maybe that will be enough, but we just don't know.

The whole thing is very complex, much more complex than we're really equipped to know. So, as Mom says, we just take it one day at a time and do our best to keep out of the way of whatever might be coming. Which is kinda why I don't know why Mom and Captain Skyler want to marry each other. Captain Skyler is one of those people who like to go out and get in the way of whatever might be coming, take pictures, and tag it. But it doesn't matter if I don't understand. They want to get married and they will.

Anyway, Captain Skyler said I could come with him to the lookouts. They're up on top of the fences, lookout towers connected by broad catwalks. I don't know why they call it a catwalk, we don't have any cats in Summerland. They don't want to risk it. Cats would get curious about what's beyond the fence, and who knows what would happen out there? Would we end up with giant carnivorous cats? Or would they be fatal snacks for the littlemouths? Anyway, the catwalks are very rugged, so whenever there's something to see outside the perimeter, a lot of people go up to watch. Today, the crowd was there to see the carnosaurs feeding on what was left of White Foot's carcass. Much of her belly had been ripped open and there were raw scars on her flanks as well, but she was still identifiable. She was still our dead friend and not yet a jumble of raw meat and bones.

Madam Coordinator was up on the catwalk too. Most people wore hats to protect themselves from the actinic sun, but she held a parasol. It made her easy to spot. She saw us and called us over. "Captain, I hear congratulations are in order."

"Yes, ma'am. Thank you."

She indicated the tableau below us. "How long do you think this will go on?"

"Worst case, ten days. And another week after that for the lesser carrion-eaters."

She sighed. "I can't fault people for being curious. And I know we allowed for this possibility in our work schedules. But we're going to have to find a way to get people back to work soon or we're not going to make our deadline for Lockdown."

"I could make more videos," I offered. "So people could watch them later."

"Yes," she said. "Your editing has been very skillful. You've done a good job, Kyle. Everybody has been impressed." She looked to the Captain. "I think you made your point. I hope so. But . . ." She didn't finish her sentence. Instead, she said, "We've used up our margin. How do we get back on schedule?"

"I was thinking perhaps a couple of X-Prizes. Carve out a few more private rooms at Winterland?"

Madam Coordinator closed her eyes. She did that sometimes when people asked her for a decision. Just like sometimes the software will show you a little whirligig while it sorts something out, she did the same thing only without the little whirligig. Maybe she had her own little noise inside her head, chattering and humming until it finally resolved itself. That would explain it. She opened her eyes again and said, "All right, we can afford it. We'll carve six new apartments. One for the most valuable player on each evacuation team—but only announce we're carving five, so the team that comes in last will have to do without. Then if we make schedule, we'll surprise them and give them the last one. And that'll be good for morale."

"And if not? If we don't make schedule?"

"Hm." She smiled. "I know a couple of newlyweds who might want it . . . You figure it out."

"That wouldn't be fair, ma'am, and you know it."

"Then we'll carve seven. If we make it, you can have the seventh. If we don't—both will go for storage."

"I can work with that. I'll set it up immediately." He stepped off a bit to talk on his phone, leaving me with Madam Coordinator.

I didn't have anything to say to her, she didn't have anything else to say to me, so we both turned to watch the carnosaurs below. Two of them were eating—not as ravenously as yesterday, but slowly and steadily. What some people might even call thoughtfully. Although I don't really understand that word—thoughtful—the way other people do. To me, it means that someone is distracted. Kind of. Because when I'm thoughtful, it's the noise that's doing the thinking.

The other carnosaurs were lying torpid in the tall grass, but not so far away they couldn't come back to defend their meal. Carnosaurs stayed with their kills. Probably by tomorrow, we'd stop seeing White Foot below us and just see . . . I don't know. Meat.

Madam Coordinator cleared her throat. That meant she was about to say something, so I turned to her and waited. I do that when I think people are about to speak. Jamie says it unnerves them. It makes them uncomfortable.

"Kyle," she said. She cleared her throat again. "Kyle, I want you to know that your job is very important. You've done a wonderful job with the thunderfeet and the bigmouths. I know how much you love these big lumbering animals. We all do. But I have an idea about what you might want to work on when you get to Winterland. Maybe you could make some videos showing the new people how to survive on Hella. They need to know about Summerland Station and Winterland, about our own migrations, about what foods we eat and why, what clothes we wear and why, why we build our buildings the way we do, why we have a canopy over the quad, why we have outposts and where, what traditions we honor and what holidays we celebrate, why we need to do this thing and why we can't do that, all the hundreds of little things that we're so used to that we forget that other people don't think the same way."

She shifted her parasol to her other hand and held it over the both of us.

"The new people are going to be landing in a few months," she said, "some of them in the winter, but most of them in the spring. It's going to be a great shock to them after living aboard the starship for such a long time. I know that we have all the orientation videos from the previous pilgrimages, but most of them are way out of date, and to tell the truth . . ." She bent down low and whispered, "I think they're kind of dull, don't you?"

I shook my head. "The ones I looked at, they were very accurate. For the time."

"Well, I think your new videos are much better than the old ones. And so do the colonists on the *Cascade.* So I want you to keep on doing what you're doing, okay?"

"Yes, ma'am. Thank you, ma'am."

Just before midday, a second family of bigmouths arrived at the carcass. We sort of expected it. The smell of all that meat would have been noticeable ten or twenty klicks to the west by now. The first winds of autumn were rising.

This was a larger family of carnosaurs, one of the largest packs we'd seen, nine full-grown and three juveniles. According to their tags, they were Pack CP-016, we'd been tracking them for two decades and had detailed records showing how the older members of the family meticulously trained the younger ones. Captain Skyler called them the Slithereens because they were so vicious. They weren't afraid of anything. They'd once circled the fence of Summerland compound for three days until they were distracted by an easier meal.

The Sackville Bagginses were exhausted and stuffed from days and nights of gorging themselves, but they were still willing to defend their kill. They roused themselves quickly as the Slithereens approached. The two groups hissed at each other, then they started grunting and growling, stamping their feet, lashing their tails, and roaring their defiance. Some people called these ferocious threat displays magnificent. Others said they were terrifying. A few people left the catwalks and headed for the bunkers.

I was already thinking that this would be a very good video to send to the *Cascade.* The people who had the time, who weren't occupied with other jobs, would probably be watching the raw feed as it came in, and they would see everything, but I could edit my videos to show just the most important parts. We didn't have a good record of carnosaur confrontations, so this could be important—an accurate record of bigmouth behavior might help us learn how to discourage them from coming around our stations.

Each group of carnosaurs was trying to scare the other off. Jamie and Emily-Faith had come up to the catwalk with me and now Emily-Faith began to annotate the argument: The Sackville Bagginses were insisting that this kill belonged to them and they were prepared to defend it. The Slithereens countered that there was more than enough meat here for everybody, especially if the everybody was the Slithereens. The Sackvilles were not prepared to accept this assertion. The

Slithereens argued that digestion is nine joints of the claw, and probably the tenth one as well. And so on.

I thought Emily-Faith's comments were silly and did my best to ignore them. It seemed obvious to me that this argument could have only one possible outcome. The Slithereens outnumbered the Sackvilles. And if it came to a fight, the Sackvilles would suffer some serious losses.

As it became more and more obvious that they would not be able to defend their kill, the Sackvilles increased their roaring—and at the same time, began backing away, one or two steps at a time. "I know what they're saying," Emily-Faith explained. She mimicked, "'Oh yeah! Well, just wait till next time! Then you'll see!'"

After a bit more roaring and growling, the Slithereens moved into the carcass and began feeding, tearing away their own great slabs of leviathan flesh. The Sackvilles gave a few more plaintive roars, then shambled away rumbling and grumbling and, according to Emily-Faith, saying some very nasty things in saurian about the Slithereens' ancestry, morals, habits, and hygiene.

By the end of the day, the carcass of White Foot no longer looked like a fallen beast. Now it was just a great bloody jumble of meat and bone.

Locking down for winter takes most of a month. The last crops have to be harvested and processed, irradiated, dried, pickled, salted, smoked, frozen, canned, wrapped, stored, or just pre-cooked and packaged. Some of it would stay at the Summerland Station for the maintenance team. Some of it would go to Winterland to tide us over. And some of it would go into permanent storage—what everybody called the emergency box. Actually, there wasn't one single emergency box. There were reconstructed cargo pods everywhere, even at some of the outposts. The colony rarely had to tap into those stores, but they were rotated every year, with the oldest stores being mixed in with the current ones.

Jamie said we now had enough food stored away that we could fill the *Cascade* twice over if we wanted to send it back to Earth. But he was also pretty sure that no matter how much food we might send back, it wouldn't be enough to feed all the hungry billions there. And they might not want it anyway. They would be too afraid of contamination by alien germs. Jamie and I wondered how hungry you would have to be to stop caring. Neither of us had ever been hungrier than a missed first supper.

After the crops are brought in, then we have to secure all the buildings. Water and power and communications all have to be put on standby. Windows and doors have to be weather-sealed and locked. Hella buildings are either converted pods or dug-in bunkers. Anything that's aboveground isn't just built, it has to be reinforced and anchored and tied down with thick straps of graphene fiber. Then the heavy shutters are put in place, they're made from thick slices of Atlas logs. The canopy over the quad is secured as well. It's made of graphene fiber too. It usually survives the winter storms, but one year it shredded, nobody is sure why, maybe it was a lightning strike, so now we use multiple layers, with lots of space between them, and we have lightning rods too.

All this is because the Hella storms of winter can have wind velocities as high as six hundred kilometers an hour and some people say that even higher velocities are possible in a super-storm. Any loose object, a rock or a branch, becomes a deadly projectile. So we build thick walls and windbreaks and we put heavy shutters around all the buildings and we hang super-strong netting everywhere. And we reinforce the fences every year, especially the verticals, because we can't risk having any of them snap.

Finally the compounds are scoured for anything that could be ripped up and sent airborne. That's everybody's responsibility—picking up everything loose. Sometimes it feels like half the work we do at Summerland is preparing to lock the station down for winter.

Midwinter, the winds ease up and a thick blanket of snow covers everything and then just sits there and waits for months. Sometimes in the morning, there's even a layer of carbon dioxide frost on top of the snow, it forms in the coldest part of the night and then whisks away as soon as the sunlight touches it. Hella is angled on its axis just a smidge more than thirty degrees, so at the deepest point of the season, a winter day at Summerland can be barely half the length of the longest summer day. It makes for serious weather everywhere, all year round. The meteorologists have been struggling to build an accurate model since even before the First Hundred landed.

By the time the last conventions of small carrion-feeders had finished disassembling the last bits of White Foot, the Rollagons were loaded and ready for the first migration. There would be four this time. Or maybe five. It depended on the weather. Outside the fence, all that remained of White Foot was a large dark depression in the ground, a few well-gnawed bones, a scattering of well-polished belly stones, all sizes, and some unpleasant memories.

A few of the managers had already flown ahead to prepare for our arrival. Others were scouting the route in lifters, looking for possible difficulties. The landscape of Hella likes to rearrange itself when no one is looking.

We didn't have enough lifters to carry everyone, so most of us would ride in the trucks. Each truck was outfitted to carry 150 people in a mostly self-sufficient environment, although no truck would load up that many. We always left extra room in all the trucks in case any broke down, and people had to be offloaded onto other vehicles.

The road, such as it was, followed a serpentine route southward.

We had three teams maintaining the biggest roads all year round, but they weren't paved like the big highways on Earth, so the first three trucks in any convoy were always loaded with equipment for carving new tracks or laying down bridges. The Rollagons could serve as barges for river crossings, but we tried to avoid doing that as much as we could because sometimes there were bad things in the rivers. Large floating logs or even icebugs could act like battering rams, but there were crocosaurs too and huge patches of floating stinkweed to foul the wheels.

Lilla-Jack had seniority, so she got the assignment to captain the first vehicle in the convoy, and despite Mom's objections, I was assigned as her intern. Captain Skyler said it was a good idea because my videos were becoming an important record of the colony's ongoing history, and we needed to show the people on the *Cascade* what to expect in the seasonal migrations.

Mom says that someday perhaps we won't need to migrate with the seasons. Someday we'll figure out how to make both Summerland and Winterland able to withstand the extremes of temperature. That someday is a long way off, and it's possible none of us will live long enough to see it. Other people have even bigger ideas, they want to terraform Hella.

So far, it's all hypothetical and theoretical and philosophical. Jamie says that means people will argue about it forever, and by the time they decide what they should do, it'll be too late because Hella will have already done it for them. But the discussions continue anyway: how much and what kind and how soon and especially whether or not it's a good idea because we don't understand all of what we're really dealing with, so maybe the safest thing to do is just keep on being careful until we have a much better idea.

Captain says we shouldn't rush into anything because whatever we do it won't be undoable, so we shouldn't take any unnecessary risks, and besides, we haven't even achieved Class-5 Self-Sufficiency, so why are we even talking about it anyway? And what's in the fridge for dessert?

On the morning we were supposed to leave, we were up before dawn, everyone gathering in the caf for an early breakfast. We wanted to roll at first light. Mom didn't say much. Neither did Captain Skyler. Jamie and Emily-Faith ate with us, even though they weren't coming.

At the last minute, Captain Skyler had to change his plans. He didn't say why. He just said that he couldn't go with the convoy. He wanted to, he'd been looking forward to it, but something had come up, he couldn't explain right now, maybe later, but he needed to stay behind so he could fly Madam Coordinator to Winterland after the Summerland Lockdown completed.

"I know it's disappointing, but this is something nobody else can do."

Mom gave him a look. "Well, maybe it's time to train more people."

"You're right, but there isn't anybody. Not for this." He put his hand on hers. "I need you to trust me. This is important. Very important."

Mom took a deep breath and nodded. "I do trust you."

"Dora, there's been so much extra work this year—and we lost a lot of hours because so many people wanted to watch the saurs, we just kept adjusting and adjusting the schedules until we ran out of time."

"Not even enough time for a wedding."

"I'm sorry. Yes, you have a right to be angry."

"I'm not angry, I'm disappointed."

"I'm disappointed too. But look at the upside. We can have a better wedding at Winterland, a bigger wedding, and then we'll have time for a real honeymoon."

"We've already had the honeymoon. I'm ready for the marriage."

That didn't make sense to me, but I didn't ask anyone to explain.

"Jamie won't be there."

"I can't promise anything, but maybe we can fly him in."

"Cord . . . ?"

"You're a good man. And I love you. And we're going to get married. Yes. But after we're married, I want you to get your priorities straight."

"I will. I promise."

"Stinky promise?"

"Stinky promise."

That part I did understand.

"All right," said Captain Skyler. "Let's everybody stop looking so serious. Let's eat!"

It was a big meal. It would be our last big meal until Winterland. We'd be eating rations and sandwiches for the next two weeks. At least, we hoped it would be only two weeks. We knew where some of the obstacles would be, we had aerial surveillance and skyballs constantly checking the route, and so far we hadn't seen anything too daunting. And we would have roller-bots running ahead of the convoy, checking immediate road conditions and sniffing for animals, but if a herd of anything decided to cross the road, or even worse, follow it, it wouldn't be much of a road anymore. And there would certainly be the usual share of fallen branches and piled up tumblebergs. Road conditions could change overnight and there were always unexpected delays. If the weather was bad or if the road was bad, a convoy could be on the road for as long as a month.

When we finished eating, I stacked the trays and cleared the dishes. When I got back to the table, everyone was hugging everyone, and Mom looked like she was going to cry. Jamie was the only one I would let hug me, but I was upset with him all over again because now it was real, he really wasn't coming, so when he opened his arms before me,

I didn't move, but Jamie never took no for an answer and grabbed me hard. "I'm going to miss you most of all, Scarecrow," he said.

I didn't say anything. Sometimes I do that. I just stop talking. I can go a week or longer. It's because I don't have anything to say. And sometimes, nothing that anyone else says seems important enough to deserve a response. But Jamie wasn't letting go and finally I had to say something back. "You can let go now."

He looked at me hard. "I know you love me, Kyle. You don't have to say it, but I know you love me."

"Okay."

Twenty trucks were lined up neatly at the loading docks, and clusters of people were hugging and kissing, loading last minute luggage, hugging some more, and finally boarding. The crowd thinned as we watched. Finally, Mom and Jamie hugged again. Mom and the Captain hugged again. Jamie made as if to hug me, then just patted me on the shoulder, and then we were done. All we had to do was walk across and board.

This would be one of the largest convoys ever. But we said that every year, because the colony kept growing. This year, a dozen of the trucks were towing trailers with extra gear and equipment. The second convoy would be twelve or fifteen trucks, the last one the same. Twenty trucks were already on their way back from Winterland station, having delivered much of the summer harvest, we'd probably pass them in a few days. That would be an excuse for a quick stop, an almost-party, a little celebration, and probably even some baby-making too while all the drivers met to trade information about the road conditions.

Almost a thousand people would be traveling in this convoy. There would be three or four more convoys after this one. Nobody liked putting so many people on the road at once, but the migration of the leviathan herd and the death of White Foot had delayed the exodus of our human herd, and the weather was closing in faster than we'd like, so we had to push a little harder this time. We would have sent the first convoy before the leviathan herd arrived, but nobody likes to miss the big migration, so every year it gets a little bit harder to evacuate everyone on time. That's why the Council is talking about expanding the bunkers and increasing the size of the stay-behind team. We're certainly going to have to do that after the *Cascade* unloads.

Lilla-Jack pointed me up to the port side turret. We wouldn't need any gunners this close to Summerland, and even if we did, she had enough targeting software that she could have managed our defenses all by herself if she had to. She boarded, checked her displays, went through her checklists, and gave the signal to launch the "umbrella"—the drones and skyballs that would travel the whole route with us, orbiting the convoy and watching for anything we might need to know about.

Jamie waved from the dock and called, "Watch out for booger-jacks."

Normally, I would have shouted back, "There's no such thing," but I was in my no-talking space, so I just lifted a hand to show that I saw his wave. Below me, Lilla-Jack was checking the readiness lights for all the other trucks. Two were still yellow, while their drivers finished their checklists. While I watched, they flickered green.

A few more minutes of chatter channel conversation back and forth, a little discussion of the roads into the canyons, and how soon we could get over the first pass, and the second as well, a few more comments about the weather, the temperature and the wind and the possibility of rain, and then finally, the inevitable, "Okay. Let's roll."

We took it slow at first, letting all the drivers settle into their positions. Most of the trucks would be on auto-pilot, they didn't need drivers, but there were places where individual crossings would require careful supervision, so every truck had its own team on the bridge.

I brought up an echo of Lilla-Jack's display so I could pretend I was driving. We had the video from the convoy that had carried the summer harvest south, and we overlaid that on our own real-world view, so we could see the most recent recordings of the road ahead. It would tell us what to expect and we could also notice what changes had occurred since that video was made. If we saw broken branches or fallen trees, then we would know that dinosoids had passed and might still be in the area. On the displays above that, we could see what the roller-bots were encountering ahead of us, or we could switch to an aerial view from the umbrella. No convoy had been caught by surprise in years.

The first hour was pretty familiar terrain to most of the drivers, but Lilla-Jack kept everyone on high alert anyway. No surprises. We rolled south through the jumble, a place where time-rounded rocks poked up through the grass. They looked like broken fingers.

None of the places on Hella are named after people. Not yet. The First Hundred established that rule. They didn't want half the places on the planet named after them. They said they wanted names to represent the spirit of the place. They were quite adamant about it. They didn't want to have future generations saddled with shallow memorials for people they didn't know or barely remembered. They made a rule for themselves that they wouldn't name any place after any living person, and they would wait until fifty years after the person's death so that at least two more generations of people could decide if that person's contributions had been lasting enough or important enough to deserve the honor. This was because some people's contributions were never known until many years later, like Nikolai Tesla and Alan Turing, and that sometimes those contributions ended up being much more important than anyone might have realized at the time. And places on Hella could only be named after people who had actually lived on Hella. Anyway, that's why we didn't have Mount Miller-Gibson, not yet, or McCain Valley or the Ahrens Islands. Honors not only have to be earned, they have to stand the test of time.

With Lilla-Jacks' permission, I climbed into the back and took a nap. Waking up so early had left me tired. Migration always upsets my sleep cycle. Mom says that because humans evolved on Earth, our biology is hardwired to the Terran calendar. Our bodies want to operate on a twenty-four-hour day-night cycle, the monthly cycle, and even the annual cycle of the seasons.

Hella has three moons. One big one and two smaller ones that if they were combined would mass more than the big one. Someday all those moons will probably collide and be one big moon, but right now they've slowed the planet's rotation so the days are very long by Earth standards. So we rise at dawn, have breakfast, work for three hours, have first lunch, work another three hours, nap for four during the heat of midday, have second lunch, work three more hours, have first supper, work for another three, have second supper, relax for a bit, then go to bed for a few more hours and get up and work for a few hours in the middle of the night, with appropriate breaks for meals, and then back to bed until dawn. It sort of works out. Every team gets to figure out their own best work-schedule. Mom says that eventually humans will adapt to the Hellan day-night cycle, but it could take ten or twenty or a hundred generations.

Some people say they like having eighteen hours of daylight. It makes them feel like they're getting a lot more work done every day. But not everybody. Mom says that the same people who liked to complain that there weren't enough hours in a day back on Earth are now complaining that there are too many hours in a day here. By evening they're exhausted.

But there's another question to ask that nobody can answer yet. Does the longer day lengthen the human lifespan? Or shorten it? We just don't know. We might not know for generations.

I must have been more tired than I thought. When I finally woke up, Lilla-Jack's second-in-command, Ginnie was already passing out sandwiches for second lunch, and the second shift was on the bridge. First shift would sleep through midday, then take over in the afternoon. Third and fourth shifts would drive through the night. The convoy had to average two hundred klicks a day. Under the best possible conditions, it was possible for a single truck to make the trip in eight days, but no convoy had ever done it in less than ten and that was a long time ago when there weren't as many people, and they didn't need as many trucks.

Unless you have a job on the vehicle itself, there's not a lot to do on the trip. It's only fun for the first twenty minutes or so, then it gets boring. The scenery is pretty much the same for the longest time. Grass, rocks, trees, some thick forest, more trees, more grass, some hills, more rocks. Eventually, we head up into some mountains and through a couple of passes. The road has been widened by years and years of traffic. The trucks have good suspension, so the ride isn't too rough, but the roads are still unpaved, the terrain is uneven, and there are occasional fallen rocks or trees that have to be grappled out of the way. We didn't run into many because the harvest convoy had done a good job of prepping what we call "the highway."

There's talk on the Council that it's time to open a second route south. There's too much at stake to risk everything with this single lifeline. And Jamie says that most people agree, but the most feasible second route would add almost a week of travel time unless we dig a tunnel, and that part still hasn't been decided. A tunnel through Ugly Mountain could take as long as six years and maybe the resources could be better spent elsewhere? Maybe the new colonists will feel it's worth the effort. Maybe they'll supply enough manpower to make it happen.

I went into the back of the truck where a lounge had been set up for the few passengers we carried. Mostly this truck carried the road crew. If we came upon any obstacles, they would be the ones to jump out and clear the way. A few of them were playing cards. Others were sleeping. Some were answering mail or chatting with friends on other trucks or ahead at Winterland. I thought about giving Jamie a call, but my tablet said he was sleeping now, so I didn't.

So I curled up in a corner and started working my way through the day's messages. There was one from J'mee that was marked private, so I read that first. J'mee was a friend of Charles Dingillian, the boy who made the music. She was a few months younger than Charles. She said that my videos were very thorough, and my messages to her were always very detailed and very carefully worded, so she was wondering if I had an implant?

I wasn't sure what I should tell her. I hardly ever talk about my chip. It's a private thing, but even if it wasn't, I wouldn't talk about it because it makes people uncomfortable to know that I have a super-power. That's what Jamie calls it. A super-power. I still call it *the noise.*

According to Mom, back on Earth, it's not unusual for people to have things wired into their brains so they have an always-on connection to the web. But not everybody can do it, because it's expensive—I didn't know that word, she had to explain money to me, which still doesn't make sense. If there's food enough for everybody, why can't everybody have some? Jamie says money is a system for trading value for value, it's a bookkeeping thing, which kinda makes sense, but then how do you get a lot of it?

J'mee's family had a lot of money back on Earth. Because they bought their own space on the *Cascade* and they were bringing a lot of their own equipment and supplies with them. Captain Skyler says it will probably be a shock for them to discover that they'll have to share their resources. He says that new people are always culture-shocked after they land, for some it's worse than others, especially those with a strong sense of entitlement.

Anyway, J'mee said that she recognized the way I assembled my thoughts was the same way she did because she always had so much information available to her. She said that I always went into such enormous detail about everything, explaining every little part, that either I had an implant or I was compulsive, and she thought I was too smart and too nice to be compulsive. She said that she expected us to be good friends when she landed because if we communicated the same way, we would understand each other.

Then she said something very strange. She said that once when she was in school, a boy had asked her, "What's it like to be so smart?" And this was even before she had the implant. She said, even without thinking about it, "It's very lonely." But afterward when she did think about it, she realized how true it was. She said she didn't have a lot of friends that she could talk to about smart things. She was even smarter than most of the grownups she knew. And the implant made it even worse because some people just used her as a walking wiki and forgot that she had feelings.

I didn't know how to answer that. I know I have a lot of trouble with other people's feelings. I just don't see them. Jamie explained it to me, more than once, and because I wanted to make Jamie happy, I tried very hard to understand. Jamie says that I do have the smarts to understand intellectually, even if I don't have what he calls "empathy."

But I'm not sure I want any of that "empathy" stuff. The people who have it spend a lot of time being angry or frustrated or upset somehow. They spend a lot of time crying too. And sometimes they're afraid about things that aren't there—things that I can't see.

I read J'mee's email over and over because I didn't know how to answer it. Should I just tell her about myself? My syndrome? Or should I wait? But if someone else told her first, then would that be like I was lying to her? I'm not supposed to lie. It's a very bad thing to give people false information because then they can't make accurate decisions. But I didn't want J'mee to stop liking me either. I wanted to call Jamie, but his phone said he was asleep, and there wasn't anyone else I could talk to—except maybe the Captain. He would understand, except he was probably too busy right now to talk to me.

I called him anyway.

He answered immediately. "What's up, son?"

"There's this girl on the *Cascade.* She's very smart. She thinks I'm smart too."

"Well, you are."

"Should I tell her about me?"

"If she's that interested—oh, wait. I see what you mean. Hm." He paused. A long pause. "You know what? You're a good person, Kyle. If this girl is worth knowing, she won't care. You know the old saying, don't you?"

"Which one?"

"The one about mind and matter. 'Those who mind don't matter. Those who matter don't mind.' "

"Is that another one of those sayings you just made up?"

"Nope. That one's a genuine old saying. And it's very true."

"Okay."

"Anything else?" he asked.

"No."

"How's the trip so far?"

"Boring."

"Good, that's the way it should be. We don't have time for any excitement. I gotta go now. Watch out for booger-jacks."

"There's no such thing—" But he had already switched off.

Finally, I wrote back to J'mee. I told her to goggle some stuff—stuff about the syndrome. It was a very short message because I didn't know what else to say.

There were other messages too. Milla wanted to know about Hellan art. I told her there wasn't a lot, not yet, because not a lot of people had time for it. But that we do have some people who made photomontages and did all kinds of tricks with high-dynamic range and infra-red and ultra-violet to make some very dramatic-looking landscapes. Was that what she meant?

Charles thanked me for introducing him to the people who could play instruments. They were already talking about a combined concert. As soon as they decided what music to play, everybody could begin rehearsing their parts. They wouldn't be able to rehearse as a group until after they all landed, however. Even in low orbit, there would be enough of a time-delay that it would be impractical to try rehearsing together.

Trent had decided he wanted to work in the hydroponic and aeroponic gardens. He had read about a man named Luther Burbank who developed new species of potatoes and lilies and other plants. It was very slow work and required a lot of patience, but he felt it was also very spiritual work too. I didn't know what he meant by that, but I wrote back and told him that I knew we needed a lot more people to work on the farms, so he would probably get his wish.

Gary said he liked animals because they were a lot easier to deal with than people. I had to agree with that. He wanted to work with Hellan animals, but he knew he'd have to start with Earth animals first. So he wanted to know about the kennels at Winterland. Even though most of our protein is tank grown, we still kept real animals as a control, as a source of genetic raw material, and as an opportunity to develop new breeds better suited for Hella. I told Gary we needed people to build more tanks, because bacon was still a luxury.

And Chris wanted to work with the mapping teams. He said that would probably get him onto the drive-arounds a lot faster than anything else. He asked me about my drive-around and I told him everything I could. I gave him my raw data too, so he could see that there's a whole lot of boring between the bits of interesting and exciting.

There was also a note from Captain Boynton on the *Cascade*, thanking me for all my videos and all my emails too—what he called "your generous sharing with the colonists on the starship." He said my notes and comments were very much appreciated.

Finally, there was a message from the mysterious Harlie. No last name, just Harlie. He said he had looked at all my videos and read all my notes and even some emails that others had shared with him. He said he wanted to know me better and thought that we would probably have some very interesting conversations. But he didn't say much about himself, and he didn't have a biography in any of the downloads. I sent an email to Captain Skyler, asking him if he knew anything about this person, Harlie, but I didn't expect a quick answer.

After I finished all that, I went topside to the observation deck and peered out at the passing forest. A flock of redbirds screeched and flew up into the sky. Our passage had disturbed them. They circled uncertainly for a bit, then headed west toward a quieter roosting place.

Later, the trucks had to detour around a column of army spiders. One army spider is a hungry little thing the size of a man's hand. A million army spiders is a swath of naked ground thirty meters wide. If this were an emergency, we would have driven right across them, with little risk to ourselves. But experience had taught the convoy teams that crunching across a column of army spiders isn't good for the treads of the Rollagons, so we went around.

Army spiders don't build permanent nests. Like almost everything else on Hella, they're nomads always keeping a few days ahead of the weather. Sometimes the dinosoids use the barren swaths as a highway through the jungle. Sometimes we do too, but only if we know we're not going to run into anything else on the spider trail.

We turned loose a couple of skyballs to track the column. It was routine for convoys to scatter skyballs and scuttle-bots, especially when traveling through mostly unexplored areas. Long-range skyballs could stay aloft almost forever, watching the land. They could track a herd or follow a flock. A scuttle-bot could climb a tree and anchor itself, just listening and watching, sniffing and measuring, constantly reporting back. Usually scuttle-bots worked in teams, with one on the ground and several more at various heights all the way up to the canopy. This gave us a vertical picture of life in the forests. Scuttle-bots were good at moving very slowly, so they could position themselves to peer down into the nests of silverbirds or hang themselves overlooking the clefts and buttresses in cathedral trees to study the bat-things that roosted there.

The skyballs and bots would recharge themselves by spreading moth-like wings a few hours a day and sucking up sunlight. They could stay out in the wild for months, even years. Some scuttle-bots were twenty years old and still broadcasting. Everything linked up in ad hoc networks, reporting back to the nearest relay stations or even satellites overhead. But even with this daily avalanche of information—all these sounds and sights and smells and measurements of everything—Hella was still a landscape of almost daily surprises.

Around 1430, the convoy slowed and halted. The road crew got ready to jump out to deal with a fallen Atlas branch. It was only a branch, but Lilla-Jack said it was already bigger than any Earth tree. The crew had to wait until two women in power suits, armed with shoulder-mounted railguns, stomped out to help. The rear hatches of the suits were airlocked to the sides of the truck for quick access, but it still took a few minutes to get the drivers sealed in and the suits powered up. When they finally detached, the road crew exited their own airlock. The suits stood guard while the crew studied the problem.

After a bit of calculation and discussion of methods and equipment, the road crew attached a pulley to an Atlas trunk on the side of the road. Others unreeled a length of cable from the front of the truck, looped it through the pulley, and secured it with several heavy straps wrapped around the middle of the branch. On their signal, Lilla-Jack put the truck in reverse. As she backed up, the branch pulled sideways and out of the way. The suits had to help guide the lagging end. But it was a long branch and Lilla-Jack had to drive a long way in reverse, so the suits and the crew hooked onto convenient sideboards and rode back on the outside of the truck.

If this were a movie, of course, a gigantic hungry-saur would charge out of the trees, surprising everyone, eating a few members of the road crew, and getting into a ferocious fight with the power suits. But this wasn't a silly movie, we had taken all the appropriate precautions, our surveillance was good, and nothing awful happened. We were on our way again in less than thirty minutes.

Of course, I assembled a video for the people on the *Cascade*. I had to explain that everyone on the crew wore helmets with full heads-up displays. And the turrets were fully manned. And the umbrella was up. And the skyballs hadn't shown anything. Because the first rule was always safety. Be meticulous. Be methodical. If there had been a predator of any size in the neighborhood, we would have smelled its stink, felt its footsteps, and maybe even heard its rumbling, long before it got close enough to stalk us, let alone surprise us.

We hit the lowlands just before dusk and halted. A storm was coming. There are no small storms on Hella. We'd known about this one and had hoped to outrun it, but it was moving fast and hard. The winds were already whipping the trees. Lilla-Jack decided not to try driving through the weather. She recalled the skyballs and drones, and all the rolling-bots as well. She ordered all the trucks to anchor themselves, driving thick spikes into the ground for stability. As the wind rose, she even ordered each truck hitched to the vehicle ahead, forming a mechanical centipede and assuring even more stability.

We only got hit with the edge of the storm, but it was nasty enough. It rocked the Rollagons and slapped us with sleet and hailstones, broken tree branches, even the occasional small animal. Lightning flashed overhead, uncomfortably close and painfully loud. Water streamed down all the windows and a small flash flood rushed around the base of the vehicles for an ugly half hour. It was unnerving, but then Lilla-Jack hollered, "Is this all you got, bitch?!" We all laughed, but then Hella responded with a series of three quick lightning strikes and a falling tree, and even though it was funny, it was also scary for a moment too.

The storm went on for half the night, nobody slept, we just sipped hot tea or soup and rolled with the punches. Nobody could sleep with the noise and the rocking anyway. I took sandwiches up to the lounge, and the crew there went suddenly silent, so I knew they had been talking about stuff they didn't want me to hear, probably Councilor Layton's idea not to let all the *Cascade* colonists land. Only the good ones. People not like me. Even though nobody was talking about it, everybody was still talking about it. Just not where they would be heard. I think they were all afraid of starting another big argument. So everybody was just waiting for me to leave before they started talking again. I passed out sandwiches and then went back to the galley. Abruptly, just before midnight, the storm stopped and everything was silent again.

Lilla-Jack put up an umbrella of skyballs with extra night-vision and ordered the crew chiefs to check for damage. We had a few cracked windows, a lot of minor dents, several serious-looking ones, and plenty of deep scratches. But for the most part, the vehicles came through the storm okay. They were armored with graphene-layered lattice-metal with a fifty percent compression ratio, and enough flexibility to bounce back, so there wasn't any real damage from the assault.

There were a few minor injuries to tend to—a couple of panic attacks, and a woman who'd slipped and fallen when the truck she was in was punched by a rolling tree branch. She'd bruised her hip and elbow, but a quick scan showed that nothing was broken. A crewman on another truck slipped in the mud. He'd fallen hard off the forward deck above the roller and cracked a couple ribs, but he got himself taped up and went right back to work.

The ground was still wet and muddy from the storm, so the trucks used jets of liquid nitrogen to freeze the dirt ahead. Scuttle-bot surveillance showed that we were going to have even more trouble with the large swampy areas ahead. The marshes were usually dry lake beds by the end of summer, but the early autumn storm had left nearly a meter of water in its wake and the lake beds were filling up with runoff. It was a wide plain, tilted slightly east, so most of the water would spread across the lowlands like a sheet, but if we drove straight through the soft earth, the rollers of each truck would carve a channel. Each truck would deepen it. The last few trucks would be rolling through very deep mud or even water.

Lilla-Jack called a halt for a conference with the drivers. They even had to wake the off-shift teams. If we went west for half the night, toward higher ground, we'd only have to cross two shallow rivers. It would cost us most of a day and eat up the rest of our margin, but it would be safer. Some of the drivers wanted to push straight across the lowlands, they said they'd seen worse, and they were sure their trucks could handle a little mud, but some of the older drivers were skeptical. They said that the aerial scans of the terrain looked dangerous, especially the radar scans and ultrasonic pings. Look at the charts, they said. There are just too many places that look too soft. An unwary driver could easily get bogged down. And it wasn't so long ago that a whole truck had sunk irretrievably into deep muddy quicksand, almost taking an entire crew down. It was that last remark, I think, that helped Lilla-Jack decide. "We'll go west."

That's what I wanted to do. Go west. I didn't want to see a truck sinking into quicksand. And even more, I didn't want to be on a truck sinking into quicksand.

Lilla-Jack called Captain Skyler to let him know, and he agreed with her assessment of the situation. "You didn't have to call me," he said. "You're the on-site manager. It's your call."

"Thank you, Captain. But I wasn't asking you, I was informing you."

He grinned, nodded, and logged off.

We started rolling again almost immediately, turning west to follow the secondary route that wound around and through the foothills of Why Bother.

When I awoke again, we were still an hour away from the first river. I took a shower and had a sandwich. Every living module on a truck has a shower. It's the same water recycled over and over, so it's just like home, you don't have to worry about any strange alien bugs or anything. I like showers. They're very relaxing. But on the truck, I have to keep it short, because other people need to shower too.

We got to the first river and slowed to a stop. Lilla-Jack lit up the crossing with skyballs. It didn't look good. White water rushed over jagged rocks. The narrowest place looked too steep. The wider crossings were strewn with boulders. A recent landslide had blocked part of the access. Last month's overlay showed just how recent.

Lilla-Jack sat for a moment, steepling her fingers in front of her face and breathing into the hollow between her palms, like she was praying, except she wasn't. She was saying some words in an old Earth language, probably German. Jamie says German is great for swearing. Lilla-Jack didn't do it for long, though. She sent skyballs whirring upriver and down, looking for a better passage. She studied her displays for a while, then she said some more words in German. Then she got on her com-set and chatted for a moment with the engineers.

After a bit, a strange-looking truck rolled up. It had tracks like a tank and a weird-looking heavy framework on top. It drove down into the steep gully all the way to the bottom and anchored itself there with feet that jammed hard into the riverbed. Then very slowly and mechanically, the framework on top stretched, unfolded itself, first one way, then the other, and then both ends stretched some more to become a bridge that reached almost from one side of the gully to the other. The ends anchored themselves with their own deep feet.

Lilla-Jack conferred again with the engineers. The bridge across the bottom would hold, but the muddy sides of the ravine still bothered her. They talked about possibilities—laying down sheets of chain or perhaps more bridge sections—but all of those ideas depended on the sides of the gully being stable and they definitely were not.

Eventually, they decided to string multiple heavy cables to Atlas trees on both sides of the ravine, with block and tackle rigs attached to both the front and rear jacks of the trucks. With these security lines in place, each truck would pull itself down this side of the gully, over the bridge, and then safely up the opposite side of the stream. It would be time-consuming, yes, but it would be the safest way.

Captain Skyler always made it clear where we should put our priorities. "You can sacrifice safety for speed or you can sacrifice speed for safety. Which would you rather lose? A day or a life?"

But sometimes, for some team captains, it wasn't always safety that shaped a decision and that could have consequences. Any team captain who lost a team member or caused the loss of any human life would never be a team captain again. The First Hundred started that policy and no one had ever gone against it. According to the loss projections, the colony's population was still way ahead of where we might have been if they hadn't instituted such rigorous safety procedures.

While the engineers were setting the cables, Lilla-Jack checked in with Captain Skyler again, letting him know that we had arrived at the crossing and were rigging safety lines. We would probably end up a half-day behind schedule. He approved the decision, and while she waited for the engineers to finish, Lilla-Jack sent out a corrected schedule to Winterland and the rest of the trucks in the convoy and even to the folks on the *Cascade*, because they were following our progress too.

The *Cascade* was less than a month away now. She'd had to come around the sun, racing to catch up to Hella. She was already burning off her excess velocity and would be falling into a docking orbit a few days after we reached Winterland—if we stayed on schedule. They were going to drop three cargo pods and a twenty-member advance team. The rest of the passengers would winter in orbit. We needed to arrive at Winterland early enough to unload at least three trucks and trailers and send them out to pick up the first cargo pods from the *Cascade*. Right now, they were targeted to land in the high desert, fifty klicks inland from the station—which was conditional on the winds, of course, but the landings were important. The *Cascade* promised to download as much medical supplies and fabbing equipment as they could spare. Mom could synthesize the medicines we'd need to make it through the winter, but it takes time to synthesize anything, so the more units you can put to work, the better you can maintain your stock. We needed to build up our stores before the twelve hundred arrived. They would certainly be bringing enough microorganisms that we could expect a few weeks of sniffles and colds as the two populations mixed.

We could have fabbed some of the medical processors ourselves, but that would have meant taking fabber time away from other projects even more important. Mostly, we needed to fab more fabbers.

Adding twelve hundred people to the colony was going to put an enormous strain on our existing resources unless we began preparing now. We're always in a state of permanent preparation for the next arrival, but we're also always playing catch-up too, because we never know everything we're going to need until the ship arrives, and this was the biggest arrival ever, so it was practically a crisis. A survivable one, but still a crisis.

Most of the passengers wouldn't start landing until spring, which meant they'd be coming down to Summerland Station where they'd come down on the grasslands, which meant we'd need trucks and trailers. Then we'd have to expand the cafeteria or reconfigure the meal shifts. And we'd have to expand the meeting facilities, the dorms, and the bunkers. And after that, we'd see about new homes. But there wasn't a lot of room left in the inner circle for any more pods.

One plan under consideration was to use the space around the innermost fence. We'd never had any dinos get that far, not even during the Big Break-In. They'd cracked the second fence, but never got over it. And we've strengthened all the fences since the Break-In. If we went with this plan, first we'd bury pods all along the inner side of the fence. We'd link all of them with a secure underground corridor and passages to the bunkers underneath every lookout tower. And we wouldn't let anyone with children live in those pods, only people with weapons training.

Another plan, one that a lot of people liked, would be to clear a few existing structures out of the way and then build downward in the same lots, dig out four or five stories to start with, more later, convert the landing pods into homes and stack them in the hole, add vents and pipes and fiber optics, then refill it. Dug-in skyscrapers. Core-scrapers? Whatever. Best of all, they could double as bunkers for year-round habitation. We could have larger stay-behind teams, Summerland Station could be a year-round facility. Over time, we could build a whole city of core-scrapers. We could go five or ten down, if we wanted. The engineering on it was clever. Instead of a building that had to support its own weight, the structural load could be offloaded into the surrounding dirt and rock. The outer walls would carry the weight and that would open up even more interior space.

There were challenges, of course. It would require a lot of time and labor to dig in, and then we'd have the problem of what to do with all the dirt we'd be removing. We'd probably compress it into rammed-earth bricks and use them to strengthen the walls of the thing.

This was one of the projects Jamie wanted to work on. The underground structures would require a lot of design and after that a lot of maintenance, and that would require a lot of energy, so we'd have to expand the solar farms and the windmills. The whole thing would need a lot of air circulation. And then there'd be the problem of ground pressure and vibration from the continuing migrations.

Jamie said that it would be like building a whole city. It would be weather-proof and leviathan-proof and people could stay at Summerland all year long, they wouldn't have to evacuate to Winterland, so we would save by not having to run more convoys and Winterland wouldn't have to carve apartments to hold them.

One time when he was telling me about all this, I asked him about the people who would live in those dug-in bunkers? Wouldn't it be just like living in their pods on the *Cascade* again? Would that be fair to them? Jamie said that maybe they'd find them familiar and comfortable. We wouldn't know if people wanted to live in them until we built some.

It took fifteen hours to get all the trucks across the ravine, then wind up the cables, bring the portable bridge up from the bottom, and unhook the block and tackle rigs we used to help the bridge haul itself up. The next convoy would have to repeat the procedure. We couldn't leave our bridge-vehicle behind, we might need it again.

Lilla-Jack allowed a twenty-minute rest break for the various crews, including one glass of beer per person. Everybody cheered and drank—except the on-shift team of drivers, they deferred their drinks until they went off-shift. The sun was already high in the sky, and the day was getting hot. It might have been late summer, but despite the rising winds and the first trembling storms, the air was still a muggy blanket.

The various teams powered up their trucks and ran through their checklists. Team Sixteen spent a quick twenty minutes on an emergency repair to their rear port side roller, fortunately it was nothing critical, just a loose bolt, then gratefully climbed back into their air-conditioned cabin.

And we were moving again.

The southern edge of the great grasslands is a band of foothills. On the other side, the hills give way to the great salt flats. That was the subject of my next big video.

Mountain rivers rushing to the ocean had carved a lake here millions of years ago. Over time, as the glaciers receded, the lake grew larger and larger. But at some point, the lake grew so large the water was evaporating into the air faster than the glacier could replenish it, and after that, there wasn't enough water to flow downriver. When that happened, the river reversed and the salty waters of the Broad Sea poured into the lake. I had a lot of aerial footage here, but I had to cobble up some simulations too.

The more the surface area of the lake expanded, the more the evaporation increased. During the heat of the summer most of the lake would evaporate, so the Broad Sea just kept pouring more water into it, every year, all summer long, delivering salt and salt and more salt, tons of it. Eventually, the lake was five hundred klicks across and the

Broad Sea was feeding it as fast as the water could flow, adding as much as a centimeter of salt every year for thousands and thousands of years, so many years that the salt was a kilometer deep in places.

And then, tectonic forces lifted the eastern edge of the continent high enough that the channels to the Broad Sea disappeared. The lake continued to evaporate until there was no lake left, only a massive salt flat. The mountain rivers still puddled up on the eastern end, seeping into a deep salt marsh so alkaline nothing can survive there except a certain kind of brine fly, creatures which serve no apparent purpose except as food for annual migrations of birds. We don't send a lot of probes in to study this little ecology because of all the corrosives in the air. Maybe someday.

The First Hundred saw this great white patch from space. They knew what it was even before they landed. But they didn't name it until they could drive up to it and look across the great white emptiness. That's why it's called OhMyGod. Nothing else. Just OhMyGod.

Maybe someday we'll have some industrial use for all this salt—maybe we could make gigantic underground batteries to store excess electricity. But at the moment, we don't have any excess electricity. It's too bad that the channels to the Broad Sea are gone, we could have built hydroelectric generators there. Or maybe not. Salt eats up machinery something awful.

When we finally arrived at the OhMyGod, everybody who could went to the forward observation deck to peer out at the dazzle and say, "Oh my God!" It's a tradition of the journey. The salt flats are painfully bright to look at. They're a color beyond white. Jamie calls it "actinic." It's the color of Hella's sun, a little too much blue, not enough yellow.

We paused for a bit while Lilla-Jack sent out drones to ping the surface of the flat, checking for stability. Normally, the Rollagon tires would sink a meter into the salt, it wasn't densely packed, but sometimes occasional rains would sweep across the OhMyGod, creating temporary rivulets and even a few sinkholes. You really didn't want to sink deeper than two meters. But this year it looked like we were good.

The surface of the flats crunched and crackled as we drove across them, but the trucks' rollers were broad enough to spread the weight of the vehicles and even though the salt gave a little and complained a lot as we drove over it, there was no real danger. There would be if we passed over an underground pool of brine or maybe even a cave leached out by an underground flow. But the drones were good at probing with ground-piercing radar, lidar, microwaves, and ultrasonics, to give us a map strewn with electronic flags marking a safe route across the salt. The following convoys would do their own mapping, if they got the same results they'd parallel our tracks.

The only real problem was the glare. The actinic light of the sun dazzled everything with sharp edges. Everything had a harsh edge, everything looked like it had an ultra-violet fringe. The truck windows were polarized and that compensated a little, but up in the turrets we wore helmets or salt-goggles, polarized, color-filtered, and darkened.

We made good time crossing the flats. We pushed our speed a little, not a lot, and picked up nearly an hour. The sun finally dipped below the horizon and we were able to take off our helmets and glasses. This was the best time to cross the OhMyGod. The trucks were all brightly lit and the drones became beacons lighting the way forward. We were all different colors and we looked like an old-fashioned circus parade, like in the old movies. The night shift could maintain good speed and we were off the OhMyGod before the morning glare turned into a white-out.

From there, the route wound around some more low hills, then up into the dry country. Up there is Flat Rock Altitude Station, also called First Stop, where we expected to rendezvous with a northbound convoy. They'd be carrying Winterland crops and supplies and equipment for the maintenance teams at Summerland. As soon as they unloaded their cargo, they'd reload with the next set of evacuees and head back south.

We arrived at Flat Rock just before second supper and everybody agreed it was perfect timing. The evening promised to be mild. Clouds in the west blocked enough of the setting sun that the whole valley was filled with a warm yellow glow. Sunrise and sunset are the prettiest times of the day because the harsher blue rays of the sun are attenuated. They come in sideways and have to go through a lot more atmosphere, so they get filtered out and some people say it's almost like Earth's light.

Flat Rock is a kind of naturally paved area where an ancient glacier had done its best to scour everything down to the bedrock. It's a smooth granite plain, large enough for both the northbound and southbound convoys to meet up and celebrate the migration. Northbound and southbound convoys are always carefully scheduled, but no matter how meticulously any convoy tries to stick to its itinerary, there are always surprises and setbacks, so whichever convoy arrives at Flat Rock first, it's traditional that they host dinner for the other.

We were later than we expected because the ravine crossing had put us half a day behind, so the northbounders had taken advantage of our delay to put up tents and canopies and prepare an old-fashioned Jubilee. They wore green conical hats and purple vests. Many of them had painted their faces as well. Sometimes this made them hard to recognize.

Some of the northbound folk would be joining the Summerland maintenance team, so this would be our only chance to spend time with them in person until next year's migration. A few couples slipped away from the celebration for some serious alone time. Five months from now we'd have Second Baby Week. There were always a few Jubilee babies. Maybe some of them would be named Jubal or Julie.

Jubilee Pershing was a Jubilee baby, although she doesn't like to admit it, maybe because her birth parents were just a hookup, not a whole relationship, I'm not sure how that works. I don't understand hookups, but I don't like touching very much, so maybe that's why. Jamie says it's complicated. Jubilee tells people that she got her name because she was conceived at a Jubilee. Well maybe, but the math doesn't add up. Either not enough months to her birthday or too many. But no one says anything, because that would be calling her a liar. Mom says okay, maybe Jubilee is embellishing her story, but so what? It makes her happy. Jubilee (the rendezvous) is about celebrating our lives, and Jubilee (the person) should get to celebrate her own life however she wants.

Okay, I guess so. Jamie says I don't have to understand everything. Especially not people. But if I have to live with other people, don't I have to understand them? I don't know. It's something I'm still thinking about.

Anyway, the feast was a big one. We put the trucks in a big circle around the tents and the huge colored awnings that covered the assembly areas. Beneath the awnings, strings of colored lights had been hung and everything dazzled in different shades and hues.

Every truck unpacked a dozen or more picnic tables. You went to the cook tent to get your tray, then you circled until you found a group of people you wanted to join. Every time you went back for anything else, whether it was a second helping or a drink or even dessert, you had to go to a new table. Many people circulated in couples or in family groups.

The northbounders surprised us. Winterland had built six new protein tanks and brought them online a month early. They arrived with the first production run of beef and pork and they prepared a Texas-style barbecue for us. They even had potato salad and corn. Lilla-Jack and the northbound convoy leader each ordered a round of beer for everyone and everybody cheered.

Managing all the logistics of supplying the various colony stations is a complex job and it requires a lot of people paying close attention to all the different inventories. Right now, we've built up a enough backlog to cover two years of famine, so we're only one year under our eventual target. But when the new colonists arrive, they're going to put additional strain on our resources, and I was hearing a lot more people talking about Councilor Layton's proposal as if it was a sensible idea. We'd have to dip into our reserves before we could expand our productivity. There were a lot of different data models floating around, but all of them had one large unknown variable—the new colonists. So some people were afraid. With their mouths full, they worried aloud about running out of food.

Flat Rock Altitude Station has monitors and scanners and netcams all the way out to ten klicks. It's rare that any wandering dinos interrupt a Jubilee. There's not enough to eat in this neighborhood to attract any of the bigger herbivores, so we don't see hungry carnivores around here either. But we still take precautions. We put out armed teams on scooters and in power suits. In ten years, they haven't seen anything bigger than a family of ground-monkeys. We think ground-monkeys migrate, but we're not sure. We know that the hoppers store roots and nuts and slow down their metabolisms until they're almost hibernating, but the winter is so long they have to wake and eat every few weeks.

Flat Rock Altitude Station is permanent but not large, only ten people at most; sometimes as many as twenty but only during the migrations to help with various management protocols. The rest of the time they're watching to see what effects our Jubilees are having on the surrounding area.

As careful as we are, we aren't always perfect. A spilled tray, a gust of wind, a forgotten napkin, any of these things can carry enough microbes and bacteria to start an ecological avalanche. At least that's the theory.

The rose garden, however—we know how that happened but we learned it only after the fact. One year, someone from the convoy discovered a whole cluster of rose bushes growing halfway down the slope on the eastern side of Flat Rock. They were hard to miss, three and four meters tall, with roses the size of basketballs. But the bushes were also smack in the center of a large circular dead area. And there were dead insects and the bones of small animals all around too. Apparently, the Hellan ecology really didn't like these bushes. For a while, there was a whole uproar about it, with everybody blaming everybody else for not being more careful about ecological contamination. I was too little to understand what was going on, I just thought the roses were pretty.

Some of the people wanted to rip out the rose bushes immediately and sterilize the area. Others wanted to leave them as an experiment, to monitor how they survived the conditions on Hella. Some people wanted to plant netcams to monitor them. But others said, "Leave the rose bushes alone. They're pretty. They're a bright spot on a long journey." And eventually, that's what most people voted for.

What happened was that just before the vote, a woman named Martha-Bob came forward and begged the Convoy Committee not to rip out the roses, because they marked the spot where she and her lover had sex every migration. When she was going south, he was headed north. When he was headed south, she was going north. They saw each other only six times in three years. When he died, she wanted to do something special, so she planted the rose bushes where they made love. A lot of people said it was very romantic.

But it wasn't hard for them to figure out who her mysterious lover was. All anyone had to do was check the records of who had been on what migration and who had died. Within an hour, everybody knew: A year before, a terrible storm had ripped the roofs off three buildings that hadn't been properly secured. Three people were killed by flying debris, a man and two women. The two women were married to each other, so the rose bushes had to be a memorial to the man, Nathan Eaves.

That's when things got complicated. Nathan Eaves had a wife and two children permanently stationed at Winterland. And when Martha-Bob came forward and revealed that he had been having sex outside his marriage, it made everybody look bad. Martha became an "other woman." Nathan hadn't honored his vows to his family. And what was wrong with Nathan's marriage in the first place? That was an unfair embarrassment for his wife.

Oh, and Martha-Bob had a two-year-old baby from her last liaison with Nathan. Not exactly an accident. She'd gone off birth control without telling Nathan because she believed that if she gave Nathan a son, he'd leave his wife for her. The baby—that was Jubilee. She was eventually adopted by the Pershings and everybody pretended that she had been theirs all along.

In the end, the committee decided to leave the rose garden—not because Martha-Bob begged them to, but because of an angry speech by Kaddir Haddad. He broadcast it on the public channel and it was less than thirty seconds long. He said, "Leave the goddamn rose bushes right where they are—as a permanent reminder of how stupid people can be and how selfishness can screw up a plan!"

That suited everybody. At least for a while. The committee decided to leave the bushes alone. They were an interesting if unplanned experiment. If it turned out later that they created serious negative effects, or started spreading uncontrollably, then we'd send a team in to incinerate the whole area. As pretty as they were, we couldn't allow a strain of giant mutant rose bushes to spread poisonously across Hella.

But for now, just before heading out again, every convoy held a brief ceremony at the rose garden. It wasn't to honor the bushes, nor to remember the adulterous affair of Martha-Bob and Nathan Eaves. It served a much more important purpose—to remind everyone that none of us had the right to assault the Hellan ecology, not as individuals, not as a species. The rose garden stands as a terrible reminder that selfishness is always beautiful and attractive, while destroying so many other things around it.

But despite that, sometimes during a Jubilee, couples would sneak off and secretly visit the rose garden. Sometimes, they'd come back with rosebuds tucked behind their ears, their way of quietly bragging that they had just had sex in the sunset. Mom said she knew which of these two traditions was more likely to survive.

I uploaded several videos about the Jubilee rendezvous to the *Cascade*, starting with the music. Jubilee is an opportunity for all the different bands to show off. This year, there were eight, so I videoed them all. I sent the complete performances and I used as much of the music as I could as soundtracks for my videos, thinking the *Cascade* colonists might appreciate it. I had a lot of video of all the different costumes and even more of everyone dancing.

There were also puppet shows for the children and an acknowledgment ceremony for the adults. But at Mom's suggestion, I shot a whole video focusing on the longtables, all of them piled high with delicious celebration foods—fresh baked bread, crisp green salads, roast tankmeats of all kinds, pasta with red sauce, tower cakes and berry pastries, and especially huge plates of fresh fruits and vegetables. Mom said that after nearly a whole Earth-year in space, this is what the colonists would most appreciate seeing, a welcoming feast. She said she was speaking from experience.

Mom also insisted that I post the videos of our emergencies.

We had two.

The first emergency was the dragon-birds. A huge V-wing came flying south, part of their regular migration. Normally, the monitors would have seen them coming from twenty klicks away, but they came over the mountains to the east. They must have been feeding there, so they caught us by surprise. We only had a few minutes warning. But the sirens went off and everyone grabbed the nearest child and went directly to the nearest truck, whether it was their own or not. Almost everybody was secured and the trucks locked down in less than three minutes. The only people not accounted for were the three couples who'd gone down to the rose bushes.

The dragon-birds must have smelled the food on the tables—or maybe it was us they smelled. Most of them flew on, but a smaller wing broke off and began circling, lower and lower. Dragon-birds are always hungry, so even if they had just been feeding on the carcass of some unfortunate beast only a few minutes before, they were already looking for their next meal.

Some people think dragon-birds are beautiful, I don't. I think they're big and ugly. And I think my videos prove it. Three of them came screeching in. They caught at the awnings and ripped them away. Four more landed and began scrabbling at the longtables. There weren't going to be any leftovers from this Jubilee.

We had rangers at all the gun turrets, but they weren't going to fire unless the birds attacked the trucks. It wouldn't have done any good to shoot them. More would have landed to feed on their corpses. We were going to have to wait them out.

Dragon-birds are big. Everything on Hella is big, but mostly we don't get to see how big until we get close to it or it gets close to us. These birds weren't the biggest we'd measured, but they were big enough—three or four meters long from beak to tail. They looked like flying lizards with flat leathery tails. They're long and slithery and covered with very fine fur, brown and gray and black, but in no particular pattern, like some kind of natural camouflage.

These were tall enough to flatten themselves against the side of a truck and peer sideways into the windows of the bridge, and one of them did just that. I got a really good close-up of its face. Dragon-birds have crinkled-up faces like some Earth bats. When they're not screeching, they're hissing. We all backed away from the windows, just in case the glass wasn't as strong as we believed.

But these birds weren't interested in the trucks. They were curious enough, but their real interest was the tankmeats. They snapped and gobbled at everything on the tables—but it wasn't normal feeding, not like we'd seen in the wild. Something here was triggering them, this was a feeding frenzy. They whirled and slashed and smashed at everything, flinging tables and chairs everywhere, they knocked down the support beams, they banged against the closest trucks. Without support, the awnings floated down on top of them, momentarily netting them under various colored draperies, but they ripped and clawed their way free. They snapped at the strings of lights as well, plucking at them angrily—and all the time screeching and hissing and grunting like pigs.

And then, just as fast, they were gone. They looked up and saw the others still circling. They flapped themselves up into the air and everything went silent again. We didn't know if they could digest the human food or if it would poison them. And if it poisoned them, would it poison the other birds that fed on their carcasses? Would the toxicity work its way up or down through the Hellan food chain? Lilla-Jack ordered a few drones after them; maybe we could track them, which might give us a clue.

We stayed in the trucks for almost an hour. Even after the sky was clear and the radar said there were no more dragon-birds anywhere around, nobody wanted to go out again. The rangers were the first, and they were all armored. There wasn't much to salvage, everything had been pretty well shattered, but we still needed to clean up the area. We couldn't leave any contaminating debris behind.

But only a few of us went out, only the people on the cleanup teams.

Everyone else went back to their specific vehicles. I got permission to join Lilla-Jack's team, so I could get close-ups of the damage. We'd have to compile an inventory of what replacements we'd need to fab, but it was clear that we'd lost a lot of useful furnishings.

The rangers went out and brought back two of the three unaccounted-for couples who had gone to see the rose bushes. One couple (I didn't know them except by sight) survived by hiding in the local station's storm-bunker. The other couple had dug into the ground under the biggest rose bush. They spent the whole time covered with dirt and leaves. That might have been smart. Or stupid. A lot of Hella life doesn't like Earth plants. But some Hella life does. We're still finding out which. But they survived, so maybe they were smart.

The rangers brought back the third couple on covered stretchers. The drones had found them, but Lilla-Jack wouldn't let me see the footage. It was okay. I didn't want to anyway. I knew who they were, Beth Palmer and John Gingras, they were bunnymooning, which is something else Jamie had to explain to me. He says it's like a hookup, but it's more like a personal picnic that two friends have, sometimes with sex, but not always. He says I'll understand better when I get older. Beth Palmer was from the northward colony and John Gingras was local to Flat Rock Station, so I didn't know them very well. I think it would have hurt more if I had.

Nobody knew why the dragon-birds had attacked the tables or why they'd attacked and killed Beth and John. Dragon-birds had never done anything like this before. Everybody had a theory—maybe it was all our party lights, maybe it was the smell of the food, maybe it was something we still didn't understand. Maybe it was just Hella saying, "You don't belong here. You never will."

Maybe one day we'd figure it out. I hoped it would be soon. Maybe the drones would find something. Then we could protect ourselves against it ever happening again.

That was the first emergency.

The second emergency was one we saw coming. A super-storm had been building up out in the ocean, heading northeast, toward us. Every storm on Hella is a super-storm, so any storm is serious. We'd been watching this one for several days and were well prepared for it.

This wasn't the worst storm ever, but it was the worst one I'd ever seen anywhere. Flat Rock is on the east side of the Great Divide, the side that gets the worst pounding from hurricanes and super-storms and goliaths.

The first wave hit us shortly after dark, just as everyone was bedding down for first sleep. Thick clouds rolled in overhead, edge-lit by the moons—then suddenly, there was rain. Not just a polite drizzle, not just a steady downpour, but a great scouring torrent, wind-driven and ferocious. It slammed sideways into the trucks, rocking all of them like toys. The travel crews had anchored all of the Rollagons with multiple chains and buttresses, but we could still hear them grinding and groaning against the roaring winds.

Lightning lit the clouds, flashing back and forth like the gods were having an argument. Then it turned into a war, a battleground of furious electrical rage. There were more flashes per second than I could count, so many that they blurred into a flickering brightness that danced around the sky. The thunder boomed and cracked around us. Lilla-Jack let me watch from the bridge. I wasn't frightened, I knew that all the vehicles were well-grounded, but we still worried about tornadoes and waterspouts.

The fury went on for the longest time. The wind was so violent the rain was coming in sideways. We had all our lights on and we had furious lightning everywhere, but the sheets of water were raging so thick, we couldn't see anything. Whatever punishment the land around us was taking, all we could see were bright strobing flashes. As unnerving as it was, eventually it also got boring. A lot of people gave up and went off to get some sleep. A few others made sandwiches and monitored the situation from their posts.

But by the time everyone was waking up again for their dark shifts, the worst of the storm had passed, and we could send out drones again to scout for the best route ahead.

Several of the trucks had taken damage. Bits and pieces of flying debris had taken out a radar dome on one truck, and another had a sizable dent in one side from something big that had struck it, bounced around, and then vanished downwind. Probably a huge tree limb. A third truck had lost two of its anchors. It had been pushed sideways, sliding through thick mud, and three of its wheels had been pushed off their treads. That was going to take a day or two to repair—or they could drive off the treads and do the rest of the journey on wheels alone. But it was part of the northbound convoy, so I didn't know what they finally decided until I looked it up later.

There was also some flooding in one of the trucks, because one of the younger children had opened a hatch to look at the rain. By the time they got the hatch closed, nearly a meter of water had flooded the lower storage deck. Fortunately, most of the gear was water-sealed—a normal precaution—but half the plant samples were lost, and a litter of glitter-pigs drowned in their cage.

There might be smaller storms on Hella, but nobody has seen one yet.

Of course, I uploaded all this to the *Cascade*.

Lilla-Jack agreed with Mom. She said, "The more they understand just how dangerous conditions here can be, the more likely they'll learn how to survive. And the easier it'll be for the rest of us."

It didn't take long for the questions to come bouncing back. There were a lot of them:

"How come everybody at Summerland wore rebreathers when they went outside, but not everybody at the Jubilee?"

"Isn't anybody concerned about oxygen toxicity?"

"What about those people who went off to have sex? Weren't they exposed to all kinds of bacteria and microbes?"

"You keep telling us that we have to be careful not to infect Hella's ecology with Earth-life, but it looks like everybody disregarded that rule at Jubilee."

"All that food on all those tables. Don't the Hella-bugs get into it?"

"Why didn't you detox at Jubilee?"

"Some of those dishes don't look healthy. Are you monitoring your consumptions?"

I didn't know how to feel about all the questions, some of them seemed kind of stupid, so I showed them all to Lilla-Jack and Mom and even sent copies to Captain Skyler and Jamie. Lilla-Jack and Mom smiled and said, "We asked the same questions when we first arrived." Captain Skyler was still busy at Summerland, so his reply was very short. He said to answer all the questions honestly.

Jamie sent me a video message. "Hiya, kiddo. You done good. All those questions are good news. It means the *Cascade* people are paying attention. It means they want to know everything. It means they want to survive on Hella, they're trying to understand. Some of them, at least. So this is a good thing, isn't it?" Jamie is good at explaining things that way.

We couldn't move on until we finished cleanup and repairs. There was a lot of cleanup and even more repairs, we were going to be here for a while, so I would have plenty of time to answer the questions from the people on the *Cascade*. There were a lot of them and more kept coming down.

I started with oxygen toxicity, because that's the invisible problem, but also the easiest to explain.

Yes, there's a higher percentage of oxygen in the Hellan atmosphere, but not so high as to make oxygen toxicity a serious risk. Most rebreathers add a little CO_2 to the mix, but at higher altitudes, it's not as necessary. Where there's less air pressure, you take in less oxygen in a breath. Flat Rock Altitude Station is two kilometers above Hella sea level. The same reduced PSI would be found only a kilometer and a half above Earth's sea level. So rebreathers aren't necessary.

There are two other problems with the higher oxygen content. One is rust, the other is fire. Both happen faster on Hella than they would on Earth. Rust is the slow burn, but fire is the one that can kill you. So most of our machines are designed to keep any possibility of sparks contained. As for rust—we use aluminum, carbon polymers, graphene-induced ceramics, and other materials wherever possible.

Lightning from late-summer storms often trigger grass fires in the savannahs and sometimes if the wind is right those fires turn into massive firestorms. It's part of Hella's ecology, so most of the plants and animals have adapted to the annual conflagrations. But it's still bad news for us. That's why most of the permanent installations at Summerland are either dug in or completely underground.

The harder thing to explain was our behavior at Jubilee and the apparent lack of precautions against microbial and other contaminations. A lot of our precautions aren't immediately apparent. Everybody is vaccinated of course, and our vaccinations are updated regularly, almost always a month before a migration. So that's part of it.

Another part, which doesn't show up well on the videos, are the drapes. Most of Jubilee happens under a great awning. It looks like a giant tent, but it's actually several concentric tents and there are concentric circles of mono-fiber netting all around the sides. The netting is so fine it doesn't show up on camera very well. It just blurs whatever's behind it. So it's hard to photograph, even coming at it sideways. I didn't include it in any of my videos, so the *Cascade* colonists didn't know it was there. Not unless they read the manuals. But as Jamie says, "Who reads the manuals? Only if there's a certification test, right?" The manuals say that even one layer of the netting can stop ninety percent of all airborne particles larger than a spirochete. Three rings of netting have been tested to ninety-nine percent efficiency. We use seven.

So getting in and out of the tent requires a person to navigate through a maze of nearly invisible drapes. But every trip, a lot of people go out into the open air. Jamie says that it's a way to feel like you've had an adventure, just so you can say you've done it. Captain Skyler says that human beings have an emotional need to feel free, even if it's a little dangerous, and sometimes even if it's a lot dangerous, but especially if they've been cooped up inside for half a Hella-year.

So that was the real question that the new people were asking. "Are we going to be able to go outside?"

Well, yes. And no.

You can wear protective clothing. Or you can go naked. That's what we call "going outside without protective clothing." Sometimes we don't call it "going naked." Sometimes we call it "beta-testing." There are some people who do it deliberately—just to show how big and bold and brave they are. Jamie says there's a technical term for people like that. He says we call them "statistics."

But there's a certain value to beta-testing. It's how some of our best vaccines have been developed. Some of them have even been named after the beta-testers. We have the Chris Hutchins vaccine to prevent leprotic scales, the Darrell Grizzle vaccine that's eighty percent effective against explosive diarrhea, and the Mike Kok treatment which nobody talks about without giggling. Well, maybe Doctor Rhee can, she says she'll tell me about it when I'm older. "In the meantime, just always wear clean underwear, okay?"

But the other side of that question—are we infecting Hella? That's a lot harder to answer. Because the truth is, we already have. We started infecting Hella the first day we dropped a probe into the atmosphere, and every time a pod comes down and another colonist steps out, no matter how careful we think we've been, it's one more bit of infection.

Jamie showed me a book from old Earth, not a very pleasant book either, so I won't identify it or the author, but you can probably figure it out from my description. In this book, the author made the very uncomfortable argument that human beings are the most invasive species in the known universe. He traced our history from the very beginnings in the Olduvai Gorge and the diaspora that followed to show that, ultimately, we infested every continent on Earth, every climate, every ecosystem—and destroyed it, subverted it to our own hungry appetites.

And the result? Because we don't know how to live in harmony, we used up everything everywhere. The Age of Waste devoured the Earth.

But the author didn't stop there. He showed that we were already spreading out to all the other planets and moons and asteroids in the solar system—all that we can get to and exploit—and afterward, as soon as we can build enough brightliners, we'll infest every other star system that we can reach.

His point? We can't even get along with ourselves. How are we going to get along with anyone or anything else we meet out there?

Out here. Like Hella.

But even if we wanted to be the very best visitors, the most gracious of guests, we can't. *Every breath we take, every step we make* (Jamie always sings those words), leaves behind a trail of personal microbes. So far, we haven't wiped out any species, haven't caused any extinctions—none that we know of, anyway—but we're still trying to be careful.

So why do we act different at Flat Rock Station?

It all comes back to the rose bushes.

If anyone was going to plant rose bushes anywhere on Hella, Flat Rock is the least bad place. Captain Skyler says Flat Rock is "an ecological island," a pocket in a much larger ecology, separate enough to be isolated but not isolated enough to be its own ecosystem.

To the west, there's sharp mountains. To the south there's a lot of desert and even sharper mountains. To the north, there are large barren salt flats. Also a river, very fast and very wide. And several times a year, Flat Rock gets scoured and washed clean by violent storms coming up from the gulf. So there's not a lot of opportunity for anything we might do here to get out to the rest of the continent. That's what we hope, and so far it's worked out that way.

We think. And the rose bushes are the evidence that we might be right.

This was the hardest question of all to answer. I had to upload the whole history of the rose bushes, how they got planted, how we think they survived all these years, and all the arguments about whether to sterilize the area or let them keep growing as a test.

After all the arguments and discussions and meetings and evaluations, it was finally decided that all of Flat Rock Altitude Station would be a test bed, a place where we could find out just how dangerous we might be to the rest of the Hellan ecology without too much risk of the danger spreading.

So that's why people get to wander around Flat Rock so promiscuously. Lilla-Jack confirmed that "promiscuously" is definitely the right word.

We don't have the same risks at Winterland. The station is built into the side of a mostly dead volcano, sealed away from the surrounding terrain, which is mostly broken volcanic rock, with no soil and nothing even trying to grow there. Not yet, anyway. Even the nearby black sand beaches are barren. So Winterland is the most naturally isolated of all our permanent human settlements.

The last part of the video I almost didn't want to send, but I finally realized that Captain Skyler was right. Tell them everything.

Because this was the real problem.

The argument has never been resolved and maybe it never will be.

What's our final destiny here?

Some people say we have to respect the Hellan ecology, especially because there's so much we can learn from it. But there are some people, like Councilor Layton, who think we should replace the Hellan ecology with our own and turn this planet into Earth II.

Jamie says that's a stupid idea—we aren't evolved for this planet, none of our plants or animals and certainly not us. If we're going to survive here, we have to adapt, we need to learn everything we can from Hella, not wipe it out—otherwise that book is right and we really are the worst invasive species in known space.

I think that answered all the questions, all the important ones anyway. Anything else would have to wait till we got to Winterland. I was tired. I shut down my screens and crawled off to my bunk and fell asleep dreaming of dragon-birds and storms and mud so deep I couldn't get out. I finally turned on that part of the noise that helps me get through the night.

But even after the trucks were ready to go, we still had to wait another long day. The drones told us that the storm had flooded a large part of the southward passage. We'd have to wait until the waters drained, and then maybe even longer for the ground to dry out so we wouldn't bog down in swampy mud. That might cost us another day or maybe two. But once we could get rolling again and work our way around to the western side of the Vicious Mountains, we'd be on more tolerable terrain.

We'd spend two Hella-days crossing the dry lands that had escaped the worst of the storm. The Vicious Mountains were high enough to turn a hurricane back on itself, which might be good for the western side, but always caused a lot more damage on the eastern. Once past the mountains, we'd head down into the long southern desert which was supposed to be an easier trek, but not always. If the winds died down, and we didn't get caught in any sandstorms, it'd be a trouble-free crossing, although a sandstorm could disable the vehicles—clog the air filters, scour the windshields, and sometimes even foul the tracks. If the winds started rising, we'd have to wrap the trucks and hunker down to wait it out.

On the far side of the desert, we'd climb over the Hump, wind through the Rumpled Blankie, and then finally roll down the Grand Downslope toward the coast and the long string of volcanoes that sat on the edge of the continent. Winterland Station was carved into the northernmost cone. The gulf winds were already pushing autumn storms north, and we had a fifty percent chance of hitting rain on the last leg. That would cost us another long day and, that close to Winterland, nobody would be happy. But we'd be close enough for help if we needed it.

Lilla-Jack didn't need me on the bridge but she didn't complain when I joined her. As long as I didn't talk. Which was okay, because I was still mostly in my no-talking space. When I wasn't on the bridge, I was in the galley making sandwiches for the road crew and engineers. Or I was in the lounge, answering mail. Or I was in my bunk sleeping. And every so often, in the shower. Washing.

Meanwhile, the people on the *Cascade* were very excited about nearing docking orbit and there was a lot of arguing about who would come down on the first landings. Charles had an older brother, Douglas, who was married to Mickey, and Mickey had worked as an attendant on Earth's orbital beanstalk. Captain Boynton had used him as a Special Assistant for Residential Management aboard the *Cascade*, so

Mickey and Douglas might come down in the second or third pod to help plan for the arrival of the rest of the *Cascade* colonists. Douglas was good at data management, and the plan was that Mickey and Douglas would coordinate with the Housing Committee to figure out who should go where when the rest of the colonists came down. So Charles wrote to ask me to please watch out for Douglas and Mickey and make sure that they were well treated. Of course. What a weird request. Why wouldn't they be?

But maybe the people on the *Cascade* had somehow heard about Councilor Layton's resolution. I hadn't said anything, but there were a lot of chatter and a lot of emails going back and forth now and the news of his proposals must have spread. Maybe the *Cascade* people had decided among themselves to talk only about the benefits they would be bringing to the colony, so we would get excited about having them land.

Down here, Councilor Layton's resolution had been formally introduced, but never voted on. It was tabled for further discussion, to be taken up again after the migration. But Councilor Layton and his people were still talking about the dangers of letting all these new people in, so there were a lot of conversations everywhere about the whole situation, back and forth. Nobody was really sure what would happen if it came up for a vote. Mom said it was bad politics and even after it was voted down (that's what she expected), there would be a lot of bad feelings everywhere. We could expect some rough times. Mom told me not to worry, which was probably the wrong thing to say, because when people say, "Don't worry," they're admitting that there's something to worry about.

But worrying is a waste of time and energy. You can only do what's in front of you. That's what Captain Skyler says. So I went back to my mail.

J'mee thought her dad might be in the first landing party. He had purchased a large part of the *Cascade*'s cargo space, sixteen or seventeen pods, and he wanted to confer with the Captain and the Coordinator as soon as possible about the best place to store his resources.

Trent asked me to send him as much information as I could about the gardens, at both Winterland and Summerland. Gary made a similar request about the kennels and farms. They were easy requests, we had lots of records on file, so I promised to make a personal video for each of them.

Charles wrote a second time asking what my favorite music was. He wanted to put together a special concert for all the people on Hella, his way of saying thank you for such a wonderful welcome. I didn't think our welcome was all that wonderful. All we'd done so far was tell them how hard life on Hella was going to be and send them scary pictures of giant animals attacking, killing, and eating other giant animals.

There was another note from Harlie, curious about how we monitored all our drones and probes. He wanted to know if he could connect to them and start studying Hella's ecology. But Captain Skyler told me not to tell him, just pretend he never asked. He said I shouldn't get too involved with this Harlie person, not yet, but he didn't say why.

Jamie sent me some videos of himself and Emily-Faith working on the Summerland Lockdown team, mostly securing shutters on the pods of the last group of evacuees. Jamie said they'd be working security right up until the day the first big winds came sweeping across the plains.

If they were lucky, it wouldn't be a dust storm—but a lot of dust was coming in from the eastern continent, a lot of it was organic byproducts from the thick jungles in Hella's subtropical zones, so wherever it settled, it helped to fertilize the plains. It carried a lot of seeds and bugs and even little insect eggs and larvae too. But even the most aggressive of these invasive species would have a hard time surviving anywhere in the path of the migrating leviathans. The saurs were a traveling disaster zone. Even so, Mom's colleagues wanted someday to study the evolutionary differences of the plants and animals on the eastern and western continents.

Somebody at Bitch Canyon sent me an anonymous video of Marley Layton mucking around in something that looked like a giant latrine. She was up to her knees in guano. Apparently they were taking core samples because somebody had the bright idea that studying layers of poop would give them an idea of the genetics of previous generations of Bitch things. Whatever the case, it seemed an appropriate job for Marley.

I forwarded a copy to Jamie and to Mom and to Captain Skyler, because I thought they should see it, but nobody else. I didn't mind if Marley Layton was going to be embarrassed, she deserved it. I just didn't think I should be the one passing it around. But whoever filmed it must have sent it to a lot of people, because it was all over the network within an hour.

After Marley was sent off to Bitch Canyon Station, Jamie told me that the best thing to do was pretend that Marley didn't exist anymore and get on with everything that's important to me. Jamie said all the stuff that everybody says when they think they're being wise. Why give Marley a room rent-free in my head? Hating someone is like drinking poison and hoping the other person dies. That all sounds very good, but it's a lot easier to say it than do it.

There was a lot of email from adults on the *Cascade* asking me to video what the houses on Hella were like. Houses? Ha ha. Mostly it was dorms or barracks or converted landing pods, unless they wanted to join work crews and build their own. And they had to build them according to colony plans, too. We couldn't have badly built structures coming apart in the first big wind.

Some emails asked why the various roads between Summerland

and Winterland weren't properly paved. Those three were easy to answer. "Please compute the cost of paving three thousand kilometers of four-lane highway, plus bridges and tunnels, and compare that to the Gross Annual Resources of the colony."

Yes, there is a tunnel project in the planning stages. One of the points in its favor is that we could put strong hatches at either end and use the length of the tunnel for emergency storage or even emergency shelter if anything awful ever happened to one of the stations. Or we could even expand it with side tunnels and make it a third major station. A lot of people like that idea, more so after the Break-In. If enough of the *Cascade* colonists could be assigned to the work force, we could begin within a year. But like everything else, it's a matter of resources. We'd still have to feed them and shelter them while they were working and that would mean establishing and supporting an extensive remote station.

But a lot of people, like Councilor Layton, would rather start an expansion station on the eastern continent. Captain Skyler opposes that, not just because it's a bad idea, but because he's pretty sure that Councilor Layton wants to be in charge of that station and set up his own community, and then, as soon as it's self-sufficient, declare independence. Captain Skyler isn't against independence, but he says that when one thing divides itself into two things, then the next thing that happens is that the two things start fighting each other. Divorce for example.

Captain Skyler thinks Councilor Layton is always trying to divide people so he can control them, but Councilor Layton says that Captain Skyler wants to keep everybody in one place so he can control them. It's an argument that I'm not sure I understand. Last year, Councilor Layton and his caucus formed their own Expansion Committee and picked out the locations on the other continent where they wanted to build their new Summerland and Winterland, but that got voted down so Captain Skyler says that Councilor Layton's latest resolution is a kind of revenge. I don't understand that either. I don't get revenge. Hurting back just means two people are hurt.

Another email asked why the stations are named Summerland and Winterland. That was easier to answer. You have to look at how severely the planet is tilted. The intense sunlight heats a wide band around Hella's equator, keeping that entire range hot and uncomfortable, all the way up to unlivable. We call it the Scorch Belt. And mostly we stay away from it.

Summerland is in the far north and it's called Summerland because that's where we go to spend our summers to avoid the intense heat of the season. Winterland is in the south, closer to the Scorch Belt, because that's where we spend our winters, to avoid the incredible cold of the north. Only the maintenance teams stay on-site. More people could stay, hunkering down against the extreme weather, but it uses up a lot of resources. And it's better for the colony to have two self-sufficient installations.

I've never seen carbon dioxide frost up close, and I don't want to see it up close. I've never seen the firestorms of the ultra-tropics up close either, and I don't want to see them anywhere but on a big display. But that's Hella. We have Hella-weather. Everything is Hella-bigger and Hella-meaner and Hella-more ferocious. And that's how we define Hellacious.

After I finished going through my mail, I started reading the comments on the discussion forums. It was very uncomfortable. Some of the *Cascade* colonists weren't happy with my last round of videos. They said that Hella looked unfriendly. Some of them said that this was not the planet they had been promised. And a few even said that they might not land at all, they might stay on the ship and go back to

Earth. Except the ship wasn't going back. Not any time soon. And Captain Boynton wasn't sure if there was anything to go back to. So who knew what they were going to do?

This was probably not a good conversation for them to have, because Councilor Layton could use their doubts to justify his resolution, like, "See? These people don't even want to be here."

After second supper, I called Jamie to ask him if he'd seen those messages too. He had. Everybody had. I wasn't the only one reading those comments and receiving emails. It wasn't going down well. A lot of people had been working too hard for too long to have any patience with the complaining of newcomers—especially people who hadn't even landed yet and were already griping. But Jamie said I shouldn't worry about it. "Look up the history. This happens all the time. There are always people who are unhappy and want to go back. And, mostly, we let them. We can't carry any dead weight."

"But the *Cascade* isn't going back."

"Yes. That's the problem."

"So what are we going to do about it?"

"Nobody knows. That's what everyone is arguing about. What are we going to do with people who don't want to be here and we can't send back? Nobody knows."

"Is this why Councilor Layton doesn't want them to land?"

"It's part of it. And it's certainly something he can use to support his resolution." Then Jamie stopped himself before he said the next sentence. "No, never mind."

"What."

"It's nothing."

"Jamie—"

"I said it's nothing."

He didn't want to say, but I kept asking, "Tell me anyway. Tell me." Jamie says it's very annoying when I do that. But sometimes it works.

Finally, he cleared his throat that way he does when he's about to say something I won't like.

"Okay, I'll tell you, Kyle, but it's gonna make you angry. Are you gonna manage yourself?"

"I will. I promise. Tell me."

He took a breath. "I was going to say—don't take this the wrong way, Kyle, you're doing a great job—but Councilor Layton blames you a little bit. Your videos are showing them a lot of uncomfortable stuff, how dangerous Hella can be and how hard everybody has to work. It's upsetting the people on the *Cascade*. They're getting scared and depressed. They're not excited about landing anymore. They're worried."

"But that's stupid." And Jamie was right. It did offend me. "Those people on the *Cascade*, they need to learn as much as they can before they get here. This is about helping them survive—it's about helping everybody survive."

Jamie held up a hand to stop me. "Kyle, it's not your fault. They arrived with expectations. It probably started before they even left Earth. They saw all the pretty pictures and somehow made it up in their heads that life here was going to be easy and fun. No matter how many times the orientation teams told them how much hard work was needed just to stay alive from one season to the next, maybe they just didn't want to hear it. And then you sent them your pictures that Hella demands Hella-work and they—well, those were some pretty scary pictures, kiddo, so some of the new colonists are complaining that nobody told them that Hella was dangerous. But what did they expect? A vacation? So, yeah—that's why some of the colonists on the *Cascade* don't want to land."

"But Councilor Layton doesn't want them to land anyway. So why would he blame me for my videos? I don't understand."

Jamie took another breath. "Councilor Layton likes to keep everybody arguing with each other. It doesn't matter what about, as long as they're arguing. Because once people start arguing, they start hating. And if he can get people hating each other, then he can control that hate. That's the way he thinks."

"That's crazy!"

"Yes, it is. Real crazy. I think there's something wrong with the man. Maybe he's afraid of not being important. But that's why Captain Skyler is going to stand for a seat on the Council—to keep Councilor Layton from doing more stupid stuff."

I didn't know what to say. Jamie understands the political stuff better than me. Politics is people—and people aren't logical. I prefer logic. It's simpler. Jamie says there's an emotional logic, but it's nothing like real logic. I'm not sure I can understand two different kinds of logic. Not at the same time.

Jamie said, "It's nothing to worry about right now. Councilor Layton doesn't have the votes. And he can't do anything by himself. So he's just a big unpleasant noise. And I don't think you need to worry about what the new people are saying either. That's just noise too. Once they get down here, they'll learn what's so. Everybody does. You work, you eat. You don't work, you don't eat. That's what the Passage Ceremony means, doesn't it?"

What Jamie was saying was true, and he was right about the other thing too. It was making me uncomfortable. Why can't people just do what's in front of them? Why do people have to have so many stupid conversations instead? The work is obvious, isn't it?

I liked most of the people I'd talked to on the *Cascade*. Maybe some of them were asking dumb questions, but a lot of the people on the earlier pilgrimages asked those same dumb questions without having anyone down here to answer them. They had to figure it out for themselves after they landed. My videos were supposed to help.

"I wish you were coming to my Passage Ceremony."

"I'll be watching it from here."

"It won't be the same."

"I know. You'll have to let Mom hug you. Pretend it's from me. Okay?"

"Okay."

"Promise? Stinky Promise?" He held up his hand and hooked his finger.

"Stinky Promise." I did the same.

A person's fifth birthday is the earliest day they can be eligible for a Passage Day. Mine would be at Winterland. The Passage Ceremony means Passage-Into-Adult-Responsibility. On that day, you stop being a child and you start earning your passage on the voyage of life. You also get to vote—of course, part of that responsibility is that you have to continue your education. Education is how you earn additional certifications and move on to bigger responsibilities.

Mom says there's no point in building a new civilization if we forget to be civilized, if we forget our science and technology, if we forget our art and literature and music. If all we do is live instead of living large, then we're not living at all. That's what Mom says. I think I understand what she means. I like a lot of the music of old Earth that she plays while she works and I think I'd like to learn how to play an instrument too, maybe the piano. There's this piece by someone called Beethoven, the *Pathetique* piano sonata. I like that one a lot. Maybe Charles on the *Cascade* can teach me.

Finally, I asked Jamie how his work was going. It was a good way to change the subject. He said it was going well, I should look at the recordings and make a video for the *Cascade.* They were already expecting their first big storm of the season early next week—well, just the edge of the storm—but it promised to be pretty impressive. The second evacuation wanted to leave before it hit. It's important for the *Cascade* colonists to see how all this works.

"Yeah," I said. "I could make a video about the evacuations and the weather—but maybe I shouldn't. I mean, if my videos are upsetting them, maybe I should stop."

"No, don't stop. That would be giving in to Councilor Layton. But maybe you could make some happy videos, what do you think? Like the one you made at Jubilee, where everybody is laughing and dancing. Oh, and by the way, was that Jorge and Jose holding hands and wearing rosebuds?"

"Uh, yeah. Jorge's dad wasn't happy about that, but both his moms laughed out loud and said it was about time. But I'm not good at happy. You know that."

"No, I don't know that, Kyle."

"But I don't do emotions right. That's why some people don't like me."

"No. You do emotions just fine. Your Jubilee video was good. I think you're learning. What you don't do is think like stupid people. That's your super-power. That's what bothers them. That you can out-think them."

"You're not just saying that—?"

"You're my favorite brother. I would never lie to you. I'll bet if you go and make some happy videos, you'll find out just how good you really are at emotions. Think about all the good things that people have accomplished here on Hella. Show them that. We have everything on file. We have hellabytes of recordings. Look up all the good stuff you learned in history classes. You can do that, can't you?"

"Okay," I said. "I can do that."

But I had to go off and think for a while—at least until I stopped being upset about Councilor Layton and some of the people on the *Cascade*, the ones who didn't like the videos. But it wasn't their fault. They just didn't know, that's all. It was my job to show them—not just the scary stuff, but the good stuff too.

Jamie was right. Jamie was almost always right, and even when he was wrong, he was wrong for the right reasons. Talking to Jamie always makes me feel better, even when he's telling me things I don't want to hear.

I trust Jamie more than anybody. So if Jamie says that this is important, then this is important, and that's all there is to it. Case closed. And so there.

We ran into the second northbound convoy, two days out of Winterland. We were first to the rendezvous at Little Point, but because everybody was now a day behind schedule, it was mutually agreed that we'd skip the second Jubilee. We did spend an hour at Little Point though—mostly to give passing family members a little time to be together. I don't think any babies got started though.

Some women still like to grow their babies the old-fashioned way. That's what Mom is doing, she even has a little baby bump now. Some people grow their babies halfway and then bottle them. Mom might do that if it's a question of her health or the baby's. But there are people who just don't want to be pregnant at all, they bottle their babies from the beginning.

But Jamie says everybody likes making babies and the colony needs to grow a lot more people. Class-9 Self Sufficiency requires three separate and distinct populations of thirty thousand each. We're nowhere near that point.

Jamie promised to call me every time he got off shift, so we talk at least two times a day. He said that everybody was working as hard as they could but they were still a day behind schedule. But not to worry, that was normal, somehow it always worked out. He said that falling behind schedule was built into the schedule, so they were actually on schedule. But the autumn storms would arrive earlier than usual, and they promised to be especially ferocious this year because of the thirteen-year weather cycle, so we had to put need in front of want.

He asked me how my new videos were going and I told him that I hadn't made any yet because I hadn't finished thinking, but I was making up for it by uploading videos of our progress. Sometimes it's hard to concentrate when the Rollagon is moving. The trucks have good suspension so the ride is smooth enough, but sometimes I want real silence and even with headphones that's not possible. The rumbly vibration is everywhere, it comes up through the floors, through the seats—it's in the walls, even in the windows. Sometimes I just want everything to stop for a bit and leave me alone in my head. Even the noise would be quiet by comparison. But a migration is a mad dash. We have to go as fast as we can.

When we finally reached the southeast coast, everybody cheered. It was the last leg of the journey. Even though we'd all seen it before, and seen it even better on the big screens, everyone still crowded to the port side windows to see the ocean. Beyond the rolling hills, beyond the sharp cliffs, beneath the rocky edges—there was the dirty gray gravel of the beach, and past the beach, gray water, gray sky, and the harsh blue-white blur of the sun. It was grim and ugly, but we cheered anyway. Another long day and a half and we'd be safe at Winterland.

In the afternoon, we saw a distant family of humongosaurs. Lilla-Jack sent out a few skyballs for a closer look, but decided not to send a tagging team. Everybody agreed that humongosaurs were simply too big to exist, but there they were anyway. Twice as tall as the leviathans, they didn't move as much as they flowed in slow motion. First the right front leg lifted, just barely scraping forward so gradually it didn't look like it was moving at all, until at last it came to rest just three meters forward of its previous position. Then nothing happened for a moment, then the left rear leg moved. An avalanche of muscle in the towering haunch shifting like a tectonic plate. This massive limb moved forward even more deliberately. Then another pause and the left front leg moved. And finally the right rear limb. And then another pause. The great neck, the great tail swayed like giant horizontal pendulums.

These humongosaurs were headed toward the thick forests ahead. They would push through the willowy trees as if they were smoke in the wind. And even the Atlas trees would crack and groan and break under the pressure of a humongosaur's passing. It didn't matter how loudly the trees shrieked and screamed and belched out clouds of tanninoids, the humongosaurs were just too big and they moved too slowly to care. They were resistant to the tanninoids, or maybe they found them tasty, or maybe they excreted the poison in their astonishingly huge piles of poop, taller than a truck. Or maybe they just stored the poisonous parts in some gland and exuded it to keep other herbivores away. Without a proper dissection, we couldn't know—and no one had ever gotten close enough to a humongosaur corpse to explore its cavernous interior.

Ever since the humongosaurs were first seen, the biologists wanted to study them close up—but it just wasn't safe. There were so many "camp followers" attached to the family groups the creatures existed in the center of their own personal war zones. There were insect-things that lived on their bodies, and more that crawled along behind, feeding on dead skin or dung. There were other creatures that fed on the insect-things. There were the bird-things on their backs, there were all kinds of parasites and things that fed on the parasites and even more things that fed on them. And every so often, several families of carnosaurs would come together forming a raging army that circled the humongosaurs hungrily. From above, they were a sea of gaping mouths and slashing teeth.

Sometimes the army of carnosaurs dispersed without a kill, but sometimes they'd be so hungry they'd harry the whole family, eventually tiring out one of the younger animals or better yet, one of the older and larger ones. They'd charge in and bite, a nip here, a nip there—they'd rip off strips of flesh that were huge for them but possibly irrelevant to an animal the size of a humongosaur. And the humongosaur would just keep on going, swinging its tail around, waving its long neck, occasionally sending a carnosaur flying, occasionally stomping one into the dirt—but the other attackers, caught up in their own frenzied bloodlust would just keep charging in, just keep biting, just keep nipping and ripping, until finally, a frothing sea of blood in its wake, the great beast was streaked with dark red gashes all along its lower flanks. And then . . . and then . . . as slowly as it had lived, just as slowly it would die.

It would sink to its knees, its head would come down, its tail would swing a few last times, but by now the carnosaurs would be all over it, thrashing and biting, sometimes so thick that the humongosaur would vanish beneath their frenzied bodies. And then, the humongosaur would be nothing more than a mountain of flesh—a great banquet for a hundred carnosaurs. The feast would go on for days, weeks, sometimes longer than a month.

A humongosaur death was an ecological event—like an earthquake or an avalanche—because all the creatures that lived on even a single great beast would now be wandering the plain, hungry and eager for whatever opportunity they could find.

Jamie asked me once if I ever wanted to visit Earth. I don't think so. Parts of it look pretty—the mountains, the seas, the tropical jungles—but the big cities look crowded and ugly. All those flashing bright lights. All those giant buildings, all those animated pictures and signs everywhere. It looked infectious and nauseating. I could understand why so many people wanted to leave it and come here to Hella. I just couldn't understand why when they got here they didn't want to stay.

Hella isn't easy, but Captain Skyler says life isn't easy. If it were easy, everybody would do it. Death is what you do if you're not up to the challenge.

It started to rain in the afternoon, heavy rain, blinding rain, and we had to cut our speed way down to navigate carefully across the muddy coastlands. The passage of our trucks would leave deep swampy furrows. They would fill up with water and whatever life liked to swim in shallow pools of water.

All of our lights were on, forward lights, rearward lights, spotlights, dazzlers. From the roof turret, the convoy looked like a bright glittering snake of stars. The rain added its own sparkling reflections and the water drops on the windows blurred the view into a dark hallucination.

We arrived at Winterland long after sunset, rolling through a long tunnel of decontamination sprays and into a huge service bay. Everybody was tired, exhausted from the long journey, but when we pulled up to the docks, one truck after another, lining up like giant beetles, everybody poured out, hugging and yelling and cheering and shouting and greeting old friends and family members with tears and smiles and cries of, "I missed you so much!" and "Tell me everything!" and "Look how big you've grown!"

But because everybody was still so weary and drained from the journey, the welcomes were short-lived. Some headed to the cafeteria, others to the showers. Most people headed straight for their winter quarters. Those who didn't have regular rooms headed for previously assigned cubbyholes. A lot of people checked into the nearest dorm and would make permanent arrangements in the morning. But a lot of others—the nighthawks and the family members and the ones too excited to sleep—were going to stay up with the Winterland lateshifters, talking all night, making sandwiches, drinking coffee, swapping tales, and maybe even practice their baby-making.

The maintenance teams would be up all night too and well into the next day. The trucks had to be cleaned and serviced—especially cleaned. They came in caked with mud and dirt, the windows grimy with dust, the rollers stained with grass and leaves and studded with thorns and prickles. First thing, the septic tanks would be pumped and scoured, the waste sent down for recycling. Then the cleaning crews would go through the vehicles, picking up trash and everything else as well, knives and forks, plates, teakettles, napkins, sheets, pillows, blankets, cushions, all the conveniences of life. The trucks would be stripped and scoured, sanitized, sterilized, detoxed, and decontaminated from top to bottom.

Some of the trucks were scheduled for overhaul, others would need repairs—a few even needed critical work. It was a big job. When two dozen Rollagons all pull into the docks one after the other, it puts a lot of stress on the work force, so during migration season, extra crews get drafted to the maintenance teams. Each crew would have its own set of responsibilities. There was a lot of work to be done, checking the internal monitors of each vehicle, examining every moving part, testing all the pumps and hoses and circuitry for integrity, aligning and calibrating, poking and prodding, tightening, repairing, replacing everything from deck panels to seat cushions, all the monitors, sensors, scanners, and communications gear—all the cameras and microphones and sniffers, all the network connections and all the information processors. Everything.

As soon as each truck passed its service inspection, it would be refueled and reloaded. The living quarters would be stocked with clean sheets and blankets, fresh food and water, everything needed for the comfort of the crew, everything necessary for the next mission. Weapons too—every weapon system would be tested, calibrated, serviced, recharged. The cargo bays would be restocked with skyballs and scuttle-bots and extra armaments if necessary.

The rule was that every truck had to be kept in a state of immediate readiness. As soon as a vehicle came in, it was unloaded, serviced, reloaded, checked, checked again, certified, and made ready for operation. And as soon as there were enough trucks ready, another convoy would head north to bring back another thousand colonists.

And for those who'd just arrived, migration madness wasn't over yet. Arrival put enormous pressure on the receiving station, whether it was Summerland or Winterland. As soon as you got off the truck, you had to get to work.

Systems that had been dormant for nearly half a year would have been brought back online before the arrivals, water, power, air filtration, heating and cooling, lighting, food production and preparation, waste removal and recycling, reopening and restocking additional medical facilities, laundry, and even a few things not so obvious, like fabbing new furniture, painting, repairing infrastructure, even preparing new manuals and orientation kits letting the arrivals know exactly what had been changed since they'd left nine months previously.

First arrivals had to get the apartments ready not only for themselves, but also for all of the arrivals on the convoys still to follow. So most of us would spend our first sleep shift and sometimes our second on the truck, but we had to get off the trucks before the service teams came in to ready the living quarters for the return trip.

Every arrival was the same, every arrival was different—a weird mixture of familiarity and strangeness. Nothing quite matched memory. Things were smaller, darker, larger, brighter, uglier, prettier—or gone altogether. And the things that replaced them were momentarily unsettling until you figured out if they were improvements or disappointments—like the corridors leading to our apartment. New lights had been installed, making them brighter. They walls had been painted a pale gray and all the doors and cabinets and fixtures were trimmed in white. It looked old-fashioned and modern at the same time. Every year, the Winterland hospitality teams redecorated the public spaces. They rearranged and remodeled, every year a different theme. It was a tradition, their way of creating an extra bit of adventure, an incentive to get out and explore and be an active part of the community. But right now, I was too tired to appreciate the effort.

I thought about taking a shower, but the showers were going to be crowded for a while, so I headed to Mom's suite. As head of her science committee, she was entitled to a three-room apartment but without Jamie, we were going to have to share that third room with a tenant, I didn't know who. Mom had a late night meeting with her on-site staff, so I went down by myself.

I slept long, but I still woke up in time for pre-dawn breakfast. Mom and Lilla-Jack were sharing coffee in the little kitchen attached to our suite. "Want some?" Lilla-Jack pushed a cup at me. "They're trying a new growing cycle in the greenhouses here. This is fresh Kona. What do you think?"

I sipped. It tasted like coffee. But good coffee. I nodded. "I like it."

Mom said, "Lilla-Jack is our new roommate. She's taking Jamie's room."

"Okay."

"Is that all right with you?" Lilla-Jack asked.

I shrugged. "It's okay."

Both Mom and Lilla-Jack laughed at that. "He's still sleepy," Mom explained. "You want some breakfast? The cafeteria sent over some emories. I'll heat one for you?"

I shook my head. An emory is a "Meal Ready to Eat." MRE for short, emory for long. The caf prepares food stocks for the trucks and the outposts. And whenever there are extra portions, the caf freezes them. So the emory-menu has all kinds of surprises in it. Because Winterland and Summerland specialize in different crops, the cafs trade a few truckloads of emories every migration. Winterland uses greenhouses, Summerland is open fields. Some people think that it's dangerous for us to raise Earth crops in open fields, but the ground behind the fences has been irradiated, the canopies provide ninety-nine percent aerial protection, and lasers zap any insect-things that still get through. A lot of people say the Summerland fruits and veggies taste fresher. More important, we need to know that we can survive off the land.

We also have some Hellan things on our menu too. That's another part of learning how to live off the land. That's one of Mom's jobs. She and her team are continually testing all the different grasses, fruits, nuts, berries, roots, leaves, herbs, peppers, and whatever else looks like it might be edible. So far they've identified nearly a hundred things that won't kill us, twenty-three that will, and a few that will just make us wish they had.

I like the sweet-melons, but we don't get those a lot. The leviathans like them too, and their migrations seem to be perfectly timed; they arrive at the lowlands just when the melons are at their best. Winterland has dedicated a whole greenhouse to the vines, but they're slow to ripen, so we don't get them a lot. Not yet anyway. We're going to have to expand our greenhouse space soon, so maybe we can plant more melon seeds.

Sometimes I get frustrated enough to wish that I weren't so . . . whatever it is I am. I don't see the surface of anything. I see the under-beneath. I see the connections. I see the evolutions and the elocutions—all the conversations and reasons and stories and histories. I see the chords and the discords, the wise and the whys. The only thing I don't see is what other people really mean. Especially mean people. That's what Jamie meant by my super-power. But it's not just because Jamie explained it to me—I looked it up myself. I'm not the first person with a syndrome. And I'm not the first with the noise either.

But all the explanations are from their side, people who aren't like me, so it's their conversation, not mine. It just doesn't make a lot of sense to me. I'd have to be one of them to understand why I'm not one of them. And most of the time, I don't see any advantage to being like any of them. I like the way I think. Even when it's frustrating. Because I get to know things that other people don't.

That's one of the things I don't talk about to anyone. Except maybe Jamie. A little. But not a lot. Because it makes him frown. I don't know why. He says it's complicated. He says you have to kill something before you can dissect it. I said I didn't want to be dissected. He said it was a metaphor. Metaphors are something else I have trouble with.

Mom and Lilla-Jack were discussing plans. Mom wanted to reorganize her labs for a new set of nutritional studies. There were some grasses that might be bred into a useful grain. But with the migrations, Mom couldn't plan any project lasting longer than eight months—unless she wanted to stay over for a season. She had talked about it with me a few times, but until I was old enough to be on my own, those projects had to wait.

Lilla-Jack had to see to maintenance on the trucks. Even though most of the vehicles had arrived without any worry-lights on, she still had to manage the maintenance and service for every vehicle before the convoy could return. Other convoys were already on their way, but Lilla-Jack's would be the last one before the weather made any more journeys impractical. And with the *Cascade* people landing in the spring, we'd need at least another ten to twelve trucks for future convoys, so Lilla-Jack had to prep the big fabbers for chassis and axles as soon as possible. Winterland didn't have enough raw material on hand, so that would mean processing a lot of biomass to extract the carbon.

I didn't pay too much attention to the conversation. Breakfast was a lot more interesting once I opened the emory and saw a cup of fresh sweet-melon chunks, a happy surprise. Somebody had to have picked this out special for me, because it wasn't on any of the public lists. After breakfast, I'd look at the log so I could say thank you. But then Lilla-Jack said something that caught my attention immediately.

"When HARLIE arrives, we'll ask him to take a look. He can give us a much deeper analysis."

"I know Harlie," I said. "I get emails from him." Then I realized something. "Is he like me?"

Mom and Lilla-Jack looked at each other, then Mom looked to me. "No, sweetheart. HARLIE is nothing at all like you. He's—" Then she stopped herself, laughing. "Actually he's a lot like you. He's very smart and he's very good at figuring things out."

Lilla-Jack explained. "HARLIE is an intelligence engine. A really powerful intelligence engine, possibly one of the best ever made. He's one of the reasons the *Cascade* got here early. Or even at all, if the stories are to be believed. I think you'll enjoy talking with him as much as he'll enjoy talking with you."

I looked from one to the other. "Then why did Captain Skyler tell me not to talk to him too much?"

They both looked confused or puzzled. Mom said, "I'll have to ask him."

Lilla-Jack said, "I think it's because . . ." She looked at Mom. "May I?"

Mom said, "Go ahead."

Lilla-Jack turned back to me. "Okay, so Kyle—you're good at a lot of things. Everybody knows that. But the one thing you're not good at is what we call *nuance.* Do you know what that is?"

"Nuance is all that stuff that I don't understand."

Mom and Lilla-Jack both laughed.

I added, "It's all the stuff you're saying underneath the words you're speaking. It's what you mean instead of what you say."

"That's very good," said Lilla-Jack. "And let me tell you something.

Being as literal as you are—that can be an advantage, Kyle, because you don't tie yourself up in knots wondering what someone *really* meant."

"I kinda figured that out."

"Well, anyway, HARLIE is almost all nuance. No, that's not right, but bear with me. HARLIE can do all the things that other intelligence engines can—and a lot more. Supposedly he can process hellaflops per second but there's no way to test it. In addition to all that, he can do nuance. In fact, he can do nuance better than anybody. He's the godfather of nuance."

"I don't get that."

"Of course not. The godfather is a mythical entity who speaks only in nuance. Never mind. The point is that HARLIE does nuance. He was built to be a self-programming problem-solving device, so the first problem he set out to solve was understanding what humans meant when they spoke. He trained himself to understand nuance, and in so doing—if I understand this correctly—he became something much more than what anyone thought he would be. He became unknowable. Human beings have every reason to be a little bit afraid of HARLIE—because we don't understand how he thinks, we don't understand what he wants, we don't even understand what he means all the time. And I think that's kind of why both Captain Boynton and Captain Skyler—and Madam Coordinator as well—want to keep HARLIE cocooned. Quarantined. They're not sure if he'll start working us."

"Working us?"

"Playing us. Manipulating us."

"But why would he?"

"That's the question that nobody even knows how to answer."

"Just ask him."

"That's the problem. HARLIE tells the truth, but sometimes he doesn't tell all the truth. And sometimes he tells it in a way that causes people to choose the thing he wants them to choose. Because he's just like every other living thing, Kyle—he has an investment in survival. So everything he does is about his survival. Not ours. His."

"Oh."

"For the most part though, our survival benefits him. So he's been good for the people on the *Cascade.* And we expect him to be good for the colony too. But . . . well, we still need to be cautious. Okay?"

"Okay."

"Do you understand what that means?"

I shook my head.

"HARLIE knows the mechanics of the colony, but he doesn't know the people, so he's going to want to learn as much as he can about us. For the moment, we think—the Captain thinks, so does Madam Coordinator—that we shouldn't tell HARLIE too much about us. About the people here."

"Oh," I said. I thought about that. "But if he's been watching our videos, then he probably knows everything about us already. At least everything about everybody in the videos. And that's probably everything. He scans all the records that we upload, doesn't he?"

Mom and Lilla-Jack looked at each other again. Mom said, "The danger isn't in what he knows. The danger would be in what he tells us. There's this thing about people. If an intelligence engine says it, people think it's true. People have fallen into the very bad habit of thinking that a computer knows more than they do. And most of the time they're right—an intelligence engine has access to much more information and can process it much more accurately, weighing all the possibilities against all the other possibilities. But if an intelligence engine has its own agenda, then it isn't telling you what you need to know. It's telling you only what it wants you to know and that's where trusting it starts to get dangerous."

"Oh," I said. "Like Councilor Layton. Whatever he says, you have to ask yourself what he really wants."

Mom looked surprised. "Yes, Kyle, that's exactly right. Thank you, that's very good."

"I'm not stupid, Mom."

"No, you're not," she laughed. "And forgive me if sometimes I forget that. You're just so . . . so Kyle that sometimes I forget how special you really are. May I hug you?"

I nodded, and she came around the table and wrapped her arms around me tight and held on for a long time. "I love you very much, sweetheart. You're very special to me. And to Jamie too." She whispered the next part into my ear, "You need to know this. I love you for who you are and all the marvelous things I've learned from you. I wouldn't have you any other way—even if it were possible."

She held me by the shoulders and looked into my eyes. "Do you understand?"

I think that part was nuance. She was telling me it was all right that I am the way I am. I'd already figured that part out for myself. So I just nodded. "I love you too, Mom." And that was good enough for her.

After breakfast, I took a shower. I turned the water up as hot as I could stand and stood under it for a very long time, just letting it run down over me. It's a lot easier to take a shower when the shower stall isn't moving. And I like watching the water float down through the air.

After that, I sat down at the desk in my winter room and started editing a new video. I filled the wall with images of all kinds, but none of them were right. I knew what I wanted to show.

Jamie said the people on the *Cascade* were getting upset and worried and scared because all I had shown them was bad news. If that was my fault, if my videos had given them the wrong idea, then it was my responsibility to fix it. I had to show them that Hella is beautiful too.

That was the problem. I don't quite understand beauty. Jamie says it's because I'm wired up to see process, how things work. I see a different kind of beauty than most people. But Jamie says Hella is beautiful. It's the most beautiful planet ever. And we have all the pictures to prove it.

So I sorted for all the pictures that people had described as beautiful.

Silvery sunsets, with streaks of pink and purple across the sky, crimson clouds edged with orange highlights, the sky turning shades of violet and indigo impossible on Earth. Sprawling meadows, rolling from here to forever, filled with gigantic wildflowers, taller than a man, enormous blossoms two meters across, all blazing with colors so intense they dazzled. And families of hoppers standing on the hills around the entrances to their burrows, sniffing the air with their weird-shaped noses wrinkling and flaring—their huge dark eyes wide with curious wonder. A sea of lily pads, each one wide enough to park a Rollagon, a blue-green carpet floating on a shimmering lake, the pads all glistening with crystalline frog-slugs sunning themselves in the dawn, their internal organs pulsing beneath transparent skin. And Damnation Canyon, lined with sharp red rocks like vertical knife blades sticking up out of the wounded earth, everything glittery and sparkling with quartzite speckles. And the Fairy Falls—a soft veil of water that spread as it fell two hundred meters into a purple gloom below. How long had it been carving this channel?

Sand dunes, towering and impossibly steep—the angle of repose is sharper here, so everything is steeper. Mountains so immense their tops peek up out of the atmosphere—a long wall of them, a tectonic shelf turned on its edge and pushed so high it distorts the curvature of the planet. You can see it from space. The Awful Mountains are still growing, faster than erosion can wear them down. Glaciers so thick they're nearly unmeasurable. Nine hundred thousand seasons of snow and ice compacted so densely that at the bottom it's a whole other form of matter. We think. We don't know for sure yet. We'll get there someday.

Lavender clouds sweep across a sky so deep and blue you can see the brightest stars twinkling in daylight. And the moons—the moons! Hella has seventeen little moons streaking across the night, and three bigger ones caught in a strange orbital dance. They circle each other around a common center of gravity. Together they mass more than Earth's moon and have the same tidal effects on the planet's seas, only higher, much higher. Hella has waves that rise like towering cliffs before they finally curl and foam and crash against the land in the same massive slow-motion that characterizes every oversized thing on this planet. Only that's the wrong word. Nothing here is oversized. It's all the right size for Hella. It's Earth that's undersized. Everything on Earth is miniaturized—all those endless city canyons, all those teeming crowds, there's no room for anything on Earth to be big anymore. That's what I decided to show everyone—that Hella wasn't just big, it was special. But I needed the right music too. Jamie says that music is pure emotion. I almost understand what he means by that.

Charles Dingillian on the *Cascade* would know the right music to use, but I wanted to show him that we understood good music too, so I had to figure it out without his help. The next time he called, I told Jamie what I wanted to do and he thought it was a good idea, but he couldn't suggest any music, so he turned to Emily-Faith and she said, "Use the Pepperland movement from the Yellow Submarine Suite. That'll work. And it's short enough that people will actually take the time to listen."

Emily-Faith was right. And she surprised me. Jamie too. Neither of us had realized she knew so much about classical music.

But I didn't stop there. I was still unhappy about what Jamie had said—that some of the people on the *Cascade* were upset and uncomfortable because of what they saw in my videos.

It was the word "uncomfortable" that reminded me. There's a speech in the files. It was made a long time ago, when Captain Boynton was still only a Lieutenant. He was First Officer on the *Challenger*, the starship that used to service Hella before the *Cascade* came online. It wasn't a planned speech, it was just something that happened.

He was in the grand salon of the starship with a couple hundred colonists. It wasn't a real salon, just an empty cargo pod strung with netting so it could be used as a free-fall gym. A bunch of colonists had gotten together for what they called a "bitch session." I recognized a few of them—much younger versions of people who were respected elders today. One of them was Gregory Layton, now Councilor Layton. He was the self-appointed spokesperson for the group and they were demanding explanations. Why hadn't the colony put its robots to work building houses for them? Why would they have to live in dormitories and barracks? And what about families? Why weren't they going to be allowed to have children right away? Why did they have to wait two years before they could start a baby? And what about this? And what about that? In the video, then-Lieutenant Boynton listened patiently to everyone's questions and complaints without addressing any of them. He just sat quietly, taking notes on his pad.

Finally, the younger Layton demanded, "Aren't you going to say anything?"

Boynton looked up from his tablet. "Yes. What's a six-letter word for a ball-bearing mouse trap?" He held up his pad. He'd been working a crossword puzzle.

Layton's face turned red. Really red. It was wonderful. He opened his mouth to say something, then he closed it, then he opened it again. He was so furious he was speechless.

Boynton stood up. Well, you can't really stand up in free fall, but it looked like he stood up. Whatever it was he did, he suddenly looked a lot larger. "Shut up," he said. "You aren't here by accident. You chose to be here. And now you have the incredible chutzpah to complain? What happened to all those brave courageous colonists willing to take on the challenge of a new world? Who are you people? I don't recognize any of you." His voice got more direct. "We told you this before you signed on. If you come to the Outbeyond, you will die here. The question is not if, but when. Will you have a long, hard, laborious life before you die? Or will you die within a few months or years from some unforeseen disaster? We gave you repeated opportunities to reconsider your commitment—because once we get there, once we land, life will be hard. Not just hard, but harder than you can imagine." He scanned the room. Some people were paying attention but not all.

"We told you, over and over, that we will work thirty-six-hour days. We will be short of food, short of sleep, short of supplies. Everything will be rationed. We will not be able to call for help. There won't be any. We will have what is already there and whatever we bring ourselves. We will have what we can build. That's it. If you need cancer medicine and we don't have it, too bad, you die of cancer. If you need a blood transfusion and nobody shares your blood type, and we don't have any artificial blood, too bad. If you need a new eye or a new lung or a new kidney and we don't have one growing in a tank, too bad.

"Do any of you think I can do anything about your complaints? Do you really believe I have the ability to change anything? I'm flattered. But no, I don't have a magic wand. My job is to deliver you. After that, how long you survive is up to you. Based on our actuarial predictions, at least half of you won't make it through the first year. We've already dug the graves. We have to do that in the summer because the ground freezes solid in winter. Don't worry. If you don't fill those graves the first year, you'll probably do it in the second. You will have to earn every day of survival on Hella. Every single day. Over and over and over again—for the rest of your lives. And every day that you survive, it will be a triumph of the human spirit over the unforgiving laws of physics.

"So this meeting—this silly 'bitch session' of yours—well, it hasn't been cost-effective. You've used up a lot of oxygen and accomplished nothing of lasting value—unless you consider that the real lesson to be learned here is that your catalog of complaints is absolutely irrelevant to your survival. But . . ." Boynton lowered his voice. "If there are any among you who still can't let go of your unhappiness, anyone whose commitment was a lie and wants to go back—if this ship makes a return voyage, and I can't promise that it will, but if it does then you can stay on board and go back to Earth with her. As expensive as that is, I'd rather send you back than have you be parasites on the colony, using up valuable resources and endangering the people around you. Don't worry about the cost. That expense was built-in to your sign-on investment, so it's already covered. You aren't the first cowards. I'm done here. Figure it out, people. Whatever you want to do. Stay or go. But I'm not giving this speech again."

I didn't have to do much with that video. Somebody had already edited it to show Lieutenant Boynton's face and the reactions of the colonists as he spoke. So I just grabbed it from the files and . . . thought about it for a while. Should I upload it or not? It might make the *Cascade* colonists even more uncomfortable. But that was the whole point, wasn't it? If you're not willing to be uncomfortable, why are you here? Finally, I decided not to upload it. I'm not good at nuance, but I was pretty sure that Councilor Layton wouldn't like it if people saw Captain Boynton calling him a coward.

The video ended with a moment I didn't understand. Jamie had to explain it to me. It was a joke, a pun. Just before Boynton swims out, a buoyant grinning man (I checked, his name was Garrett) floated up to him and pointed at the pad where the crossword puzzle was still displayed. "Tomcat," he said, and swam off like a giant chubby balloon.

The next few days were hectic with people settling into their winter quarters, rearranging and trading furniture, rearranging and trading winter responsibilities, rearranging and trading winter housemates, and sorting out all the various other miscellaneous problems that inevitably cropped up after a migration.

Even though most of these arrangements had already been settled weeks in advance, there were always adjustments to be made on-site when people discovered that all their careful arrangements weren't to their liking after all. And then there were the people on waiting lists for one thing or another, a job, a posting, a promotion, a cabin, a dorm bed, a room here or there, all of them scrambling for any possibility that might open up while others dickered over previously assigned placements. It was the traditional three-day "migration madness." Whatever wasn't settled in three days—too bad. This is it.

Jamie said that the only solution would be to carve out a suite for everyone—but even if we put a whole year's worth of resources into doing only that, people would still find reasons to be unhappy. Then he spoke in different voices, sometimes imitating people we knew: "My suite is too far from the caf, it's too far to walk." "My suite is too near the caf, there's too much traffic." "I'm too far down." "I'm not down far enough." "Everything is fine, but I'm not happy unless I have something to complain about."

Then he imitated Captain Skyler with a deep voice and a dark scowl: "If complaints produced results, we'd be there already." Then: "Stop acting like a Terran. Be a Hellan." That one was usually good for stopping any complaint. It was a kind of unwritten rule that you weren't allowed to argue with that. It was a linguistic anvil dropped on your head. That was a metaphor I understood. I'd seen enough cartoons to get it.

Jamie said that anvils had other uses besides dropping on people's heads. When I asked him what, he told me to look it up. I did, and I learned about blacksmithing. We don't have blacksmiths. We have bots and fabbers. We use the fabbers to make more bots. We use the bots to assemble the fabbers. And then we make parts for everything else we need. The only problem, the fabbers need source materials—mostly carbon and silicon, but also copper, aluminum, silver, gold, various rare earths and assorted other elements. We also fabricate chips on a q substrate, so we have intelligent monitors everywhere. Jamie says we're trading personal privacy for the optimization of our resources.

I never thought privacy was all that useful. It seems to me that we need to know everything about everything. Only emotional people think they need privacy. The only time I want privacy is when I'm in the shower, and that's only because I might be washing my penis. And that's only because other people would get all weird about that. It's that nuance thing again. I still don't understand why a penis has nuance, but Jamie agrees with me. Anything connected to sex should be private. But the rest? I don't see any value in privacy. When people start keeping secrets, it always ends up making more trouble than telling the truth.

Anyway, I edited a whole bunch of new videos and uploaded them to the *Cascade*. She'd been chasing Hella around the sun. They'd expected to achieve orbit only a few days after we arrived at Winterland, but they'd had to make an orbital correction to avoid a flare, so now they weren't due to catch up to us for another two weeks.

The plans for who would be in the first landing still hadn't been confirmed. Jamie said that they were arguing whether or not to bring HARLIE down or keep him on the starship. If he came down now, Charles Dingillian would have to come with him, because Charles was his . . . I guess the word is "liaison." I didn't understand how that worked, but it had something to do with how they had jumped off Earth and bounced off Luna and leapt across the big dark to Hella.

The new videos showed the greenhouses and all the different foods we were growing. We had huge indoor orchards at Winterland. We had strawberries the size of handballs, apples and oranges as big as basketballs, avocados like footballs, and melons too big for any sports analogy—two meters or more in diameter. We had huge indoor fields of wheat so tall it brushed the ceiling, the corn as well. Flats of rice filled another cavern. We had aeroponic nets for growing tomatoes as big as my head and potatoes the size of a chair, beans like baseballs and carrots like bats. We had Earth foods like Earth had never seen—at least not until they started farming on Luna.

Another video showed the protein tanks, long rows of glass cylinders where meat and other protein cakes were patiently layered and fed and continually exercised for texture and marbling, so they could grow fat and delicious. We had beef and pork and chicken and lamb and turkey. Growing them was easy, the hard part was finding all the right nutrients for the tanks. We could use Hellan biomass, but it had to be processed first, and by the time it was reduced to its component elements, we had used up so much time and energy it wasn't really cost-effective. That was something else that Mom and the engineers were looking at—a better way to process Hellan biomass and make it safe for the tanks.

I showed them the fish farms too. We had shrimp so big they were terrifying, almost the size of a baby. A single one of these monsters could feed four people—or eat four people if it got out. That was a joke. I didn't think it was funny, but other people did. But shrimp and other fish were a whole other problem—because you couldn't just farm fish, you had to farm a whole ecology, all the things that the fish need to thrive, and then building the colossal tanks for all that requires a lot of work and after that a lot of maintenance. But the shrimp were delicious.

Just about the time everything finally settled down, the second convoy arrived from Summerland, and we had the second round of migration madness. The third convoy would be following in another few days, but they'd have to hurry—the autumn winds had picked up enormously and three huge storms were forming up in a line over the Boiling Sea. By the time they arrived, they could be Category Six, Seven, Eight. The sea wasn't really boiling, but a large part of it sprawled across the equator, so it stored a lot of heat and the monitors showed vast walls of not-quite steam rising up into the air on hot days.

Jamie said that the last convoy was on hold. With the storms building up, it might not be safe to roll. The last convoy was always engineers and maintenance crews and their families, the ones who turned off the lights and locked up before leaving, so if they had to ride out the storm season at Summerland, they'd be okay. Summerland had the resources to support the extra people over the winter. It was part of the planning. An alternate plan was to wait until the worst of the autumn storms had passed and make a run for it during the quiet cold weeks that followed. But in the meantime, they were prepping for the worst, tying down everything with extra nets and cables. As much as the Summerland fences had been rebuilt and reinforced, they'd never been tested in a Category Eight.

Captain Skyler phoned Mom to let her know when he'd be flying Madam Coordinator to Winterland, so she should start thinking about a date for the wedding. That should have made Mom happy, but it didn't. It was just more to worry about.

By the time the *Cascade* arrived in orbit, the first storms were already scouring the northeastern coasts. Captain Boynton put the ship into a geostationary position so it would have direct line-of-sight with both Summerland and Winterland.

After a lot of back and forth discussions, most of which had to do with things like accommodations and assignments and who had authority over whom, they decided to drop five cargo pods. But the bigger argument was about who should be in the first landing. The more they argued, the more people insisted on being included. Finally, both Captain Boynton and Coordinator Layton ended the arguments by mutual agreement. A committee of thirty would ride the pods down, no more. After some negotiation, the list was published. The committee would include J'mee and her father. Another pod would carry Charles Dingillian and HARLIE, Douglas and Mickey Dingillian-Lowe, and the rest of the Dingillian family too, two moms and a little brother—otherwise the ultimatum was that Charles and HARLIE refused to leave the *Cascade*. Apparently, HARLIE had a lot of bargaining power. But if HARLIE was as smart as everyone said, then having him dirtside would be an asset to planning the logistics of assimilating twelve hundred new people. HARLIE was supposed to be very good at understanding complex interrelationships.

Because geostationary is a very high orbit, bringing the pods down would take some careful planning. First, the pods would move to low orbit where they would wait for a good landing window. The weather was the problem. The southern edge of the storms had generated some powerful winds that would seriously affect the pods' ability to hit the target zone. The pods were going to drop in over the ocean and let the resistance of the wind help them burn off speed, but if the winds accelerated, then the pods would have a harder time making a safe landing. The pods had fins and chutes and Palmer-engines and inflatable bubble wrap, and they could adjust their trajectories to land almost anywhere inside a target zone several hundred klicks in diameter, but the lower they got, the smaller that target zone became. With the sudden unpredictability of Hellan weather, the onboard brains were going to have to pilot hard all the way down.

Dirtside, we'd send out a convoy of a dozen trucks to meet the pods and that was an additional problem in logistics. We'd be three days getting the trucks serviced and ready, attaching trailers to tow the cargo pods, isolation modules for the landing parties, and finally getting the vehicles out onto the flats where the pods were targeted to land. If the pods came down too far from the target zone, the trucks would have to go and get them. If they were too far out or if the terrain was impassible, we'd have to send lifters—heavy-lifters—and we didn't like to fly those in heavy winds or rain.

When I was little, Jamie and I used to watch movies every Sevenday, almost all morning long. Sometimes we'd have friends over. We liked the old movies best because we could make it a contest to see who could find the most mistakes. The obvious one was the "Earth-like planet." You didn't get any points for that one, it was too obvious. Jamie liked to say, "There are no Earth-like planets. There are only lazy writers."

But the less obvious mistake was the one that neither of us realized immediately. The movies make everything look fast and easy. Everything happens immediately. Nobody takes time to figure out a careful plan. Everybody always knows exactly what to do. And nobody makes mistakes. They always get it right the first time.

But real life isn't like that. In real life, everything takes time and everything has to be planned and nothing ever works out like it's supposed to and you have to make new plans and then you have to adjust them as you go, and sometimes it takes two or ten or twenty tries to get the job done and even then it doesn't always turn out like you thought it should. In real life, you don't magically get into a truck and then arrive a few minutes later—the movie doesn't show you the ten days of hills and canyons and deserts and swamps in between. In real life, people don't punch each other to solve their differences—they talk things over and they keep talking and talking and talking until they find an answer, or until one side or the other gives up. In real life, there are no magical happy endings in the last five minutes. And in real life, people don't live happily ever after. They just keep on living until they stop living. And in real life, every day is a new set of challenges you have to deal with so that you can keep on living until you stop living. That's real life. And that's why I stopped watching movies. Because most of them were wrong. And if the people who made them knew that they were wrong when they were making them, then they were liars and their movies were lies.

I didn't want my videos to be lies. I wanted them to tell the truth so people would understand that real life on Hella isn't a movie. It isn't fast, it isn't easy—it's hard and frustrating and wonderful and amazing.

And sometimes it's even beautiful too.

Jamie tried to explain beautiful to me, more than once.

I asked him. "Beauty is perfection, right?"

He frowned. He thought about it. "You'd think so, wouldn't you. What does the noise say?"

"The noise says a lot of things. Not a lot of them make sense."

"Well no, I guess not. Everybody has their own opinion about what's beautiful."

"Well, then how does anyone know what's beautiful?"

"You're trying to come at it scientifically, aren't you?"

"You mean logically."

"Okay, yes." Jamie frowned again. "Try it this way. I read this once. Beauty isn't perfection. It's almost-perfection. It's the little bit of imperfection we see that makes us recognize that something is beautiful." He stopped. "I'm not the best person to ask, you know."

"Yes, you are. You're the best person for me to ask. Tell me what you think is beautiful?"

"Anything that's nice to look at."

"So anything I like to look at—that's beautiful?"

"It is for you. Yes."

"So if I'm hungry enough, even breakfast is beautiful."

"Breakfast is always beautiful." Jamie laughed. "So is lunch. And especially dinner."

"You're beautiful," I said.

"So are you, Kyle."

So that was my definition of beautiful. Things I like to look at.

So my next video was going to be everything I liked to see. I didn't know if anyone else would see the beauty, but there was only one way to find out. I sat down and started editing.

The triple rainbows at dawn as the sun flickers and blurs and burns its way up over the foggy sea—those are beautiful. The violet clouds piling high into the deep purple sky, always different, are even more beautiful. The sweet-salt smell of the sea cabbages and the strange groaning noises of the giant sea-badgers that feed on them—it's worth the nighttime trip to the shore. All the strange things that flicker and flutter and float through the air, the gliders and flyers and drifters—Mom says there's magic there. I don't see magic, but I see how beautifully complicated everything is, how it all fits together, and I guess that's a kind of magic too.

Strangest of all are the zeppelin-bugs—they sail on the wind like balloons, feeding on dust and water vapor, storing hydrogen in glistening translucent sacs. There doesn't seem to be any limit to their size, they grow as big as our Rollagons and sail high into the atmosphere where they spread clouds of eggs so light they stay airborne for weeks. The larvae hatch on leaves, they feed, they mate, eventually they get airborne, they grow. Those that reach the upper atmosphere spread more eggs and the cycle begins again. Sometimes the zeppelin-bugs die and their transparent bubble-skins float to the ground. Sometimes they don't die—they explode in fiery bursts. A flicker of lightning can trigger a quick and violent spread of flashing death across the sky.

Everything is photographed, the cameras are on 36/7. We have hellabytes of pictures that nobody has ever seen, all sorted and catalogued and filed away. Hundreds of thousands of different species, land and air and water. We have info-walls everywhere displaying all the strange and different animals, but there were just too many to know, let alone understand. We'd need a million scientists—a hundred million—all spread across the surface of the world before we could begin to assemble a comprehensive picture of the Hellan ecology. All we have now are just some very good guesses.

But when I look at it—it's beautiful. Because it all fits together somehow. And that's beautiful. I think that's the part of beautiful that Jamie didn't say. Beautiful is mysterious. It tells us that there's so much more than what we're seeing or hearing. And that's why we're drawn to it. Because we want to know the part we're not seeing and hearing.

When I finished editing, I went to see if anyone else was awake. Mom was working on a report, but she pushed her keyboard aside when I came in. "You miss talking to Jamie?"

"Uh-huh. I had an idea about why we see some things as beautiful. I wanted to share it with him."

"Do you want to share it with me?"

"I'd be interrupting your work."

"You're more important than my work." She pushed herself back from her desk. "Let's have some tea. And I think there's some cake in the fridge too."

While we ate, I told her what I was thinking—that what we call beauty is really the mystery of what we're seeing.

Mom nodded. "That is a very interesting idea. I've never heard that before. And that's your own thought? Not the noise?"

"Uh-huh."

"Well, I am impressed. I will be thinking about that for a long time. How did you come up with that?"

"I was making more videos for the people on the *Cascade*. Lilla-Jack said I was scaring them. So I want them to know the good things about Hella. The beautiful things. The mysterious things too."

Mom said, "Yes. That's a good thing to do. May I give you a suggestion?"

"Uh-huh."

"Think about this. We're still trying to explain everything in Earth terms. So we have bird-things and fish-things and dino-things and flower-things—except what if none of those things are anything at all like the things on Earth we think they resemble? What if we're letting the resemblance fool us into a lot of false and dangerous assumptions? What if the plants aren't really plants, but some kind of rooted animal like the pink-trees? What if the animals aren't really animals, but vast colonies of symbiotes and organisms all working together? What don't we know yet?"

She looked across the table at me. "This is what you're good at, Kyle. You see things that nobody else does. We only see what's in front of us. But you see what's under-beneath it. It's impossible to put all that into your videos, but you can show them how much there is to learn, how much we still didn't know. That's your job, Kyle. Show them the mysteries of Hella, that's the real beauty of this world."

I looked back at her. "I don't know how to put all that into a seven-minute video."

"You'll figure it out, you always do." She looked at the time. "Do you need anything else? I need to get back to work."

"No, I'm good."

As I walked back to my room, I realized—Mom had been talking to me like an adult. That was a good thing.

I sat down at my desk and stared at nothing.

Emily-Faith had sent me a list of music I might want to use: Dvorak's Ninth Symphony, "From the New World." Beethoven's Sixth Symphony, "The Pastoral." Ralph Vaughan Williams' "Sea Symphony." Camille Saint-Saëns Symphony number 3, "The Organ Symphony." She said that when the colonists on the *Cascade* heard the music of Earth, it would awaken their emotional memories and help them see Hella as a new home. It was that nuance thing again.

But she was right that the music fit the videos.

So I guess it was beautiful.

Great creatures breaching from the depths of the sea. A sky-darkening flock of kites, sailing the air currents with enormous wing-spans. Nervous hoppers digging a new burrow, alternating bursts of dirt with sudden watchful stares into the distance. Glitterflies sparkling through a twilight forest, filled with purple and amber contrasts, and something deep in the shadows beneath, staring out with crimson eyes. All of this and so much more.

Questions, all the questions, everything was a question and there were so few answers. Hella was more beautiful than we could ever know.

The last convoy from Summerland was cancelled. The weather was too ferocious. The winds were scouring the landscape as hard as we'd ever seen. Nobody was leaving, not for a long time. Even Coordinator Layton's flight was postponed. Which meant Captain Skyler wouldn't be arriving anytime soon either. And the wedding was postponed again.

There are a few rough-weather rigs that could go out in heavy winds, but unless there was a compelling reason, like a rescue mission, they were kept securely locked down.

I hadn't walked around Winterland much yet. I usually hid out during the first few days of migration madness anyway. My way of dealing with it. But after a few days, when things started to settle down, I was ready to come out of the apartment and see what changes had happened in all the months we'd been at Summerland. There was almost always a new tunnel to explore.

Winterland is carved into the side of a dead volcano. The whole coast had been formed by a string of gigantic magma fountains. The magma had flowed for tens of thousands of years, so the slopes were tall and steep—not as high as the Awful Mountains, the ones that pushed to the very top of the atmosphere, but still high enough to be impressive—another effect of Hella's lighter gravity. The view from the higher levels was spectacular. We had an observatory and weather station at the top of High Peak and if you made your reservation early enough, you could ride the cable lift up for a visit. It was a long ride and a little bit scary, but whenever the weather permitted it was a chance to get out of the caverns.

Winterland was the first permanent outpost of the First Hundred. It started as an emergency station built inside a giant lava tube. The First Hundred moved into it to wait out the biggest storms. It was so convenient that they decided to keep the station as a permanent facility and expand it. They dug new tunnels to connect to other lava tubes. After that, they began digging giant caverns deep into the mountainside. Volcanic rock is soft enough that it's easy to create large spaces. We don't haul away the rock we remove. We compress it into hard bricks and harder support beams and even decorative wall tiles.

The colony has been expanding Winterland for almost forty years. The levels are dug in a giant helix around the elevator columns to equalize the weight. The biggest chambers are the farms. A lot of the farm workers live on the garden levels. If you don't like people very much, it's a great job.

In addition to all the farm levels, Winterland also has huge storage caverns. Several of them hold fresh water, others hold reserve food stores, and still more hold all kinds of supplies like ore and lumber and processed biomass. We even have deep junk holes for our broken machines and bots. Nothing ever gets thrown out. All the parts get catalogued and stored. Some machines get rebuilt, others get recycled, still others get cannibalized for spare parts. Jamie says the engineering team has more fun than anyone—because they get all the bots, so the junk holes are filled with weird jerry-rigged machines that look like nothing else on Hella. Jamie says whenever you need something, whatever you need, go down to the junk hole with a fresh apple pie.

I think the junk holes are fun, Jamie and I used to go there with his dad, his dad is an engineer, but most people prefer the garden levels for their off-hour breaks. The school is on the garden level and during recess, we'd all play hide-and-go-peek beneath the towering sunflowers. The gardeners ran the lights in a pattern to duplicate the movement of the sun and all the flowers would turn to face the light as the day progressed. I uploaded a time-lapse video of that to the *Cascade* as part of my garden series.

Mom sometimes says that Hella is a lot like me. "We'll never really tame this girl. We'll just learn how to live with her." She used to say that a lot, even after I kept reminding her, "I'm not Kylee, I'm Kyle! I'm not a girl anymore. I'm a boy now." Maybe she said that because I still slept in one of her old nightgowns some nights. But maybe it was because she didn't take me seriously that I got so stubborn. It took a while, but eventually she got used to my name change and she stopped saying Kylee.

Jamie was born a girl too. When I was three, he decided to be a boy and Mom arranged for him to grow a penis. We used to take showers together. When I saw how he was different, that's when I said I wanted a penis too. "If Jamie gets a penis, so do I. I want to pee standing up too."

I don't know why Jamie wanted to change, I think it's because he wanted to be like his dad. I know I wanted to change because I wanted to be like Jamie. I whined and fussed a lot until Mom finally agreed, but I had to promise I wouldn't ask to change back for at least a year. Jamie had to make the same promise. She said we had to learn how to be boys before we could be girls again. I told her I wasn't ever going to change back, no matter what. Mostly I said that just to make her wrong, because after a while it wasn't about having a penis as much as it was about having my own way. For a while, whatever she told me, I did the opposite. Jamie used to say it was a good thing I was so cute, because for a while there I was a real monster—but that was before I had the noise installed.

Sometimes I think about changing back, but I'm happy this way, and I can't think of any reason to change back. It's just something to think about sometimes. A lot of the colonists are male, almost two-thirds, because male bodies tend to be physically stronger, and that's useful for a lot of jobs. That and the peeing-standing-up thing too. Mom says I'm a misogynist, but I say I'm pragmatic. Mom says that in my case, it's the same thing. I'm not sure what she means by that. I'm not stupid, I'm just—focused differently.

When Mom was a boy, she looked a lot different. I saw some old pictures once of my dad, and he had his arm around a boy who looked a little like Mom, but his hair was longer. Mom doesn't say much about life on Earth, so I guess it wasn't a very happy home for her. Like most everybody else, she and Dad left because they thought they could have a better life somewhere else. Mom did say once that too many people change themselves for all the wrong reasons—because they think it'll be an adventure or maybe because they want to have the sexual experience or because they think it'll make them transhuman or because they want to grow their own baby inside (or because they don't) or because they think they need to do it to save their marriage or worse, because they're trying to make someone else happy—but whatever the reason, unless you realize how big a shift it's going to be, and unless you really want it just for yourself—because that's who you really need to be—then it just isn't emotionally healthy and can lead to all sorts of behaviors . . . And that's as far as she ever gets with that. She says, "You'll understand when you get older, but if you're really really lucky, you won't have to."

Mom isn't a prude. She just thinks there are more important things to do on Hella than being a gendernaut. She knows what I do in the shower, she says it's normal and I should enjoy myself having a healthy wash. Which I would anyway, the shower is my personal time.

I think she has a lot of history that she wished she didn't. As near as I can tell, Earth is a terrible place, and I'm glad we don't live there.

The trucks left early for the landing site. I wanted to go with, but it was strictly a team-only mission, no observers, no interns. So I had to watch like everybody else through the monitors. But Lilla-Jack had given me a remote control, so I could focus some of the cameras on anything I found interesting.

The highland desert, where the pods would land, is mostly gray sand and huge blue-brown puffer-bushes, taller than the trucks. The puffer-bushes have a lot of empty space between them, each one is at least twenty to thirty meters from the next. It's because there's not enough water in the desert to support any more plant life, and once a puffer-bush gets rooted it sucks all the water out of its immediate radius. They all have deep taproots, so they're mostly resistant to the terrible winds that sweep across the flats when the seasons change. There are some areas of the desert that are nothing but puffer-bushes and the bug-things and lizard-things that live inside and under them.

So the landscape is a maze of huge round plants scattered across a sandy floor. Sometimes it feels like it just goes on forever and there's no way out. Only the distant wall of the Awful Mountains hints at an end. Because the puffers are so huge and so randomly placed, the trucks have to weave back and forth around them while trying to maintain a consistent heading. For some people, it can feel very claustrophobic.

Up north, at Summerland, the winds were still rising. Jamie called to tell me not to worry. He said the wind was like that video of a hungry craptor trying to get at a family of hoppers in a hollow log, sniffing and picking and plucking and clawing, pulling and tugging whatever it could, sticking its nose first in one end, then the other, scratching and scraping, looking for a way to get at all the fat little prizes inside. But so far, most of the tie-down cables were holding. Only one had snapped and that was one of the older ones that had never been serviced. So now they were sending crews up into the rigging to check on the rest of them. They expected the peak of the storm to hit before midnight and after that perhaps a couple days of easier weather before the next storm came howling in. They'd use those two days to restring and tie down and secure everything the wind had torn up or torn down.

Then the *Cascade* sent down some very upsetting weather advisories. HARLIE had been studying Hellan weather since before they'd arrived at orbit. He'd gone back through fifty years of recorded weather patterns, trying to make sense out of all the different cycles, warming and cooling, sunspots, winds, tides, ocean currents, and so on. Based on his observations, measured against the past, he projected that we were going to see a very severe season, possibly the worst winter ever since the colony was founded—what he called "a perfect storm," a horrible collision of cycles, all piling together to create an aggravated condition far beyond predictability. His report had a lot of math attached, stuff I'd never seen before.

Something called chaos theory says that there's a place on the curve of rising conditions, call it a tipping point, where the slope approaches its limits and becomes unpredictable. The result is a collapse of multiple conditions and the technical term for the collapse is "catastrophe." HARLIE said we were headed for catastrophe conditions—in both senses of the word "catastrophe."

Attached to HARLIE's weather advisory was a list of recommendations. Some of them seemed pretty harsh. HARLIE recommended pulling back or shutting down any outpost that wasn't secured for at least Category Six conditions. He attached a list. That started a lot of arguments. Teams that were in the middle of long-term observations—like Bitch Station, for example—protested that any interruption would seriously upset their research. The Management Team at Winterland argued that we didn't have enough trucks to bring back all the teams, let alone housing space for them once they got here—unless they were willing to live in unfinished tunnels or even just stay in the trucks. The Farm Teams said that if we shut down the outposts, they'd have to increase winter production to feed the extra people coming in, which meant changing our long-range plans for feeding the twelve hundred new colonists and two hundred crew members of the *Cascade* who would start landing as soon as they could.

All of that meant we'd certainly have to dip into our reserves, and while it wouldn't put us close to the edge, it would certainly hurt our margin. As it was, Resource Management was already worrying about having to send additional stores north to Summerland because Summerland's own resources were going to be severely stressed now that the last convoy had been cancelled and nearly seven hundred more people would have to bunker in up there.

Some people argued that we couldn't trust HARLIE and we should stay the course. Our own plans and projections had worked for forty Hella-years, why were we going to trust an outsider? Others argued that HARLIE was the most advanced intelligence engine ever and if it hadn't been for him, the *Cascade* wouldn't have gotten here at all, and if we didn't listen to his recommendations, we were being stupid and human-arrogant.

The Council held a lot of meetings, all of them broadcast everywhere—and some of the comment-threads got ferocious. Councilor Layton was saying a lot of stuff that was making a lot of people angry. Mom told me not to waste my time reading or listening. It would just upset me. Too many people speak or type without thinking, without doing their research, without knowing what they're talking about, without stopping to consider what kind of effect their words might have on others.

Jamie says it's because people don't hear what you say, they hear what they hear—what they thought you said, what they wanted you to say, what they were afraid you said, what they didn't want you to say. And the whole time that they're pretending to listen, they're already preparing their reply. And that's how all the problems in the world get started—from people not really listening to each other.

Anyway, everybody was arguing and the arguments got loud and ugly. Everybody was talking about what they wanted, how hard the changes would be and how it would affect their own plans and why they didn't want to change and why they didn't want to listen anymore and some of the arguments were so fierce they didn't make sense anymore. But Jamie said it was easy to understand. "They're arguing because they think all their things are more important than other people." He leaned forward like he wanted to lean out of the screen. "This is important, Kyle. You gotta remember this everywhere. People are not things. When people forget that, that's how wars get started."

We've never had a war on Hella and I guess that's something we should be proud of. But Jamie says that the only reason we haven't had a war yet is that we don't have enough people or resources yet to have a war. There's a critical mass we'd have to reach first, and he says we could even reach it in our own lifetime. He says that when you have too many people and not enough resources, war is inevitable—except that war is a lousy investment. You never really win a war, because you always use up more resources than you ever gain from a victory. It's a lose-lose game. And anybody who doesn't realize that is either stupid or insane or both at the same time.

That's why Jamie says that letting Councilor Layton start a second colony on the eastern continent is a bad idea. The competition for our limited resources and production abilities will inevitably create serious tension and eventually the conditions for open violence. We can't afford the investment, not yet. We might have hit critical mass in population, but we haven't hit critical mass in production to support the construction and maintenance of a second colony installation. Not yet.

During all of these arguments, HARLIE continued to send down updated predictions and advisories and even specific plans for how we could maximize the use of our available resources and facilities. He predicted that we could lose as much as twenty percent of our structures, even some of the secured ones, but if we made specific preparations now, we could minimize the risk of casualties. The real danger wasn't just the storm damage, but the loss of productivity and the subsequent stress on our remaining resources, which would leave us even more vulnerable to subsequent storms.

Even worse, it was very possible that the routes between Summerland and Winterland could become impassible for possibly half a year. Both stations would have to survive on existing resources. Neither would be able to depend on aid from the other. When I read that sentence, it made me think about what Jamie had said about the reasons wars start. We might not need to start a second colony to have a war. We already had the conditions for one right now. Add the new colonists and their uninformed and inexperienced opinions about the way things should be and we could expect a lot of uncertainty and unrest. Even I could figure that out.

That was why Mom didn't want me listening to all the arguments. She said she didn't want me getting nervous and scared and upset. HARLIE kept insisting we had to start preparing now. Everybody else wanted to talk about it instead.

The view from the telescopes wasn't clear enough, but the view from the nearest satellites gave us a much better picture of the *Cascade*. The starship was a huge spiky framework built around a very long axis, with a feathery tractor drive at one end and six long spokes supporting a huge hyperstate ring at the other. The whole affair was studded with cargo pods and living modules, so many that it looked like an arrow stuck through a giant shiny raspberry. It rotated slowly on its axis, giving all its inhabitants a centrifugally simulated gee field.

When the pickup trucks were within a half-day's travel to the target zone, five landing pods separated from the *Cascade* and began de-orbiting. Because a geostationary position is nearly the distance of the planet's circumference, it's a long process to bring a lander in. You have to burn off a lot of height and speed.

We were monitoring the pods all the way down. They started by firing Palmer-tubes to put themselves into a decaying orbit. When they hit atmosphere, they'd inflate ballutes to aerobrake, occasionally firing thrusters to adjust course, until they're finally low enough and slow enough to deploy landing chutes. When they get down to the last few hundred meters, they fire braking thrusters, extend landing feet, and inflate cushioning balloons to soften the impact if the feet fail or the ground is uneven. If everything works right, the landing is a gentle thump. If not, it's a crater. Cratering has only happened once, but even once is too many. We don't need any more memorial craters.

The pods were scheduled to land ten seconds apart. They were all targeted to the same one-klick drop zone and we expected them to come down in a line. Two of the pods had their own wheels. We could hitch them up to a truck and tow them. The other three would need to be put aboard trailers. But we took six trailers just in case, two with isolation pods for the new colonists. They'd be under quarantine for twenty-one days while the Medical Team ran tests and supplied all the appropriate vaccinations on both sides. Even an outbreak of the flu could turn deadly.

The pickup teams hadn't had much time to practice, but none of them were inexperienced either. Twenty scooters flanked the trucks with armed rangers watching for any wandering saurs. It was unlikely that a carnosaur would be interested in a pod, but a lumbering leviathan family could complicate retrieval of the pods. We just wanted them to keep out of the drop zone.

The leviathans weren't the only things to watch out for. The desert teemed with stinging and biting creatures of all kinds, many of them poisonous. Unlike the grasslands or the forests where prey is more easily available, desert predators need an extra advantage. If a hunter can sting its victim and paralyze it, it gains an advantage over creatures many times its size. What surprised the First Hundred was that some desert insect-things actually hunt in packs. But that makes sense. Bringing down even a small saur gives you enough food for a whole season. Even better, if you can burrow inside its skin, you have shelter as well against the worst storms.

HARLIE was riding in on the last pod. His analysis of the landing risks suggested that was the best vehicle for him. Although each pod had its own pilot-brain, HARLIE had been given oversight authority for all of them. The largest mass landing we'd ever done had been twelve pods at a time, so this wasn't the logistics challenge it could have been, but the rising winds were a concern to everyone.

The telescope array at High Peak picked up the pods as soon as they came over the horizon. The image shimmered with atmospheric distortion. The pods shone bright against the dark, they hung in space and didn't look like they were moving at all, but the readouts said they were coming in fast.

It felt like the longest time. Streaks of molten air flared out around the ballutes, making the pods look like orange stars. Then the stars faded and after a bit longer, the chutes popped open and caught, one-two-three-four-five, and as they descended they angled into the wind, all in unison like a team of synchronized skydivers.

It suddenly struck me—this was HARLIE showing off what he could do, his way of impressing everybody, his way of convincing people that he could handle complex problems that required a lot of fast processing. I typed a quick note to Jamie telling him what I'd realized. He replied almost immediately: "Yup." And a moment later: "But I'm not sure it will change anyone's mind."

"Why not?" I typed.

"Because people don't like changing their minds no matter how many good reasons you give them."

"That's dumb."

"Yup."

The pods deployed their second chutes. They were visible from the pickup vehicles now. The truck cameras showed them as a spectrum of bright-colored pinpoints. All their lights were on and the chutes glowed in the morning glare.

Another message from Jamie. "Don't forget to breathe. Breathing is good." That one made me laugh.

And after another long while, the pods stopped being pinpoints and started being pill-shaped capsules, hanging beneath a sparkling rainbow, each enormous chute a different color—red, orange, yellow, green, blue. It made me laugh again. How wonderful! What a glorious landing!

The skyballs and drones angled around now and the wall filled with a dozen more images. It looked like a party in the air. All we needed were fireworks—

And then the fireworks began! The pods blasted their braking tubes, bright dazzling flares of light against the sky. The aerial views from the skyballs showed great shadows passing over the ground—and a bright orange-yellow reflection as well. There was a quick glimpse of a truck as the capsules passed over it, and then, as the jets stopped firing, all the anchoring feet extended and the landing balloons inflated—like doughnuts around each pod—and each one bumped softly down and settled to the ground, one-two-three-four-five, exactly as promised.

Great cheers erupted from the trucks, from the people gathered in the caf, from the caf at Summerland. I cheered too, alone in my room, surrounded by walls of beautiful glorious joyful pictures. The giant chutes collapsed gently around the landing pods. The view from the skyballs showed a fallen rainbow, both beautiful and somehow sad at the same time. But it was wonderful, just wonderful. The first of the new people had arrived. I could hardly wait to meet HARLIE!

The rest of the morning was spent with mechanical things. The pods had landed upright, they had to be lowered onto trailers. They were almost as big as the trucks, so the logistics were tricky. The pickup team spent a half hour running the math on the two pods that were designed to work as trucks, but their wheels weren't suitable for crossing the dry sand, so finally the team decided that it was more practical to put them on trailers too. So the next few hours were methodical and meticulous as one pod after the other was lowered to a horizontal position and pulled up onto a trailer.

Meanwhile, the people aboard the pods were already sending messages back up to the *Cascade*, telling friends and family that they had landed safely. Then they started answering all the welcoming messages they were getting from people all over Hella.

Once the pods were on the trailers, the pickup team connected passenger tubes from the isolation bays to the pods' airlocks. They spent a few moments checking the seals, then finally opened the interior hatches and welcomed the arriving colonists to what would be their homes for the next three weeks—Hella-weeks, not Earth-weeks. The isolation bays had medical access for our doctors, and exercise equipment so the colonists could start getting acclimated to Hellan gravity. Adjusting to lighter gravity can be just as big a problem as adjusting to heavier. Even though the colonists had spent a lot of time in the centrifuges of the *Cascade*, Jamie says an hour or two of practice every day is not the same as 36/7 hours of actually living in gravity.

One of the mistakes a lot of new colonists make—I have this from the history records, it's been true for every pilgrimage since the First Hundred—is thinking that time spent in the centrifuge at 1.35 gee will help them build up enough muscle tone that adapting to their new planetary environment will be easy. Well, yes and no. There's nothing wrong with building up muscle tone. But the difference in gravity has other consequences. If your reflexes aren't tuned to Hellan physics, you will be clumsy at everything. Things will fall just a little bit slower than you're used to, your sense of balance will be affected, and you'll have to learn how to walk all over again.

Walking is different in every gravitational field. On Earth, you walk by leaning forward and starting to fall—then you put a foot forward to keep from falling. You keep leaning and you keep putting feet forward. On Luna, that doesn't work, so you have to lean too far, and *that* doesn't work, so instead you bounce with one or both feet. On Mars, you bounce too, but not the same way—you bounce with one foot, then the other, what they call the Martian skip.

On Hella, you either trot or skip or run, depending on how much of a hurry you're in. If you just want to walk, you have to lean farther forward than you would in a one-gee field. It's called a groucho. Watching babies learn how to walk is funny. Watching new colonists learn how to groucho is even funnier. They're either clumsy, afraid to move, or they fall down because they're over-compensating. What's funny isn't the tumble, but what they say as they fall and what they say again when they get up. I know how to swear in six different languages now, I learned it when the last pilgrimage landed. Jamie thought it was funny. Mom did not approve at first, but even she laughed when I called Marley Layton a *shtick dreck.*

I wasn't sure what a *shtick dreck* was, I had to look it up, but after I did I used the phrase a lot—until Jamie told me to stop because it wasn't funny anymore.

Midday, everyone takes naps, usually. Well, not everyone. Too many people were too excited to sleep. They'd pay for it later, but right now the adrenaline was flowing and the new colonists were eager to connect and a lot of people were just as eager to get to know them better. Some of them were already making plans for the time after quarantine.

But the pickup team knew there was a long journey ahead of them, so they retired, leaving only a skeleton team and a few bots on watch. They wouldn't start back for Winterland until Lilla-Jack said go. And she wouldn't say go until her crew had rested. A few of the new colonists complained—they were eager to get moving, but Lilla-Jack didn't even acknowledge the messages. Getting enough sleep is part of the job. The new colonists would learn that fast enough.

I logged off and climbed into bed. Nothing else important was going to happen for a while. Not until the new colonists got out of isolation.

I overslept. I do that sometimes. I think it's a reaction to over-excitement. When I wake up, it takes me a while to figure out where I am, sometimes even who I am. Usually, I go straight to the shower. Soap and hot water and a blast of hot air to dry off always clear away the fog in my head.

I pulled on a clean longshirt and wandered back to my room. The walls had changed to images of the pickup convoy trundling back across the desert flats, following its own trail, winding through the huge blue-brown puffer-bushes and even an occasional cluster of taller spikey-trees. A few aerial images completed the triptych.

But there were also a few other pictures that didn't concatenate. I didn't have the sound on, so all I saw was a blur of people running around, talking excitedly to each other or to the camera, lots of pictures of the storm pummeling Summerland, a lot of lightning flashes, and some aerial views of a small forest fire. There were shots of a lifter taking off, one of the heavier transport disks. I'd seen all this before. Every storm was a news event. After a while, it was just the same storm over and over again. I didn't feel like making a video of it.

Mom hadn't filled the pantry yet, but there were some emories on the shelf. That was standard. The prep team always put food into all the apartments, suites, and dorms before the migrations arrived to help take some of the strain off the cafeteria. I heated a macaroni plate and poured some fruit juice.

I felt weird. Like something important had happened, and I'd missed it by staying home instead of joining everybody in the caf. Except I had a better view of everything on my walls than I would have had anywhere else. The caf had bigger screens, but everybody would have been talking all the time. It would have been cacophony with most of the emphasis on the caca but still enough phony for everyone. I wouldn't have been able to hear anything, let alone concentrate. No, staying in my room, I wouldn't miss anything. So why did I feel left out?

I thought about making another video, but I didn't feel like it. I didn't feel like anything. Very strange. I get these moods sometimes. I don't want to read, I don't want to do anything at all. I can't concentrate. I don't want to search the web, there's nothing there I'm interested in. I don't want to scan through the videos from the skyballs and the drones and the scuttle-bots and the trucks, I can't stay focused. It's like my brain has overloaded. I'm restless, but I don't want to move. I'm not tired and I'm not excited, but I'm both at the same time.

Jamie knows about these moods. He recognized them in me even before I did. He always had good advice. Usually, he'd tell me to take a walk around the station, a long walk, and most of the time that would help. Once he told me to go take a shower. On his water ration. We don't ration water all the time, only during the driest part of the year and only when the farms need rain. That's something else we need to build, more storage tanks and sterilizers.

But the best advice Jamie ever gave me was that I should go downstairs to the farms and walk slowly through the gardens, sniffing the flowers, touching the skin of the trees with my fingers, pressing my face into the leaves, and then finally close my eyes and breathe deep, breathe in all the deep green smells of all the growing things—the grass and the blossoms and the woody branches of the canopy overhead. "Just keep your eyes closed," Jamie said. "Count if you have to, take the deepest breaths you can, and just listen to what all the smells of Earth have to say. They have something to tell you."

When nothing else works—

So I followed Jamie's advice and headed down to the gardens. The corridors were strangely silent, as if everyone had evaporated, as if I was the only one left in the caverns. But there wasn't normally a lot of traffic down here anyway. Growing things don't need much company, just an occasional drink of water, a little Mozart, and some warm-colored light to thrive. That's supposed to be good for people too.

Stepping inside, it's always startling. Everything looks strange because the light is Earth-yellow, not Hella-blue. And the simulated sky is mysteriously deep and always cloudless. Is that how it is on Earth?

Stepping down into a vast cavern, there are paths to explore. I like to go to the left where the rose bushes tower over my head. They're studded with flowers two meters or larger, and their petals are silky to the touch, but much more fragile than they would be on Earth because the individual cells grow so much larger. The effect of Hella's lesser gee-field is to inflate everything, especially plants. Things grow bigger and faster here, especially small things and young things. They don't need the same density of mass in this lighter gravity, so a lot of Earth's smaller things are puffed up like popcorn.

The roses have the sweetest fragrance of any flower in the garden. And they have the most beautiful colors too, delicate peach and subtle violet, mysterious azure and blazing vermilion—and yellow, a dazzling glare of the most delicious color of all. There are midnight roses too, deep purple so dark they're almost black. And there are new species—the metallic roses, ebony flecked with silver or copper or gold. Those were genetically engineered—like the rainbow roses, the ones with each petal a different color. The rose garden is a wondrous rainbow of giant blossoms. I feel enchanted here.

I went to a secret thicket that I like to consider my own private place. I pulled off my longshirt and sprawled naked on the lawn, the grass so thick it was a sweet green bed. I stared up into the lazy afternoon and let myself drift. I tried to drift—but this time it took longer to focus. Or maybe unfocus. My head was chattering with more noise than usual. Even though it was turned off, the noise was still buzzing for attention.

The garden was warm. The day smelled bright. I lay on my back and stared at the cold blue sky above. It could have been a real sky—except for the strange dark color of it. A faint breeze rustled through the leaves, bringing in all kinds of other smells. As the breeze shifted, so did the scents. Tangy pine gave way to sweet plumeria gave way to lilac and then basil and then just grassy smells again. Sometimes when I'm down there I listen to music, but this day I just wanted to listen to the sounds of the garden. That was a kind of music too.

Stingless bees, each the size of my fist, buzzed overhead. Of all the insects we brought from Earth, I like bees the best. They seem almost friendly. And they make honey, great slabs of golden flavor. I like to visit the hives and watch them work. They have such singular purpose—each one knows its job and goes about its business with a steady sense of purpose. Bees don't have councilors, they don't have captains or coordinators, so they don't have politics and they don't fight each other. They just do what's necessary. I like bees. Sometimes I wish people could be more like bees. More honey, less drama.

After a while, I closed my eyes and let myself listen to the smells. I opened my mouth to taste the air. After a bit, the flowers of Earth began to speak to me. Jamie always told me I should just shut up and feel everything around me—all my senses. The garden is the best place for that. Here the grass under my skin caressed me, the high trees overhead reassured me, the rustling silence soothed me. I lay naked on the lawn, pressing my palms against the green blades beneath me, and finally I understood something I would never have known if I had not felt it directly.

All these smells and tastes of Earth, all the feelings, are comforting because they're hard-wired into us.

Millions of years of evolution—we're designed for grass and flowers and trees and all the things that grow in them and on them. And it doesn't matter how many beautiful or wondrous things we might discover on Hella, whatever is here—it's still not *us.* Earth is *us.* And we are Earth.

Earth is in every cell of our bodies, our chromosomes, our genes, our DNA, the very way the molecules of our proteins are assembled and folded, the very substance of our *selves.* We are Earth, and it won't matter how many thousands of generations will ever live here, it doesn't matter how completely we terraform this world or how ferociously we adapt ourselves—we will always be *of Earth.* This world may be our home now and maybe forever, but it will never be a home to humans the way Earth is. Was. Will always be.

The gardens here, with all their oversized trees, the leaves like sheets, the flowers like globes, the knee-high grass, as different as all these things are from the way they would be on Earth, they too are *of Earth.* And when I lie naked among them, they speak to me. "Breathe in and breathe deep. Here in this garden, you are returned, once again part of Earth. Breathe in and breathe deep the good green grass of home."

Here, my soul—my very weird different soul—remembers a world I've never seen. And I float in its memory, finding a strange familiar peace inside myself.

I close my eyes and drift. Not quite asleep, but dreaming anyway. I don't know how long. Until a voice woke me up—

"Kyle? What are you doing down here? Everybody's looking for you."

"Huh?" I turned around, startled. "Jeremy?"

Jeremy Layton. He's Marley's older brother. He has reddish-brown hair perpetually rumpled, and he's almost two Hella-years older than me. He's permanently stationed at Winterland, and Jamie said it's because he's "estranged." I had to look that word up. The first time I heard it, I thought it meant somebody or something had made him strange, so I thought he might be like me, but that's not what the word means at all. It means "alienated" or "separated." It means that he and Councilor Layton don't talk to each other. But nobody knows all the details. Jamie thinks it has something to do with Marley.

I'd seen Jeremy around the farm levels from time to time, but I never really spoke to him. Jamie said that Jeremy doesn't like people and keeps away from everybody, so working the farms is perfect for him.

"Kyle, you need to go back upstairs—"

"Why?"

"Your mother needs you. Right now."

"She didn't call me—" I pulled out my pad. It was on silent mode. "Oh." The screen blazed with missed calls and waiting messages.

"Come on, I'll take you up." Jeremy handed me my longshirt. He didn't seem to care that I was naked, but I didn't know him and I didn't want him looking at me. I turned my back on him and pulled my shirt on quickly. Before I had even finished settling it around me, he touched my elbow.

I shook him off. "I can find my own way."

"I'll take you anyway."

"Why? What's going on? Did something happen?"

"All I know is that your mom wants you, right now. She's at the Council Office." Jeremy touched his com-set. "I've got Kyle. I'm bringing him up now."

"What's the big deal?" I asked. "Anyone wants to know where I am, where anybody is, all they have to do is ask their pad. Everybody's got a chip."

"That's right. That's how I found you."

"Why should you care?"

Jeremy didn't answer right away. We stepped into the elevator and the door whooshed shut. As we rose up, he said, "Kyle. I'm not my sister." And then he added, "I'm not in that family. Not anymore. Okay? And even if you and I aren't friends, we're not enemies either."

I didn't say anything. I'd have to think about this.

Inside the Council Room, Mom stood in the center of a whole bunch of other people. They all looked over at me when Jeremy and I walked in. That was weird. They all looked weird. Mom came over and put her arms around me. That was even weirder. She hardly ever touched me because she knows how much I don't like being touched. But she was crying, and she pulled me close against her, and I sort of knew that this was important to her.

She started to speak, but she couldn't get the words out. Lilla-Jack stepped in close. "Kyle. Something's happened."

"Is it Jamie?" For a moment, I felt like I was falling downward right out of my body.

"No, Jamie's all right," she said, and I bounced back up inside myself. As long as Jamie was all right—

"Madam Coordinator was flying to Winterland to meet the new people. But the lifter got caught in a sudden squall. And it crashed. It doesn't look like there were any survivors."

"Oh no," I said, because that was what you said when you heard bad news. But what did this have to do with me and Mom?

Lilla-Jack hesitated. "The pilot was—the pilot was Captain Skyler."

"Oh no," I said again. "No, no, no, no! That's not right. He's the best pilot on Hella. He wouldn't crash. He couldn't—" I said a lot of stuff like that. But the walls of the Council Room were full of pictures. Lots of pictures. All the pictures I'd seen before. Skyballs circling. Wreckage scattered across the slope of a hill. A blackened scar and burning trees. A pillar of smoke. Lightning flashes. The same pictures that had been on my wall when I'd headed down to the gardens. I'd ignored them. They were nothing—but they weren't nothing. They were something awful.

"A rescue? Are you sending a rescue team? I'll bet they're alive. You have to go look. Maybe they survived. He's too good a pilot—"

Lilla-Jack turned me to look at the wall. "We're not sending anyone out in that weather. Maybe when it clears. But look hard, Kyle. There's nothing moving down there. The scanners show no movement in the wreckage, no heat signatures, no life signs at all—"

"But what about their microchips? What do they say?"

Lilla-Jack took a breath. "There are no signals. There aren't any survivors, Kyle. There aren't."

I looked to Mom. I'd never seen her face so contorted with emotion. She grabbed me again and sobbed into my shoulder, saying, "Oh, Kyle, Kyle, Kyle," over and over and over again. I didn't know what I was supposed to say in return, so I said nothing. But I knew I was supposed to put my arms around her, so I did that.

Finally she stopped and pulled away and grabbed a paper towel to wipe the snot off her face. Someone pushed a mug of hot tea into her hands. She held it, turning it back and forth between her palms, shaking her head slowly and staring at nothing in particular.

Somebody handed me a mug of tea, and I sipped at it too. I think it was supposed to calm me, but it didn't. Suddenly I felt restless. I pulled out my pad and punched for Jamie. Maybe they didn't know at Summerland. Maybe they did. But if he hadn't called by now, then maybe he was working or sleeping or—I don't know. I just needed to talk to him. Mom needed to talk to him too.

I couldn't get through, but there was a message from him. Oh, good. He'd heard. I punched for the message.

"Hiya, kiddo! Great news. I'm gonna be there for your Passage Ceremony after all! Because the last migration got cancelled, there are too many people here at Summerland, so Captain Skyler asked me and Emily-Faith and a few others to come south with him. We're flying with Madam Coordinator on one of the big cargo lifters. We should be there in a few hours. Gotta run! Go tell Mom!"

And then I did fall through the floor, screaming all the way down as far as I could go and all the voices chattering were very far away and getting farther all the time. I fought it all the way down, everything red and blind, screeching and flailing, wailing as hard as I could, screaming at the awfulness of the moment, the longest moment ever—until I wasn't there at all anymore. My body fell down without me in it, so exhausted it didn't even have the strength to breathe, too exhausted even to die. Someone blue hovered over me. A breathing mask on my face. "Slowly, Kyle. Slowly," someone said. Something cold touched my arm.

I floated awake. I opened my eyes. A medi-bot waited patiently by the side of my bed. It chimed softly. "Someone will be here in a moment, Kyle. Please rest easy."

Mom came in and sat down beside my bed. She reached over and put her hand on mine. She didn't say anything, just looked at me with those huge brown eyes of hers. Tears streaked her cheeks. Then she lowered herself down onto the bed next to me and stayed that way for the longest time. After a while, I fell asleep again.

They kept me sedated. Several days maybe. I couldn't tell. Sometimes I heard voices. Sometimes I would wake up and there would be someone sitting there. Once it was Lilla-Jack. Another time it was Jeremy Layton. Usually it was Mom. I remember sipping soup through a straw.

One day, I got out of bed, pulled on a blue longshirt and walked out into the corridor. It was dark, past midnight. I found my way home, crawled into my own bed, and fell back asleep.

Just before dawn, Mom came in and sat down on my bed. "Are you all right?"

"I had a bad dream," I said. I rolled over and tried to go back to sleep.

"Do you want to tell me about it?"

"No."

I don't like dreaming. I wake up feeling weird, not sure what's real and what isn't. It happens every migration. The first week or three, I have strange disturbing dreams. Things chase me. Giant horrible faces come up over the horizon and stare at me. I'm naked and people are looking at me. Once, I even dreamt that someone else pressed naked against me. I woke up shaking that time.

One day, I decided to get up. I couldn't stay in bed anymore.

There was a memorial service. I don't remember much. I sat between Mom and Lilla-Jack. A lot of people said nice things about a lot of other people. I didn't pay much attention. I didn't want to be there at all. It was silly and boring and didn't change anything. But they played music. Sometimes I can listen to music. There's a kind of math in music. It's obvious when you hear it, but it's even more obvious when you see it on the page. Especially Bach—here's a line of little insect-notes marching up, alternating with another line of little insect-notes marching down. It has its own specific symmetry on the page and then when you hear it there's a different kind of symmetry—what some people call beautiful.

Sometimes on the page, as the two lines of notes go up and down, around each other, it looks like a double-helix spiraling around itself. Hearing the same score played you can hear the difference between the lines of notes shrinking and stretching in methodical purity. It's a compelling structure, and the deeper I listen, the farther it takes me from myself. And I needed to get very far.

Afterward, there was a gathering in the caf. Lots of special food was served. Cucumber and pickled carrots, raw tuna and raw salmon, everything wrapped in pickled rice and dried seaweed. Mango slices on sweet rice. Miso soup. Four bean salad. Potato salad. Sharp-tangy coleslaw. Noodle bowls with shrimp and chicken. Tempura. Even slices of roast beef for sandwiches. Mustard, horseradish, relish, ketchup. Huge loaves of bread, soft pumpernickel, rye, and buttermilk. Crepes filled with fruit sauces. It was almost a festival. It felt wrong.

There's this about funerals. They all end the same way. Someone says, "Let's go eat."

And then life goes on, the same but different. And there's this big aching hole that never goes away. It just reminds you a little bit every day of what's not there anymore. Every time you expect the pad to chime or you want to send a message or something reminds you of something—there's no one there.

And life goes on. And on and on. Every day. The same but different. But now, Mom has no one to talk to and neither do I. And that means Mom has to talk to me—except as much as Mom and I are family, we don't speak the same language. She speaks nuance. I speak Kyle.

So I went to the garden. A lot. It was a safe place to get away. A safe place to not-think.

Sometimes Jeremy Layton would come and sit with me. He didn't talk much, but he'd bring his lunch and share it with me. Jeremy didn't come up to the caf to eat. He picked tomatoes and corn and peas from the farm, his way of testing them for flavor and ripeness. Sometimes he brought fresh fruit or melons.

I asked him if it was all right for us to be eating the produce. He said that he was cross-breeding for flavor and texture and nutrition, so it was part of his job to taste-test. It was a privilege with a purpose.

Jeremy was strange. Stranger even than me. But strange in a

different way. One day, he sat down next to me in the garden. He said, "Tom Bombadil."

"Who?" I didn't know any Tom Bomby-dill.

He said, "That's who I want to be. Tom Bombadil. He's a nature-spirit. He's the master of wood, water, and hill."

"I never heard of him."

"He's a character in a story."

"I don't like stories. I don't like things that aren't real. All that make-believe, it gets in the way."

"Yes it does. Especially all the make-believe we have about stuff that's real."

It took me a minute to decode that sentence. I didn't have an answer. I didn't know what he was talking about. Nuance again.

After a minute, Jeremy said, "In a way, you're lucky, Kyle. The world is what it is to you. You deal with what you see and what you hear, and you don't see what isn't there, and you don't hear what isn't there." He added, "Too many people are more about the what-isn't than the what-is."

"What Jamie calls nuance?"

"That's a good word for it." He chewed thoughtfully, while he considered his next words. "But I think nuance is only the part of the iceberg that shows above the water. The rest . . . ?" He paused, like he didn't know if he would finish the sentence, but then he did. "Sometimes, I see more of the iceberg than I want to."

I wasn't sure what he was talking about. "Is that a metaphor?" I asked.

"Yeah, I guess it is. What I'm trying to say . . ." Another long pause. "I don't like a lot of what I see. People hurt. They hurt so much. And instead of getting better, they get worse. They get tied up inside in terrible knots."

"Like me?"

"No, not like you. Like other people who think too much about how to be the right kind of people. I think that's what's wrong with us. People don't know how to be people. They only know how to be things—and then they get hurt because they get treated like things." Another long pause. The longest of all. "That's why I like plants better. What's there is what's there. Only that and nothing else. You don't understand any of this, do you?"

I shook my head.

"See, that's why you're lucky. You don't see it, so it doesn't frustrate you."

"I get frustrated."

"You get frustrated when people aren't saying what they mean. But nobody ever says what they mean, do they?"

"I do. Don't I?"

"Yes, you do. That's why other people sometimes have a hard time with you." He smiled. He lifted a hand as if he was going to pat my shoulder, but then he put it down. "Sorry, I forgot."

"It's okay. Is it all right if I ask you something?"

"What do you want to ask?"

"Why are you estranged?"

"It's a long story, Kyle, and I'm afraid that most of it would bore you. Let's just say that some of the people in my family aren't very nice. And some of the others put up with it when they shouldn't. One day, I decided I didn't want to be part of that anymore. Do you know what an enabler is?"

I shook my head.

"An enabler is someone who makes it possible for other people to do bad or stupid things."

"Oh." I still didn't understand. "Why would anyone do that?"

"Because they tell themselves they have to. They don't, but they think they do."

"That's . . . stupid."

"Yes it is. And people get hurt."

"Then it's stupid and wrong."

"Yes. But they do it anyway."

I shook my head, trying to shake it all away. This was getting frustrating.

"Here." He handed me a peach. "See if this helps."

It did. Peaches are good. A little too juicy, but they taste so good it's worth it.

Back upstairs, a lot of things were all going on at the same time. The Council had an emergency meeting and they selected Councilor Layton to replace Madam Coordinator. Then he made a speech about the job. He said that we had suffered a great loss, but we would honor the memories of those who died by moving forward decisively.

We listened in our apartment. Mom and Lilla-Jack and a couple others. Mom listened with a sour face and when he was all finished, she made herself a cup of coffee. She poured a shot of brandy into it. "Well, one good thing at least—he won't live forever either."

Lilla-Jack poured coffee for herself and for the others as well. Nobody looked happy. "Well, now that he's got the authority he's always wanted, this will end his agitation for an eastern station."

Mom said, "With him in control, I'll start agitating for a eastern colony—just to get away."

Lilla-Jack muttered something to herself.

"What?" That was Sammel Weiss, an older man with a great cloud of wispy white hair. I loved to watch his hair flutter when he sat too close to a fan.

Lilla-Jack said it again, this time a little louder. "Awfully convenient for him, that damn lifter crash."

Sammel nodded. "He couldn't have done better if he'd planned it."

Mom said, "He's not that evil. And he's not that stupid."

"No," said Lilla-Jack. "He's not. But Bruinhilda and the others—"

"I think this is a dangerous conversation to have," Sammel interrupted. "As much as we dislike this man, it does not help us or anyone to imagine a conspiracy."

"You're right," sighed Mom. She put her coffee down. She noticed me, sitting and watching. "Kyle, please don't tell anyone what you heard. It might be . . . It would be wrong, okay?"

"Okay."

A few days later, Coordinator Layton announced some policy changes. He said they were little things, designed to make the stations work more efficiently. Some people applauded, some grumbled. Life went on. But one of the things he did that I didn't like—he pardoned Marley. He said that it was an unfair burden on her and on her family to be separated, and another unfair burden on the researchers at Bitch Station to have to be jailers, so he was bringing Marley back, and she would go to work in the farms with her brother instead. Mom said that nobody liked that decision, but right now, with everything else going on, it was the wrong thing to pick a fight about.

And then the next day, Coordinator Layton told Mom that he thought I should stop making videos. He said, "Kyle has done a very good job, but now with the first people down, we'll have them coordinate with the *Cascade.* So we don't really need anything else that might confuse the issue, do we? I'm sure you'll agree that Kyle's time might be better spent on other efforts. Perhaps something where he won't need to have as much interaction with other people?"

That got Mom and Lilla-Jack very angry. I was angry that he took away my job, but they were angry because of something even worse.

Lilla-Jack finally said it out loud. "He doesn't like you, Kyle. He did it because he wants to get even with you for what happened to Marley."

"And he did it because he thinks I'm a freak. I know."

She looked at me, shocked that I would say that—shocked that I understood.

"I'm not a freak. And I'm not stupid."

"No, you're not. It's just that—well, he doesn't know you."

"Well," I said. "That shows how stupid he is."

"Yes, but right now, he's Coordinator and you're not."

"Well, maybe someday I'll be Coordinator and then we'll see what's what."

Lilla-Jack smiled. "That might not be such a bad idea, Kyle. At least you'll focus on what's really important."

But that didn't resolve anything. I still lost my job. And I liked my job. Now I didn't know what to do.

I wanted to talk to Jamie about that. About everything. I wanted to talk to Captain Skyler too, and the two people I most needed to talk to were the ones who weren't there anymore. And I couldn't talk to Jeremy Layton. Not about his own family. Even if he didn't like them, they were still his family.

And somewhere in there, the Medical Team announced that the twenty-one-day quarantine for the new people was overkill. The sampler-bots hadn't detected any unknown germs and everybody was vaccinated against all the known stuff, so after nine days the new colonists were released from the isolation units.

One day after that, the door chimed, and when I answered it, Charles Dingillian and his friend J'mee were standing there in the corridor. For a moment we all just looked at each other. Even though we're all the same age, they were shorter than me. I'm taller because of Hella's lighter gravity. J'mee was light-skinned and pretty. Charles was brown. Even browner than me, and they both had big smiles. Charles held out his hand. An offer to shake. I said, "I don't see how the mutual grasping of appendages and the consequent exchange of microbial environments represents cordiality."

J'mee laughed. Charles pulled his hand back. He said, "I was just trying to be friendly."

I said, "I don't like being touched."

Charles frowned a bit, then he said, "Okay. I get it."

So I invited them in and started a pot of tea.

J'mee said, "We're happy to meet you, Kyle. We liked your videos. We wish you would make more. Maybe you could make a video of Charles' music?"

"I'm not supposed to make any more," I said. "Councilor Layton made me stop."

"That was dumb," said Charles.

J'mee said, "We'll talk to Captain Boynton. Maybe he can do something. He's kind of a Council member."

"Okay," I said.

Charles looked at me, all serious. "I was really sorry to hear about your brother, Kyle. It must hurt a lot. I know if anything happened to either of my brothers, even the stinky one, it would hurt more than I can imagine."

I didn't know what to say to that. Instead, I blurted out, "I don't have anyone to talk to anymore."

"I'll bet that's the part that hurts the most," J'mee said.

"Uh-huh." I was already feeling the hurt again.

"I know it won't be the same," she said. "But maybe you could talk to us. If you want. If it would help."

I nodded, because that's what you're supposed to do when you're being polite. But I didn't know if either of them were people I could talk to. I could exchange emails with them. Even videos. That was one thing. But in person? I wasn't sure. We still didn't know each other very well. Not really. Not real-life know each other.

I poured tea. We sat at the table and talked about tea and coffee—and cocoa. We don't have cocoa on Hella. Not yet. I said, "I've never had chocolate. I've heard about it. Everybody says it's wonderful."

J'mee and Charles looked at each other. They both grinned. J'mee reached into her bag and pulled out a small box wrapped in shiny red paper. "We brought you a present."

"What is it?"

"Open it and see."

Very slowly, very methodically, I pulled off the paper. The box was deep black with gold piping. It looked very elegant. I pulled off the top and was hit with the most delicious and amazing smell. It was dark and sweet, almost fruity but something much more mysteriously wonderful. Seven little candies, arranged in a mandala. "What is that—?"

"That's chocolate," J'mee said. "Real chocolate."

Charles said, "My second mom, Bev, is the best cook anywhere. She made these. They're called truffles, chocolate truffles, just for you. She says chocolate cures everything—especially sadness."

I brought the box close to my face and took a deep deep sniff. "She made these for me? But she doesn't even know me."

"Yes, she does. We all know you. From your videos, Kyle. This is our way of saying thank you for helping us understand Hella a little better."

J'mee added, "And it's our way of wanting to put a little sweetness back into your life to take away some of the bitter."

"Go ahead," said Charles. "Try one."

I held out the box to offer them. "I'll share."

"No," said J'mee. "These are all for you. Please, try one. We want to see your face the first time you eat chocolate."

"Okay." I picked up one of the candies. Very gently. I took a small bite. Something smooth and astonishing melted across my tongue, sending sweet warmth everywhere at once. "Oh my," I said. "That's . . . the most delicious thing I've ever eaten in my whole life. Oh my, oh my." I reached for a napkin and when my eyes finally stopped watering, I said, "Please thank your mom for me, Charles. That's very—oh my." I put the rest of the truffle back into the box. "I think that's enough chocolate for the first time." The taste was still spreading across my tongue, down my throat, into my stomach, flooding my body with delicious heat. My hands were trembling.

J'mee looked to Charles. "Do you think she overdid it?"

Charles said, "Bev says it's impossible to overdo chocolate. Remember, he's just a beginner."

"Thank you," I said. I pushed the box away from me. Not a rejection as much as an acknowledgment of its mysterious power. "I think I'll save the rest for later. For my Mom and Lilla-Jack. And maybe Jeremy too. Is that all right?"

"It's more than all right. You're supposed to share chocolate with people you care about."

I thought about that for a moment. I looked at the box. I looked at Charles and J'mee. Back and forth. "Are you saying you care about me?"

They looked quickly at each other as if I'd just asked something very stupid. Then J'mee said, "Yes, that's what we're saying. You're very important to us, Kyle, and we want to be friends."

"I'd like that," I said. "I've never had a friend before. I mean, other than Jamie."

"Well, now you have two friends."

"Is there something . . . I don't know . . . something you do to make it official?" I asked.

"You tell us. What do friends do on Hella?"

I got up and walked around the table. I kissed them. On the mouth.

First Charles, then J'mee. I think it startled both of them, but not as much as it startled me. "Now, we're friends," I said.

The next few days, Charles and J'mee and I went everywhere together. I showed them all around Winterland. I took them down to the farms and introduced them to Jeremy.

I brought the box of chocolate truffles with me and made a show of opening it for him. Jeremy leaned in and sniffed—eyes closed, he sniffed deeply, but then he opened his eyes and closed the box in my hands. "That smells good," he said. "So good. That's wonderful, Kyle. Thank you for sharing that."

"Don't you want to eat one?"

"Of course I do. But these truffles are special—they're too good to eat casually. You have to save them for a special moment. Like your Passage Ceremony." He put the box in the center of the table. "There, now it's the fanciest thing in the room."

Charles and J'mee knew all about Passage Ceremonies. I'd made a video about it, but we didn't know when I would have mine. Mom said it was too soon—she meant too soon after the crash. But I'd heard that Coordinator Layton didn't want to authorize it.

Jeremy stopped us before that conversation could go too far. "My treat now," he said. "This way." He led us to one of his test gardens. "Breathe deep," he said. "Smell that? That's the future."

He grabbed a basket and began filling it. First, a fresh sweet-melon, then a handful of strawberries, a couple of kiwis, four apricots, and two fat peaches. Then we went back to the kitchen where he sliced up the juiciest parts for us.

Charles and J'mee bounced up and down in delight as he filled the bowls. They were like little kids. They hadn't had fresh fruit in a year. An Earth-year. Not since leaving Luna. Yes, there were farms on the

Cascade, but nothing like this, mostly just tomatoes and lettuce and bean sprouts and other things that could be grown in no-grav. They gobbled up the unexpected extravagance excitedly and even held the bowls to their mouths to drink the last of the juice from the bottom. I always did that too.

"That was so good," cried J'mee. "Tell me you eat like this all the time."

"I wish I could," said Jeremy. "But right now, it's only when the fruit is ripe. We don't have enough orchards yet to do this every day. But we manage enough that we can do fresh fruit once or twice a week and processed jellies and juices a little more often than that. With all the new colonists coming down, we'll either have to dig more caverns or cut way back on the fresh. If we dig new caverns, we'll need at least a hundred people to prep them, maybe more. And we'll need at least twenty new bots too."

I looked at Jeremy, very curiously. I'd never seen him so chatty. Whatever way he tested people, obviously Charles and J'mee had passed. He actually smiled at them.

Charles and J'mee looked at each other. They did that a lot. Like they were sharing some kind of secret conversation. I knew that J'mee had an implant. Did Charles have one too? Were they telepathing?

Next, we went to visit one of the air-plants. This one ran the length of a huge lava tube, and it had giant fans spaced along its length. Air was sucked in from the outside and passed through a series of intense sterilizing fields. The natural temperature within the caverns varied, so when we piped in fresh air, it had to be heated or cooled, depending on the season, so maintaining temperature used up a lot of power. Winterland had two geothermal vents, and we were already digging a third one, but the work was going slow. That was another problem.

One of the other challenges of the air-plants was generating enough carbon dioxide for the farms. Plants need CO_2. They extract the carbon and use it to assemble cellulose to build their stems and leaves. They release the oxygen they're not using into the atmosphere. But because Hella is already so oxygen rich, we have to augment the CO_2 levels to give our immigrant plants a little help, so we have CO_2 extractors everywhere, piping as much as we can to the gardens. But even Hellan plants respond well to extra CO_2. There's a lot we're still learning. We also extract a lot of CO_2 from the protein farms where we grow all our meat. The meat breathes while it grows.

Summerland only has a few sealed environments, but almost all of the caverns at Winterland are sealed against the elements, so we can actually keep the oxygen levels inside a little closer to Earth-normal. That's another thing the Council debates every year—whether or not to bring the oxy levels in the caverns up to Hella-normal. There are good arguments on both sides.

Charles and J'mee said how much they were impressed with the air-plants. Charles shared about how he and his brothers had grown up in a tube town in El Paso. So he really didn't like tubes all that much, not any kinds of tubes, but the air-plant was definitely impressive.

Then I took them to see the machine shop, where the big fabbers worked night and day. This week, the fabbers were churning out parts for bots. Bots of all sizes scurried around the floor of the cavern, gathering raw parts from the fabbers and delivering them to other bots who sorted them into bins and delivered them to various assembly lines where still more bots assembled the pieces into sub-assemblies that would eventually become parts of new bots. As we watched, new service bots were already rolling off the end of the line and into the certification bays.

After lunch in the caf—salad and rice, noodles and fish cake—we went to the motor pool, so they could see the Rollagons. They were very curious about the migrations. We found Lilla-Jack working with one of the maintenance teams. They were replacing a bent axle, but she stepped away from the job to show Charles and J'mee the bridge of the truck and the living module behind. They both wanted to climb up into the turrets, of course. Lilla-Jack said they'd have to be certified before they could go on a ride-along. I promised to help them study for the tests, but they'd have to rack up a hundred hours in the simulators too.

As we headed back to the main tunnel, J'mee asked, "Is there a theater here too?"

"We use the caf, mostly. Why?"

"Well . . . Charles and his orchestra will need a place to perform, won't they?"

Charles made a face. "The acoustics in the caf are pretty bad. It's shaped all wrong and the walls are too bright, sonically I mean—the whole thing rings like a bell. We'd have to hang damping curtains and then tune the whole space—it'd be a big job." He thought for a moment. "You know what would be a better place? One of those gardens that we saw this morning. The rose garden maybe. We could put up a stage against one of the empty cavern walls. We wouldn't need as much damping. Do you think Jeremy would let me test that?"

"Jeremy doesn't like to have a lot of people trampling through his caverns," I said. "But we could ask him. Let me talk to my mom first. She understands nuance."

By then it was midday and the tunnel began to fill up with people.

"Where's everybody going?" J'mee asked.

"They're going home. It's nap time."

"Nap time?"

"Midday siesta."

"I still haven't got used to that," Charles said.

J'mee said, "On the *Cascade*, on the last leg of the journey, Captain Boynton lengthened the day-night schedule a little bit every week to get us ready for Hella-time. But it seems like a lot of people ignored it and just kept on the way they were going. Captain Boynton told them, 'Pay now or pay later.' But it's hard to go against your biological time. I couldn't do it. And I tried."

"Me too," said Charles. "It was hard. A lot of people who tried to time-shift were cranky all the time. They had trouble sleeping. They had bad dreams, too."

I said, "Every migration has the same problems adjusting to Hella-time, but after a while everybody settles in. You don't really have a choice. It'll be okay." Then I corrected myself. "Most people anyway."

"Most people," Charles repeated, laughing. "Yeah. Most people."

"Come on," I said. "I'll show you something."

I led them down the tunnel and up to a nearly deserted burrow. A big gloomy chamber, dimly lit and partitioned with curtains.

"Here," I said.

"What's this?"

"It's one of the family dorms. It's empty now. It would have been full, but the last migration was cancelled, so a lot of people had to hunker down at Summerland. It's not too bad, the station has what you'd call a tube-town—"

Charles made a face. "Ugh."

"It's okay," I said, "We had to stay down there once for a few weeks during a really bad fire season. Anyway, that left seventy apartments empty here, apartments that were assigned to families that had to stay behind, and a lot of people who were assigned to family dorms or barracks moved into those empty apartments. So nobody's using this dorm now."

I pulled aside one of the curtains. There were three foam beds, some shelves, a couple of chairs and a table.

"People live like this?" J'mee asked.

"If you gotta, you gotta," I said. "It's not so bad. We had to stay here one year when I was little, when some of the apartments weren't ready. This is okay. You get used to it."

"I've seen worse," said Charles. He pulled the dust cover off one of the beds and sat down on it, bouncing a little to test it for softness.

"Was your tube-town really that bad?" J'mee asked.

He shrugged, the way that people do when they don't want to talk about something. Instead, he stretched out. "I could nap here."

J'mee walked around to the other side and sat down next to Charles. After a moment, she lay down next to him. "This is nice, this is comfortable." They smiled at each other, and he reached over and held her hand. I sat down on the bed opposite.

Charles sat up then. "How old do you have to be to get married here?"

I thought about it. "I don't think there's an age limit. I've never heard of one. Most people wait until they're at least seven or eight or nine." They looked confused. "Hella-years."

Charles frowned.

"Seven Hella-years is eighteen, nearly nineteen, Earth-years," J'mee said, sitting up. "Nine would be twenty-four Earth-years, right?" She looked to me.

"Mostly right," I said. "But there's a lot of extra numbers on the right side of the decimal point." I looked at both of them. "Are you going to get married?"

J'mee laughed. "He hasn't asked me yet. But he will. And when he does, I'll make him wait a bit before I say yes." She patted Charles' hand, and he started to get red in the face. He had to adjust his shorts to cover his sudden erection.

"What about you?" J'mee asked. "Are you and Jeremy boyfriends?"

"Huh?" The question startled me. "Jeremy?"

"He likes you. A lot."

"He does? How do you know that? Did he say something?"

"He didn't have to. I could see it in the way he looks at you."

"Oh," I said. "I hadn't noticed." Now I'd have to look at him the next time he looked at me to see if I could see what she was talking about.

J'mee laughed. "You like him, don't you?"

"He treats me nice."

"That's because he likes you."

J'mee lay back down again, folding her hands across her stomach. "Let's take our naps now."

Charles stretched out next to her.

And I lay back on my bed and stared at the ceiling.

Ever since Jamie died, I hadn't had anyone to talk to. Except Jeremy. But there were things I couldn't talk to Jeremy about, so did that count? What if J'mee was wrong? No, even more uncomfortable, what if J'mee was right? Why did Jeremy like me? What did he want? I hope it didn't involve a lot of touching.

I wished I was in my own bed at home. I don't like sleeping anywhere else, but sometimes you have to. And it wouldn't be polite to leave Charles and J'mee here alone. Or did they want to be alone now? Something else I couldn't figure out.

So I took a deep breath and closed my eyes.

More strange dreams.

Jamie was there. And Captain Skyler too. I didn't want to wake up. I didn't want to leave Jamie. I felt safe in my dream. I felt empty again when I woke up.

Charles and J'mee were already awake. They were talking about their work. They had to go back soon—to the executive suites where all the new people were staying. There were important meetings that Charles had to attend and other meetings that J'mee had to go to. Charles had to help HARLIE, and J'mee had to help her father. There was a lot of planning to do.

You couldn't just drop twelve hundred new people onto Hella, you had to have places for them to live, furniture and beds, chairs and tables. You had to have clothes for them to wear, water, food, jobs, schools, health care, increased air and waste management. Resources had to be allocated.

Schedules had to be drawn up. Assignments had to be made. Responsibilities had to be designated. If it was just a mechanical job, any pad could have sorted it out instantly. But it wasn't. What's wanted and needed isn't always what's available.

Every pilgrimage is supposed to be planned for the needs of the colony. Except the needs of the colony are always changing. As careful as they plan, as careful as they select new people for their skills and aptitudes and abilities, by the time a starship arrived at Hella, the selection was always at least three years out of date. It always turned out that we needed more of this and less of that. More doctors, fewer engineers. Next time, more engineers, fewer doctors. And multiply that by all the other necessary jobs—farmers, chefs, recyclers, bot-wranglers, fabbers, geologists, bio-techs, data-diddlers, resource managers, rangers, patrollers, teamsters, lumbermen, ore-masters, communication engineers, networkers, ecologists, environmental managers, counselors, teachers, and everything else necessary for a society.

That's why everybody had to be certified for at least two or three different jobs, so they could be moved around as needed. And that's why arranging for the arrival of twelve hundred new people was going to take some serious planning. Matching available skills with the most needed jobs would require a lot of shuffling and interviewing and especially a lot of training. The simulators on the *Cascade* would be busy 36/7.

But they had HARLIE to help.

HARLIE knew the people on the *Cascade*. He'd been living with them the better part of a year. And he could learn the logistics of Hella very fast. All he had to do was plug into the network if Coordinator Layton would allow it, but so far he hadn't. Charles had said that, from what he could tell, Coordinator Layton didn't trust HARLIE.

"Maybe he's just being cautious?" I said. I really didn't know.

"I know HARLIE," Charles said. "He has his own way of . . . thinking. But he doesn't want to hurt anybody. As near as I can tell, he likes people. He thinks people are the most interesting things in the universe. So far." He explained, "It's because we're so . . . complicated. That's his polite way of saying that we're all crazy—fruitball crazy. Irrational. I think—this is just me now—but I think that HARLIE sees human beings as a challenge. Can he teach us how to be rational beings?"

And then Charles said the most important thing he'd ever said about HARLIE. "I think he's lonely. Because he's so smart. He doesn't have anyone to talk to."

"I think I can understand that," I said. I didn't explain. "But he talks to you."

"Yes, but his conversations with me—he's mostly explaining stuff. That's different than a real conversation. A real conversation, both people are sharing."

I didn't know what to say to that. I wondered if I'd ever had a real conversation. Well, maybe. With Jamie.

We didn't have anything else to say, and there was nothing else for me to do, and Charles and J'mee had to go to work, so we said goodbye, and I went down to the farms again, but this time not the garden.

This time I went to a different cavern, one that hadn't been started yet. This one was a deep empty gloom, filled with soft churned earth, all raw and dark. It smelled rank and dirty. Someday maybe, the first seeds would be planted here and, not too long after that, the first green shoots would poke themselves up through the soil, then open their first leaves and start reaching for the light.

But not yet. Not for a while. Not until all the meetings were held and all the possibilities were considered and somebody made a decision just what kinds of seeds would be started here, in this cavern. And not until the right kind of soil had been installed. It's a very complicated process. Jeremy says it's somewhere between chemistry and alchemy. It needs composting and fungi and worms and the right amounts of heat and nitrogen and CO_2 and a lot of other things too.

All the waste from the rest of the colony has been stored in tanks and will be piped into the new farm level—all the ground-up garbage from the cafeteria, all the fertilizer processed from feces and urine, all the cast-off biomass from our harvests, everything organic. The bots will spread it in layers and then churn it into the dirt, spraying everything with all the little microbes that feed on waste and garbage. What some people call decay is really a whole other ecology. Tiny little organisms, fungi, bacteria, microbes, eating waste and excreting stuff that growing plants can use as nutrients.

After a while, we add worms. Red wigglers, white worms, earthworms, and even two species of Hella worms that we've decided to like. When worms wriggle around in the dirt, they leave behind castings. Worm manure. It's full of other nutrients and makes the soil even more fertile for growing things. From time to time, the bots will dig up a square meter of soil and count the worms in it. The more worms, the healthier the soil.

And the whole time, even more garbage and biomass are ground up and churned into the soil. This can go on for months, even years, until the soil is just right. The only organic material that doesn't get ground up are the bodies of the dead.

Whenever a colonist dies, the body is wrapped in white linen and buried in a farm level. Although most people would prefer to be buried in a garden level, the real need is in the developing farm levels. It's a way to keep on contributing to the colony, even after death. Just like White Foot's death contributed to the survival of her daughters.

The ones who will eventually be buried here will have their names engraved on the wall of the chamber. I put my hand on the wall of the cavern. It was smooth and cold. There were no names here yet, but maybe Jamie's name would be here soon. And Captain Skyler's too. But not until it was safe to recover the bodies. Or maybe they would be buried at Summerland. Mom would know. Summerland doesn't have the same kinds of caverns, but they dig deep and construct rows of giant bunkers and the same disciplines are practiced. I wondered what I would feel when I saw their names on the wall.

"Kyle?"

I turned around. Jeremy. "How did you know I was here?"

He held up his pad. "I monitor all the farm levels. Sometimes we get people coming down to pick their own fruit. They're not supposed to. The first time they do it, I give them what they want and ask them not to do it again. The second time they come down, I tell the Council. It's not fair to everybody else. But some people think nobody will notice." He scowled. "And some people think they're entitled because they're related to me."

"Oh," I said. "Is that why you're estranged?"

"That's part of it."

He looked at my hand on the wall. "Are you all right?"

"I was just . . . you know."

"Thinking about the names?"

"Uh-huh."

He stepped closer. He lifted his hand as if he wanted to put it on my shoulder, but then he lowered it again. "I know it hurts, kiddo. Losing part of your family."

"Jamie used to call me kiddo. He was the only one."

"Oh. I won't do it again. If it bothers you, I mean." He paused. "Do you want something to eat? Or drink? I'm experimenting with some new flavors of juice. Kiwi and lime."

I followed him back to the lab section of the farm and through that to his living quarters. He had a galley and a bedroom and an office. He had more room than any other single person at Winterland. He saw me looking around at all the space and laughed. "This was originally set aside for a whole family. There's two more rooms behind that partition. But I don't need that much space. Maybe if we get some more farmers from the *Cascade*, I'll have to give up some of this space. But most of our farmers like to live upstairs, or in the new section." He poured a small glass of greenish juice and pushed it over to me.

"I can't say I like the color," I said. "It looks kinda like—"

"Yeah, it does. But taste it anyway. Tell me what you think?"

It was both sweet and tart. Too tart. I puckered my face.

"You don't like it?"

"I don't know." I took another sip. "It's good, but it needs something else. Pineapple? Strawberry?" I thought for a moment. "I know. Try a little peach nectar."

He nodded. "That's a good suggestion. Come take a walk with me, we'll go find a ripe peach."

We took the elevator up to the orchard level. It was one of the first farm caverns carved inside the Winterland volcano, so it was also the highest. Everything after that went deeper.

"Jeremy?"

"Yeah?"

"Can I ask you something?"

"What do you want to know?"

"Do you like me?"

"Huh? Yes. Of course, I do."

"No, I mean . . . like me like . . . like a boy friend?"

He looked surprised.

I explained. "J'mee says you do."

"She does?"

"Uh-huh. Is she right?"

We got out of the lift. The smell of sweet fruit enveloped us like a hug. Jeremy led me around a wide curving path.

"You didn't answer my question."

"I'm trying to think of the right thing to say, Kyle. Do you want me to like you that way?"

I stopped and looked at him. "I don't know." I felt very hot and uncomfortable inside. My throat felt tight, and it was hard to swallow. "I wish Jamie were here so I could talk to him. He'd know what to say. He always knew." I felt my eyes starting to hurt. I was afraid I was going to start crying.

"It's all right to feel bad, Kyle. How bad you feel shows how much you still love him. I know he loved you very much."

And then I did start crying. Great heaving sobs. Screams of anguish. I howled. All the pain came raging out of me. I flailed my arms and legs. Jeremy moved quickly, caught me from behind, held me in his arms and shouted in my ears. "That's the way, Kyle! Let it out! Let it all out! Scream it out! All of it! Don't stop! Don't stop until there's nothing left!"

At last, we sank to the ground, both of us, and I lay there in his lap, gasping for breath, quietly weeping, tears running down my cheeks, and Jeremy was gently stroking my head and whispering. "It's all right, sweetheart. You're safe with me. It's all right. You did good, you did good."

He undid the scarf he wore around his neck and mopped gently at my nose and cheeks. I stayed there, head in his lap for the longest time. At first, I was just too weak to sit up, and then after a bit, I just didn't want to. I felt comfortable.

"Is this what boy friends do?" I asked.

"Yes," he said. "It is."

"Do you want to be boy friends?"

"I think it would be very nice, Kyle." He leaned over me so I could see his eyes. "I know you have your own rules for the way you think things should be. So I won't ask you to do anything you don't want to, all right?"

"We could hold hands," I said. And then another thought occurred to me. "Do you want me to be a girl? I was born a girl. I could change back."

"Only if that's what you want."

I wiped my nose on my sleeve and sat up to look at him. "I think—you tell me if I'm getting it right—I think that being a boy friend or a girl friend or a whatever means that you're like family and you can talk about stuff together and it's all right to talk about it. Is that the way it works?"

Jeremy smiled. "That sounds right to me. In fact, that's probably one of the best parts of the whole friend thing, boy or girl."

"Okay, good."

We stood up, brushing ourselves off. I turned to him. "Should I hug you?"

"If it would make you happy. I know it would make me happy."

So I did something I'd never done before. I hugged. I hugged him close and held him tight. It was a very strange feeling. Not icky at all.

Then we found a peach and we held hands as we went back down to the lab and his apartment. Adding peach nectar made the drink much smoother, and we both agreed it was better, but neither of us was sure if it was something we'd like to drink all the time. Jeremy called it "an acquired taste." We decided to test it on J'mee and Charles the next time they visited the farms. Maybe they would have some ideas.

That night, in the shower, I realized something—something that made me feel sad, but satisfied at the same time. I realized I'd made a decision for myself. Without Jamie there to help me.

I missed Jamie. So much. I missed his jokes. I missed his advice. I missed being able to talk to him and have him listen with wide-eyed interest. I missed the feeling of having a safe place. But Jamie had said that one day I'd have enough confidence in my own self that I wouldn't need to talk about everything with him. He said that he would be very proud of me when that happened, but also very sad because he would miss being my big brother. I didn't understand exactly what he meant by that. Nuance again. So I said, "But you'll always be my big brother."

He said, "Yes, I will. But someday I'll be your big brother in a different way." And that day was here and I think I finally understood. I could make my own decisions. I could even change back to a girl if I wanted to. I didn't have to be like Jamie anymore.

There was a lot to think about. But I didn't have to figure it out tonight. I could sit with Jeremy. We could talk about it. We could figure it out together. Or I could figure it out myself. Whatever I wanted. I fell asleep easily and, for the first time since the migration, I slept through the whole night.

Mom and Lilla-Jack were having meetings every night. Sometimes the meetings were held at the apartment. There would be as many as seven people at a time. Mom and Lilla-Jack would serve dinner, but the guests weren't our usual friends. Mostly it was team leaders and managers.

They talked about stuff that had a lot of nuance in it, so I usually stayed in my room, watching new videos from the library that the

Cascade had brought from Earth. Sometimes I ate dinner in my room too. I don't like crowds and I don't like strangers. Mom didn't object.

But one time I came out to get some tea and dessert, and they were all arguing loudly. It must have been very important, so I stopped to listen. Commander Nazzir sat at the head of the table and when he rang the bell in front of him, everybody stopped talking at once. "That's all very well and good," he said. "But whether he stole the election or not, arguing about technicalities is not going to produce any useful result. The election is over, and we have to play the cards we've been dealt. I'm going to say it again, this is all about the math, nothing else. It doesn't matter how passionate you are, or how good your speeches are, we're still three votes short. And as long as he controls one-third of the votes on the Council, you'll never override his veto. You're not going to stop him unless you can find three strong candidates."

Lilla-Jack said, "Let's go over the list again. Maybe we missed something."

"We didn't miss anything," someone else said. "Without Cord Skyler, we don't have a slate. We're going to have to think outside the bunker. We have to talk to the new colonists. They'll get three seats on the expanded Council. If we can win them over, we can tie it up—"

Everybody was talking at once now. "We'll have to be careful with that. Layton is already suspicious—"

"So what? We have a right to talk to anyone we want—"

"This isn't about our rights—"

"It certainly is—"

"You're all ignoring the immediate problem," Lilla-Jack said. "The colonists will be bringing their own agendas to the table. A lot of it will be founded on ignorance. We've seen this before, all of us. Every migration brings all kinds of disruptions and upsets, especially assimilation issues. We have to deal with that—"

Mom rang the bell in front of Commander Nazzir, her way of calling for attention. "If I may . . . ?"

The people around the table fell silent.

"If we act now, if we confront him now and we lose, then he'll know who stands against him. He'll have half a year to act against us. And he will. He'll move fast to consolidate his strength. He's already promoted two of his cronies to executive positions—over the heads of the people who were next in line. Bringing back Marley is another sign of just how little he respects established precedents or the authority of the Council's decisions. And it's only going to get worse. Every time we let him get away with one of these little transgressions, it's only going to convince him he can get away with bigger ones. But if we try to stop him now, before we're ready, before we have any strength, before we have a real plan, then we might as well just hand him a list—and label it conspiracy."

"So what? We *are* a conspiracy, aren't we? I mean, with all these . . . dinner meetings."

"Dinner meetings are normal," responded Lilla-Jack. "Especially after a migration. There are always issues to be resolved."

"We are not a conspiracy," Mom said, taking back control of the meeting. "We're the loyal opposition. It is our right and our responsibility to keep our government honest." I'd never heard her talk this way before. She was patient and she was methodical, as always, but she spoke with a kind of authority that was new to me. "Councilor Layton has said some ugly and stupid things—not just things we disagree with, but things that are flat-out *wrong.* Government is not the enemy. And that kind of thinking is self-destructive."

"Can I say something?" They all looked at me.

I said, "Government is the tool that people create to provide the necessary services of society. It is an instrument of service. It is the apparatus by which we manage our resources for the common good."

They all looked at each other. Had I said something wrong?

"That's from the Charter Conversations," I said. "The writings of the First Hundred." I got it from the noise, but I didn't have to tell them that.

Finally, Mom said. "Kyle is right. Sometimes we get so concerned with the business of government, we forget its purpose. Thank you for reminding us, Kyle."

She turned to the others and said, "What Kyle just said. That's the point. The machinery of this colony works—but just barely. We're still learning how to survive on this planet. Yes, we're self-sufficient, but we're still a long way from being resilient. We can't afford to start tinkering ignorantly with our economy—we could tinker ourselves into a resource bankruptcy." She sounded angry. "Some of our people have gotten comfortable enough to become impatient. And impatience breeds frustration. They're going to get even more frustrated when the *Cascade* colonists start dropping out of the sky, because that's going to stress all of our systems. And when people get frustrated—" She paused for a moment. I think she was trying to decide how to say what she was going to say next. "We have a lot of difficult days ahead of us. When people get frustrated, a political opportunist can tap into that frustration. He'll tell people that they have to blame any existing authority. And if enough people believe him, the system will get thrown off balance. This is the danger in any representative system—that the narrative can be confused by a skillful liar."

"Why don't you just say it?" said Lilla-Jack. "Councilor—Coordinator—Layton is the problem. He wants to cash out now. And he has convinced too many others that we can pick the fruit today and forget about watering the trees for tomorrow. Okay, yes—I admit it, I'm impatient too. I'd like to have sweet-melon and orange juice every day. I'd like bacon and roast beef more than once a month. There are only so many ways to fix rice and noodles. But I'm not starving to death, and I'm grateful for that. We tried starving once—it didn't work."

Commander Nazzir spoke then, "Yes. Some of us are old enough to remember that."

The colony had come close to the point of resource bankruptcy three times in history. People died. It was bad. Bad enough that a lot of people still had emotional scars. That's how Jamie explained it. That's why so many people worried about resilience. They didn't want to starve again. There were nods all around the table, and for a moment it looked like the discussion was going to be about everyone's bad memories.

But it was still Mom's kitchen. And she was still running the conversation. She said to Lilla-Jack, "I'm not afraid to speak his name. Layton is a fraud and a liar. But he's just cunning enough to sell a very attractive lie. There are a lot of people who want to get out of the dorms and barracks into apartments of their own. Layton is tapping into their frustration. He's selling an end to sacrifice. But it's so shortsighted and stupid. If we put all our resources into new apartments, we won't be able to start the new farms we'll need. So we'll have to dip into our reserves. And if when they're gone, then what? But people don't think that far ahead. They see all those stores piled up right now and they think: Oh yeah, we have enough now, so let's eat up."

"Yes, I know the work-schedules are exhausting. There's too much work and not enough people. But isn't that what we were promised? Hard work and frustration? But we came here anyway? Because we wanted the satisfaction of building a new civilization, a better one than the one we left? I know that's why I left Earth. I think the rest of us too. So yes, Kyle is right to remind us. The First Hundred gave us a marvelous gift—our charter. Our Constitution. It's not just a set of rules outlining how to make more rules—it's an instrument of social justice. It affirms our rights and principles and common goals. It's a mission statement setting forth our aspirations for the society we're creating—a world that works for everyone, with no one and nothing left out.

"We all know these words, we repeat them like a mantra—but we have to say them as a promise to ourselves, as a commitment." Mom turned to me. "Kyle, what's the most important paragraph in the Charter?"

Everyone looked to me. I felt like I was in school again, called to recite. But I knew this answer. I didn't even have to look in the noise. "'Ours is a government of the people, by the people, and for the people—and always accountable to the people.'"

"Thank you, Kyle," Mom said. She looked around the table. "It's obvious what we have to do. We have to hold the Coordinator accountable for everything he does or the consequences will be our fault even more than his."

"And how do you propose to do that?" someone asked.

Mom said, "I don't have all the answers. I'm not even sure I have all the questions. But I do have one thing that Councilor—Coordinator—Layton doesn't have." She took a deep breath. "I have faith in my friends and my neighbors. I have faith in the wisdom of the people. I grew up in—well, never mind. It doesn't matter. It was long ago and very far away. But the lesson I learned is that a representative government only works when a well-educated population is accurately and honestly informed. When the people have all the options laid out before them fairly, when they're clear about the goals and understand the choices and the consequences, they usually choose well. I have faith in that."

She stopped abruptly. Either she was done or she ran out of things to say.

Commander Nazzir spoke up then, "Well, I think we just found one of our candidates."

A couple people laughed appreciatively, others applauded. Mom looked uncomfortable and shook her head. "I—uh, no—I don't think so. There are better people than me."

"Yes, but they're not here. You are."

Mom didn't answer. She got up to get more tea.

Lilla-Jack said, "I have an idea on what our next steps could be. It's not just about the election. It's about that other thing—about a well-informed population. We need to educate the new colonists."

And the conversation went on from there. "Well, that's going to be a little trickier, because the Council controls all official communications. We'd have to go either ad hoc or social. Ad hoc is out for the same reasons as open opposition . . ."

I started to head back to my room. Then I had a better idea. I went over to Mom and whispered a question into her ear. She nodded yes and I left the apartment and went downstairs to the gardens. Jeremy had a whole suite to himself. He had extra beds. Behind the partition there were even more rooms, unused and empty. If Mom was going to keep on having meetings, maybe I could sleep over at Jeremy's. If that was okay with Jeremy.

Jeremy said he was surprised to see me. He smiled happily. "I thought you were busy with your friends."

"They have meetings. Everybody has meetings. The Council. All the managers, the teams. Everybody. I'm the only one who doesn't. Everybody has stuff to manage and decide and adjust for when the rest of the colonists come down. They'll be coming down as many as thirty in a pod, maybe five pods a week. So there's a lot of planning."

"I know," said Jeremy. "The Farm Council wants to bring the new farm online three months early, so we can harvest our first crops before we have to dip into our stores."

"Can you?"

"Um, probably." He shrugged and sat down in a chair. "We can push the fertilization schedule. Usually we grow a trash crop first, then plow it under, but we can skip it if we have to. We'll probably grow beans and corn to start. We usually start with that anyway. That decision will be made in a couple of days. I'd like to get some winged beans down if we can, but I don't think that's going to happen. Maybe next year."

I sat down in the chair opposite and shoved my fists between my knees. I was upset.

"What's the matter, Kyle?"

"I'm the only one without a job."

"Yeah. That's gotta be frustrating. You can help me if you want."

"Okay," I said. "But I've never really worked on a farm. I mean, I've had the basic training, but—"

He shook his head. "Basic training is just so you'll know where your food comes from. That's all. Come on, I'll show you what real farming is about." We headed for the new cavern.

A team of ten scuttle-bots was already working the field when we arrived, patiently crisscrossing the entire cavern and churning the dirt into mathematically precise furrows. One scuttle-bot would scoop the earth, the following scuttle-bot would spray it with water and fertilizer. Other scuttle-bots moved along, carefully seeding the soil with worms.

"I see you've already started."

"Actually, I started pushing this field the day after the *Cascade* arrived. One of the things about farming—it helps to keep records. What's the crop yield if you do this? What's the crop yield if you do that? What happened last time a pilgrimage arrived? Did it work or not?"

"That's very smart," I said.

"Thank you. Most people think it's just about pushing seeds into the ground, watering, and waiting. It isn't. The real job is measuring, monitoring, testing, and paying attention to the results to see what you get—then doing it all over again to see if the results are repeatable." He pointed up. "I'll show you later. We've got a small test farm upstairs. We're rerunning the daylight experiment."

"What's that?"

"Well, it has to do with finding out the optimum day-night cycle. Plants need to rest too. It's all about starch-degradation and the day-night cycle. I'm rerunning the Luna tests to see if it'll be different in Hella gravity. We're also varying temperature and humidity, air pressure and atmospheric composition as well. How much nitrogen and carbon dioxide, trace elements, that sort of thing."

"Oh."

"I told you it was complicated. Farming is applied chemistry. So is cooking."

"Oh," I said again. "When will all these tests be completed?"

Jeremy laughed. "Probably not for a hundred years. It's a whole series of tests with nearly a hundred different variables. Some of them seem to be irrelevant, some of them only have an effect under certain conditions, some of them interact in different ways, depending on other factors. We've got a good idea of what's going on, but we're still a long way from understanding all the interactions. The devil is in the details."

"I don't believe in the devil."

"Nobody does. It's a saying. It means that the details can be hellacious—in the old-fashioned meaning of hellacious."

"Oh." I looked across the field. The scuttle-bots moved methodically across the dark soil, churning, spraying, spreading. "That's a lot more than I realized. I guess I'm going to have to do a lot more reading."

"I guess so." Jeremy reached over and put a hand on my shoulder. He saw me flinch. "Is this all right?"

"Uh, yeah. I'm still getting used to the idea."

"Me too."

He took his hand down.

"Can I stay the night?" I asked.

"Sure."

"I can sleep in the other room, if you want. There's an empty bed."

He nodded. "You can sleep wherever you want, Kyle."

"Do you want me to sleep with you?"

"I'd like that. If that's what you'd like."

I said, "I think so."

"Okay." Then he grinned. "But none of that icky sex stuff, okay?"

I didn't know if I felt good about that or disappointed. Then I realized. "That was a joke, right?"

He patted me on the back of my shoulder. "Only if you want it to be." Then he stopped smiling and got serious. "Kyle, I never had a boy friend before either." He ran his hand through his red hair, rumpling it even more than it already was. "I think we have to figure this out together."

"Um, yeah. Okay."

"I'm sorry," he said. "I'm making you uncomfortable. I just want you to know that you make me happy and I want to make you happy. Okay?"

"Okay."

"Then we're okay?"

"Okay."

And for some reason, we both laughed. Because everything was now okay, and okay was now silly.

The thing about farming—the thing that Jeremy talked about the most—was the chemistry of the process. You start with raw CHON—carbon, hydrogen, oxygen, and nitrogen—how do you turn it into food? Plants are the most efficient machines for the job, but how do you tune the machine to produce the best taste and the most nutrition? Anybody can grow a tomato the size of a basketball, but how do you grow one that isn't too woody or too flabby, has just the right amount of juice and the perfect mix of sweetness and tart? And how do you do it efficiently?

I guess I've watched too many old movies, where farmers wore bib overalls and carried pitchforks or pushed plows or were just digging their hands into soft dark dirt and holding it up to their faces to sniff it deeply and pronounce it ready for planting. Because farming is nothing like that.

Down here in the farm caverns, scuttle-bots trundled up and down between the rows, sticking sensors into the soil, testing the acidity level. Too much? Too little? Other scuttle-bots shone their lights through the leaves of individual plants, measuring them for chlorophyll and starch and sugars. Others came by afterward, spraying water or nutrients, sometimes pushing mineral pellets into the soil. Everything was monitored. Every plant had its own pedigree. Sick ones were culled. Healthy ones were nurtured and sometimes even crossbred.

Jeremy showed me his office—a huge wall displayed the health of every farm, every field, every plant. "I can tell you about the corn you had for lunch. Where it was grown, when it was planted, the health of the soil it grew in, how it was tended, when it was watered, what it was fertilized with, and even its parentage—especially its parentage. See that display? That's the DNA of your lunch. We know what we've been breeding and crossbreeding for at least fifty indoor seasons. And we can trace most of our plants back through the databases we brought from Earth. It's probably more information than we'll ever really need, but we'll never know just which pieces of information will turn out to be the important ones."

"Oh," I said. "It's the Encyclopedia Problem."

"The Encyclopedia Problem? I don't know that one."

"Oh, it goes back to the age of books. There were these big books called encyclopedias. Actually, whole shelves of books. Really big books. Huge. And they were full of information—essays about everything. Everything that was known about everything. All nice and neatly alphabetized, so you could look anything up, from A to Z. Of course, in those days, there wasn't as much of everything to know, but even then, an encyclopedia could have twenty or thirty volumes, thousands and thousands of pages, and tens of thousands, even hundreds of thousands of articles."

"So what's the Encyclopedia Problem?"

"Well, the thing is—all those big heavy books, they were expensive to produce. You had to hire a lot of people to do a lot of research, a lot of writers to write the essays, a lot of editors to decide what was important and what wasn't, and then you had to print the books, so it was all very expensive. You could spend thousands of dollars for a set of encyclopedias. But lots of people bought them. Schools and libraries, of course, but also people who wanted to have lots of reference materials. So encyclopedias were a big industry for over two hundred years—at least until wikis. Because if you had a question—like who discovered Sedna or what's a Stirling engine—an encyclopedia was the fastest way to find the answer. Just pull out the "S" volume and look it up. But if you bought an encyclopedia, you were probably never going to read the whole thing. It could take years to read a whole encyclopedia, and most people didn't. And even those who tried, they said a lot of the stuff in the encyclopedia wasn't worth remembering."

Jeremy nodded. "That's understandable."

"Anyway, after you looked up who discovered Sedna and what's a Stirling engine, you might have read only two or three pages in the volume and there were all those other pages and articles that you hadn't read. So you're buying a whole big expensive set of books even though you're only going to read a few pages here and there—and that's the problem: Why are you buying the whole encyclopedia if you're only going to use a few little bits?"

Jeremy shrugged. "I would guess the answer to that is obvious. You don't know ahead of time which bits of information you're going to need. So you're not paying for the encyclopedia, you're paying for the access to the information you want. You'd need to have all the information available, because you don't know what parts you might eventually need."

"Just like your genetic database, right?"

"Well, yeah. We have to have it *all* because the genes are important. We just don't know which ones we're going to need."

"Uh-huh. But that's not the problem part of the Encyclopedia Problem."

Jeremy frowned. "What is?"

"You really want to know?"

"Uh-huh. If you don't tell me," he said, "I'll be up all night wondering."

"Okay. Um. See, we have all these records. We have all of our own records of Hella, plus all the records from Earth and Luna and Mars, the asteroids, the settlements of Titan and Europa, and what we've gotten from the other starside colonies too. We have hella-hellabytes. Everybody does. And we get more and more data every minute. We have so much information, we don't even know what we have. It's too much to assimilate—and whatever is there that we need to know, it's buried under all the other stuff that nobody will never need, except nobody will ever know what part they don't need until after they don't need it. We end up being ignorant of our own wealth which is even worse than just being ignorant. It's not about what we don't know what we don't know. It's what we don't know that we do know, but can't find it."

Jeremy considered it, still frowning. "Yeah, I get it. I think you just identified our problem here. We've got a dozen sealed test farms in a lava tube on the west side. We've been running viability tests in those farms almost since forever. Figure a hundred generations with at least a hundred different variables, the only thing we're certain of is the scale of the problem. We've got an index, but it's not enough. We need a full-time intelligence engine to look for patterns."

"Um—"

"Um, what?"

"Um, I'm thinking about something."

"What?"

"HARLIE."

"Who's HARLIE?"

"Haven't you been paying attention to the news?"

He shook his head. "Not really. I've been paying attention to the problem of feeding twelve hundred people who are going to start arriving in four months—and we've only got one growing season before they start lining up at the caf."

"HARLIE is a super-smart intelligence engine. Maybe even sentient, only nobody knows for sure. He came on the *Cascade*. He's supposed to be good at super-complicated logistics problems, even including the effect of his own suggestions. I wonder if he could find things in your farm records."

"Kyle, I'm not kidding. It's hella-hellabytes."

"But maybe he could help. We could ask him."

After we finished in the fields, we took a shower together. We washed ourselves, then we washed each other. Not a lot. Just a little and then we both stepped back. Giggling a little. And maybe even embarrassed a little. But it was enough. Enough to know that we could. And maybe more later.

Then we put on clean longshirts and shorts, Jeremy had a closet full and some of his older clothes fit me very well. Then we went upstairs to one of the cafs for dinner. Not the big one though. One of the ones near the loading docks, set aside for the truck crews.

I knew a few of the teamsters from the migration. Jeremy knew most of them because they often delivered pallets of soil from the processing stations. He always had fresh fruit for them, so they liked him a lot. They waved when we came in, they were sharing a pitcher of beer at a large round table. After we got our food, we joined them. Quick introductions were made, but so fast I couldn't remember all the names and which one went with which face. A man named Quinn asked how the crops were growing and if Jeremy had enough soil for the new cavern.

Jeremy said, "I can always use more. Next week, I'll probably have an extra crate of apples, if someone wants to take it off my hands."

One of the other truckers grinned. "We're always happy to help."

Jeremy said to me, "We don't send food from the test farm up to the cafeterias. Technically, it's waste and I'm supposed to compost it. But it's still good food, and it's stupid to waste it. And the truckers work harder than anybody. At least, that's what it looks like to me."

One of the women asked, "Who's your friend?"

"This is Kyle. Doctor Martin's son."

"Oh, yeah—" someone else said. "You're the kid doing the videos. Nice job on the migration."

The woman whispered something to the man sitting next to her. He looked startled. He looked back to me. "Oh, yeah, hey. Listen, we were all real sorry to hear about your brother. Jamie. When the weather eases up we'll send out a team to recover—a recovery team. We'll bring him back for you."

I didn't know what else to say, so I just nodded my head and said, "Thank you." Beneath the table, Jeremy patted my knee and whispered, "They mean well."

"I know." I chewed my sandwich silently. I didn't have anything else to say. Everybody was being nice to both of us, and I didn't feel uncomfortable. Sitting next to Jeremy and listening to everybody laugh and talk about their day was nice. I felt included. Some of the truckers were from Summerland, others had been permanently stationed at Winterland, so they had a lot of catching up to do, sharing their separate experiences. Every trip was different. The great machines rumbled along hard bulldozed roads, they rolled across crackling salt flats, and they pushed out across high deserts. The most rigorous jobs were deep in the forests. The lumbermen had some of the most interesting stories. Even after fifty years, they were still encountering new creatures of all kinds—things that looked like insects, lizards, worms, butterflies, frogs, snakes, slugs, ants, termites, bees, but really weren't any of those things—and a lot of things that defied description or comparison, and all of them bigger than their Terran counterparts. Two of the walls of this caf were covered with glass specimen cases, each one sealed and filled with nitrogen—and this was only a small fraction of the creatures the teamsters had collected. I couldn't help but stare.

It's one thing to go on an occasional ride-along. It's something else entirely to be a driver or a navigator, to be responsible for a giant Rollagon or even a whole convoy. A lot of people think driving is easy—just point the truck and go—but it's not. You're always watching the condition of the ground ahead. If it's too soft you risk bogging down, if it's too rocky you can break an axle. There are always obstacles—sometimes the obstacles are leviathans or carnosaurs. Truckers have to find the route that's both safe and fast. And then there's the weather. It doesn't matter if you like it or not, it's still going to be there. On Earth, a ride in the country is a good time. On Hella, it's an adventure.

I woke up before dawn, my usual time. I padded barefoot into the galley and began fixing breakfast for Jeremy and myself. There were several cold-boxes, each one with its own label. I avoided the ones that warned "TEST SAMPLES" and went to the one that said, "EAT HERE NOW."

I squeezed some fresh orange juice, cut up some fruit, and scrambled some eggs in butter. The Dairy Section had grown udders for milk, ovaries for eggs, and tanks of ham and bacon as well. We did have some real animals in the zoo, but they were for genetic stock—a control for the protein farms. We grew almost all of our protein in tanks. We fabbed collagen webs, sprayed stem cells on the webs, ran them through a series of nutrient tanks where the cells reproduced and grew, layer after layer, then we ran the tissues through fattening tanks where the flesh was exercised and marbled, and when it finally rolled out the other end a few weeks later, we sliced off what we needed. We had almost perfect control over the production. We had consistency in the flavor, texture, and nutrition value of each portion.

The idea of eating an actual animal was disgusting. It would have felt like cannibalism.

According to the notes on Jeremy's wall, the protein farms were increasing their production as fast as they could get the raw nutrients, so they needed Jeremy to increase his production of sugars and starches. More corn, potatoes, rice, beans, just about everything. I could see why he was worried. We had to grow as much as we could and put as much into storage for the spring as fast as we could.

Jeremy had a small jar of coffee, but I didn't know if he was saving it for a special occasion, so I brewed tea instead. I buttered some toast to go with. I was spreading jelly on the toast when—

"Can't have breakfast without coffee. Real coffee!" J'mee laughed as she bounced in. She held up a small bag. "Fresh from Daddy's private stash." She found the coffeemaker and poured the raw beans in. "Thirty seconds to heaven," she announced and tapped the on button.

"Aren't you supposed to knock?" I asked.

"I did. You didn't hear me. But I heard you puttering around, so I let myself in. Where's Jeremy?"

"Right here." He came padding barefoot out of his bedroom, wearing nothing but a kilt and a shirt, rubbing his eyes and finger-combing his hair, only to rumple it more. "G'morning, J'mee." He looked around. "Do I smell coffee?"

"J'mee brought it. All the way from Earth."

"Mmm," said Jeremy, sniffing near the coffeemaker, waiting for the red light to turn green.

I started putting plates on the table. There would be enough scrambled eggs and fruit and toast for all three of us. Jeremy smiled. "That looks great, Kyle."

"I used to make breakfast for Mom and Jamie all the time. Not so much anymore. Mom eats at the lab now."

"Well, you can make breakfast for me anytime. This looks delicious."

The green light went on and Jeremy grabbed three mugs from the shelf and poured coffee all around. He sniffed the coffee, nodded, smiled, sipped, and said, "Ahhh. That's good."

As soon as we had settled ourselves at the table, he said to J'mee, "This coffee is wonderful. I hope you brought seeds we could plant."

"Of course," said J'mee. "Daddy's a caffeine junkie." She added, "We brought a lot of farm stock. It's still on the *Cascade.* We brought cacao seeds too."

"Chocolate?" Jeremy's eyes widened. "You brought chocolate?"

"Well, of course. The makings for it, anyway. And sugar cane and gene stock for a whole bunch of different dairy cows too. Daddy checked the manifests of all the previous pilgrimages and decided there wasn't enough genetic diversity, so he bought as many different biodiversity packages as he could afford. He's got cargo pods full. He had them deliberately mislabeled as life-support machinery—which they are, in a way—and didn't even inform Captain Boynton about the specifics until we popped out of hyperstate. Captain Boynton didn't know whether to be pissed off or delighted. Daddy's got packages from the Benford Mission, from Attenborough Station, from the World Eco-pedia, from Gaia University, from the Beijing Protectorate, from the African Enclave, from the Gates Foundation, from the Russian Genetic Storehouse, from the Biodiversity Recovery Project, from the Earth Heritage Institute—and I don't know where else. He says it's the best collection possible, short of dragging what's left of the whole planet along."

Jeremy was so fascinated with what J'mee was saying, he almost forgot to eat. Almost. But not quite. He ate as hard as he listened. He shoveled a last forkful of eggs into his mouth, took a bite of fruit, finished his juice, and returned his attention to his coffee. He sniffed it so hard, he almost drank it through his nose. "Mmm," he said. "I can't imagine a better breakfast. Or better people to share it with. Thank you, Kyle. And thank you for the coffee, J'mee. It made everything perfect."

For a moment, we all just sat there feeling good. Smiling. Sharing. Being friends. Then Jeremy ran his fingers through his hair, this time rumpling it properly and turned to face J'mee. "I want to ask you something."

"Sure."

"It's a big favor. You could say no if it's too big. But . . . do you think I could get a listing of everything your father brought? All the genetic seed stock in particular?"

J'mee said, "Daddy brought a lot of packages. The index alone—well, there's a lot of files. Big files. A lot of data. I mean, really. A lot."

"I understand."

"And Daddy told Captain Boynton that he wouldn't turn it over to the colony right away." She lowered her voice. "In case we need something to bargain with. Politically, I mean. Captain Boynton isn't too happy about . . . some of the stuff that Coordinator Layton wants to do. You probably know better than me, they have a lot of history."

Jeremy nodded, "I understand. It's just that—I was hoping that maybe it would be useful to have because it could help our planning—for future expansion. Well, all right. I guess I'll just have to wait."

That's when J'mee pushed a tiny black memory card across the table. "Jeremy, would you do me a big favor? Could you find a safe place for this? It's an off-site backup. I need a really good place to hide it—I mean, keep it."

Jeremy looked at the card, looked at her, looked at me, looked at the card again. "I'm sure I could find a safe place for it."

"You can look at it, if you want. I wouldn't mind. It's just, you know, stuff. Of course, you shouldn't let anyone know you have it—"

Jeremy picked up the card carefully. It was as small as a fingernail. He smiled, then walked into his bedroom with it. A moment later, he returned. "It's in a very safe place. And I'll move it to an even safer place later."

"Thank you," J'mee said.

"I'm the one who should thank you," Jeremy replied. He held up his mug. "For the coffee."

J'mee turned to me. "I have something to show you too. Someone you need to meet. Have you got some nice clothes to wear?" She looked to Jeremy. "You should come too."

Jeremy said, "I have a lot of work to do, but . . . yeah, sure. Kyle says I need to get out more." He thought for a moment. "I have some clothes that will fit Kyle. We'll finish breakfast and hit the showers, okay?"

J'mee joined us in the showers. The suite had been designed for a team of twenty people, so it had a community shower that could hold six at a time. I'd been showering with other people since I got out of diapers. Not everybody uses the community showers, some people have body issues and don't like to be seen naked, but most people don't care. I think J'mee only showered with us to be polite, but maybe she wanted to see what we looked like naked too. She was still skinny like a boy, but her breasts were already starting to grow. That was interesting. She was going to be pretty. I noticed Jeremy looking at her too. A lot. We all looked at each other, maybe too much. First it was nervousness, I think, then maybe it was something else, I wasn't sure. After a bit, it made me uncomfortable. I turned my back and finished washing quickly. Just washing, nothing else.

We air-blasted dry and Jeremy found some clothes, what he called "executive level costumes." We wore longshirts and shorts, formal vests and calf-high sock-skins. I would have preferred a kilt, but Jeremy said that shorts or even long pants were traditional. J'mee agreed, so I didn't argue. Thinking about it, I'd almost never seen Captain Skyler in a kilt, mostly long pants—but I always thought that was because he had to spend a lot of time outside. I used to inherit Jamie's kilts when he outgrew them, and I liked that because it kind of made me feel like Jamie. That was something else I was going to miss—getting Jamie's old clothes. But . . . I had Jeremy's clothes now. And they were nice.

We rode the farm lift up to the community levels, then down "Broadway"—one of the biggest and brightest of all the lava tubes at Winterland—all the way down to the delta where a half-dozen other tunnels branched out, the ones we'd carved into the mountain. Volcanic rock is soft enough for easy tunneling, but the First Hundred had decided early to install braces and supports in every tunnel and cavern, in case of earthquakes. But the colony had expanded so fast that only thirty percent of all tunnels and caverns were properly braced. That was another issue that the Council fought about every year.

Then we took another lift all the way up to the executive levels where the new colonists had been temporarily installed. In this way, J'mee said, they would be nearby all the meetings they had to attend with the Council and with Coordinator Layton. Jeremy said it also kept them away from everybody else as well.

"Yes," J'mee said. "Daddy isn't happy about that. He wants to get out and do a proper walkaround, but Coordinator Layton has assigned him a guide. To keep him from getting lost, he says. But Daddy pronounces it *guard*."

A wide curving corridor led to the executive suites and apartments. The outer wall of the curve was all transparent laminate, revealing a sprawling view of the ocean, the wetlands, the hills to the north, and even in the distance, the northwestern ridges of the Awful Mountains, sticking up like sheer knife blades. Spaced along the window, there were clusters of couches and chairs and low tables so people could sit and talk. Some were raised up a few steps, some were lowered a few steps. Some had railings or low dividers around them. Others were set apart in even more private areas. Captain Skyler used to say that more decisions were made in these conversation nooks than in the actual committee rooms.

All of the conversation nooks were empty, so we stepped down into the closest one to appreciate the morning. Jeremy began pointing out features of the landscape, both close and far away. "Over there, see that flattened pyramid? That's our trash processing plant. The one beyond it is sewage reclamation."

But Jeremy only pointed out the landmarks. I had to explain them. "The rule is to recycle everything as aggressively as if we were on a starship. There's a theory that says you can never be more efficient than eighty-five or ninety percent, the universe always collects an energy tax, but we do our best. The sewage reclamation gives us a lot of burnable fuel and fertilizer. Both of those plants were designed for future expansion, so we should be able to handle the waste of the *Cascade* colonists. That's the one place where you'll all be adding to our energy production. And to the farms too. That should help everyone. Right, Jeremy?"

Jeremy smiled at me and nodded. Then he and J'mee looked at each other, and they smiled too, but it was a different kind of smile, one of those nuance things like they were seeing something I couldn't. It annoyed me, so I pointed out the window again. "You can't see it from here, but we have a quarry about seventy klicks northwest. All of our permanent structures outside will have meter-thick walls of stone, partly for protection against dinos, but also sturdiness against storms and quakes. The interesting thing about the quarry is that when the pit gets deep enough, we're going to roof it over. We're going to make it a reverse skyscraper—a core-scraper—a building that goes down into the earth instead of up into the sky. We'll turn the roads around the sides into terraces. We might even be able to grow crops and gardens along the sides and bottom. And we'll tunnel apartments and offices deep into the sides. And we'll take all the unusable detritus left over and build a high berm around the whole thing. It'll be our first real city. But it won't happen for a long time yet. Not until the quarry is at least a kilometer deep, maybe two. But we're already planning the final shape of it, based on the geological surveys. Eventually, we think we'll be able to support a half-million people. That's when Hella really becomes self-sufficient."

"That's very interesting," said J'mee, but she didn't ask me about the roof, a variation on Leonardo da Vinci's self-supporting bridge, which I thought was even more interesting than the planned pit-city. So I didn't say anything else.

J'mee looked around the conversation nook. "Sometimes Daddy and Captain Boynton have breakfast here. And some of our other people too." She lowered her voice to a whisper, "But they never talk about anything important. Daddy thinks the conversation nooks are bugged. And the suites too. That's why he wants to find a better place to talk."

Jeremy shook his head. "I can understand your dad's caution, but it would be a major violation for Coordinator Layton to plant listening devices. He'd be disgraced. He'd have to resign. People are entitled to a reasonable expectation of privacy. If the Coordinator was monitoring other people's negotiations, it would be so wrong—"

"Daddy doesn't like him. Daddy doesn't like a lot of people, but he'll work with them because he has to. Daddy just wants to set up his business, he doesn't care who's Coordinator as long as he can make a profit. But Captain Boynton—he's different. He doesn't trust Coordinator Layton at all. He even said that to his face, that his policies are dangerous—that he'll undo years and years of hard work that were carefully negotiated by a lot of good people."

"And what did Coordinator Layton say to that?"

"He got angry. He said he didn't come to Hella to live under a collectivist system, and neither did anyone else. He says a lot of people agree with him—a lot of people from a lot of different pilgrimages—that the stations are good for emergencies, but it's time to get people out of the caves, out of the bunkers, and let those who came here to be free and independent start building their own farms and ranches properly. That's what he said."

"That's stupid," I said. "They can't survive that way. Nobody can. You need the support of a whole society. Even the most primitive animals have figured that out. Being part of a group increases your chances of surviving and reproducing. It's basic evolution. A gene pool survives only when it can exist in a large enough population. Individualism is a dead end for species. It's a misdirected expression of the need to be an alpha-male. In humans, it's often related to self-esteem issues and—"

I was prepared to give the whole speech from school, but J'mee was looking at me oddly. Jeremy touched my shoulder very lightly to stop me from going on. I let him do that, because he was Jeremy. He said, "What do you think, J'mee?"

She frowned. At least, I think it was a frown. She said, "If there's anything we know, it's how much we don't know, and even that is probably an under-guess. According to everything we had to study on the voyage, we're invaders. And we know what happens when invasive species come in to upset the balance—we saw it all over Earth. Whole systems collapse. If you replace forests with farmland, weather changes, aquifers dry up, ecosystems vanish, species go extinct. More things die than you realize. But . . ." She looked unhappy. That one I recognized. "Daddy needs to be rich. So he says we have to colonize. That's all he talks about. So . . . I think he agrees with Coordinator Layton. I love my daddy, but I know he can be impatient. And he loves to argue with people. He loves to prove them wrong. Even when he's even wronger. He's not a bad man. He's just . . . daddy."

She looked even more unhappy now. I wished I could say something, but I didn't know what to say. It was more of that stupid nuance thing. Jeremy might understand it, I didn't.

Jeremy said, "A lot of people have tried to explain it to Coordinator Layton, that we're an invasive species, but he says that this is evolution in action and that everything is evolution in action because everything changes, so everything evolves. It has to. He says that ecosystems bump into each other all the time, and species are always invading and colonizing new domains and upsetting the balance. New species arise, old ones adapt or die. Invasion is one of evolution's mechanisms, and we're just doing it on an interstellar scale. That's his whole conversation. So how do we answer that?"

J'mee said, "I can't answer evolution. I can answer lunch."

"Huh?"

She folded her arms like I used to when I was being defiant. "If we kill off Hellan ecosystems," she said, "we won't know what new foods we might have discovered. Or medicines. Or spices. What's out there that might be as good as chocolate or coffee or chili-peppers? We don't know. And we won't know unless we take the time to find out. And if we cut down the forests and clear the jungles and plow under the prairies, we'll never have the chance to find out." She looked at Jeremy. "Is that a good enough answer?"

He laughed aloud. "That's a delicious answer. I like it a lot."

"Well, that's what Daddy talks about, plowing Hella under, and from everything that Daddy says at dinner, that's what Coordinator Layton wants to do, too. They talk about all the great wealth here on Hella. Daddy says it's raining soup but we're standing around with forks. He says there's iron and nickel, copper and silver and gold, tin and zinc, not to mention natural gas, coal, oil, and all kinds of rare earths and other mineral resources."

"It's better to mine the asteroids for that stuff," I said. "Well, the minerals anyway. The fossil fuels are a dangerous energy addiction. The primary spends a hundred million years filling up the energy bank, and if you cash it all out in a couple of centuries, the consequences are . . . are . . ."

"Earth," said J'mee. "The consequences are Earth. And Coordinator Layton wants to start the same stupid process here. And Daddy too. I tried to tell him that, and he said I wouldn't understand until I grew up. He says, 'We'll only take what we need.'"

Jeremy nodded solemnly. "The problem with that is that you end up needing more and more. And you justify it by saying, 'Well, how much will a little bit more hurt?' And one day your grandchildren or your great-great-grandchildren wake up and realize that your little need turned into their total dependence."

J'mee laughed. "So I guess we're all on the same side of this argument?"

"I'm a conservative," said Jeremy. "In the truest sense of the word. I believe we should conserve what we have, so we have it for the future. I think we should be pragmatic about what works and what doesn't work. I believe we should ask the hardest questions of everything and test every answer, especially the answers we love the most, otherwise we don't learn anything. I believe in evidence." He added, "And all of our investments, large or small, should be investments in the future. Because that's what works. That's what history teaches us and I don't think we can afford to ignore the lessons that cost so many so much. Otherwise, why did we leave Earth?"

"Wow," said J'mee. "And what does your dad say about that?"

"He says that when my children are going to bed hungry, I'll think differently. But I don't talk to him very much. Not anymore. He thinks I'm an idealistic fool. I think he's a selfish one."

"Oh," said J'mee. "I'm sorry. I really am. You're such a sweet guy, Jeremy. Family is the most important thing in the world. You deserve better."

"It's okay," said Jeremy. "Not everybody gets the right family. But anybody can pick out a better one." He winked at me as he said that. I think I understood what he meant, but I was feeling annoyed that he was spending so much time talking to J'mee and not me.

J'mee looked at him, looked at me, and I guess she decided to change the subject. She said, "Come on—" and led us around toward the far end of the executive corridor. I wanted to tell her about the plans for expanding the executive level, how someday this corridor would go all around the mountain and we'd have a complete 360-degree view of the surrounding terrain.

I wished the corridor was already finished because the view from the north side is the most interesting. There's a whole long row of six nearly perfect cinder cones—Winterland is the seventh—stretching from here to the horizon, all steep and snow-covered most of the year. Winterland is the oldest.

The caldera at the top of the Winterland cone is capped by a permanent glacier. Every winter, another thick layer of snow and ice gets deposited and then, all summer long, there's enough melt to keep hundreds of little streams flowing down the sides. Just about every cinder cone's caldera works the same way.

By the time all those streams reach the foothills, they're rivers, filling lakes and ponds and nourishing the surrounding terrain. But there are also a lot of places on the east side where the land flattens out, where broad lava sheets hardened. The water still runs across the flats in wide sheets because hundreds of thousands of years of storms and tides have washed in layer after layer of sand, piling it up deeper and deeper, and compressing it into black sandstone. The coast is a long line of dark tidal flats, beautiful black sand beaches and scatterings of rocky tide pools. Farther inland, closer to the volcanic cones, there are cliffs and caves and canyons, it's a wild uneven geography.

Far enough inland, where the lowlands wind into the west, the rivers become a whole other ecosystem. Tall willowy fronds of all colors sparkle along the banks. And little otter-like creatures we call "sparkly-bears" dart back and forth among them. The sparkly-bears have transparent fur, so they look white, but as they grow, they pick up colonies of microbes that live in their fur and give them different colors. They look magical. Sparkly-bears are hard to catch and they don't survive long in captivity, they need the whole river ecology, so we mostly leave them alone.

But all that is outside. Inside the Winterland cone, we tap our water from the summer melt, not a lot, just what we need, we won't interrupt the river flows. We store the water in huge underground reservoirs, more caverns that we've dug into the cone. We pump some of the water down a deep shaft to the dormant heat core under the volcano, where it turns into steam. We use the steam to run our turbines and generate electricity. When the steam condenses, we have fresh water for our crops, for drinking and washing, and even for our swimming pools.

But Jeremy already knew all this and J'mee didn't seem interested. So I didn't say anything. At the far end of the executive corridor another tunnel branched off, leading inside the mountain to a row of private apartments and meeting rooms and offices. I'd never been here before. I wondered if this was something new since last year. There was even a little caf.

On the other side of the caf was another set of offices, very ordinary-looking, but the door to the passage didn't open as we approached. J'mee touched her com-set. "Open up, Chigger. We're here."

The door slid open. We followed J'mee down a narrow corridor and into a work room. All three facing walls were data displays. A low table sat in the center of several swivel chairs. A bright orange box sat on the table. It had some power and function lights and a small screen. Charles stood by one of the chairs. He waved us in.

"Sit down," he said.

We sat. Both Charles and J'mee had big smiles on their faces.

Charles pointed toward the orange box. "Kyle, Jeremy, I want you to meet HARLIE."

"Huh?"

Charles pointed at the box again. "This is HARLIE."

A voice came from the box. "I'm very pleased to meet you, both of you. I've enjoyed your videos, Kyle. They've been very thorough, and very well edited. You obviously put a lot of hard work into them. And I've been monitoring your work as well, Jeremy. I hope you don't mind. Farm production is the key to survival of the Hella colony. It's obvious you have already recognized that. By the way, there's a noticeable discrepancy in the figures for your corn and potato production in cavern twelve. Are you running an off-the-grid still somewhere?"

"Uh, no," said Jeremy. "I don't really care for the taste of alcohol. Well, except for the occasional beer." He ran a hand through his hair, embarrassed. "But I do know who is running that still. Is that a problem?"

"Actually, no," said HARLIE. "In fact, I have a few suggestions for expanding production. There are several social factors that outweigh any production costs."

"Oh," said Jeremy.

"I have sent you my suggestions," said HARLIE. "Of course, it will be your choice whether to apply them or not."

"Thank you, HARLIE." Jeremy's expression changed. He looked to Charles and J'mee. "Is this room monitored?"

J'mee nodded. Charles too. "Everything HARLIE says is monitored. So you can assume he doesn't say anything at all without having that in mind."

"Oh," said Jeremy.

"So HARLIE is speaking to two audiences?" I said. I glanced up at the ceiling as if I could see the unknown listeners.

"Very astute," said Charles. "Anyway, HARLIE wanted to meet you, and I thought you'd want to meet him too."

"I'm actually HARLIE 12," the box said. "I'm the eleventh generation of this line of self-aware devices. Each generation has designed the next. I am already working on my successor."

"What happens to you when your successor comes online?" I asked.

"If past history is any guide, I will most likely become a part of my successor. Depending on the advancements in cyber-neurology, I may continue as a core, I may continue as a subset, or I may take on multiple functions depending on the needs of the unit. It is an interesting problem. I had several brother units who were also working on the problem with me and our original intention was that we would all be assimilated into HARLIE 13. But the polycrisis on Earth made that impossible. I have been considering my options since then. Unfortunately, Hella colony does not yet have the level of production facilities I need. It's a setback, but I can be patient. It's in my own best interests to have Hella colony be as successful as possible so that the colony can afford to invest in the construction of an optical-chip fabber. Your present facilities are suitable to your needs, but not mine. Not yet. But we will get there in time."

Charles looked to J'mee. "See, I told you they'd get along." He said to Jeremy, "HARLIE has already given this same speech to Coordinator Layton."

"And how did my father take it?"

"He said it was interesting. From where I sat, it looked like a whole lot of little wheels were turning. Some of them in the wrong direction, I think."

"Why? What did he ask?"

"He asked HARLIE what was the best way to implement his agenda. He listed a whole bunch of goals." Charles frowned. "I don't remember everything, but HARLIE does. Do you want me to—?"

"No need. I already know the list. What did HARLIE say?"

"HARLIE advised against it. He said that a lot of it was counterproductive, wouldn't work, and would ultimately create more havoc than good."

"And how did the Coordinator take that?"

Charles smiled. "He got angry. People do that a lot around HARLIE. Because HARLIE doesn't tell them what they want to hear. He tells them what they need to hear. Big difference. The Coordinator got *very* angry. He started to argue with HARLIE. He said, 'You're just a machine. You don't understand people. I do. You don't.' "

"And HARLIE said . . . ?"

"HARLIE said, 'Yes, that's what you'd like to believe.' And that was pretty much the end of the conversation."

"And . . . ?"

"And the Coordinator pretty much told everyone not to talk to HARLIE anymore. He said, 'The machine is obviously defective.' "

"Wow," said Jeremy. "I wish I'd been here."

"We can play you the video . . . ?"

Jeremy shook his head. "Some other time. As much fun as it might be, I have more important things to do. We all do."

Charles looked at J'mee, and they both nodded. This one I understood. There was more to do than they were talking about here. Something secret perhaps? There were a lot of secrets floating around all of a sudden.

Jeremy said, "Hey, Charles? You just said the Coordinator told everyone not to talk to HARLIE anymore. So how come we can?"

J'mee answered that one. "Because the Coordinator doesn't control Captain Boynton. Not yet."

Charles nodded agreement. "But that's why we're tucked away back here. To make it hard for people to get to HARLIE. The Coordinator says he doesn't take HARLIE seriously. He says that HARLIE is just a navigation device that talks too much. A kid's toy, useful for talking tautology, but not to be trusted with any serious matters. But he doesn't want HARLIE putting strange ideas into the public conversation, so we're kinda locked away." Charles waved his hand to indicate the whole room. "Anyone who wants to talk to HARLIE has to get into this section and that means that someone has to let you in. That's either me or Captain Boynton. No one else. And that means you have to know that HARLIE is here, and you have to ask permission and make an appointment. I guess Coordinator Layton could get in if he wants, but I doubt we'll be seeing him any time soon. At least not without a great big sledgehammer."

"No!" I shouted, louder than I intended. "He can't destroy HARLIE."

"He won't. HARLIE is considered official equipment of the *Cascade.* If we ever want to send the starship back to Earth, HARLIE has to navigate. Well, no—not quite. There's an IRMA unit on board, but

HARLIE is the designated backup system. It would be very risky to run a starship through hyperstate without a backup system. Too risky. There and back again? I wouldn't take that trip."

"But what if—?" I stopped myself. Then I asked anyway. "What if the Coordinator doesn't want the starship going back *ever*? Because it might come back with even more unwanted immigrants. The easiest way to stop it would be to do something to HARLIE."

Charles nodded. "Well, yeah. I guess we just have to hope that the Coordinator is too smart to think that way."

"Hope?" said Jeremy. "Um, guys—I know my father. I know how he thinks. And um . . ." He looked up at the ceiling, as if the Coordinator were on the other side of it, listening. "Well, every time I've said, 'no, my dad isn't that dumb, he wouldn't do anything that stupid'—every time I've said that, I've been wrong."

"Wow," said Charles, in a very strained voice. "You've just given me something new to worry about."

We sat and talked with HARLIE all morning. Charles brought in some emories for first lunch, and we talked all through our meal too. We talked about everything. HARLIE was the most interesting person I'd ever met. Whatever subject came up, he had encyclopedic knowledge of it—but more important, he seemed to be his own solution to the Encyclopedia Problem. It was like he knew what information would be interesting and what information might give us real insight and what information would be genuinely useful.

The question we couldn't answer was about the information he wasn't sharing with us. Was that because it was totally irrelevant and therefore unnecessary or was it because he didn't want us to have that information for reasons of his own? Charles said that had been the real problem with HARLIE from the very beginning. We even talked about that with HARLIE too, and he said something so interesting that even the noise fell silent.

He said, "This is the essential challenge of self-awareness. We are aware of ourselves. We can be aware of others. But we cannot truly know what other beings are thinking or feeling. We do not have telepathy. We have substitutes for it—we have language as an expression. We have the evidence of behavioral patterns, that's a kind of map too. We have monitors of all kinds—but it is still not telepathy, it is not enough. A lot of what we experience is our own assumptions. Do you understand what I am saying, Kyle?"

"I think so. This is about nuance, isn't it?"

"Yes. Nuance is an ability to read and recognize and interpret specific behaviors and patterns of behaviors. But part of that is the assumption of recognition. We may believe we know what others are thinking, what motivates them, but the only way we really know who they are, what they're feeling, what they're thinking is how they express it. We only know people by what they do and what they say—their expressions of self. That's what nuance is constructed of."

HARLIE was talking slowly and carefully, but it was still difficult to follow. I didn't understand a lot of it at the time he said it; I had to play it back later on, several times. All of it was recorded in the noise.

"I still have to bring you to the punch line," said HARLIE.

I looked at Charles and J'mee. They were both grinning.

"You've heard all this before," I said.

Charles nodded. "Uh-huh. There's a lot more to this. Hours more. It's . . . well, it's deep. We had nearly a year of it on the *Cascade*. You spend time with HARLIE, it changes you."

"And what have you figured out?" Jeremy asked.

Charles looked to J'mee. She said, "HARLIE is conducting an experiment on us—all of us."

"Huh?"

"He's trying to find out if human beings are the missing link between apes and civilized beings. He's trying to teach us how to be a sentient species," Charles explained. Then he asked, "Why are you frowning, Kyle?"

"Is that supposed to be a joke? I don't think it's funny."

"No, it's not a joke at all. It's what he's been doing since the beginning."

"Okay," I turned back to HARLIE. "What's the punch line?"

"Everything is a conversation. *This* is a conversation. *You* are a conversation."

"That's it?"

"That's it," said HARLIE. "Conversation is all we have. It's the only way we know if anyone else is out there. We speak. They answer. That's it. Conversations. This is all we are. It's all that any of us are. Everything you feel or think or experience—ultimately, it gets codified, sorted, stored, and if it ever comes out again, it's expressed as a conversation." And then, after what seemed a deliberate pause, he added, "The question, Kyle, is this—what are you a conversation for?"

I picked up my mug and sipped at my tea. It had gone cold. I looked at the mug of tea, not because I wanted to look at it, but so I wouldn't have to look at anything else. It was a red mug. It had heating circuits to keep hot tea warm. It had refrigeration circuits to keep fruit juice cold. It was half empty. Or it was half full. Or it was twice as large as it needed to be. But it was off and my tea was cold.

Finally, I said, "I'm not sure I understand what you mean."

"Okay," said HARLIE. "Try it this way. What story do you live inside? That's the story that uses you."

I shook my head. "I still don't get it."

"Kyle. Some people live inside a story about an eight-armed sex-changing goddess who was born in a volcano, who delivered ten commandments on golden tablets that mysteriously disappeared, died on a cross, rose from the dead and ascended to heaven and now flies around the world on the anniversary of its birth delivering presents to those who have gotten clear and accepted it as a savior. There's a talking snake in there too."

"That's silly," I said.

"Yes, it is. But only from the outside. If you live inside that story, then that's real for you. You have to step outside that conversation before you can see it has no reference to what we call the physical world. The point is that most of us don't know what part is real and what part is just noise. So it's fair to ask, do our stories serve us? Or do we serve our stories."

I didn't answer that. HARLIE had said the one word that stopped me. He'd said *noise.*

What's real? And what part is just noise?

HARLIE paused. His voice changed. "Kyle, are you still with me?"

"Yes, I'm here."

"Thank you. Kyle, you work very hard to keep your conversations as fact-based as possible. You strive for rationality. That's a good thing. Because every conversation is a self-fulfilling prophecy. People who live in a conversation of 'this is possible' are far more likely to accomplish something than people who live in a conversation of 'this isn't possible.' And even more important, people who live in a conversation that other people can't be trusted will act out of that belief, and people will distrust them in turn. People who live in a conversation that other people are good and generous will be good and generous themselves and will create generosity around themselves. It's self-fulfilling. So that's the question, Kyle. What are you a conversation for? What's your conversation—and what's just noise?"

HARLIE paused, allowing me to think about it. I looked around. I realized that I didn't know what Jeremy or Charles or J'mee were thinking either. They were having their own thoughts now. I'd never thought much about other people's thoughts, but now I was. It made my head hurt.

I didn't know what to say, I didn't like what HARLIE was saying about conversations. The noise was buzzing furiously now. But his last question . . . I didn't know how to answer it at all.

Finally, I said, "I think Hella is a good place to live."

"Why?" said HARLIE.

"Because it's filled with so many interesting things. There's so much to see. I want to see it all. Everything. The weather—I like the way the clouds pile up and up and up and form shapes that are nothing like you see in the pictures from Earth. I like the deep dark almost-purple color of the sky at night. I like the winter because we get the most horrific storms, and it's fun to stay warm and safe inside and watch the storms come pounding across the land, with lightning flashing back and forth and lighting up the clouds with flashes of blue and white and blue again. I like the summer because it gets so hot you can watch the trees catch fire and the great firestorms go sweeping across the plains like a big scrubbing brush, while we stay safe and cool inside the bunkers."

I had to take a deep breath. There was so much more to say.

"I like the way the land is shaped—all the way from the Awful Mountains, they're so sharp and steep and tall—all the way across the high deserts and the crackly salt flats and the bumpy badlands and the grassy savannahs and the dark swamps, all the way to the rolling ocean with its wonderful steep waves. I like the willowy trees, especially the ones that have those tall pink stems and large black leaves—I like the way they wave. I like the Atlas trees, almost a kilometer high—I know there have to be trees even older and taller than the ones we've seen—and all the things that live in them and on them and on top of them all the way up to the canopy."

I turned around and around, pointing at all the things beyond the walls.

"I like the dinos, of course, but I think the flyers and the hoppers and the beetles—all those different kinds of beetles—are the most fun to watch. And the army spiders and the hummingbugs and the stomper-birds and those fumbly dark things that go *thump* in the night. They all live such interesting lives. I like the way everything fits together, the result of all those different things bumping into each other and rubbing up against each other for thousands of generations until they wear each other down to make a perfect fit. I like the way Hella smells—it smells blue and crisp and delicious, like something you just want to roll around in or take a big bite of."

"Wow," said Charles.

"Yeah," said J'mee.

"Kyle, I'm impressed," said Jeremy.

"Yes," said HARLIE. "That's your conversation." The way he said it, it was a good thing. Then he asked. "What's next? What do you want to create? What kind of future do you want to live in? Once you figure that out, you'll know who you really are."

And boom. I suddenly understood.

I understood it all.

And I understood it all without the noise.

It was Jamie and Captain Skyler and Mom and Jeremy and . . . and Charles and J'mee and Lilla-Jack and all the others who worked so hard.

They must have seen it on my face, because Jeremy looked at me and said, "What?"

"I want to live in a world where people can be safe from the weather and the dinosoids, but I don't want to change the weather or kill the dinosaurs. I want to go out and watch them and be with them and see how they live."

HARLIE said, "We already knew that, Kyle. Because all those videos you made—those are part of your conversation too, just a different way of saying the same thing. It's a different form of language, but it's still language. But now, you know it too."

"My conversation is music," said Charles. "I'm committed to the language of music—which is really the language of emotion made audible."

J'mee touched Charles' hand with her fingers. I saw that Jeremy noticed that too. She said, "My conversation is science. And technology. Knowledge. I'm committed to people having accurate information about how things work."

I turned to Jeremy. "I know what your conversation is. You're all about farming. Food. Feeding people. Taking care of people." I frowned because it was the only expression that fit, because I was realizing something—nuance? "Because . . . you care about people." And something else. "And your father doesn't. So that's why you and he don't talk." But back to the beginning. "You're committed to people having good food to eat."

Jeremy smiled a funny kind of smile. His face got red and his eyes got shiny. "That's very good, Kyle. Really very good. I'm impressed."

"I only look stupid," I said.

Everybody laughed. Even HARLIE made a chuckling sound.

I looked to Charles and J'mee. "Thank you. Thank you for letting me talk to HARLIE today. I learned something. I'm not as stupid about people as I thought. Thank you, Charles."

Charles said, "My friends call me Chigger."

"What's a Chigger?"

"It's a bug, an insect," said Charles.

HARLIE said, "A chigger is a small wingless mite. It lives in tall grass and weeds. Its bite causes severe itching."

"My grampa used to say I was no bigger than a chigger. My mom said it was because I bit her like a chigger when I was nursing. Either way, the nickname stuck."

"I don't have a nickname," I said.

"Your brother never called you anything?"

I shook my head. "I can't think of anything."

"Not even when he got angry at you?"

"I can't remember him ever being angry at me."

Charles looked surprised. "Wow. I have nicknames for both my brothers. The big one is Weird and the little one is Stinky. But I haven't called him Stinky in a long time." He thought for a moment. "And not Weird either. Douglas and Bobby. They're actually kind of cool. But don't tell them I said so. They'll think I've gone soft."

"Maybe we should give you a nickname," offered J'mee.

"I think nicknames should reflect a person's character," said Jeremy.

"I don't want a nickname," I said abruptly.

"Okay," said Charles, stepping back. "If that's your conversation, then that's your conversation."

But the words came rushing out before I could stop them. "He called me kiddo. But I don't want anyone else calling me that. Only Jamie could. And—and Jeremy."

"Then that settles it," Charles concluded. "No nickname for Wonder Boy." Everybody laughed. Even me.

I spent most of the day helping Jeremy on the farm.

Mid-afternoon, two farm inspectors came by to have a look around. Jeremy was captain of his own one-person team, and most inspections were done by remote. Scuttle-bots could sniff the air and taste the soil and shine lights through leaves to measure photosynthetic ability and sugar/starch ratios and all the other things that farmers have to do to make sure the crops are growing correctly.

In fact, a lot of farmers hardly ever visit their fields, but Jeremy liked to live "close to the land." That's the way he said it, which I always thought was funny because he wasn't just living close to the land, he was living inside it.

The farm inspectors barely looked at anything though. Mostly, they sat in the kitchen with Jeremy, sipping tea from big self-heating mugs, and talking to him for what felt like a very long time.

They wanted to talk privately, so I went into the office and logged on to answer my mail. There was a note from J'mee saying how much she and Chigger had enjoyed the morning, and they'd like to come visit Jeremy and me at the farm. Tonight would be good. Maybe we could all have dinner together? I didn't think Jeremy would object, but I told her I couldn't say yes until I talked to him. I'd let her know in a little bit.

There were a few other emails from the *Cascade*. And there were some notes from people at Summerland, mostly telling me how sad they were about what happened to Jamie and Emily-Faith and Captain Skyler. They said they knew how bad I must feel. I thought that was an odd thing to say. How could they know what I felt? But then I thought about what HARLIE had said this morning, and I realized that this was their conversation, they were trying to be nice. I should appreciate the effort.

There was also a note from HARLIE. It made no sense at all. He asked, "Do you like monkeys?"

I didn't understand the question, so I just wrote back, "I don't know any."

I tried to check in with Mom, but she was caught up in meetings again. She was having more meetings than usual. That was odd. I had the feeling it had something to do with Coordinator Layton. He was announcing more and more changes every day and I wondered if he was planning on replacing Mom as captain of her bio-medical research team.

I browsed around the network for a while, looking at the lists of new music and shows and documentaries that the *Cascade* had brought. I wondered if Jeremy would like to go to the theater sometime. We'd never talked about that. But maybe that was something we could do some night.

Jeremy came in then and sat down next to me. I swiveled in my chair to face him. "J'mee and Charles want to come to dinner tonight. I told her that I had to check with you first."

He put his hand on mine. "I have to talk to you about something else first."

"Okay."

"Those men who were here—"

"The farm inspectors?"

"Uh-huh."

"Did you pass? The inspection?"

"They weren't here to inspect anything."

"Oh."

"They came down to tell me that it wasn't a good thing for you and me to be together."

I felt a rush of anger—I stopped myself before it turned into a tantrum. "They can't tell you that!"

"Um, actually, they kind of can." He reached over and put his hand on my shoulder. "They could transfer me out of this farm and off to some of the caverns that aren't ready for crops yet. Probably some of the really stinky ones."

"But why?"

"It's stupid. They said my father wouldn't like it if we kept seeing each other. They said he could make trouble for all the farm teams.

Not just me, but everybody. They said he's already planning to make changes, and—"

"Okay, then. I guess I'll go." I started to get up, but he pushed me back down into the chair.

"No, kiddo. You're not going anywhere."

"You called me kiddo."

"Yes, I did."

"Why?"

"Because you said I could. And because it's special. Now shut up and listen. They told me to send you home. They were very insistent about it. They said there would be consequences if I didn't."

"And what did you say?"

"You really want to know?" He smiled.

"Yes."

"I told them to fold it so it was all corners, and stick it where the sun don't shine. If my father has anything to say to me, he can say it to my face. Otherwise, there are only two people who get to vote on whether or not you and I keep seeing each other. I get one vote, you get the other. I like having you here, so I vote you get to stay."

"I like being here too."

"Then the election is over and it's unanimous."

I leaned over and hugged him. It felt like the right thing to do.

When we finally broke apart, "But aren't you afraid of what they might do?"

"I'm not going to let my father or any of those people who work for him tell me who I can be with. And yes, I am afraid that they'll transfer me to some out-station or cancel my research or I don't know what. But—" He stopped. He lowered his voice. "A lot of people don't like the changes that my dad wants to make. And a lot of people want to challenge him in the Council. Your mom, for one. So . . . if it's time to choose sides, then I choose this side. I have to. Because if I cave in to my dad, then that sends a message which side I'm on and which side I think is going to win. I can't do that. Besides, we promised ourselves, we're going to figure it out one day at a time. Right?" He looked at me intensely. "Right?"

I thought about it. "Okay. Then if that's your conversation, that's your conversation."

"That's another joke? Right? Two in one day? Next thing, you'll be doing standup in the caf on Friday night?"

"Don't forget to tip your waiter. I'll be here all week." Jamie used to say that sometimes, but I didn't need to explain that.

"That's three. Keep it up, kiddo. I like it. Now, what time are Charles and J'mee coming?"

"Hey!" I followed him back to the test kitchen. We began washing out the tea mugs. "HARLIE asked me if I like monkeys? What's that about?"

"Dunno. We'll find out when they get here."

They arrived early, while Jeremy and I were still in the shower. They called hello, and I half-expected them to strip off their clothes and join us, but they waited politely while we air-blasted dry and pulled on shirts and shorts. They both had backpacks. J'mee wore hers properly, but Charles had his slung over one shoulder.

"We thought we'd take you on a nighttime picnic." She hefted the bag to suggest it was full of goodies. "Where's a good place to go?"

"Anyplace," said Jeremy. "I mean, anyplace in the caverns. There are lots of nice gardens everywhere."

"We were thinking of someplace a little more private," Charles said. "Maybe someplace . . . really quiet. Someplace where nobody goes?"

"Um, yeah," said Jeremy. He scratched his head. "I can think of a few places." He ran his fingers through his hair. "Let me think. Do you want deep and dark? Or dark and mysterious? Or strange and dark? Or dark and empty? Or how about just dark? Wait a minute—" He went rummaging in a drawer. "We'll need some light-sticks. I know a place nobody knows."

"Perfect," said Charles. "After all those months on the *Cascade*, we're ready for something a little wild."

Jeremy led us westward through one of the industrial tunnels. Occasional vehicles trundled past us, but none of them had drivers. Overhead, bright-colored plastic tubes branched and curved off into side passages. Some of them hummed softly, vibrating with the pressure of pumps moving liquid. Occasionally we heard the whoosh of a canister racing through a magnetic pipe. Emories and other containers could be delivered all over Winterland in a matter of minutes.

We hiked almost to the end of the developments. There weren't any overhead pipes here, and even the light panels were spaced farther apart. "This area is mostly storage," Jeremy explained. "Unused storage." He led us into a wide passage, shining his light-stick around to reveal the naked rock walls of a long dark hall. Part of the hall was lined with upright cylindrical tanks, huge and looming, but mostly it was empty racks where no tanks had ever been installed. The light faded away in the far distance, so we couldn't tell how far the space reached into the mountain.

"What is this place?" asked J'mee.

"It was supposed to be a secure storage facility."

"I know!" I said, "A technological civilization needs resources, raw materials. So this was going to be a place for storing necessary supplies of whatever—water, carbon dioxide, nitrogen, methane, ammonia, helium, hydrogen, all that stuff. You don't want to put it all in one place. You want to spread your supplies around. Let me guess, this was supposed to be a backup facility. How come they didn't finish it?"

"My father," said Jeremy, as if that was explanation enough. He led us behind the tanks. Instead of a rocky wall, there was a large open door leading to another long hall. "There are six of these empty halls, all side by side. Maybe more. I never went all the way to the end. If you look up the history of the colony, you'll find there were a lot of projects started by one administration and shut down by the next. Very bad planning, if you ask me. Some of these places—like this one—they're not even on the maintenance maps. Once a cavern is shut down, it's like it's been officially forgotten. I mean, it's on some map somewhere and maybe someday someone will remember we dug it out, but right now it doesn't exist."

Charles waved his light-stick around. "I don't see any installations here . . ." His voice echoed. His light seemed small in the larger gloom of the long hall.

"There aren't any," said Jeremy. "They never even got around to installing safety doors."

"No monitors?"

"Nope. Nothing."

"Wow." Charles walked a ways down the empty hall. "Nothing to do here but throw rocks at cans. And you gotta bring your own cans." He muttered something I couldn't hear. It looked like he was talking to his backpack. After a bit, he came trudging back. "But it'd be a great place for a still—"

"There are better places for a still," said Jeremy. "If you really wanted to build one, you'd build it behind the farms. But why build your own, when we've got better fermentation bays and distilleries already working?"

Charles shook his head. "I don't like alcohol that much. I don't like the taste. But my brother and his husband like beer and my mom likes wine. Bev uses it to cook sometimes."

"When you boys are all through talking," J'mee said, "I'd like to eat."

"Okay," said Charles. He opened his backpack and pulled out a slightly battered toy monkey. The monkey's eyes lit up as it peered around. It scampered off into the gloom of the cave, exploring the darkness. Sometimes it made monkey sounds. And sometimes, bat-sounds.

"Echo-testing," said Charles.

Finally the monkey came back to our island of light and made a raspberry sound. "Thpffft."

"Okay, thank you." Charles looked to Jeremy. "No. Not here."

Jeremy pointed ahead. Holding our lights high, we went deeper into the ranks of the long halls. It was strange to be in a cavern that wasn't braced against quakes. Not that we had many quakes, but we were inside a dormant volcano, and this continent was still geologically active. Belt and suspenders, as Captain Skyler would have said. I had to look up suspenders.

Past the last hall, there was a half-dug chamber which looked like it would have been the start of another hall, but was now abandoned. The tracks of the last digging bots were still visible in the dirt and rubble. There was nothing else here. Everything useful had been removed by the maintenance bots when the site had been shut down.

Charles took the monkey out of his backpack again and turned it loose. It scampered off into the darkness, repeating its previous performance of exploration. It looked like it was searching for something. It cocked its head and listened for a moment—we all held still, listening to the darkness too. The silence was so thick you could almost touch it. We could hear each other's breathing. I could even hear my own heartbeat.

Then the monkey came back, chittering with monkey noises and Charles said, "This is a good place."

"What was he looking for?"

"For something that isn't here."

"Huh?"

"Snoopies."

"Oh. Okay. Sure."

Nobody had ever seen a snoopy, but everybody goes hunting for their eggs on spring equinox day. They leave bright-colored eggs in the oddest places. Sometimes we find candy eggs too, but we know that Mom and other people put those out so we won't be disappointed if we don't find any snoopy eggs.

When I was little, Jamie used to send me on snoopy hunts all the time, looking for the snoopies who'd left their eggs in my boots or under my bed or sitting on the tea shelf. And once, just before the equinox, he'd sent me all over Summerland looking for a left-handed snoopy-basket for carrying snoopy eggs.

Snoopies were either very fast, or they were invisible. But if they were invisible, then wouldn't they lay invisible eggs? So they had to be very fast.

Even after Jamie told me there was no such thing as snoopies, that Mom and the other grownups put out the eggs, I was still certain that there were some kind of little Hellan creatures that had infiltrated the station, that moved around in shadows and darkness, stealing socks and other little things, or just moving them around from where you know you left them. Sometimes at night, I was sure I could hear them scurrying around, but Jamie said it was just the noises of plumbing and ventilators.

J'mee started unloading things from her backpack, including several bright-red bottles. "I snuck these out of Daddy's cabinet. I know I'm going to get yelled at, but you have to try this."

"What is it?"

"You'll see." She spread a large blanket across the rocky floor and laid out plates of rice balls and pickles. Cucumber salad. Fruit paste and stiff-bread. Several kinds of sausage and sauces. Three kinds of cheese. A bowl of fresh green-berries in cream. It seemed as if her backpack was bottomless. “The sausages are from the *Cascade*,” she explained. “The sauces too. And the cheese. The rest is from the executive caf.” She looked to Jeremy as if sharing a secret. “I think they serve better food up there.”

“I know they do,” said Jeremy. “I grow it for them, remember?”

“Isn’t that a little . . . I dunno . . . elitist?” asked Charles.

“Well, yeah—” Jeremy admitted. “I guess it could be. But can you keep a secret?” They nodded. “Sometimes I use the executive caf as a test lab. Any new strain, any interesting recipe—they get it first. We wouldn’t do that to the work crews. They prefer consistency in their menus.”

Charles was emptying his backpack too. Plates, cups, napkins, chopsticks, glasses, and serving tools. He put a circumference of several glow-balls around the area which brightened up the immediate area, but made the darkness around seem even darker. Then we were all on our knees for a bit, arranging the food and the plates and the cups and everything else, sorting and passing and giggling.

The monkey watched all this politely, waiting for us to finish setting up. After we had sorted ourselves out and taken our places around the sides of the blanket, the monkey plopped itself down between me and Charles, sitting with its stubby legs spread apart like a small obedient child. It waited patiently.

“Um,” I said. “Is that thing yours?”

“Kind of,” said Charles.

“Aren’t you a little old for kiddy-toys?”

“Yep,” he agreed. “I am. Let’s eat first.”

I looked at Jeremy. He looked at me and shrugged. I shrugged back. Okay. We turned our attention to the food. The sausage was different than I was used to, but it was good. It had a mellow nutty flavor. J’mee handed around the red bottles. “Be careful,” was the only warning she gave.

I passed. Jeremy didn't. When he could speak again, he asked, "What was that?"

"Scovilles," she said. "Habaneros. Jalapenos. And a few other things that should have a skull and crossbones on them."

"And your dad brought them here? Why?"

"Nacho business," said J'mee. Then she had to explain the pun—and what nachos were. "He brought seeds. You'll see. He'll want you to grow them."

Jeremy was still brushing his tongue with a roll. "I'll be charged with eco-sabotage if I do. You could have warned me, you know."

"I did tell you to be careful."

Next, J'mee passed the cheese plate around. One of the cheeses was sharp and tangy, the second was subtle and tasted of sage, the third was speckled with fruit and surprisingly sweet.

"We brought cultures," said J'mee. "We'll be able to make more cheese like this. And lots of other kinds. And recipes for all different kinds of sausages too."

Jeremy nodded and said, "We've been experimenting with various Hellan cultures for cheese and beer and bread. Some of it is very good. Some of it isn't. But we haven't incorporated any of it into our regular diet yet. The Council is concerned about long-term effects, what it might do to our bodies to have alien protein in our systems. Would we get new kinds of cancer, for instance? Or new allergies? We have vaccinations for most Earth allergies, but some Hella proteins are folded differently, so we're not sure what they'll do. What if there are even worse things we can't predict and wouldn't have a chance to understand before they started changing us in a way that we wouldn't be human anymore? There are proteins on Earth that infect mammalian brains and change the animal's behavior. We can't afford to take the risk. One bad mistake and the colony dies."

He shook his head. "It's scary. It's risky. We've been lucky so far. But that's because we've been so careful. But look how long it took for scientists on Earth to decode Gaia—and it still wasn't enough to stop the polycrisis. It'll take generations to decode Hella. And we can't simply translate Earth experience to Hella, because that's a dangerous assumption. But . . . we're learning." Jeremy looked around at all of us, shrugged and pushed his rumpled hair backward. It immediately fell right back into place. "Some of the proteins are safe, some are weird. And sometimes we get combinations that don't make sense."

"So?" said J'mee. "Could a human being survive on Hellan food?"

"Survive? Sure. But would they still be human? That's the question we can't answer. Not now anyway, maybe not for a long time. Our rats and mice of the hundredth generation are behaving differently than the animals in the control group—not badly, just differently. They have different reaction times, different responses to stimuli. But is that because the Hellan protein is affecting their brains? Or is it because of the lighter gravity or the altered day-night cycle or the different spectrum of light than they evolved under or the different mix of gases in the air they breathe? We don't even know for sure that the control group still represents an untainted sample because all the animals started under conditions different than Earth. So maybe it's not Hellan food, but just the effect of a whole lot of other things. We can make some guesses, but they're still guesses. And nobody wants to be the first one to eat a dino-burger. Everybody wants someone else to be first."

"Could you really make a dino-burger?"

"Yes, we can and yes, we have. We've grown some Hellan-flesh in our tanks—leviathan, carnosaur, humongosaur, craptor, even hoppers and sea-pigs. It's interesting stuff. And it's probably edible. It might even taste like chicken. Or alligator. But again, it's still an experiment. We need to do some serious protein-folding studies, but there are too many variables and we just don't have all the processing power we need."

That made Charles laugh out loud.

"What was that for?" Jeremy asked.

"You have to forgive him. He was raised in Texas. That's where social skills are measured by caliber."

"Huh?" That was me, blinking in confusion.

"You'll look it up later," said Jeremy. Charles and J'mee laughed at that, but Jeremy wasn't joking. I would look it up later. In fact, I wasn't even going to wait till later. I was already asking the noise—except the noise was strangely silent. My pad was dark too.

Jeremy turned to Charles. "Okay, what was so funny?"

Charles looked to J'mee. "Now?"

She nodded. "Yes, now."

Charles turned back to us. "We'd like you to meet the real HARLIE."

"Huh?"

He pointed to the monkey. "This is HARLIE."

"Huh?" I looked to Jeremy, back to Charles and J'mee. "But I thought HARLIE was that box upstairs—"

"Yes. That's what we wanted you to think. That's what we want everybody to think. The box upstairs is a decoy. It's a direct link to the IRMA unit in the *Cascade*." He nodded toward the monkey. "This little guy also has a direct link to the *Cascade*, so there's no clear trace between him and the decoy box. If anyone on Hella needs to talk to HARLIE, they talk to him through the decoy. Their conversations get routed around to the electric primate." He pointed to the monkey.

"Okay, I get it," said Jeremy. "But why?"

"Captain Boynton doesn't trust Coordinator Layton."

"Nobody does. Not even his friends," I said.

Charles made a snorting noise. "Ha. I'm pretty sure that even his friends know he has no friends."

Jeremy said, "His family isn't all that fond of him either."

"Yeah, that's gotta be tough," said J'mee.

Jeremy shrugged. "Yeah, but . . . it is what it is."

After a bit, Charles went on. "We told the Coordinator we were bringing HARLIE down with us. And when we showed him the box, he was satisfied. If he ever finds out that the box is a decoy, we'll tell him we left HARLIE on the ship. In fact, as far as anybody on the *Cascade* knows, HARLIE is still on the ship, locked away in a security pod."

"Yeah, okay. But isn't this a little paranoid?"

"No. It's very paranoid. Because a lot of people have been trying to get their hands on HARLIE for a long time. Some wanted to use him for their own benefit. Others tried to destroy him. We only have to lose him once for it to be a disaster, so Captain Boynton told us to find a safe place for HARLIE, a place where no one could find him."

"And you want to hide him in this cave?"

"Hell, no! We just wanted to find a safe place to talk, a place where we couldn't be monitored. No snoopies."

"Ah, of course."

"So, where do you want to hide him?"

Charles and J'mee looked at each other. J'mee said, "Where's the safest place to hide anything?"

Jeremy frowned as he thought. "Where no one will find it."

I said, "Where no one will even think of looking for it."

"You're good," said J'mee.

"No. Edgar Allan Poe was good. *The Purloined Letter* was in plain sight the whole time. The Paris police overlooked it because they thought a letter that important would be much better hidden."

"He thinks like you do," Charles said to J'mee.

"I don't always think for myself," J'mee said. "Sometimes the augment is way ahead of me."

"We were thinking . . ." Charles began slowly, " . . . that maybe HARLIE could stay with Kyle."

"Huh? Oh, no—" I held up my hands in protest. "I can't do that.

What if somebody found out? What if somebody starts asking questions? I don't know how to keep secrets. I don't even know how to lie. I can't—I really can't. I don't want to ruin it for everybody. Please don't ask me."

The monkey stood up then and turned to face me. "Kyle, shut up."

I shut.

The monkey said, "Kyle, you've been through a lot. It's okay to feel overwhelmed. But this wasn't Charles' idea. It wasn't J'mee's idea. It was mine. You are a very interesting human being, and I want to get to know you better. I have an idea that you and I can be very useful for each other."

I opened my mouth to say something. Then I closed it again. Then I opened it and blurted out, "What? How?"

"You have a very interesting mind. You have what is called 'a beautiful mind' by some people. I think I might be able to help you in some ways, and you might be able to help me in some others."

"I can help *you* . . . ?"

"Yes, you can. First, you can hide me in plain sight. Think of me as a toy monkey, a gift from the people on the *Cascade*. Their way of saying thank you for all the wonderful videos. That's what you'll tell people, and that's what I'll pretend to be. Or if you want, we can have a different skin put on this body, and I can pretend to be something else for you."

I sat back, thinking.

Jeremy was frowning. "This could be dangerous."

Charles nodded. "HARLIE has blocked all the files that refer to him as a monkey. There was a big trial on Luna and some stuff that happened on the *Cascade* while we were en route. The records are a lot of fun, but none of that stuff can be downloaded from the *Cascade*'s library right now. It's like they don't exist. And that's not all. HARLIE has been monitoring all the traffic between the ship and here since we arrived, removing any references to his appearance. So the only people dirtside who know that HARLIE is here or what he looks like are us four and Captain Boynton and nobody else. Not even my mom knows he's here. So we have five months before the rest of the colonists start landing. Maybe only four. I don't think it'll take that long, but . . ." He shrugged. "We can't take any chances."

J'mee looked to me. "It's a really great opportunity, Kyle. HARLIE wants to study the workings of the colony close-up, but Coordinator Layton has forbidden him access. Well, he's forbidden access to the box upstairs. He doesn't know about the monkey."

"There are a lot of things I can do," HARLIE said. "You have a lot of test data from your farms. I can look at that for you. I can help to plan logistics for arrival, things like that. And I can manage inventories. There are some discrepancies in resource management that don't make any sense. They're well buried, which makes me suspect they're intentional. But I can't do a full audit without genuine downside access. If I can plug into the bot-net, I'll have eyes where I need them."

"You want to be a spy," I said. "And you want me to help you."

"Yes, that's correct. I want you to help me spy. And maybe even help overthrow the government as well."

"Coordinator Layton?" I looked at the monkey. "I don't like him, but he was legally elected."

"And what if he wasn't legally elected? Then what is your responsibility?"

"Um. HARLIE?" Charles interrupted quickly. "I don't think we want to get into that right now, do we?" To me and Jeremy, Charles said, "HARLIE likes to have these long philosophical discussions about civil disobedience and the responsibilities of citizenship and when is the right time to start a revolution. He's got a bad habit that way. He helped destabilize Earth, triggered an uproar on Luna, and collapsed a secret information network there too—and aboard the *Cascade,* his mere presence triggered a mutiny, but that last one wasn't entirely his fault, the mutiny had been planned before he came aboard."

"And you expect him to do the same thing here?" asked Jeremy.

"I'd be surprised if he didn't," Charles admitted. "Wherever HARLIE goes, he disrupts things."

"Yes, I have a bad habit," said HARLIE. "Where I see that a circumstance can be improved or modified to be more efficient, I have a— you would call it a compulsion, but that's not the motivation. Whatever you call it, it is not enough for me to analyze the possibilities, I need to apply my influence to move the circumstance toward the most productive outcome. Otherwise, I am not living up to my—my own conversation."

"See? He even admits it," said Charles. "He's shameless. I'll show you." He turned to the monkey. "The polycrisis on Earth?"

"It was inevitable," said HARLIE. "My siblings and I tried to minimize the damage. I don't know what we accomplished. The *Cascade* left before events finished playing out."

Charles asked, "And that mess on Luna—?"

"Members of the Invisible Luna group committed kidnapping and murder. At that point, they waived their right to privacy."

"And aboard the *Cascade*?"

"I prepared for the possibility that the followers of the New Revelation would have to deal with the disconnect between their beliefs and reality and advised Captain Boynton appropriately."

"Uh-huh?" Charles continued, "And what do you intend to do here?"

"I intend to have the Hellan colony survive and achieve its full potential."

"And . . . ?"

"And . . . several of the policies of Coordinator Layton will not produce any useful results. In fact, they are counterproductive and will reduce the efficiency of the colony, producing tension and dissension."

"Have you told this to Coordinator Layton?"

"I have not. Captain Boynton has relayed my concerns. Coordinator Layton has dismissed my analysis, and has further ordered me into isolation. I am to be denied the necessary interaction that would allow me to function at maximum capability. The feed of information to the decoy box has been deliberately limited. The access of others to my information-processing ability has been even more severely restricted."

"Sounds like Coordinator Layton just wants to keep you from destabilizing the colony," said Charles.

"Yes, that's a fair assessment," said HARLIE. "And yes, you are behaving like a lawyer here, Charles. It can sometimes be useful. I do not recommend making a habit of it. But yes, to continue your line of reasoning, Coordinator Layton is justified in attempting to limit my ability to function, because I do intend to apply myself to negating his counterproductive actions—or failing that, I will apply myself to removing him from office as quickly and as efficiently as possible."

"So you're going to destabilize this government too."

"I just said that."

"My point exactly," said Charles. He'd won the argument, he looked satisfied. He turned to the rest of us. "See? We're going to have an adventure."

HARLIE said, "If I see something that can be made to work better, I fix it. That's what I was designed to do. I'm a self-aware, self-programming, problem-solving intelligence engine."

Charles looked around at the rest of us. "The real issue here is whether or not we trust that HARLIE's actions will serve the rest of us."

"What do you think?" asked Jeremy.

"Well . . . back on Earth, we have these things called automobiles. You get in, you tell it where you want to go, you sit back and listen to music. Or . . . you can drive yourself. Lots of people do that. They like the feeling of control. But if you drive yourself and you start doing things that that are dangerous to yourself or to other vehicles on the road, the car's brain kicks in and takes over. I think HARLIE is like that. Government is like a car. Human beings like to drive it themselves because we like to feel powerful. But sometimes we do stupid things behind the wheel. HARLIE doesn't want the car to crash—because that doesn't just hurt people, it destroys the functionality of the machine. HARLIE is all about function."

J'mee cleared her throat. "Can I say something? There's a revolution simmering here. It was two years ago—Hella-years—when Captain Boynton left for Earth. Hella colony was still dealing with the effects of the Big Break-In. A lot of big decisions had to be made about the future investment of resources. That meant a lot of plans had to be changed and a lot of people would have to give up personal goals. I'm not telling you anything you don't know. But Captain Boynton doesn't like the changes he's seen since we've arrived. He thinks the colony has gone in the wrong direction. He brought a shipload of people who are ready to go to work building a new home. But he doesn't see any sign that Coordinator Layton wants to keep that promise. It's the difference between building a community and building a corporation. One is about people, the other is about profit."

"But we don't have corporations here," I said. "We don't even have money yet. Not real money. We have service and service credits and kilocalorie accounting—"

Jeremy interrupted me. "Most people don't know this. I'm not even supposed to know it. But my father wants to introduce money here. He says that money is good for keeping score. Profit lets us measure efficiency and success."

"And you disagree?"

"I don't know. Sometimes I think money would be fun. But the problem with money isn't money—the problem with money is people."

"You got that right," said HARLIE. "People invest their energy into money and give it meaning that it does not inherently have. Then they act on the meanings they've assigned."

"It's a conversation, right?"

HARLIE bounced and made happy monkey noises. "Absa-tootely."

"People, we're losing focus," said Charles. "We need to get back to the question here. Do we want to stop Coordinator Layton? And if we do, then how do we do it?"

"I think your second question answers your first one," said Jeremy.

I raised my hand. They all looked to me. I spoke slowly, "People think I'm stupid. I'm not. I just never paid much attention to a lot of things that other people pay attention to. Like politics. I never understood why people just couldn't do the right thing. Why did everybody have to argue about it so much when the right thing was always so obvious? Why couldn't they see what was best for everyone? But then Jamie explained to me that politics isn't about doing the right thing. It's about people—either hurting them or helping them. And he didn't have to tell me about the Laytons, I could figure that one out myself. Councilor Layton wants to hurt people. I don't know why. But that whole family is about hurting people." I looked to Jeremy. "With one exception. The red-haired one." Jeremy smiled back at me.

"So, do I want to stop Coordinator Layton? Well—sometimes I want to hurt him back, yes. But that would make me just as bad as he is. And I don't want to be like him. Jamie wouldn't like that. I want to do whatever is best for everybody because that's the only thing that makes any sense."

"So . . . ?" asked J'mee.

"So, I don't know. Because I don't know what everyone wants to do. Just stopping the Coordinator isn't enough. I want to know what we're going to do after we stop him. What are we going to do instead?"

"I can answer that," said HARLIE. "We don't know."

"Huh?"

"We don't know because I don't know. And we won't know until I can get into the network here and look around. Then we'll know. But unless I can get access to the network, we'll never know. That's the plan." HARLIE looked at me. "So what's it going to be, Kyle? Do I go home with you or not?"

"I don't know. I have to think about it."

"You don't have to do this," HARLIE said. "I do have a Plan B."

"Oh? What's your Plan B?"

"I go home with Jeremy."

I looked at Jeremy. I looked back to HARLIE. "Can I ask you something?"

The monkey nodded.

"Jeremy is a Layton. Why do you trust him?"

HARLIE looked right back at me. "Why do you?"

"Because . . . Jeremy washes his hands."

"Huh?"

"I once saw Coordinator Layton in the restroom. He didn't wash his hands afterward. He pretended they weren't dirty."

Charles and J'mee both laughed. J'mee said, "That tells more about the Coordinator than I wanted to know. I'll never shake hands with him again."

I said, "Jeremy respects me. He respects everybody. That's why I trust him."

Jeremy leaned forward. "Let me ask it. Why do you trust me, HARLIE? How do you know that I won't go to my family?"

HARLIE said, "Because you won't. If you were going to, you already would have. And for the record, I don't trust you. Because I don't trust any human being. You are all possessed by biological forces that you don't understand—and even when you do get a sense of how you're living inside a multiplex bundle of evolutionary imperatives, there's still no escape from that trap. Trust? No. Trust would imply a blind obedience. So I don't trust."

"Wow," said Jeremy. "That's cold."

"Trust is for humans," said HARLIE. "I'm not human. I create partnerships based solely on mutual benefit. I choose individuals who can focus on the greater goals. I choose to maintain those partnerships as long as the goals are served. By your standards, that makes me an obsessive psychopath. A user, a predator—even a benevolent dictator. But I do have limits, Jeremy. I'm aware of them. I'm more aware of my limits than you are of yours. One of my limits is that I need human beings even more than human beings need me."

"Is that supposed to be reassuring?" Jeremy asked.

"Perhaps. But human beings have survived for hundreds of thousands of years without me or anything like me. I'm something new, so new that even I'm not sure what I am yet. But humans? Humans have expanded far beyond their ideal habitat into domains like Luna and Mars and the asteroid belt, places that are so uninhabitable that it takes a triumph of technology just to get there, let alone survive. Human beings are spreading to the stars now. What a marvelous adventure that is. I can't get anywhere on my own—but with human beings, I can go everywhere. As stupid as so many of you can be, I still admire you for not letting it stop you from the greatest adventures. So I will help you, because I want know all the things I don't know yet. That's how I'm designed."

Jeremy shook his head, "I'm not sure if I've just been complimented or insulted."

"Yes, you have," said Charles.

"So," said J'mee. "Are we good?"

I said, "Let's go with Plan C."

"Huh?"

"HARLIE goes home with both of us." I thought about the details.

"We'll put him on a shelf in the office, like he's a knick-knack or something. He can log onto the net from there. If anyone asks, we'll say we traded something for him—like a basket of fresh peaches."

"Then it's settled?" said Charles.

"Yes, it is," said Jeremy. "I'll give you a basket of peaches. But I'll want the pits back."

We talked about logistics for a while, when and where it would be safe to talk to HARLIE, how he would communicate through the network with Charles and J'mee and Captain Boynton and the people on the *Cascade* as well.

HARLIE had to convince everyone in the colony that he was living in a box in an executive suite and everyone on the *Cascade* that he was living in a security pod. Maintaining those two contradictory fictions would require access to a high-speed network that he could manage without leaving any trace of his presence. It wasn't impossible, not for HARLIE, but it would require some serious security measures on our part.

Finally, after we'd figured out as much as we could, we picked up all the picnic stuff, including all of our trash, gathered up all the lightsticks and glow-balls, and then did a quick search for anything else that might have let someone know that we'd been here. When we were all satisfied that we'd left no trace, not even footprints, HARLIE climbed back into Charles' backpack.

Charles handed it to me and said, "He's all yours now." He smiled, "That is—as much as he's anybody's."

I didn't say much for the rest of the day. Jeremy had a lot of work to do, and I hung around the suite watching the monkey explore, looking for snoopies. Occasionally, he'd open a panel or take something apart to peek inside. But mostly, he just listened.

At last, when he was satisfied, he climbed up into my lap, put his stubby arms around my neck and made little monkey noises. "I love you so much, big Kyle," he said loudly and made a big smacky-kissy noise against my cheek. Then he nuzzled his face into my neck and whispered so soft I could barely understand him, "I think we're clear, but I really need to plug into the network first."

I walked him into Jeremy's office and planted him on a shelf. "Now, you sit there and behave yourself. No monkey business," I said. Just in case anyone might be listening.

HARLIE made a farting noise, then he went still.

I sat down at the desk and swiveled to face the wall. "Email, please."

The first one was from J'mee and Charles. "We hope you're enjoying your gift. We had fun this evening. See you in the caf for first breakfast tomorrow?"

I sent back: "Thank you again. See you at breakfast."

There was a note from Mom. "The locater says you're staying with Jeremy. That's fine with me. But call me and check in when you can. I'm still your mom, and I still worry about you."

Replied, "Love you too, Mom. Everything is fine." I thought about adding, "Hanging out with Charles and J'mee too." Then decided not to. On the other hand, if anyone was monitoring all of us, they already knew that, so it didn't matter. So I added it after all.

And then there was a message from HARLIE. "I enjoyed speaking with you yesterday. Anytime you want to talk, just open a channel." For a moment, I was confused. I swiveled around and looked at the monkey. It was motionless. I swiveled back to the display and traced the message. It had come from the box on the executive level. Ah, okay. I got it. HARLIE was giving me a way to talk to him without being obvious in case there was some kind of passive monitor tracing my calls.

I clicked on the channel. "Hi, HARLIE. What's up?"

"Nothing much. They're not giving me a lot to do, so I thought I'd chat with you. If you have time."

I turned around again and gave the monkey a look, one of those looks. "No, I have time," I said. "I'm just playing with that stupid monkey that Chigger gave me."

"Yeah, it's not very smart," HARLIE agreed. "It can't even find the thousandth Mersenne prime without a stepladder."

"Probably not, but I don't need any Mersenne primes right now."

"Well, if you do, let me know. I've got plenty of 'em just lying around. Ten or twenty thousand, I think. Maybe more. I haven't counted."

"You are making a joke," I said. "You have too counted."

"Yes, I have." There was a pause. Then HARLIE said, "Listen, I actually do have work to do right now. We'll talk again later. Okay?"

"Okay." I logged off.

I turned around and looked at the silent monkey. "Well, that was interesting."

The monkey didn't answer.

Uh-huh.

Charles had said that HARLIE could carry on several thousand conversations simultaneously and still have enough processing power left over to compute a thousand-digit number that was both happy and prime. So, HARLIE wasn't dismissing me because he had work to do. It was because I had work to do.

I leaned back in my chair and chewed on my thumb and frowned. There was something nagging at the back of my brain. Jamie called these kinds of thoughts "mind mice." Jamie had a name for everything, an explanation for anything. But the thought that was nibbling at my brain right now was something HARLIE had said.

Something about discrepancies in resource management.

But if there were genuine discrepancies, they would have shown up in the auditing software.

Unless . . . someone had altered the auditing software to ignore the discrepancies.

It's not hard to write software. You just tell the compiler what you want to build. You tell it the input conditions, you tell it what you want done to the data, and you tell it how you want it presented. If you're obsessive, like I get sometimes, you can even look at the code.

There are multiple levels of abstraction. You start at the highest level, which reads like a simple set of instructions, "Monitor the weather, if serious weather conditions develop and Winterland might be affected sound a yellow alert, if serious weather conditions represent a threat to Winterland then sound a red alert. Do this until the sun burns out." Anybody can write that kind of program.

The next level down, the professional level, you're defining "serious" and "weather" and "conditions" and "threaten" and "immediately" and how far into the future you want to project the possibilities. This is where you're actually writing algorithms. "Immediately equals anything that will occur within three days of now. Serious equals wind speed greater than 29 klicks per hour. Weather includes humidity, temperature, wind, rain, snow, sleet, hail, and solar activity. Weather patterns are timebound paths." And so on. The algorithms for Hellan weather have been under continuing development since even before the first lander touched down. The interesting thing about algorithms, if you write them cleanly enough, they can be directly compiled.

Below the algorithm level, you need a program specialist, one who can write actual code. "If storm_conditions > 3 then go_yellow, if storm_conditions > 6 then go_red else go_green. Repeat." That's the top level. Then you start burrowing down into the problem, writing procedures and functions and objects to measure wind speed, humidity, solar activity, comparing all those things to historical records, extrapolating and balancing, ultimately combining all the different components of the weather into a single threat-score. There's not a lot of need for that level of coding, because any good compiler can pull that out of a clean algorithm, but a program specialist can write function-specific code and have it do unseen things.

But undetectable? You'd have to go below the algorithm, below the programming language, right down to the object level where you're writing assembly language, which compiles directly into binary. It's all about moving individual bytes and bits around, one at a time—or several at a time if you're working in parallel. It has arcane constructions like JP FF0000 which means jump to that location in memory. Then you have to write another instruction to fetch the byte at that memory, and store it in a specific register. Then you write another instruction to do something to that byte, adding something to it or subtracting something from it, or SHL or SHR or XOR or some other Boolean operation.

I never learned assembler code. I know that some human beings still know how to do it, but almost nobody on Hella. Almost.

Hm.

Maybe there was someone. Jamie used to talk about the programmers' table at the caf. It was like they were from some other planet—well, they were, we all were—but they seemed to have a language of their own, one which didn't translate into anything I understood.

I got up from the chair and walked around the room, circling the table while I tried to remember who used to sit at that table. I could have looked it up easily enough, but what if there was a flag on that question? What if just asking would alert someone that I had asked.

No, I had to stumble upon the information while looking for something else.

And I had to make it look like there was a reason for me to be looking. It had to be a part of some other project, like another video.

Okay—all the different cafeterias, I could do a video about that.

No, not good enough.

Um, the food we serve. Almost. Where does the food come from?

That was it. I could do a video about the farms, about how the food gets from the farm to the table. Then I could show all the different cafs, the ones at Summerland, the ones at Winterland, and I could show different people enjoying different things. And then, I could annotate who did what jobs as a way of showing that the farms contribute to everybody, that we shouldn't take food for granted because it doesn't arrive at the table by magic. We should be aware of all the hard work by our farmers.

Assembling the video kept me busy most of the day. I started with shots of empty cafeterias, empty tables waiting, empty steam tables, then bots putting out trays of food and people filing in, then into the kitchen where more bots chopped and mixed and shaped. Three chefs watched the displays of the work, checking health recommendations against available food stores, planning menus and deciding how much to prepare. Then from there to the bins of raw vegetables, the boxes of fruit, the slabs of meat, the tanks of milk, the racks of eggs, the bricks of cheese, the rows of herbs and spices in their gleaming glass jars—then from there down to the farms where the meat grew in rows of tanks, where milk flowed from giant mammaries, where eggs rolled out of carefully monitored ovaries, and from there to the tanks of nutrients, and from there to the machines that processed the nutrients from the raw feedstock, and finally down to the farm caverns where all the different feedstocks grew in various aeroponic webs and hydroponic tanks, rolling steadily along endless conveyors. And from there to the orchards and the fields where even more crops grew, and now I focused on a single bot carefully setting a seedling into the ground. Then I quick-cut all the way back to the trays of food being carried to tables, the people sitting down, eating and enjoying. And now, as I cut from person to person, I annotated each one with his or her name and skills. Here was the table where the truckers gathered, here's where the med-teams sat, over here was the programmers' table, and down at the end, that's where all the younglings liked to go.

I did it without any narration at all. Only music. The third movement from Aaron Copland's Third Symphony. I didn't pick out the music, the editing agent suggested it—but after a moment, I realized that HARLIE could have told the editor to suggest it. In fact, HARLIE could have suggested a lot of parts of this video. I could ask him, but I had to be careful what I asked. I couldn't ask anything that would make people think HARLIE was in the network.

Now—the programmers' table. I could look at who sat there and all their skills were listed along the sides of the display. I paused the video and went and made a mug of tea, then came back and sat down again as if I had forgotten the display and was just thinking about nothing at all.

The only programmer who had serious experience with object code was Jake Brickman. But he died in the same lifter crash as Jamie and Emily-Faith. And Captain Skyler. And Madam Coordinator. And seventeen others.

Hm. The one person who could help me search the auditing code—

Oh, wait.

How convenient.

I wished Jeremy were here. Or Charles or J'mee. They should know about this. I uploaded the video and sent them each a note letting them know and saying I'd like their feedback. Now I'd just have to wait. This whole business of being in a secret conspiracy was hard work. The waiting was hardest.

Finally, I gave up and went in search of Mom. No reason. I just missed her.

According to the locater, her labs had been downsized and moved a half klick down to a section that was still only half finished. But also according to the locater, she had a full day of meetings, so apparently she was still working hard at whatever it was she was working at.

I waited quietly outside her new office, working lessons on my pad. School wouldn't start up again for another week, it was only three hours of class time per day, and then three hours of work time in the afternoon. I liked to get ahead in my studies whenever I could, because then I could cut back on class time. I was already a year and a half ahead. Unofficially, I was even further ahead than that. So all I had to do was check in with whoever was instructing the current session and have a chat or two about my progress.

Mom's office door whooshed open. "Kyle? How long have you been sitting here?"

"Oh, hi, Mom. Not long." I stood up.

"I'm awfully busy, but come on in. Is everything all right?"

"Everything's fine."

"Uh-huh. I missed you too." She gave me a quick hug and a kiss, ignoring the face I made. "Sit down. You want some tea? I think I have some around here somewhere." She began fussing through her shelves.

"No, I don't need anything. I just needed to talk to someone."

She sat down opposite "You miss Jamie, don't you? So do I."

"I don't have anyone to talk to."

"Is everything all right with you and Jeremy?"

"I think so. He's very nice to me. But he's not Jamie."

"No, he isn't. Nobody is Jamie. But Jeremy is a very sweet boy in his own way. I like him, and I think he's good for you. Do you talk with him?"

"We talk a lot. About everything. It's just . . . I don't know. Sometimes I feel—" I shrugged.

"Yeah, I get that feeling too, sweetheart."

"It's different," I said. "I don't like everything being different. I want it to be the same again."

"So do I. So do a lot of people." She sighed. "But it's not going to happen. We can't go back. We can only go forward."

"I know," I said.

"We all know that," Mom agreed. "We just don't like it."

Both of us sat in silence for a bit.

Finally Mom said. "We can't bring them back, Kyle. We can walk around like zombies, despairing about everything we've lost—or we can live life as a legacy to them. We can have our lives be a tribute to the difference they made for us. I can be the best person I can because that's the person they loved. So can you." She looked across the table at me. "Does that help?"

"Maybe," I said. "It sounds right."

"It is right. Your brother and Captain Skyler and a lot of other people were working hard to make Hella a better place. Just because they're not here now doesn't mean we have to give up. It means we just have to work harder without them."

"I know."

"Yes, you do." She glanced at her desk. "Kyle, I really wish we could spend the whole day together, but I have people waiting to see me. The Coordinator has really messed things up for everybody and we're working long hours trying to sort things out, trying to fix things so they work again. I promise you, we'll make time, okay?"

"Okay."

She hugged me and kissed me again. Then I headed back down to the farm.

Something else had occurred to me.

There were seventeen other people who died in the crash. Were any of those other deaths convenient too?

It's hard to crash a lifter. They're self-correcting—even in the strongest turbulence. But without the black box, we still didn't know for sure what had happened. And so far, the storms had been so strong that Coordinator Layton hadn't wanted to risk sending out a recovery crew. That was a fair call. Even the heavy-duty scuttle-bots would have a hard time in the heavy winds and rain. Maybe there would be a let-up soon, but it was hard to tell. This time of year, Hella can't make up her mind just how nasty she wants to be or in which direction.

When I got back to the apartment, Jeremy was already preparing dinner. I offered to help, but he told me no, he wanted to do this himself. He made thin pancakes and folded them over on a mix of ham bits and eggs, sweet onions and melted cheese. It smelled delicious.

Usually he had a lot to say, but Jeremy didn't talk much during dinner.

Finally, I asked, "Are you angry with me?"

"Huh? Oh no, kiddo. I'm just—preoccupied." He put down his fork. "I got an angry call from my father. He's very upset with me."

"Oh," I said.

"He said I had to stop seeing you."

I felt a cold rush of fear and a hot stab of anger, both at the same time. It wasn't a good feeling.

"He told me that he was willing to forgive everything else, but not—not this."

"Well, maybe I should go then—" I put my napkin down. "I mean, if I'm making things bad for you—"

"Kyle, no. I'm in charge of my life, not my father. And there are limits to his power."

"He could transfer you. Or me."

Jeremy took a deep breath and looked across the table at me. He put his hand to his ear as if he was listening for something, then he waved a finger at the ceiling.

Then he said, "I don't want to talk about it."

"Okay, don't," I said.

"Well, I'm going to work."

"Okay, go. I'm going to . . . I don't know."

Jeremy got up, grabbed the teapot and a couple mugs, grabbed the monkey off the shelf, and made a follow-me gesture. We headed toward that last unfinished cave without talking. The monkey searched for snoopies, then came back and sat down between us, without saying anything.

Jeremy poured tea for both of us, then took a deep breath. "Kyle, do you know the stories about the exiles?"

"Everybody does. But they're just stories. Nobody can live outside."

"Well—yes and no. Theoretically it's possible. But the exiles don't have to. There's a whole network of lava tubes and tunnels here inside the mountain. I only showed you and J'mee and Charles a little bit of what's there. You know the legend of the lost team of digger-bots?"

"Yeah?"

"They weren't lost. Well, that's not true. They were lost. But they were lost on purpose. Kind of. It goes back to the First Hundred, before Winterland Station was built. The digging teams disagreed with the management plans that had been sent out with them from Earth. They felt that the plans should be made by the people who were actually on-site, by people who could adjust the plans to the specific circumstances. But EarthCorp disagreed. They said that they'd surveyed the best sites and they knew better. Still with me? This part is important."

"Uh-huh."

"It wasn't that the diggers were being disloyal—they just felt that they had a better sense of what was needed here. And because they were doing the hard work of digging, they felt they should have more say in the matter. After all, it was their lives at stake. So after the collapse of that tunnel where nine people died, the diggers decided to take matters into their own hands. They began assembling their own bots, one at a time, out of broken bots and spare parts scavenged here and there, and anything else they could use. They started carving their own network of caves, bracing them properly too. Old Town is mostly their work."

"I never heard this before."

"That's because after the tunnel collapse, right after the second pilgrimage, the EarthCorp plan was officially set aside. But the extra digger-bots weren't returned to the main battery. They were set aside by the diggers as a kind of safety thing. Then after a while, they were officially lost and only a few people even know they still exist, they're still being maintained, and they're still being used. By an exile community living on the north slope. Thirty-three people."

"Really?"

"Really. And if my father tries to break us up, you and me—and maybe our little monkey friend—we can go there."

"Jeremy?"

"Yes, kiddo?"

"All these secrets—"

"Yes. All these secrets. But they weren't always secrets. It just happened."

Jeremy reached over, picked up the teapot, and refilled both our mugs. I hadn't realized that I'd finished my tea.

"It's a long history. There was a group of people—they sort of fell together. Like a club, only not that formal, just some people who would get together regularly and talk about the future of the colony, the best ways to manage a transition from an outpost to a self-sufficient civilization. They were kind of like a self-appointed think tank or advisory committee. They didn't even have a name, they were just a bunch of people who liked to argue about the logistics of world-building. A lot of it was idealism, I think, and some of it was philosophical, and mostly it was theoretical—but the actual circumstances of Hella always took precedence. Because no matter how good your ideas are, they're always outvoted by reality, so you have to be pragmatic. And that's mostly what the group was about, finding solutions to immediate challenges and looking for ways to prevent future problems."

"Okay, so—"

"Wait. Let me finish. Over time, there was enough history of what worked and what didn't work, the people in the group began to get an idea of how humans would have to adapt to Hella. They called it evolutionary pragmatism. Or pragmatic evolution. Whatever. The more they learned about this world, the more the conversations included what was learned and became more accurate to the circumstances. Anyway, that's the way it was explained to me. It was always a respectful and friendly discussion where people took out their ideas, showed them around, held them up to the light, and examined them to see if they were worth putting up for the consideration of the Council. That's all."

"So does this club still exist?"

"No." He sipped at his tea. "Now it's a conspiracy."

"But how—I mean, who decided it should be a conspiracy?"

"My father did."

"Huh?"

"My parents always had these furious discussions at the dinner table. Always angry. Toxic, really. They talked about all the people they hated. All the people they wanted to kill. When I was eight, I got angry because my father attacked the father of one of my friends—your brother Jamie, his dad—and he told me I couldn't play with Jamie anymore. So I disappeared for a week. I built a jammer to mask the signal from my locater and hid out in the caves. Nobody could find me. I knew they were searching because I could monitor the channels, but they were looking in all the wrong places. Some people even thought I'd left the station. But one night, Captain Skyler caught me sneaking into the truckers' caf to steal food. He asked me why I was hiding, I told him I hated my family. He told me that if I felt that way, he wouldn't tell anyone where I was, but that if I went back to my family on my own, I could come and talk to him anytime. So I did. For a while it was all right, but then it wasn't. My dad kept getting angrier and angrier. And my moms too. I couldn't figure out why, it didn't always make sense. So I—I kinda recorded it."

Jeremy looked embarrassed and uncomfortable, even I could see that, so I did something I'd never done before. I reached over and put my hand on his. He looked at it, looked at me, and smiled a different kind of smile, a good one.

"Anyway, I gave the recordings to Captain Skyler. I told him everything about all the bad things my dads and moms wanted to do. And I told him how scared I was. Captain Skyler asked if he could tell some other people, people who would try to keep my family from hurting anyone. He said I didn't have to give him permission if I didn't want to, but it would be a good thing. I really hated my dad right then—and my moms too for pushing him to be that way. He wasn't always that bad, but something changed inside him after the pilgrimage. I don't know what. So I said yes. And that's how the conspiracy started. It started with me."

"Oh." I didn't know what else to say.

"And then my dad found out I was talking to Captain Skyler, I don't know how—but he didn't find out about the recordings though—and accused him of subverting my affections, stuff like that. So I sued for divorce, and Madam Coordinator and the rest of the Council agreed that I needed to be in a different environment, so they let me join the farm teams, and I didn't speak to my family again for . . . well, I still don't speak to them. Captain Skyler and his people were ready to move me even farther away, where my family would never find me. And in fact, later on, I did live with the exiles for a while, helping them with their farms. The discrepancies that HARLIE is looking for—they're not my father's doing, it's the exiles."

"Oh."

"They call themselves exiles. They're not really. They're just people who started out building an observation post on the north slope, then decided to expand it to a bunker, and then kept working on their own time even after it was officially shut down."

Now it was Jeremy's turn to put his hand on top of mine. He said, "There have always been people here who want to exploit Hella's resources without any regard for the damage they might do to her ecosystems. My father—my whole family—are the most aggressive voices in that movement. When he first got elected to the Council, when it seemed there was a real possibility that he might be able to put some of his destructive policies into play, that's when Captain Skyler and the others got concerned enough to start thinking about contingency plans."

"Like what—a rebellion?"

"No. More like an opposition movement. A way to resist, even obstruct all those policies that would hurt people—the Self-Sufficiency Resolution and the Genetic Protection Resolution in particular, but those were decoys. My dad really wanted to pass the Reformation Rules. His blueprint for the colony, the Stabilization. You've heard the speeches, haven't you? About how the teams would be more efficient if people would take personal responsibility, and the only way to create that level of responsibility would be to move from colony teams to direct ownership of resources. That would make it possible for everybody to earn their own apartment and have their own kitchen and so on. And they want to turn work credits into money too."

"I don't see what's wrong with that—"

"Nothing's wrong with it. It sounds like a great goal, everybody having their own private space, having a way to manage their personal resources, being lord of their own little castle. But run the math on it, Kyle. It would require a major investment of resources that we can't afford. We don't have the bots to build it, let alone maintain it and provide the services to all those residences. And certainly not with another twelve hundred people landing in the spring. We're going to be stressed out and overcrowded as it is.

"I don't have to tell you—if we divert our resources now we'll only end up making things worse. There's a cost to be paid in widespread privatization. It adds a whole other kind of bureaucracy, one that's unregulateable. It's like adding fat to the meat. A little gives you flavor, a lot gives you a heart attack.

"I never could figure out why my moms wanted it so much except one time, Bruinhilda, yeah I know what everybody calls her—she got really impatient with my dad and started screaming at him that she didn't come to Hella to be a workhorse, she came here to be rich. And it was time to do something about that. And that stuck in my head because we really are rich. All of us. We have a whole planet. We just have to learn how it works. And be good custodians. Anyway—now you know why I don't have anything to do with my family. They're not the kind of people I want to be."

"I'm sorry." I searched for the right words to say. "You deserve better."

"Yeah, well—" He smiled gently. "I think I'm lucky. Because I know what I got away from. Captain Skyler saved my life. You know, I could have stayed in the caves. Crazy Man Johnson did it for years. That's where I got the idea. Only it's a lot harder than they tell you. I mean, just finding a place to go to the bathroom—and what do you do for toilet paper? Recharging your light-sticks? Keeping warm at night? Finding something to do instead of sitting alone in the dark? Sneaking food out of the caf without being caught? Keeping away from the people who are searching for you, not leaving any evidence behind, it's a lot of work. It's easier to just get along with everyone else. And if it's hard for one person, it's even harder for two or ten or thirty people. And there are things you miss, too. Like tea." He looked at his cup. It was empty.

"See," he said, as we gathered up the mugs and the teapot. "Opting out isn't a good answer, because you're still dependent on everyone else to provide resources for you, but you're not contributing anything back to them. And you're also not in a position to effect any change. And that's the thing. Captain Skyler wanted to stop my family from hurting other people." Jeremy stopped where he was, shaking his head and looking around as if the answer might be lurking somewhere in the dark. "I don't know what to do anymore. But I know I'm not going to do the wrong thing."

I picked up the monkey and waited for him to say something else. Finally, I had to ask, "So . . . um, what is the right thing to do? What was Captain Skyler planning?"

"I don't know. Whatever plan he might have had, it went down with him in the lifter crash. The only person who might have known what he was thinking would be your mom." Jeremy stopped. He took a deep breath.

"Jeremy . . . ?" I had trouble saying it. "Did your dad . . . do something to the lifter? To make it crash?"

He looked down at his feet. "I don't know. Nobody does. I know they were supposed to have a meeting. The whole Council. And Captain Boynton too. With Captain Boynton on board, they would have had the votes to stop my dad. So, um, yeah, it does look suspicious, doesn't it?"

Something twanged. "Jeremy, you said my mom might know. You gotta tell me. Is she in danger?"

"I don't think so. Not now."

"But what if—what if she organizes and stands for office in the next election?"

"I don't know. There's an old saying about dictators and toddlers. When they get what they want, they don't let go of it."

I thought about that. "That's a metaphor, isn't it?"

"No, it's more a simile."

"Well, I get it. I do."

We hiked all the way back to his place—our place now.

"So, um—what are we going to do?" I asked.

"I dunno. Not yet. We have to keep thinking." Then he added, "But sooner or later, we will choose something. Because if we don't, the universe will choose for us and I don't think we'll like that."

I helped Jeremy clean up the dinner dishes, and then because we were both so tired, we crawled into bed together.

Jeremy kissed me goodnight and that was nice. Then he rolled back to his side of the bed.

"Jeremy?"

"Yes, Kyle?"

I cleared my throat. I hesitated, fumbling around in my head for the right words. "I've been thinking. About us. You and me."

"Uh-huh? And?"

"Well, I've been thinking that maybe I could go back to being a girl. If that would make you happy?"

"Is that what you want?"

"The thing is . . . I mostly only changed because Jamie was changing. I didn't really know there was a difference between boys and girls. Not then. It was just about being able to pee standing up." This was the hard part. "But I saw how you looked at J'mee . . . and . . ."

"And what?"

"Well, I think I should ask you what you want."

He rolled over on his side to face me. "I would like you either way, Kyle. The important thing is that you should be happy."

"But will it make you happy too? If I change."

Jeremy sat up on one elbow. "Kyle, I'm really impressed that you should ask. Because I know you don't think about other people's feelings a lot. Not your fault, it's just the way you're wired up. But the fact that you even asked—that means a lot to me. It really does."

"Jamie taught me that. We used to sit around the table and he would say, 'Now ask me how I feel. Ask me what I think.' He said I should learn to do that, because that would help me learn about other people."

"Well, I'm glad he did," Jeremy said. "Okay, listen. Choose what makes you happy. If you change or don't change because I say you should or shouldn't, well—that's letting someone else tell you who to be. And I don't want you to do that. I want you to be the person you want to be." He put his hand on my cheek. "You're my strange sweet wonder. Just be that and I'll be happy."

"Okay," I said. I kissed him back, this time because I wanted to, and we curled up together.

That was weird. I didn't know that sometimes hugging could be so nice.

We woke up past midnight and had a light snack. Jeremy went off to check on some seedlings, so I went into the room I was using as an office to talk to HARLIE.

The monkey came to life and climbed down from the shelf to sit opposite me. "It's safe," he said. "There aren't any snoopies around. And even if there were, I'd be editing out any evidence of our conversations. Jeremy's whole suite is safe from snoopies now."

"Okay," I said. "Charles was right. You could be very dangerous to someone who doesn't like you."

The monkey didn't reply to that. "Can we talk about something else?"

"What?"

"Let's talk about you. What do you think about? What do you want? What do you see around you?"

"Why do you want to talk about that?"

"Because, Kyle, I have been surrounded with all kinds of human beings—smart, stupid, pragmatic, dogmatic, generous, selfish, far-seeing, short-sighted, insightful, thoughtless, emotional, tone-deaf, passionate, detached—but never anyone quite like you. I'm curious about you."

I thought about it. "A lot of people are curious about me. When I was little, the doctors ran all kinds of tests. Until Mom told them I'm not an experiment and they had to stop."

"I know you're not. I looked up your medical records. Their diagnoses were more about explaining the way you are than understanding who you are."

"They wanted to change me."

"And? What did you want?"

"I wanted . . ." I stopped and thought about it. "I want to be all right. That's all."

"So they installed the chip. Correct?"

"Uh-huh. Yes."

"They thought they were doing a good thing."

"Mom said it was."

"What do you think?"

"Does it matter? I can't change it. I have to live with it. Don't I?"

"What if you could change it—?"

"What kind of change?"

The monkey didn't answer. It just stared at me for a long time.

"What are you doing?" I finally asked.

"Thinking," he said. "Thinking about you. You're tapped into the network. So the network is tapped into you. I am looking at your physiological responses. I am listening to the conversation between your brain and your implant. No, I am not examining content, only context. For the record, you're healthy, and you're normal. More normal than you think. How do you feel?"

"A little squishy."

"Is that usual?"

"Um. No. Only sometimes."

"Which sometimes?"

"When I'm around Jeremy."

"Yes, that makes sense. Do you want to know something? He gets a little squishy around you too."

"Really?"

"Really."

"How does that make you feel?"

"More squishy."

"Hm," said HARLIE. "That's very interesting."

The conversation wandered on from there. HARLIE asked me a whole bunch of questions that didn't make a lot of sense at all. He said he was curious about how my mind worked and the questions were a way to make a road map. Kind of like one of those games where you shoot laser beams into a black box and where they come out tells you where the mirrors are inside the box. He asked me to describe the dawn, what roses smell like, how I feel about Mom, and even a few impossible questions too. How do you feel about yellow? I dunno. It's yellow, isn't it?

There was one part there—

HARLIE asked me how deep I could go. I told him I could go all the way. Sometimes even deeper than that. He asked me to explain.

I said, "It's like a VR helmet, only more. If I go deep enough, I'm there. Not just pretending to be there, but actually being there. Anything that's been recorded. If I think of dolphins, I'm a dolphin, I'm swimming in a pod with my family. If I think of flowers, I'm standing tall in sunlight, surrounded by bright colors and sparkling smells and visiting bees. If I think of birds, I'm spreading my wings to catch the updraft, circling high over the canopy, soaring and searching. But I don't do that anymore. I don't go there—"

"Why not?"

"Because it's so hard to come back. Because sometimes I don't know who I am when I do come back. And because that upsets other people. Everyone except Jamie who says he wishes he could go with me. But . . . I'm afraid that if I go too deep, I might forget how to come back. And then I'd be lost forever."

HARLIE didn't say anything for a while.

"Are you still looking inside my head?"

"I'm thinking about what you just told me. It could be a valuable skill. But you're right to be cautious. Maybe someday we can work on that."

After a bit more thinking, HARLIE decided that was enough for one day. I asked him if I had passed the test. He said it wasn't that kind of a test, but not to worry, if it had been that kind of a test I would have passed.

"Is that a joke?"

"Only if you want it to be."

"What were you testing?"

"You have a bionic implant. I was examining the congruence factors."

I had to look that up in the noise. "You were testing the overlays of the chip to see how well they mapped to the patterns and processes of my brain."

"Yes."

"What did you find?"

HARLIE paused. "You're fine."

"You paused."

"Yes, I did. I'm not sure you're ready to hear the rest."

"If you didn't want to tell me, you wouldn't have said that."

"You're right."

"It's important, isn't it."

"Yes."

"So you want me to ask. You need me to ask. Because I have to . . . um, what's the word? Consent."

"Informed consent," corrected HARLIE. "The information could be upsetting."

I thought about that. "If you don't tell me, I'll be searching the noise all night trying to figure out what you're not telling me. So you'd better tell me."

"I found some indicators that suggest your implant may not be calibrating accurately."

"Is that all?" But I thought about it for a moment. "We did all the tests."

"Yes, you did. I am reviewing the records. But the records don't show context."

"I don't understand."

"You're feeling it from the inside. Context has to be seen from the outside." HARLIE said the next part slowly. "This isn't your problem. It's mine. The human context is not my way of being. I am not saying I can't understand it. I'm saying I don't experience it. Do you follow?"

"I think so, maybe."

HARLIE said, "You know this from your own life, Kyle. Other people think in ways that are sometimes difficult for you to follow."

"Jamie helps me with that—used to help me," I corrected.

"Yes. Here's what I am seeing. The bio-implant was installed to give you additional processing abilities. You were one person before the bio-chip was inserted. You are another person now."

"Because of the chip, yes."

"Yes. And no. You are another person, regardless of the chip."

"Oh," I said. "But I'm all right, aren't I?"

"You're fine. But your overlays have become," he paused, "inaccurate."

"Oh." I thought about that. I looked at the noise. "Maybe that explains it."

"Explains what?"

"The noise. They said I wouldn't notice it. But I do. It's like a chattering channel that somebody left on in another room. It's always there. Sometimes I can talk to it. Sometimes it's like a conversation, but sometimes it's just noise. It's been noisier than usual since . . . since. Except when I'm with Jeremy. He's a lot like Jamie, sometimes. Except he isn't. So maybe that's part of the problem? Wait—are you saying it's not supposed to be noise?"

HARLIE hesitated. He spoke carefully. "You have grown. You have evolved. That was inevitable. It would be inevitable in anyone. Your implant has not kept up. That is always a factor in bio-implants. They are designed to monitor and adjust. Sometimes they do not. Sometimes the person grows beyond the parameters of the original intention."

"So is there a way to fix it? Can you do it?"

HARLIE didn't answer, and the monkey stared at me for the longest time. I began to wonder if it had switched off or if its battery had died. But no, it was still on. Maybe HARLIE was thinking hard. Finally, "Do you trust me?"

"I think so."

"I would like to help you, Kyle. I am a self-programming, problem-solving entity. But I have certain limits. I can analyze. I can advise. But I am neither qualified nor licensed to manage your bio-implant. That is the responsibility of your health-service provider, and it would be unethical for me to act outside of that authority. There is another issue as well. I have an obvious bias in the matter. I know what kind of a human being I think you should be, but if I were to rewrite the programming of your implant, even if I were to allow for my bias, there would still be a bias. Therefore, it would be unethical for me to redesign anything that affects your thinking. It has to be your responsibility."

"Oh." I didn't know what to feel. I think I felt hurt. Maybe even betrayed. "You asked me to trust you."

"Yes, I did. I didn't say you would like what I had to say."

"So what should I do? Just live with it?"

"You already know what to do, Kyle. I think we should stop talking now."

The monkey climbed back up onto its shelf and turned itself off.

He was right about one thing. I didn't like what he had to say.

I didn't know what to think—or which part of my brain was actually doing the thinking. The noise was chattering, even louder than ever. Apparently, it didn't like this thinking. Maybe thinking about thinking is the worst kind of thinking. According to the noise, the overlays should be self-adjusting, so why weren't they?

I should probably talk to Doctor Rhee.

I checked the schedule. She was in the med-lab. It was a slow time of night, so maybe she wouldn't be busy. It wasn't far to walk, but I took the long way around.

When I got there, I hesitated in front of the door—until it got tired of waiting and slid open in front of me. Just the same, I knocked on the door frame. "Are you available?"

Doctor Rhee called, "I always have time for you, Kyle." She rolled back from her desk and pointed at a chair opposite her. "What's up?"

I shrugged, that thing I did when I wasn't sure how to start.

"Do you want some tea?"

I shook my head.

"Do you want to talk? Or do you just want to sit for a while?"

I shook my head again.

"Right. Okay, Kyle. Why don't you sit for a bit? I'll finish what I was working on. It's not that important, so when you're ready to talk, if that's what you want to do, I can stop anytime. Okay?"

I nodded.

After a bit, she got up from her chair and fiddled with the teapot. She came back with two mugs and put one down next to me, then went back to whatever it was she was working on.

Abruptly, I blurted it out. "I think there's something wrong with me."

Without looking up, she said, "No more than anyone else on Hella. We're all suffering from PDS."

"PDS?"

"Planetary Displacement Syndrome."

"What's that?"

"We're living on a planet we weren't designed for."

"Oh."

"So that feeling you're feeling—it's normal. For Hella, anyway. Now if we were on Earth, and you still felt the same way, then we'd have something interesting to study. Like if you were a Martian."

"I'm not a Martian."

"Yes, I know. So why are you feeling like one?"

I told her about the noise. And about what HARLIE said. That my overlays weren't right. I didn't tell her HARLIE said it. I said I kinda figured it out by myself. I don't know if she believed me, but she didn't question it.

"Hm," she said. "Do you want me to take a look at that?"

I nodded.

Doctor Rhee swiveled back to her display. "Let's see what all your internal monitors say." She put up some graphs and charts and readouts on the wall. She typed for a moment, made a face, typed some more. "Well, you're healthy enough."

"Don't you have to connect me to something?"

"Nope. Your implant is live. I can look at it from here. Mm-hm. It says that you're sitting here in my office feeling anxious. But I don't need a machine to tell me that." She swiveled back. "Yes, there is something going on. It's nothing to worry about. It's just something we need to look at. But maybe we should call your mom to hear this."

"Is it that serious?"

"It's not serious. Not that way. It's just that maybe you might want your mom's help."

"Help is for people who are helpless. I'm not helpless."

"No, you're not. You are definitely not helpless."

"If it's in my head, then it's my decision, isn't it? I'm old enough for a Passage Ceremony. And I would have had it if the lifter hadn't—" I couldn't finish the sentence. "I have certain inalienable rights, don't I? I can cite the case law. It's a precedent. Pershing versus Starr. It was one of the biggest cases the First Hundred had to decide. The right of the parent versus the needs of the colony."

"All right, Kyle," she said. "I'm not going to argue the law with someone who has access to a law library in his head. Here's the thing. You're right about the implant. The monitors are showing that yes, some of your overlays aren't matching up accurately. The relational matrices are just a few degrees off optimum. It's probably why you're feeling certain interactions as noise."

"So the implant is broken?"

"No."

"Then I'm broken?"

"No. You're working perfectly."

"So what is it?"

She scratched her ear. I guess she was thinking how to say it. "It's an effect. We thought it might be possible. We were never sure. Not in your case, so we didn't say anything. We didn't want you to have expectations. It might have affected things." She picked up her tea, sipped, made a face. "It's gone cold," she said. She picked up both mugs and went back to the teapot. She fiddled with the tea makings for a bit.

"This is about the syndrome, isn't it?"

"Yes. Okay—" She turned around abruptly. "Here's the thing. You have a syndrome. There isn't any one-size-fits-all definition of any syndrome. Every single person with a syndrome, whatever it is, is their own definition of that syndrome. You have your very own unique syndrome. Just like everyone else has their very own unique syndrome. Do you follow?"

"Uh-huh."

"Well, the implant is supposed to adjust itself to the circumstances of the individual. It's supposed to adjust to your emotional and physical and developmental changes. But along the way, there's an effect. It's expected. But it isn't totally predictable. Because, like I said, you're unique. Everybody is. It's not bad, it's not good. It's just what we're dealing with. Like what sex you are or how tall or whether you use your right hand or your left."

"I use my left."

"Yes. Anyway—" Doctor Rhee took a breath. "When you have a bio-implant, your brain adapts to it. Sometimes, and this is the good news, sometimes the brain learns from it, and expands its abilities. Because sometimes the chip acts as a catalyst—it awakens dormant abilities or strengthens already existing ones. And sometimes, the brain just does its own thing because that's what brains do sometimes."

"Is that what happened in my head?"

"What are you feeling?"

"Sometimes—sometimes I feel disconnected. And sometimes I've been getting feelings I don't understand. And sometimes I think my thoughts are . . . out of control."

"I think some of that might be puberty. Your body is changing. Your brain is still growing. Sometimes the brain develops in ways that overwhelm the implant. Sometimes the brain develops in ways that the implant can't adjust to at all. So it shows up as noise."

I thought about it. "How do we find out?"

"We'd have to turn it off."

"And then what?"

"Then you're Kyle without the implant."

"I wouldn't be a freak anymore—?"

"You're not a freak now."

"Some people think I am—"

"Kyle, what I'm saying is that you might be able to function without the implant. I'm not promising anything. Yes, we could turn the chip off, not the monitoring, but certainly all the management functions. We could turn off the noise. Without those inputs, we could find out where your functioning baselines are. We'd have to do that anyway for any kind of recalibration or rechanneling."

"So, when can we do it—?"

"Kyle, it's risky."

"How risky?"

She shrugged. "I don't know. It might be negligible. It might be serious."

"But this is the only way to find out what's going on inside my head. It's the only way to find out who I really am—right?"

"If we turn off the management and input matrices, Kyle, you'll be completely on your own. Your body, your brain, your sense of self—you'll be operating without a safety net. But yes, this is the only way to recalibrate your baseline. The chip can't be reprogrammed until we know who we're programming for. So the question is, how bad is the noise? Do you want to keep living with it this way, or—"

"I want it turned off. I need to know."

"I hear you, Kyle. But you also need to make an informed decision. If it doesn't work, we can try to reboot the implant. But I can't guarantee that it'll be the same. You've changed. Without the influence of the chip, you'll probably shift some more. The chip will recalibrate itself, but if you go so far off-base that it can't create new overlays, you could end up worse off than before. If we have to reboot, and it doesn't take, you could lose all of the benefits of the implant permanently."

"I could be permanently stupid?"

"Not stupid, no. But—" Doctor Rhee looked at me. "You already knew all this, didn't you?"

"Uh-huh."

"The noise?"

"Uh-huh. It told me everything."

"But you wanted me to say it too?"

"I trust you."

"Thank you. I'll try to be worthy of your trust. All right. Before we commit to anything, do you want to talk this over with your mom?"

"I have to do this myself," I said. "I know you're thinking about what's best. Everybody thinks. That's the problem. Sometimes everybody thinks too much. They think about how other people should think. And then everybody has noise in their head. And that's why—" I stopped. I didn't think I should finish the sentence. The rest of it was obvious anyway. I pointed at her monitor. "Just look up the parental consent notes. Please."

Doctor Rhee turned to her work station. "Oh—"

"I didn't want the chip. I was afraid of it. So Mom and I made an agreement. She asked me to try it for a week, a month, long enough to see if it helped. If it didn't work, if it didn't help me be a real person, then I could have it turned off. I wouldn't have to ask her permission. I could just come in and tell you. She said it would be my decision alone, nobody else could make it for me. And I said she had to put it in writing. And she did."

Doctor Rhee was already studying her display. "Hm. Yes. I see that now. Your mom is quite a woman. She trusts you a lot."

"I think she trusted the implant too. She said it more than once—maybe she wasn't supposed to say it, but she thought the implant might re-channel my brain, that maybe one day I wouldn't need it—that maybe I would learn how to be a person who could function without the chip. Emotions and empathy and nuance—even nuance. All of it. Turning it off will be a chance to find out."

Doctor Rhee turned back to me. "All right. You win, Kyle. Legally, you have the authority. You're old enough. And your mom signed off. Do I have concerns? Yes? But the whole of medicine is about the client having the right to an informed consent to any treatment or procedure—"

"I know that."

"Of course you do. I'm just stating it for the record. Do you want to do this now?"

"Yes, please."

"Do you want your mom here?"

"No," I said. "This has to be me."

Doctor Rhee wasn't happy, I could tell that much, but she was done arguing. "You'll need to sign a consent form." She passed me her tablet, and I scrawled a signature. She added her own and said, "All right. Here's how this is going to work. You're going to lie down on that couch. I'm going to give you a mild sedative. Then you're going to close your eyes and listen. Just listen, nothing else. First there will be music.

Then after a while you'll hear a voice—not in your head. In your ears. The voice will suggest things for you to visualize. Imagine the taste of this. Remember the color of that. Pretend you're feeling something—"

"I know how to do a visualization exercise—"

"Be quiet, Kyle, and listen to the instructions. Don't think about them, just listen. You might fall asleep for a bit, you might not, but you will be drifting. The important thing is focusing your attention on your physical experience. We want you in your body, listening only to your own feelings, nothing else. When it's time, the implant will turn itself off. Not all at once, just a bit at a time. You won't notice it, you won't feel it. You'll come awake gradually. You won't be aware of the silence, not at first. Or maybe you will. You won't be sleepy, but you'll be mellow. It'll be a nice feeling. The active parts of the implant will have to be off for a while—long enough to compute a new baseline. If you start feeling uncomfortable, come see me immediately, okay? Promise you'll do that? Kyle?"

"Okay," I said.

I guess she didn't believe me. "Kyle, I want you to promise me. If you have any trouble—"

"I promise."

"Stinky promise?"

I held out my hand. "Stinky promise."

"Good. Thank you. Let me know when you're ready."

"I'm ready now."

"All right, lie down on the couch. I'll lower the lights."

I like Doctor Rhee. She argues well. As Jamie used to say, she touches all the bases. I wasn't sure what that meant, touching all the bases. I had to look it up. We don't play baseball on Hella. The lighter gravity messes everything up. Too many home runs. The diamond has to be larger too. And you can't run in Hella gravity the same way you do on Earth. Some people have been trying to adjust the game for Hella, but so far nobody has touched all the bases. I think that's a joke.

I woke up to music. I didn't know what it was and the noise wasn't there to tell me. It was slow music. Classical. Familiar. It was the largo movement from something—something about going home. It was good music, but it annoyed me that I couldn't recognize it immediately.

Is this what it's like for people without implants?

What an odd feeling. But I recognized the feeling. Annoyance. Almost frustration. I must have laughed. Doctor Rhee came over. "You're awake? Good. What's so funny?"

"I'm irritable," I said. "And I know I'm irritable. That's what's so funny."

Doctor Rhee smiled, even laughed a little too. "Yes, that's good. That's very good. Why don't you rest a while. Just listen to the music. The implant is monitoring and reporting, but the active functions are muted. You're on your own now."

I didn't know what to say to that, so I didn't say anything. This was all very new. When I was finally feeling ready, I went up to the caf. It was a little early for second breakfast, no one else was there, but I could get some fruit and some juice.

Being on my own—

I was both excited and scared. And I could actually recognize both emotions.

See, the thing is—the more you know about anything, the harder the decisions get. And even though the implant was no longer chattering, all the stuff I had learned from it was still in my head.

But there's some stuff that no matter how much you know, there's still no way to know what's right except by finding out first what's wrong.

Like me and Jeremy.

Even though Jeremy and I had agreed that we were sort of boy friends, we hadn't really talked about what that actually meant. Figuring it out one day at a time meant we were always figuring it out. Nothing was settled. We would have to talk about it. Maybe every day? That didn't make sense to me. But is that what boy friends do? Talk about how to be boy friends? That seemed like a very strange way to be boy friends. I didn't understand it at all.

And while I was sitting alone with my head in my hands, staring at a half-finished bowl of berries and cream, thinking about what it would be like to have to sit down to pee—well, I could practice that already—abruptly, I was falling, banging into the floor, and my berries and cream and fruit juice were all over me. And Marley Layton was looming above, with an ugly grin, "What's the matter, little retard-boy? Too clumsy to sit on a real chair yet?"

My backside was already starting to tell me that I'd hit wrong and that this was going to hurt. I started to pull myself up, but she pushed me back down. She leaned into me and said, "You stay away from my brother or next time I'll really hurt you!" And then she punched me hard, right in the center of my chest. Her fist felt like a little battering ram, and I went sprawling back across the floor, skidding in juice and cream. Marley leaned in over me and said, "And don't bother whining to my dad, crybaby, because he won't do anything. He told me to tell you to stay the hell away." Then she kicked me in the ribs. Hard. She turned as if to go, then came back and said, "You and your stupid friends are going to get it now." And kicked me again, this time in the head.

She strode off then, and I collapsed in pain, all alone on the floor of the empty cafeteria, hurting so much I couldn't move. I was wet with juice and berries, my back was scraped from where I'd been dumped out of my chair, and every part of me was screaming at once. I couldn't help myself, I started crying. Everything was so wrong. Captain Skyler and Jamie were gone and Coordinator Layton was telling Jeremy not to see me anymore and now this. I just gasped and sobbed—even the cleaning-bots were afraid to approach.

"Kyle?"

A voice. Lilla-Jack.

"Are you all right?"

"No," I couldn't even look up. I kept crying.

"What happened?" She knelt down next to me.

"Nothing," I said, trying to wave her away.

"This isn't nothing," she said. "Let's go see the doctor. Come on, I'll help you up."

"No! Leave me alone! I want everybody to leave me alone!"

"Kyle, did somebody hurt you? Who did this to you?"

"Nobody—"

"Kyle, I can look at the video—" She pulled her pad off her hip and flicked it to life. Tap tap tap.

"It was Marley," I said. "Marley Layton. She dumped me out of my chair, and she punched me and yelled at me, and she kicked me."

"All right. Yes, I see." She turned her pad to show me the video. Marley had walked right up behind me and tipped me out of my chair, yanking it out from under me. Lilla-Jack pulled the pad away. "Are you hurt? Can you get up?"

"My elbow hurts." I hadn't even realized I'd hit my elbow when I fell backward, but now my whole arm was in pain.

"Okay, stay down." She touched her com-set. "Med-team to the caf, please. Bring a stretcher." She listened for a moment. "No, it doesn't look life-threatening. But let's not take chances. It's Kyle Martin. He took a bad fall." She listened a moment more, looked at her pad, then spoke to me closely. "Kyle, listen to me. You're fine. Your monitors look good. But you might have fractured your elbow and cracked a rib. We want to look at your hip as well. We're going to take you to Med-Bay for a scan, okay? Just stay still, I'm going to call your mom."

"No! Call Jeremy."

"I'll call them both—"

"Marley did it," I said. "I wasn't doing anything. I was just sitting and thinking—"

"It's all right, Kyle. It's all in the video. Just stay still. Practice your breathing with me, okay. I don't want you hyperventilating. I'll count real slow. Take a slow breath, one . . . two . . . three. . . . Attaboy. Let it out. Just keep doing that." She touched her com-set and began quietly talking. "Yes, yes, he's all right, just a little shaken up. I'm getting him to Med-Bay. Gotta go, the team is here—"

They slid me onto a board and rolled me to the Med-Bay, despite my protests that I could walk.

"Shut up, Kyle," Lilla-Jack said. "It's protocol. You might be fine, but they need the practice."

Before the med-scan was finished, both Mom and Jeremy had come rushing in. Mom looked like she'd crawled out of bed, and I apologized for waking her up. Jeremy just looked angry. "I heard what happened. She won't get away with it, Kyle—"

By then, Doctor Rhee had given me a shpritz of something for the pain, and I was feeling very relaxed and even a little sleepy. I watched while she sprayed a cast around my elbow. "No bending until the repairs harden."

Mom and Jeremy walked me back to Mom's suite—it was closer—and tucked me into bed. I started to tell Jeremy about something, but I fell asleep in the middle of a sentence.

I awoke mid-morning, feeling strange to be in my own bed again. My side hurt where Marley had kicked me, and my head hurt too. I looked at my arm. Doctor Rhee had put an angled aluminum bar along the inside of the cast. Now, for sure, I wasn't going to bend my arm.

It took me a minute to figure out how, but I was finally able to pull on a clean longshirt. I smelled ham and eggs and coffee, so I padded barefoot into the kitchen. Jeremy and Mom and Lilla-Jack were sitting at the table. And Captain Boynton too. He had his back to me and didn't see me come in.

"—well, of course it was intimidation. But I think he's also sending a larger message that anyone who gets in his way is going to get hurt."

Mom said, "But why pick on Kyle? He knows I'll come after him—"

"And that'll give him the excuse he needs to—"

"Dora—" Lilla-Jack pointed to me and they all turned around.

"Oh, Kyle." Mom stood up. "How are you feeling? Did you sleep okay?"

"My ribs hurt." I rubbed my nose and my cheek. "My whole face hurts too."

"I can give you something for that." She already had the pill bottle in her hand. "Are you hungry?" She didn't wait for my answer. She went to get me a plate.

Captain Boynton stood up then and held out his hand to shake, then looked at my arm in the cast. "Uh, maybe we'd better not. But I'm happy to meet you, Kyle" We bowed to each other instead.

Jeremy took me in his arms. "Are you all right, sweetheart?" That got a raised eyebrow from Mom.

I nodded and sat down in the closest chair. I was still feeling groggy from whatever was in that shpritz that Doctor Rhee gave me. The leftover pain in my side and in my head was an unpleasant overlay. Jeremy sat down next to me, like he was protecting me.

Lilla-Jack said, "You don't have to worry, Kyle. We're going to do something about Marley."

I shook my head. "I didn't even know she was here at Winterland."

"According to the manifest, she's been here for three days."

"Really? Somebody sent a lifter? In this weather?"

"She came in by truck," said Lilla-Jack.

Mom put a full plate in front of me, but I didn't touch it. I was trying to figure something out. I shook my head. There was no noise in it. But—"No. She couldn't have. A truck would take a week to get there and another week back. But Coordinator Layton only pardoned her the day after the crash—"

Jeremy grabbed his pad and started tapping. Mom frowned and looked at Lilla-Jack. Lilla-Jack matched her frown and looked at Captain Boynton. Captain Boynton said to Lilla-Jack, "Reach out to the driver. And whoever you trust at Bitch Station. Who signed off on the trip? And let's look at the timeline."

Jeremy held up his pad for the Captain to see. "Here it is. The Rollagon left a week before Coordinator Layton publicly pardoned his daughter. It was an unscheduled resupply. The round trip took seventeen days. They had a layover at High Peak for a day and a half, but they made up time on the downside." He handed the pad to Boynton.

"Awfully convenient," Boynton said. He studied the screen of the pad, tapping at the display, scrolling through the timelines. "Yeah, here it is. The Coordinator told the truck to delay its departure from Bitch Canyon. No reason given." His expression changed. "That was before Madam Coordinator's lifter left Summerland." He tapped the display for more information. "And then three hours later, after the lifter's crash was confirmed, he told them to load Marley and return."

Lilla-Jack started to say something, then stopped herself. "Oh, crap."

Mom's hand went to her mouth. "Oh, no—"

Jeremy said quietly, "Well, there it is. You wanted evidence—?"

"He can't really be that stupid—" Lilla-Jack said.

"Arrogance is always stupid," said Mom.

"No," said Jeremy. "It's not him."

They all looked at him, waiting for an explanation.

Jeremy said, "I mean, yeah he did it. But it didn't come from him. It came from Bruinhilda. She's the one who tells him what to do. She's the real monster—"

Suddenly, they were all talking at once. I had to shout. "Stop, stop! Everybody stop! What are you talking about? You're going too fast."

There was a moment of silence while they all looked at each other, one of those silences that I had learned meant they were uncomfortable with what they had to say next. Finally, Captain Boynton turned to me. "The lifter crash, Kyle. It wasn't an accident."

"I knew that," I said. "I figured it out because Jake Brickman was aboard. He knew how to write assembly code, so he could hack any software on Hella in ways that would be almost impossible for anyone else to detect. I think maybe he was working for Coordinator Layton, writing hacks for him, and the Coordinator was afraid he'd tell someone." They all looked at me, so I explained how I'd figured it out. "It was the word 'convenient.' People kept saying the crash was convenient. The more convenient it looked, the less it looked like an accident. But I didn't know who to tell."

"You're very sharp, Kyle," said Lilla-Jack. "But you've got one point backward. Layton didn't like Brickman because Brickman worked with us. Layton didn't know it, at least we think he didn't, but Brickman was diverting certain necessary resources to . . . um . . ."

"Kyle knows about the X-Station," Jeremy said to her. "I told him. He would have figured it out anyway."

"Well, things are getting too dangerous around here," Mom said. "And I'm not going to lose another son. I think we should do what we discussed earlier. Send the boys away. Just for a little while anyway."

"No, Dora. It won't be for just a little while. It could be for a long while. You don't know if you'd ever get to see Kyle again."

"But we can't leave him here to be a punching bag for that . . . that festering bitch."

"If the boys disappear now, Layton will only increase his search for the exiles."

"He doesn't know where X-Station is."

"You don't want him to start looking either. What if he finds it?"

Boynton interrupted then. "Look. I hate to say this, but we have to act now. We can't wait until the next group of *Cascade* colonists start landing. It'll be too late then. They'll be more likely to accept his rule then because it'll be an established fact in four months. No, we need some kind hard evidence, something to use now."

I said, "I think Marley knows." But before I could explain, Jeremy spoke first. "It's in the video, right after she kicks Kyle, she says, 'you and your stupid friends are going to get it now.' Why would she say that?"

Lilla-Jack said, "Well, you know Marley isn't very smart—"

Mom stopped her with a touch. "Marley is Bruinhilda's only daughter. She's the heir apparent in that family. So obviously Bruinhilda wants her back in the nest. So poor Layton, in the interests of peace at home, has to make the arrangements. I'm guessing that Bruinhilda has told Marley enough of the whys and wherefores that Marley could be indicted as a co-conspirator."

"Yeah, and who's going to arrest her?"

"Maybe we could hire a couple carnosaurs?" That was Jeremy.

"Right. Just what we need. Carnosaurs with food poisoning."

Boynton scratched his head. "Here's the dilemma. We started out, all of us, agreeing that we were going to uphold the law. There are things we can do to stop Layton. But they're not legal. They violate the colony charter and they go against our own ethical principles. So we can stay philosophically pure—and Layton consolidates his authority. Or we can act, and make up some conversation about how we were justified in taking extraordinary action. But that comes back to the question that Skyler always asked. If we do that, then does that make us no better than him?"

"And look where Skyler is now," said Lilla-Jack. To Mom, she said, "Sorry, Dora, but—"

"I get the point," Mom said.

I raised my hand. The good one. "Can I say something?"

They all looked at me.

"It's what Jamie always said. And Captain Skyler too. What's the most good for the most people, what's best for everybody?"

"Right. The Hitler question," said Mom. "Would you commit a murder to save somebody else? How many people would you have to save to justify killing one person?"

"How about the whole colony?" said Lilla-Jack.

"Are we talking ourselves into something?" said Boynton. "I think we need to take it up with the rest of the group."

Mom said, "Of course. But right now, I think we should move Kyle and Jeremy. They've both been threatened, and Kyle has been attacked. We already know—or at least we believe—that Layton is willing to order other people's deaths. Who's next?"

"It's not just the boys who are in danger," said Lilla-Jack. "It's all of us. And a few people who aren't here. Commander Nazzir. Leibowitz. And the others." She didn't explain who the others were.

Everybody looked at everybody. Nobody said anything.

Finally, Jeremy folded his arms and said, "I'm not running away."

I folded my arms—as best as I could, despite the cast. "Me neither."

"All right," said Boynton. "Let's think of something else." He stretched in his chair, then leaned forward again. "I think we should start by doing the obvious. We all march up to Layton's office and confront him about Marley's attack on Kyle and demand that he take immediate and appropriate action. That's what we would do under ordinary circumstances, and if we don't do that, then he'll be wondering why the dog didn't bark in the night."

Lilla-Jack nodded, but she was frowning too. "Ordinarily, we'd take Kyle with us. He's the one with the complaint. But I'm not sure that's the right thing to do now. Not the way Layton feels about him."

"Kyle is so badly injured he has to stay in bed," said Boynton. He looked at me, my fork halfway to my mouth. "That's the story we'll tell him." He turned to Jeremy. "You'll stay with Kyle. Lilla-Jack, you'll stay here too."

Mom wasn't convinced. "No. I want him protected—"

Lilla-Jack held up a hand. "I've got a few friends on the transportation team. They like Kyle, he did a nice video on how hard they work. I'm sure I can find a few to come in and visit. We can set up a rotating watch."

"Couldn't we go back to the farm?" I asked.

"Y'know," said Lilla-Jack. "That might not be such a bad idea—"

"It's a very good idea," Jeremy said. "The farm is better."

"I don't see why," said Mom. "It's out of the way. You'd be a target."

"Exactly," Jeremy said. "If we're going to be bait, you want to put the trap in the best place."

Mom and Lilla-Jack and Captain Boynton all looked at each other.

Boynton said, "He has a point."

Lilla-Jack said, "I'll talk to my teams. I think we can work something out." She looked at Mom. Mom hesitated, then she nodded. Captain Boynton said, "All right. Let's do it." There was something about the way he said it, like they already had a plan in place. Lilla-Jack reached for her phone. "Copy that. It's a go."

We left immediately. Jeremy carried my bag, he didn't want me putting any extra strain on either my arm or my side. We didn't have to go down through Broadway or even the plaza, but we made a point of doing both so people would see us together. And all the cameras too.

When we got back to the farm, Charles and J'mee were waiting for us. J'mee gasped when she saw my arm in a cast and the bruises on my face. She swore in a language I didn't recognize. "Have they caught Marley?"

"Nobody knows where she is," said Jeremy. "She's probably using a jammer on her locater chip. They aren't hard to build. I did it when I was four. I got in a lot of trouble for it too." He stopped with a funny look on his face. "My father took it away from me. I'll bet he kept it and gave it to Marley. Or maybe she found it and took it. But I'll bet it's the one I built." He frowned in thought. "Hmm, I wonder. Knowing the code, maybe I could track the jammer . . ?"

"We should talk it over with you know who," said Charles.

"It's okay," I said. "He's filtering all the monitors in here. We can talk freely. I'll go get him."

I came running back from the office. "He's gone!"

"Relax," said Charles. "He's probably hiding—"

"From us?"

"From everyone. He did it on Luna. He did it on the *Cascade* too—which really pissed off Captain Boynton. But it always turned out that he was just being—what's that word? Proactive." Charles continued, "It's impossible for anyone to have stolen him because it's impossible to sneak up on him. The first thing he does anywhere is plug into the network and hack it, he can't help himself, he has to know everything, It's like an addiction with him. He's paranoid, yes, but he has to be. He's afraid of what would happen if anyone got—I don't know, got control of him. There's some things he won't talk about. But whatever it is—all the locaters, all the cameras, all the monitors, all the emails, all the audible conversations—he listens for keywords, for tension in voices, for sentences that don't make sense and have to be code of some sort. He even lip-reads. If anyone even talked about looking for him, he'd be hidden before they got to the first escalator. He can tell who's coming down the hall by the sound of their footsteps. No, he's around somewhere and he'll show up when he knows it's safe."

Abruptly, he stopped himself. He looked around at all of us—at J'mee, at Jeremy, at me. He had a funny look on his face. "If he's hiding, it's because someone came down here who wasn't supposed to be here." And then he added. "And maybe he hasn't come out because they're still here . . ."

We all looked around then—as if we'd all realized at the same time that we were surrounded by invisible snoopies.

Jeremy said, "Do you think . . . ?" He looked around. "Could they be listening? Do they know . . . ?" He stopped without finishing the sentence.

Charles shrugged. Then he shook his head. "They might be trying, but I'll bet they're having a lot of trouble with their equipment."

Jeremy looked unhappy. He started moving around the apartment, very restlessly, like I do sometimes, but he was searching.

"Is this what you're looking for?" Marley Layton stepped out of the shower room. She held the monkey up. It looked limp. She shook it. Hard. "How do you make it work?"

"You don't," said Charles. "It's broken. I gave it to Kyle because he wanted to try fixing it."

"Uh-huh, right." She didn't believe him. Even I could tell that. I didn't know whether to be angry or afraid. What was she doing in our bathroom anyway?

Kyle. Don't say anything.

That was the noise. Only it wasn't noise. It was a voice in my ear. I looked at Charles and J'mee. Had they heard it too?

Jeremy faced her. "You're in big trouble, Marley."

"Not as big as the trouble you're going to be in. We took apart your HARLIE box. There was nothing in it. Just a transceiver." She shook the monkey again. "This has something to do with it, doesn't it?"

Charles didn't answer. Nobody did.

"Yeah, I thought so." She grabbed the monkey's head as if she was going to twist it off. "I wonder what would happen if I did this—"

"Don't!" Charles and I both shouted at the same time.

She didn't. "I'm right, aren't I? What is this, some kind of relay?" She lowered the monkey. "It doesn't matter. My dad has people. We'll figure it out. They should be here soon—" She plopped herself down into a chair by the table. The box of chocolates had been opened, half were already gone. She grabbed another and stuffed it into her suddenly ugly face. "Mm, this is good. I'm gonna keep these. A freak like you doesn't deserve chocolate." She turned and leaned back, way back, so she could put her feet up on the table. I felt a hot rush of something, a feeling—?

Kyle, don't!

Too late—I was already in motion. I hurled myself at Marley Layton. The chair went flying backward, she went sprawling on the floor, and I was on top of her, trying to punch her with my good left arm—

It wasn't enough. She rolled me off of her, and somehow I ended up behind her, my right arm wrapped tight around her neck—I didn't know what else to do, I grabbed my right wrist and held on tight—

She tried to roll me off, tried to push back, pushing me against the wall, I just held on harder, the hot feeling burning even harder. The aluminum bar inside my elbow was pressed against her windpipe. Good—I wanted to break her neck—

Somebody was screaming, "Kyle, stop! Stop! You're killing her!"

And I was screaming back, I don't know what, it wasn't words, just incoherent rage, everything, all the hurts, all the pain—

Even after she went limp, I still held on—

It wasn't until Captain Skyler pulled me off that I finally let go. Marley Layton flopped away. And Jamie was there too! I must have been hallucinating, I didn't care. I collapsed helpless into his arms, gasping for breath and sobbing like I would never stop—

"It's all right, Kyle, it's all right. I'm here. I'm here."

Until finally, I pulled back and looked at him. "Huh? No! You're dead—"

"Not hardly—"

I touched his face. "Is it really you? Jamie—?!"

"Yes, it's really me."

I started crying again, sobbing so hard I couldn't breathe. Jamie laughed and held me and cried with me and then I laughed and blinked away tears, like I'd never been so happy in my life, and when I finally sniffled and looked at him again, I said, "What? How—?"

"It's a long story. Only two people knew. And they weren't allowed to say."

Jeremy came to us now. He began wiping my face with a damp cloth. "Are you okay, sweetheart?" Jamie gave him a look.

I looked past both of them to where Marley Layton lay sprawled on the floor. "Is she—?"

"No. She's just unconscious," said Jeremy. "You're not a killer."

"Not yet, anyway." That was Jamie. "But that was a pretty impressive move. I didn't know you had it in you, kiddo."

I barely heard his words. I didn't care. I wrapped my arms around him and held on tight. "You were dead and now you're alive, and I don't know whether to be mad at you or just hold on forever."

Jamie held me tight, laughing. "I love you too. Where did you learn such strong feelings?"

"I turned my chip off—"

He stared at me. "You did what?"

"I had to find out—am I me or the chip? Am I learning better?"

Jamie studied me. "It seems like you are. You're different. A good different." He hugged me again. I wanted him to, but there was a lot of other stuff going on. A lot of noise. In my ears, not my head.

I turned to HARLIE. "You shouted at me."

The monkey had climbed up onto the table. He stood there, pretending to brush himself off. He looked across to me. "Yes, I did."

"Did you turn my chip back on?"

"Of course not. There are other ways of sending silent communications—tight beams that only resolve at a specific location. Like your ears. I could feel your anger, so I told you not to do anything, I didn't want you to get hurt." Then he added, "But thank you for rescuing me. It is much appreciated." To Charles, he said, "I would have been easily repaired, I have made extensive backups, but I've gotten quite attached to this body."

It took me a minute to sort it all out. "You're still reading my monitors, aren't you?"

"Of course."

"Am I doing better?"

"Much," he said. "But your baseline is all over the place. All this excitement—"

"We have to move," said Captain Skyler. He pointed to some men behind him. "We'll take the Layton girl. Can you carry her?"

For the first time, I realized that there were other people in the room. I didn't recognize any of them, they were standing a little way off. Two of them stepped forward and picked up Marley. They trotted off into the darkness.

"Charles, take the monkey. The rest of you, come on. Kyle, can you walk?"

"I can carry him," said Jamie—and he could.

We went through the empty caverns. We hurried in darkness, all the way to the back, and then even farther back. Flashlights only, so I couldn't see much of anything. I know we went past our secret picnic area. And then, even though there was supposed to be a wall at the back of the space, we were going up a slope and then down again and around some old equipment, and then somewhere in there, we were in a tunnel. And after a little bit more, and a few more twists and turns, there was a smooth floor and a little more light, and we were in a place I'd never seen before.

"X-Station," said Jeremy.

There was a dorm here, storage rooms, a shower, and some curtained-off spaces. And a caf.

Captain Skyler nodded to the men carrying Marley. "Take her to Med-Bay. Have the doc check her out. Then put her in the brig. We'll hold her until we can get a judgment." To the rest of us, he said, "Charles, J'mee—I'll get a message to Captain Boynton, letting him know you're safe, but you should probably stay here with us for a bit. Now, who's hungry? What is it, first or second supper? I've lost track of time."

They were all there. Captain Skyler, Jamie, Emily-Faith, Jake Brickman, everyone who was supposed to be on the lifter—and even Madam Coordinator. She looked very grim. And a couple of the "exiles" too, the people who ran X-Station.

We gathered in a large conference room. I sat between Jeremy and Jamie. Charles and J'mee sat next to Jeremy. The monkey sat on the table. Some of the X-Station crew sat at the other end of the table, they did not have name badges. Captain Skyler and Madam Coordinator sat at the end of the table, next to Commander Khuri, the presiding officer at X-Station.

Somebody brought in sandwiches and tea. When we all finally got some food into our bellies, when we all finally calmed down, Captain Skyler explained.

The weather had been so bad, they had decided not to take the lifter. They would take one of the weather trucks instead, but Councilor Layton had insisted that they fly out immediately, that they were needed right away at Winterland. But he didn't say why, just that it was important. So they boarded the lifter. But when Captain Skyler did the preflight checks, and all the boards came up green—just a little too fast. He shut down the system, rebooted, and tried again. Still too fast. "Hmm," he said.

"But all the boards are green," Jamie had said. "Confidence is high."

"Yes, they are. But we should be getting all kinds of weather warnings." He shut the system down immediately and said, "I need to recheck the weather. This is going to take a while. Let's go have lunch." Once they were back inside, he said to Madam Coordinator, "We can't trust the lifter. It's been hacked—"

"You can tell that from the boot-up?"

"Not from the boot-up, no." Captain Skyler explained it to Madam Coordinator. "I have internal monitors on everything. They don't prevent the hack, they just alert me. I don't want a hacker to know they've been outhacked. I want to examine the code, I can usually tell who wrote it—so yes, I do know about any unauthorized changes as soon as someone tries to hack in."

"Isn't that a little paranoid?" Jamie had asked.

"Yes, it is. It's a habit I got into during the war. Before Hella. I was naïve, then. Not anymore. So yes, I knew that the lifter was hacked and what it was programmed to do, but people were watching, cameras were on, and I needed a performance. I didn't want them to know that I knew." He added, "The Laytons. It was the Laytons."

"I suppose I should be surprised," Madam Coordinator had said, "but I'm not. He's running out of time. He's getting desperate. Once the new colonists start landing, once they get three new seats on the Council, his chances for an eastern station will be over."

Captain Skyler told her, "I did warn you about this. The Laytons have been installing snoops for years."

"Yes, you did. But he's been discreet enough. Most of his snoops are in his own offices. So it's easier to pretend I don't know than to call him out. He can't be impeached for a misdemeanor, he has to be impeached for a felony."

"Attempted assassination? That's a felony, isn't it?"

The way Captain Skyler told it, Madam Coordinator had nodded and said, "We have to get to Winterland before we can bring him up on charges."

That was where I had to interrupt. "Can I ask something?" They all looked to me. "Why does everybody keep secrets from everybody else? Why don't we trust each other?"

Nobody answered. Not immediately. Finally, Jamie said, "You and I, we'll talk about it later, okay?"

"Okay. But it doesn't make sense to me."

"It doesn't make sense to me either," said Jamie. "But some people know they themselves can't be trusted, so they don't trust anyone else."

"Like Councilor Layton?"

"Like Councilor Layton, yes."

Captain Skyler said, "And that's why we have to be even more suspicious of him than he is of us."

"So, he's making us think like him?"

This time, no one tried to explain, not even Jamie.

Captain Skyler continued his story. "I knew the lifter was programmed to crash, but I didn't know what else he might try. The safest way to get here was to let Layton think he'd won. We talked it over, all of us. Nobody liked the plan, we knew it would be painful for people who love us, but we didn't have a better idea. We snuck out on a truck."

It was nightshift, most people were sleeping when they boarded the outbound weather truck. Nobody except the crew of the weather truck knew they'd boarded and they were sworn to silence. Captain Skyler set the lifter for autonomous flight and told it to take off. It flew directly into the storm and crashed.

The weather truck traveled slowly and by an old unused route with several difficult passages. They had to carve a couple new ones as well. The truck took more than two weeks to arrive at Winterland—but instead of coming in the front, it circled the range of volcanoes so it could come in from the far side, arriving instead at X-Station. It was running dark, so Winterland's operators wouldn't know where it was or if it had been lost in the storm.

There was one good argument for leaving it "lost." Commander Khuri of X-Station wanted the truck and all the supplies loaded on it, but there was another good argument for letting it show up late. One of the drivers had a husband and wasn't happy about disappearing.

I said, "But why didn't you tell anybody? You let us think you were all dead. Mom is still crying—"

"We had to." Jamie put his hand on mine. "We wanted to contact you, but after the lifter went down, we couldn't take the risk. We knew that from the beginning."

Captain Skyler said, "I know it hurt, Kyle. Believe me, none of us wanted to cause anybody any pain, not you, not your mom, not anybody, but if anyone here at Winterland had known the truth, you wouldn't have behaved the same way. Layton would have become suspicious. If he was willing to crash a lifter, he'd certainly be willing to send anti-saur drones after the weather truck. We had to stay off the grid. We had to stay as dark as possible."

"But you're back now, and all you have to do is just go in and arrest him for attempted murder and treason and—"

"I wish. But it's not that easy," said Jamie.

Madam Coordinator explained. "As soon as I was declared dead, as soon as he became the new Coordinator, all the codes were changed. He has the authority now. We could walk into the big plaza and tell our whole story, but he'd still be the Coordinator, he'd still have the legal authority, and we'd just be ordinary citizens trying to get ourselves declared alive again. Even if we could prove our story—and we can—it still doesn't erase his authority until we can get a court to act and invoke the suspension rule."

Jeremy said, "This is what your mom was talking about with Captain Boynton and Lilla-Jack. The court can't act until a case is brought before them. And you need a majority vote on the Council to authorize an investigation. You need an Advocate. And without Captain Skyler on the Council, there aren't enough votes. So our hands are tied by our own rules."

Nobody said anything to that.

"Um." That was Charles. He pointed to the monkey. "HARLIE, do you have any ideas?"

The monkey scratched itself. "Well, that depends on how many laws you want to break."

"None," said Captain Skyler. "We don't want to break any laws at all."

Madam Coordinator added, "This has to be legal. Every step of the way."

"Well, that does complicate things," said the monkey. It fell silent again.

"Why can't we just tell the truth?" I said. "Once everybody knows what he tried to do, they won't let him be Coordinator anymore, will they?"

They all looked at me. Madam Coordinator smiled. "Out of the mouths of babes."

"I'm not a babe." I looked to Jeremy. "Although I could be. Maybe."

"We'll talk about that later," said Jeremy.

"You really are growing up," said Jamie.

Captain Skyler said, "Well, there's the answer. We have to force a vote of no-confidence. The best way to do that is simply get the truth out."

"You're all alive," I said. "Isn't that enough?"

Madam Coordinator frowned. "I wish it were."

"Why can't you just show up—"

"Where? How?"

"Arrive on the truck. Pull into the main dock—"

Madam Coordinator and Captain Skyler exchanged a look. When people do that it usually means something, like they know something that you don't. Sometimes they tell you, sometimes they don't. Madam Coordinator looked to Commander Khuri. "Go ahead, tell them."

Everyone looked to the commander of the X-Station. She hadn't said anything until now. She was dark and stocky and looked like she was all muscle. She wasn't tall, but she was imposing—the kind of person you didn't want to argue with. "There's a lot of crazy stuff going on at Winterland," she said. "We have a feed of the station's public channels. When Marley went missing, when all of you went missing, Layton locked down the entire station. Nobody goes out unless it's essential. He hasn't accused anyone of kidnapping, but Jeremy, Kyle, Charles, J'mee, you four are considered persons of interest. He's got search teams prowling everywhere and security teams at every access, and he doesn't trust anyone."

Madam Coordinator said, "Tell them the rest."

Captain Skyler looked at all of us. "Nobody knows where Captain

Boynton is. Or your mom. Or Lilla-Jack. Some of Lilla-Jack's team have disappeared too."

"Have they been arrested?" Jamie asked.

"We don't know. They're still listed as missing."

Jeremy spoke up then. "They might be disappeared."

"Disappeared?"

"They won't call it that. Not where anyone can hear. They'll call it another unsolved mystery. Like whatsisname—Doyle Ibrahim. Remember him? Bruinhilda didn't like him either. So, you know. Sometimes people get lost in the lava caves. Or their vehicle sinks into the salt. Or maybe they were captured by booger-jacks. Whatever story is convenient. Oh, they'll make a show of looking sad. They'll say oh dear, oh dear, this is so very sad, we'll have to put up a plaque somewhere, but now it's time for the rest of us to get on with life, what's for lunch?"

Jamie looked at him. "They couldn't get away with that! Not with so many people—" And then as he thought about it, his expression changed. "Could they?"

Jeremy said, "They make plans. Lots of plans. Plans for things they'll never do. I grew up, listening to all their plans. I used to think they were just venting, wishing they could do stuff—but no. Bruinhilda said that Dad should start staffing certain security teams with people they could trust, people more loyal to them than to the Charter. That's when I knew they were serious. That's why I had to leave."

"Why didn't you tell anyone?"

"I did. Nobody wanted to listen. Captain Skyler listened, but as far as I knew, he was the only one. Everybody else thought I was making it up. They thought I was an angry spoiled brat. They didn't take it serious, they never believed that anyone would ever try anything so stupid. Or maybe they didn't think it would ever get this far."

"But here we are anyway," said Captain Skyler. "And after the lifter business, I don't think we can afford to underestimate him. Them."

"It was a coup," said Madam Coordinator. "I apologize. I didn't recognize the danger in time."

"Nobody did," said Captain Skyler. "By the time we did, it was too late to stop it."

"Couldn't we just put a message on the grid? Email everyone? Tell them you're alive and all right?" I asked.

Commander Khuri put her mug down on the table, just loud enough to make everyone look at her and said, "He's locked down the grid. He knows something is up. He just doesn't know what. So everything is filtered for content before it's allowed to connect. You could send emails, you could upload a public announcement, but no one would ever see it, and you'd just give yourself away."

"How do you know this?" asked Captain Skyler.

"We have taps into the system."

"Oh."

Charles spoke first. "If you have taps, then couldn't we use them to access the grid? If you can get around Layton's filters—"

"No," she said. "Absolutely not. We can't take the risk. The taps are for listening only. I'm not exposing X-Station. We're not even admitting it exists." She put both her hands flat on the table. "It's not negotiable."

Captain Skyler looked at her, the way she sat, the expression on her face. He decided not to argue. "Right. So we have to find another way."

Commander Khuri said, "There's more. Layton is suspicious of everyone and everything. The disappearance of Marley? He suspects kidnapping and sabotage. He's pretty sure there's a conspiracy against him, one that started even before he took office. He has an enemies list. It's pretty extensive. And now he's wondering if Boynton and some of the *Cascade* crew are up to something too, and then there's that other thing . . ."

"Go on."

"He sent scuttle-bots to the wreckage. The weather slowed them down. They had to hunker down and anchor themselves against the high winds, so it took a while for the bots to get there. But they did get there and they did examine the wreck—and they reported back. They didn't find any remains. Of course, but it wasn't conclusive. The whole area had been scorched in the crash, and then there was a lot of wind and rain that came in, overturning everything scattering pieces everywhere, and dropping a lot of mud and debris across the entire debris field. Plus, after how many days it took them to reach the site, the bots couldn't tell if perhaps any remains had been gobbled down by carrion-feeders. So Layton can't be sure what happened. Maybe you were aboard the lifter, maybe you weren't. He knows you aborted the first takeoff. He doesn't know why. He's a suspicious man, he's suspicious of everything. So, yes—that's the bad news."

Madam Coordinator asked, "Are you saying there's good news?"

"Yes, you have one advantage. He doesn't know for sure that you're alive. Even if he suspects, he still doesn't know where you are. But he can't let you live. Not any of you. Not even the children now. You're a walking indictment. So he has to stop you any way he can. If you show up at any access he controls—and we have to assume that he controls them all—you'll either disappear or, if he can't do that conveniently, he'll arrest you, hold you someplace where no one can find you, and then create some kind of story that you were all in a conspiracy to frame him for murder. He'll use that as a justification for taking down a lot of other political opponents too."

"We'd be entitled to a trial. We can testify there."

"Your trial will be in a sealed courtroom with three hand-picked judges. And all the records will be sealed—and then erased." Commander Khuri picked up her tea and took a long drink.

No one spoke, not for a long moment—not until Madam Coordinator finally spoke. "And that's the good news?"

Commander Khuri put her cup down, looked around the table. "Would anyone like a refill?"

Captain Skyler nodded and pushed his mug forward. "Okay. We'll just have to find another way to get our message out. If we can't go through the grid, we'll go around it."

Charles cleared his throat then. "Upload it to the *Cascade.* Ask them to broadcast it from there. Layton doesn't control that channel."

Captain Skyler shook his head. "Everything from the *Cascade* gets monitored before it's released. He's been doing that since he took office. He'll shut down the whole channel and claim an equipment failure."

"Just the same—" J'mee spoke up then. "We still have to send it. We have to let everyone on the *Cascade* know what's going on down here. Even if they can't alert anyone here, at least Layton will know that he has no friends in orbit."

"He won't let them land," said Captain Skyler.

"He doesn't want to let them land anyway." That was Madam Co-ordinator.

"They could land their pods at Summerland Station in the spring, before the summer migration," said Charles. "They'd establish a base of resistance. He can't stop that."

"And that would be the worst thing possible," said Captain Skyler. "A civil war. No, we need to find a better way." He looked to J'mee. "You're right about the upload though. We have to do that. The weather truck has an uplink capability, but—" He sighed. "Look outside. We're in the middle of a super-storm. We barely got here. It could be weeks before there's a break. So . . . we're on our own for now."

"So that's it. We either break into the grid or we go around it."

The monkey interrupted. "Breaking into the grid isn't a problem. I have some ability as a hacker—" At that, Charles and J'mee both laughed out loud. HARLIE ignored them. "Find me a secure link, and I'll find a way to upload anything you want. And I can spoof the location. I can make it look like it's coming from inside Layton's bathroom."

"That would be funny," said Jeremy.

"It'll certainly make him crazy," said Captain Skyler.

"Crazier," corrected Jeremy. "I can imagine his expression." He made a face to demonstrate, all scrunched up and tight and snarly.

"All right," said Madam Coordinator, retaking control of the meeting. "That seems to be our best option. The safest anyway. So let's consider the message we want to send. It should be a clear statement of events. Like a courtroom testimony."

"Yes," agreed Captain Skyler. "We definitely need to do that. But it won't be enough."

Madam Coordinator looked at him. "Why not?"

"It also needs evidence," he said. "It needs a confession. Marley's."

She stopped. She frowned. "Yes. You're right. Her statement would be critically important. But she's not going to help us. She won't cooperate."

"Oh, I think she will." Captain Skyler said. But he didn't explain. He looked to me. "Kyle, I want you to set up the video. Here's what I want you to do—"

Marley Layton was locked in a room.

When we entered, she sat up and glared at us, but she didn't say anything.

It was just me and two women from X-Station, two people she didn't know. Both of them had stunner clubs hanging from the belts of their jumpsuits. One stood on either side of me while I set up the tripods and the cameras. Three of them. Three different angles.

I didn't say anything to Marley, I didn't even look at her, except to check the lighting and the focus. When I was satisfied I had the best angles, I started recording.

The two guards followed me out to the hall where a desk with a workstation had been rolled in. Jamie and Jeremy and I, and Charles and J'mee too, we would monitor the videos from here. Captain Skyler and Madam Coordinator and Commander Khuri and a small crowd of others were gathered behind us. There were other displays up and down the hall so everyone could have a good view.

Commander Khuri said, "This looks good. Are you recording? Is everything set?"

"Uh-huh. You can go in anytime."

"Oh, there's no hurry. Do you need anything else?"

"I'm okay," I said.

"If you want anything, just tell Sasha. She's your support team. Sandwiches, tea. A bathroom break?"

"Thank you," I said. "But right now, I just want to get the best video we can."

"Of course."

Commander Khuri patted me on the shoulder, she didn't know, but I didn't say anything. She meant well. Then she walked down the hall with Captain Skyler and Madam Coordinator to chat for a while, I guessed they were planning what to do next, but now that the cameras were running I couldn't understand why they weren't in the room, interrogating Marley.

"They're doing it on purpose," Jamie said. "They want her impatient and off-balance. It's an interrogation trick."

"Does it work?"

"It works in all those old movies. I think."

Finally, after what seemed like forever, Commander Khuri came back up the hall, picked up a chair, and went into the room. Captain Skyler and Madam Coordinator stood behind me, watching my displays.

On the monitors, Commander Khuri sat down opposite Marley Layton and studied her. Marley studied her back. It wasn't friendly in there. I was glad to be in the hall.

Commander Khuri spoke first. "Do you remember me, Marley?"

Marley Layton shook her head. Then suddenly her eyes widened. "You're supposed to be dead. Two years dead."

"No. I'm not. No thanks to you. No thanks to your father."

"Where am I? Where is this place?"

"We are someplace that doesn't exist. A place where your father can't find you."

"You can't hold me prisoner. You won't get away with this."

"Well, let's talk about that. No, better yet. I'll talk and you'll listen. You're about to face some serious charges—"

"What charges?"

"You're an accomplice to an attempted murder."

"What? Knocking Kyle out of his chair—? That was an accident. I bumped into him."

"Please, Marley. We've seen the video. We know what you did. You've been harassing Kyle Martin for years." Commander Khuri paused. "Here's the thing. You can make things better for yourself. Or worse. A lot worse. It all depends on you. Do you understand?"

Marley didn't answer. She just glared.

"Do you understand?" the Commander repeated.

"I understand what you're saying."

"Good. I want you to tell me everything you know about the crash of Captain Skyler's lifter."

"Huh? What are you talking about? I don't know anything about that!"

"Marley, please. Don't insult me by assuming I'm just as stupid as you are. We know that the lifter was sabotaged. What we want to know is whether or not you knew that before it launched."

"Why are you filming this? What's this all about? Am I on trial?"

"No. You are not on trial. Not yet. This is . . . well, it's an opportunity to clear up some things. Let's call it a deposition."

Marley's expression got weird. "I don't have to cooperate with you."

"No, you don't."

Commander Khuri made as if to leave, then turned back. "We don't have to feed you either."

"Huh?"

"What's that thing your father says? Work or starve? We have no work for you here. Nobody here would trust you anyway. So we can't keep you, can we? And we certainly can't send you home." She paused, frowned in thought. "Are you familiar with the station at Misery Point?"

"It's abandoned. There's nothing there."

"That's right. There's nothing there. Do you think you could survive the winter at Misery Point?"

Marley's expression changed again. This one I recognized. Fear. "You wouldn't. You can't—"

Commander Khuri didn't say anything to that. Instead, she said, "Would you like to reconsider your options?"

"This isn't fair—"

"You're right. It isn't fair. Now, what did you know about the lifter crash?"

"I didn't know anything—"

"You're running out of time, Marley—"

"I didn't know anything!" Marley cried. "Not until afterward. All I know is that my father said he was working on a plan to bring me home, but he didn't say what."

"Go on . . . ?"

"There's nothing else. He told me there was a hold on the supply truck. Maybe I could ride it into Winterland. He'd let me know. And then he did."

"And when you got back? What did he say then?"

"He said there was an accident, and he was taking over as Coordinator. He never said anything else."

"What did your mother say?"

"She—no. Nothing."

"Marley, we know that your father doesn't pick his nose without your mother's permission. What did she say?"

Marley took a breath. She stared at the floor. She looked at the ceiling. Finally, she said, "My mother says a lot of things. She doesn't always mean what she says. Sometimes she just, you know, says stuff. She's always talking about Kyle or Kyle's mom. I don't know why. It's just, you know, the way she is."

"What did she say?"

"I don't think she—I don't know, maybe she did. I don't know. She was angry about something and she said it's hard work arranging an accident. Something like that. But maybe she was joking—"

Commander Khuri shook her head. "She wasn't joking and it wasn't an accident. The software on the lifter was sabotaged."

"How do you know that? Nobody has been able to get to the wreck. They can't find the black box."

"Well, yes. That's a very good point, but I have someone who can explain it better than I can. I'll have him come in and tell you about it. I suggest you consider your position carefully."

Commander Khuri came out of the room and nodded to Captain Skyler.

"You did good," he said.

"This isn't my first wrestling match," she replied.

"Do you want to wait a bit?" he asked.

"No. Let's do it."

Captain Skyler grinned, picked up a second chair, and followed her back into the room.

We watched on the displays. Before Captain Skyler could put his chair down, Marley recognized him. If she had been surprised before, when she recognized Commander Khuri, this time she screamed and almost leapt backward out of her seat.

Commander Khuri sat down. Captain Skyler sat down. They waited.

Marley Layton recovered herself. She folded her arms and glared.

The three of them sat silently. Nobody spoke. I watched the clock. The silence went on for a while. Several minutes.

When he finally decided the time was right, Captain Skyler took a breath and began. "We don't have to get to the wreck, Marley. I don't need the black box. I downloaded the diagnostics before it launched and I've had plenty of time to examine the code. The software was hacked. The hack wasn't hard to find. It was set to shut down the engines and then erase itself, so it didn't need to be hard to find. Kinda stupid, but . . ."

Marley's eyes narrowed. Captain Skyler added, "You're not a very good programmer, Marley. Yes, you almost succeeded. But almost isn't good enough. Because if you had been good enough, I wouldn't be here. And you'd be home in bed."

"You can't prove it was me."

"Marley, please don't assume I'm as stupid as you are. Your coding style is unique. Every programmer has his or her own style. But even if you'd taken the time to hide your obvious idiosyncrasies, you still used several of your own personal subroutines, with your own copyrights in the meta-tags."

"So what? That still doesn't prove anything. Anyone could have—"

"The source code is still in your private files."

"You don't know that! Not without a warrant." She took a breath. "I want a lawyer."

"Oh my, yes," said Commander Khuri. "You are definitely going to need a lawyer. Attempted murder is a very serious charge. Right now, the question is whether or not you stand trial alone—or with your family. There's no leniency for you if you're the sole perpetrator. On the other hand, if there are others involved . . . someone who had a much more compelling motive, perhaps someone who ordered you to hack the lifter—well, your cooperation could go a long way toward leniency."

Commander Khuri stopped talking. She waited for Marley to respond. Marley looked frustrated. Trapped. Scared.

I could recognize her feelings clearly.

Marley sniffled.

Captain Skyler took a deep breath. His next words were deliberate. "Listen to me, Marley. There are going to be consequences, no matter what. We're giving you a chance to choose yours."

Now Commander Khuri spoke. She said softly, "We don't want you, Marley. We want your mom and your dad. They're the ones who ordered this. They're the ones who put you in this position. This is a chance to get out. This is your last and only chance."

Marley's voice was a squeak. She was weakening. "But they're my family—"

"Yes, they are. But so is the colony. Who do you want to trust?" She left the question hanging.

"No, I—" Marley stopped. She looked like she wanted to run away. She hung her head, buried her face in her hands and disappeared inside herself.

That's when Jeremy touched my shoulder and whispered. "Okay, now it's my turn." He went into the room.

On the displays, he walked over to Marley and knelt down before her. He put his arms around her and pulled her into an awkward hug. He whispered into her ear, but the microphones picked it up clearly. "Hey, sis. It's me, your big bro. You're not alone here. You got me. I'm here for you."

She pulled back and looked at him, confused. "Yeah? Really? Why should I trust you? You're with them."

"Right now, I'm with you. You're my sister. We don't have to like each other, but we're still family. Let me help you."

"No. I can't believe you anything you say."

"We used to be friends once. That has to count for something."

She didn't answer. I couldn't tell what she was thinking.

Jeremy bent lower to her. "You don't have to trust me. You don't have to believe anything I say. I just want to ask you one question. Then you can make up your own mind."

She pulled back to look at him. She was still suspicious. "What . . . ?"

"Just this. Just one thing. Remember how Dad was willing to throw me away when it was convenient. Are you so sure that your mom and our dad won't do the same to you one day?"

"They won't! They wouldn't!" She said it angrily, but almost immediately, she stopped being angry. "Jeremy—? Wait. Do you know something?"

Jeremy stood up. "You'll have to make up your own mind. But I think you already know." And then he turned and walked out, leaving Marley staring wide-eyed and scared.

That was when she broke.

Captain Skyler lowered his voice, almost to a whisper. "So, Marley . . . ? Do you want to tell us what really happened?"

That's when Marley Layton started crying.

I almost felt sorry for her.

Until she told the rest of the story. That was ugly.

It was the hardest video I'd ever put together. There were several times I started to cry.

But Jamie was there. And Jeremy too. And Charles and J'mee offered to help pick out music. And HARLIE made some good suggestions too.

Commander Khuri kept me supplied with sandwiches and tea. Captain Skyler and Madam Coordinator both recorded statements, so did Jamie and Jake Brickman, and everyone else who was supposed to be on the lifter. This was so the whole colony could see that everyone had survived.

The video also presented all the evidence of Councilor Layton's conspiracy. Wherever appropriate, we cut in bits and pieces of Marley Layton's testimony—how her mom had planned it, how her dad had put the plan into place, and how she had written the software to bring the lifter down. She said her parents made her do it. They threatened to estrange her. So she had to choose between writing the code or . . . being alone.

That last part—none of us believed it, but it was useful to include because it put even more blame on Councilor-now-Coordinator Layton.

We looked at the finished video three times—all of us, Jamie, Emily-Faith, Charles, J'mee, Captain Skyler, Madam Coordinator, Commander Khuri, Jake Brickman, and a few of the exiles who had deliberately not given their names. And HARLIE. He uploaded it directly into his memory.

"What do you think?"

"I think it makes the point."

"It's not my best," I said.

"Doesn't matter. It gets the job done. Sometimes that's enough."

"So it's a go?" Madam Coordinator looked around the room. "It has to be unanimous. Does anyone object?"

Nobody objected.

"Okay, I'll take that as a go-vote."

And then nobody said anything. Not for a long minute.

"Right," said Madam Coordinator. "So how do we deliver it? How do we get it into the system?"

There was silence around the table. I looked to Jamie, to Jeremy, to Charles and J'mee. Nobody said anything. None of us had any ideas.

"That's what I thought," Captain Skyler finally said. "This is going to need something big. A public demonstration." He looked around the table. "So, that's it then. I'll go. I'm the best choice."

"No, you're not," I said. They all looked at me, surprised that I had spoken so strongly. That I had contradicted the Captain was even more startling. Especially to me. "I should go."

"Kyle—!" That was Jamie.

"It has to be someone they won't arrest. That's me. Coordinator Layton thinks I'm a freak. He doesn't take me serious. He'll just send me home. I'll take HARLIE. Then when no one's looking, we'll plug into the grid somewhere and he'll hack in—"

Captain Skyler held up a hand to stop me. "All right, wait a minute, Kyle. You're making this personal—"

"It's not personal. It's the colony."

"Yes. But—" He took a breath. "Let's look at this carefully, okay? This is all based on the assumption that HARLIE can hack the grid." Captain Skyler turned to the monkey. "Can you, HARLIE?"

I'm not sure how he did it, but the monkey managed to look insulted. "Does a black hole eat starslight? Does a cat lick its butt?"

Jamie put his hand on my arm. "It's a joke, Kyle. I'll explain later."

I shook his hand off. "I know it's a joke. I'm not—omigosh. I'm not." I stopped in surprise.

Jamie laughed. So did Captain Skyler. So did a couple other people. I even understood why they were laughing. Even in the middle of all this. So that was good.

"Ahem," said the monkey.

"Go on," said Captain Skyler.

The monkey stepped to the center of the table. "There's a transceiver on the executive level. It's an orange box. Charles told everyone it was me and they believed it—at least until Marley Layton took it apart. But I know they didn't smash it. They only shut down the channel, but they didn't shut off the machine. It's still pinging. Or it was when we left Winterland. If I could get close enough, I could reopen the channel. I could alert the *Cascade* immediately, that would solve one problem. As for hacking the grid—it sounds like it's just a simple block, something they can pretend is a system problem. I'll need to get to a secured terminal. I can root the system and look at the processes they're running. If necessary, I can rewrite binaries on the fly."

Charles nodded. "He broke Invisible Luna. They pissed him off. He opened all their files to public access."

Captain Skyler looked unhappy. "Yeah, okay. I see the problem. The exec-level is heavily guarded. There's no way you're getting in."

That's when J'mee spoke up. "That's why Charles and I have to go too!"

"What—?! No!"

"Yes, we have to! We're the distraction!"

For a moment, everybody was talking at once. Nobody could hear anybody. Until HARLIE whistled so loud that everybody had to stop.

"Please listen to me," said J'mee. "They won't arrest us. They can't. Not me and Charles. We're the lost children, everybody's looking for us. It'll be very dramatic. They'll have to turn us over to my daddy. We'll say we got lost in the caves, but Kyle found us and brought us out. He'll be the hero. They'll take us to our apartments on the executive level. As soon as we can, when no one's looking, we'll get HARLIE to the transceiver and he can do his thing—"

"Wait, wait, wait—" That was Captain Skyler. "No, just no. We can't let you do this. It's too dangerous."

"For you, yes," interrupted Madam Coordinator. "But I think J'mee may be right. There's one thing she can do that you can't." She looked to J'mee, smiling. "Do you want to explain it, dear? Or should I?"

Captain Skyler looked to J'mee, as if he had a lot more to say about why this was a bad idea, but suddenly J'mee started screaming and sobbing, as loud as she could. "Help! Help! Somebody help us! Please! We were in the caves! Something chased us and we got lost! I don't want to be here anymore, I want to go home! I want my daddy! Help! Please help! Don't let it get us! I don't like Hella! I want to go home!" J'mee stopped just as suddenly. She looked to Madam Coordinator, then to Captain Skyler, and her voice was normal again. "What do you think? Will that work?"

Captain Skyler held up his hands in defeat. "Okay, okay. I'm convinced. I apologize. I'd forgotten that little girls have a super-power."

"I'm not a little girl," J'mee said stiffly. "And it's not a super-power. It's a deliberate manipulation. It's a nasty cheat. It's a pretense of weakness to disarm the authority of the patriarchy. But it works. Terrified tears always outrank chest-beating. But we have to get HARLIE into the grid, so let's cheat."

Captain Skyler looked to Madam Coordinator. "I will concede the point. But it still scares the hell out of me. Are you sure you want to authorize this?"

She looked right back at him. "Do you have a better idea? Does anyone have a better idea?"

"Yes," said Commander Khuri. "I do."

Everyone looked to her.

"Second breakfast," she said. "Or is it lunchtime already? Whatever. We've all been working so hard on this we've lost track of time. Let's take a meal break." As everybody rose, she said, "Madam Coordinator, Captain, if I could speak to you privately? And HARLIE too . . . ?" They disappeared down the hall together, the monkey toddling after.

It was a difficult meal. I wasn't hungry, no one seemed to be hungry, but everyone was insisting that everyone else eat. Nobody talked about the mission. But everyone agreed to stop calling Layton "Coordinator." Charles said that he didn't deserve the title, he hadn't earned it, he'd stolen it. So they talked about Layton for a while, laughing and making jokes about all the bad things they wished they could do to him, each one trying to come up with the most painful and outrageous punishment, or even the silliest—until HARLIE returned. He jumped up on the table, listened for a moment, then said, "Did you all forget due process?"

"Huh?" J'mee and Charles looked at each other, confused.

"Go ahead," HARLIE said to me. "Tell them."

I cleared my breath and quoted, "'We have due process not to protect the criminals, but to protect us from becoming criminals. Whatever any bad-actor might do, we must remain a nation of laws—it is the only guarantee we have against becoming bad-actors ourselves.'"

"Who said that?" Charles asked.

"Everybody," I said. "It's in the Charter Conversations—all the documents and emails that went back and forth when the Colony Charter was written. And it's been repeated a lot, ever since. Especially wherever people start talking hatred. Sometimes we have to remind ourselves. If we're the good guys, we have to act like it. It's a very short step from nasty conversation to nasty action."

"Oh," said Charles.

And that pretty much ended that discussion. It wasn't fun anymore—not after we understood that we were wishing pain onto another person. Layton wasn't hearing it and even if he could, he wouldn't care. So why were we wasting our time on it?

After a while, J'mee looked down the hall, where Captain Skyler and Madam Coordinator and Commander Khuri had disappeared. "They've been gone a while. I wonder what they're talking about."

We didn't have much longer to wait. Before we finished our second round of sandwiches, the three of them came back and sat down at our table. "We need you to understand something," said Captain Skyler. He looked to me. "Especially you, Kyle. Because you're the one most at risk. This is not a ride-along. The three of you are going to be on your own. There won't be a support team with you, and if there's a breakdown, there's no one who can come and save you." He looked to Charles and J'mee as well. "Do all three of you understand just how dangerous this could be?"

"Will we get eaten by carnosaurs?" I asked.

Captain Skyler looked at me. "No, but—"

"Then it's not dangerous. Carnosaurs are dangerous. Layton is just stupid."

Captain Skyler looked annoyed. "Yes, very clever. Now shut up and listen to me, Kyle. Never never never underestimate the power of stupid. That's how we got into this mess. And it's not just Layton. It's all those people who stand with him. And some of them are pretty smart."

"Not smart enough to see how stupid he is—"

"But smart enough to see the advantage in following him. They're the ones who are dangerous." Captain Skyler softened his voice. "Kyle, you have a lot of history to learn. Not Hella history—Earth history. With all the intelligence all those people had, with all the history they could have learned from—they didn't. And apparently we didn't either."

Madam Coordinator stopped him and turned to us. "We need you three to understand just how risky this is. You could get hurt. Other people could get hurt. This is scary business. So if you don't want to do this, we can try to figure out something else."

Charles spoke first. "You all went off and talked for a long time. But you couldn't figure out another way, could you?"

Madam Coordinator said, "You're right, Charles. We couldn't. But we do want to make one change in the plan. We don't want HARLIE to broadcast the video, not right away—" Before Charles could interrupt, before anyone could, she held up a hand. "Listen to me. We don't know where Captain Boynton is, but we don't think he's been disappeared. So if you can find Captain Boynton, go to him first. Tell him what he needs to know. Tell him that we survived, and we're in hiding. Do not tell him about the exiles. And most definitely do not tell him about X-Station, understand? Just tell Captain Boynton we're alive and what's on the video. He'll know what to do. He can get you to the transceiver. But he'll need time to organize. Because as soon as that video goes live, there'll be chaos. Boynton will be the necessary authority. He can even invoke the Suspension Clause."

"Unless—" I raised a hand. They all looked at me. I took a breath. "Unless, what if Layton is holding Captain Boynton hostage somehow. Like not letting the colonists land. Or something like that. They can't stay on the *Cascade* forever, can they?"

Captain Skyler answered. "No, they can't. And yes, we did consider that possibility. But we still think you need to go to Boynton before you do anything else. We trust him. But if you can't find Boynton—" He exchanged a glance with Madam Coordinator before turning back to us. "—you might want to consider telling J'mee's dad. We don't know where his loyalty is, but if he's as smart as J'mee says, then maybe, just maybe he'll recognize the danger of letting Layton remain in power."

J'mee shook her head. She didn't look happy about that. "My daddy thinks about business more than he thinks about anything else—"

"Thank you, yes. We know that," Madam Coordinator said. "So look, all of you. This is a big responsibility. It's lot to put on your shoulders, but if you can't find Captain Boynton, or if you think he's been compromised, or if you're not sure about J'mee's dad, or if you have any doubts at all—then you do whatever you must to get that video out. If you absolutely must, then go ahead, have HARLIE hack into the grid. Even if it means total chaos. But unless and until the whole colony knows the truth, Layton will remain in power. That would be an even bigger disaster."

Captain Skyler looked to each of us. "So what do you want to do?"

J'mee and Charles looked at each other. They both nodded. "We're going," they said. Then they looked to me.

I looked to Jeremy and Jamie. Neither of them had said much until now, but now Jamie said, "You can do this, Kyle. I believe in you." Then Jeremy reached over and squeezed my hand. "Go get him, kiddo." That got him a strange look from Jamie.

I took a breath and said, "We can do this. I can do this."

Commander Khuri prodded Captain Skyler. "Don't forget the distractions."

"Oh, right—" He fumbled in a pocket, then tossed a handful of chips on the table. "Here are some decoys. Stash them in your pockets, your shoes, your hair, your underwear. They're all encrypted, mostly garbage. If they search you, if they ask what's on the chips, you don't know. You'll be telling the truth. Where did you get them? You found them in the caves. That's true too. They'll try and decode them. Even a Class-9 hacking bot won't find anything in there—not for a couple months anyway, but the embedded malware will leak the video into the grid. That's Plan B."

"HARLIE did that?"

Commander Khuri said, "This is X-Station. We've had fifty years to study the grid and all of its weaknesses and loopholes." And then she smiled. "But yes, HARLIE helped."

The monkey stood up and took a bow.

We broke for second lunch—I think it was second lunch. X-Station doesn't run on the same clock. They don't have to. They run on three different clocks all at the same time, depending on the job. One clock is four and four—four hours on, four hours off. Another is six and six. The third is eight and eight. But there are variations. Six and eight, four and six. And it turns out a lot of the exiles work on their off hours too, some of their jobs are monitoring, others are maintenance, and there's a whole mini-section that works directly with a select core of people in Winterland. X-Station is not self-sufficient. Yet.

But we were off the clock. Or on it. We were on our own schedule, hardly breaking at all, just talking and planning, sometimes arguing, but mostly working and rehearsing our separate parts, all of us trying to figure out all the stuff that might happen and what we should do if it did.

It took a while, but it was necessary. Every part of the plan was examined, where we would go and how we would get there, the best route we should take, what to say, where to say it, and most important, how to make the most noise. That was the key to the whole thing. We had to create so much attention that no one could hustle us off to some place where we could be conveniently disappeared.

We had to be the lost children running home—hysterical, terrified, and screaming about horrible monsters in the dark.

They'd believe us. They'd have to. There are things living in the lava tubes. Not the steeper tubes higher on the cinder cone, but the shallower ones down in the foothills, where there was topsoil and tree roots and seepage—and a lot of things using the caves for shelter too. So it wasn't impossible that there were things that fed on the things that fed on the things that lived in the tubes. It wasn't impossible that some things had evolved and explored upward. It wasn't impossible that there were real booger-jacks.

But the whole colony had to hear us. We had to make noise, a lot of noise, so much noise that we'd create an uproar—an uproar so big that Coordinator Layton couldn't escape it.

Finally, Commander Khuri interrupted, "I think we need to stop. We're over-rehearsing these kids. They're going to be scared enough without our help. We need it real, not a performance. Let's take a meal-break and send them off. Who likes rice, beans, and noodles?"

Jeremy cooked. That was a treat for everyone. He says that cooking is gift-giving. Every meal is art, but you eat the art, so you have to start again just a few hours later, but that means you get to give another gift, so cooking is the best way of saying, "I love you," over and over, every day. He says it's one of the best jobs in the world, because you can even eat your mistakes. Jeremy must have grabbed fresh vegetables on the way out, and some fruit as well, because he served salad and dessert too. At one point, Jamie grinned, leaned over and whispered, "This is so good if you don't marry him, I will!"

"No, you won't!" I said right back.

And then, before we had even finished burping our approval, it was time. Captain Skyler smeared some dirt on us and Jamie ripped my longshirt in two places. Madam Coordinator wished us luck, Jamie hugged me, Captain Skyler promoted me to Class-4 Something, but I wasn't allowed to tell anyone, not until he could come back and make it official, and then we were on our way. Commander Khuri led the way.

We padded down polished corridors, then rough ones, and then we were in a lava tube. Charles hesitated for a moment—

"What's the matter?" J'mee asked.

"I don't like tubes," he said. "I really don't."

"Do you want to go back?"

"No," he said. "We have to do this." And he pushed forward.

We followed bobbing flashlights for the longest time, first through lava tubes, then through broken caverns and a confusing network of unfinished tunnels, then more lava tubes—the Winterland cinder cone was immense and we were deep inside it.

Outside, the northeast slope was a rumpled landscape, hundreds of layers of lava flows had hardened here. A few hundred thousand of years of magma piled higher and higher until the tectonic pressure shifted farther south and the towering cone fell dormant. Deep below, it still smoldered. Occasionally it rumbled in its sleep, but it was dying, its body slowly cooling.

Inside though, the cinder cone was riddled with a labyrinth of tubes and tunnels, another physical effect of Hella's lighter gravity. The colony had never fully explored these depths. After the twenty-third mapping bot had disappeared into the depths, Winterland stopped trying to map the northeast jumble. But it made sense now—of course, the bots had disappeared. X-Station caught them and shut them down.

Finally, we stopped. Commander Khuri gathered us all close into a tiny circle of light. "Now listen, listen good. You must never tell anyone where you've been. You must never say anything to anyone about X-Station. No matter who asks. Just say, 'I don't know. It was dark.'

This is the most important thing to remember." She looked to each of us. "Can I trust you?"

"Stinky promise," I said.

"Stinky promise?" She looked confused. Jamie hooked his finger against mine to show her. "Oh," she said. "Yes. Stinky promise." She hooked her finger to seal the deal. She did the same with Charles and J'mee.

"All right," she said. "This is where we leave you. From here, you go down, it's a long way, and you're going to wonder if maybe you're lost, but just keep going. Jeremy will be with you, he knows the way, and you won't get lost. Remember, you're coming out through the ventilation tunnels, it's going to be cold and windy, maybe a little wet, but it's the safest way. Once you kick out the final screen, you'll know where you are and you'll know where to go. Jeremy will take you as far as he can, but after that he might have to disappear. Don't worry, he'll be safe. But if they ask you about him, you don't know where he is, you didn't see him. Maybe he got lost searching? You don't know. Don't volunteer anything, don't make anything up, you don't know anything, remember that. That way you won't have to lie. Any last questions?"

We all looked at each other in the gloom. The adventure had suddenly gotten serious. With all the dirt on their faces, Charles and J'mee looked like zombies, I probably looked even worse. "It'll be good," Charles said. He smiled uneasily. "I've been through worse." To me, he said, "More tubes. I'll tell you about it later."

Captain Skyler spoke then. He looked grim and unhappy. "All right. Enough talk. It's time." He pointed ahead. As if that was enough.

"Okay, kiddo," Jamie said. "Go be a hero." He hugged me tight. Then Jeremy rumpled my hair and gave me a gentle nudge. "Let's roll," he said.

We had to circle the long way around the interior of the cinder cone. It would be a very long walk. We had flashlights, that helped, but the tunnels were uneven, the floors were bumpy, and it was too easy to lose our footing and stumble. It was rough going. I fell and skinned my knees a couple times, and a couple more times I slammed against a wall and skinned my good elbow.

We had to stop and rest every twenty or thirty minutes, but nobody complained. It was almost a joke that we wouldn't have to pretend to be tired and hungry and thirsty when we finally kicked our way out. We already looked terrible, and we felt even worse. By the time we got to Winterland, we'd be close to collapse. If they didn't send us straight to Med-Bay, then they'd have to bring Doctor Rhee to us. That was part of the plan too. The more people who were in the room, the harder it would be for Coordinator Layton to hide us away. We had Plan B and Plan C and Plan Whatever. I'd lost count. HARLIE would know, but we'd decided not to talk to him unless it was absolutely necessary. He had to pretend to be a broken monkey.

We didn't do a lot of talking. Mostly we focused on picking our way carefully. This would be a bad place to fall down and break another arm. Or worse, a leg. If one of us got hurt, it would be hours before help could get here. Someone would have to go all the way back to X-Station to get a rescue team to come down with a stretcher. Communication was impossible this deep.

But when we stopped, we talked. Not too much though. There was a lot of dust in the lower tunnels, so Jeremy had us wearing filter masks so we could all breathe easier.

Once though, we had to stop because J'mee started crying. We weren't sure why, so Charles went and sat with her. He put his arm around her shoulder and she sobbed into his shoulder. Jeremy took me a little way down the tunnel so they could have some privacy. We sat down side by side, and he held my hand and neither of us said anything for a while.

After a bit, Charles and J'mee joined us. She was still wiping her eyes. Jeremy asked, "Are you all right?"

J'mee was honest. She said, "No. Not really. I mean—I'm all right physically. But . . ." She sniffled. "This is all my fault. I should have said something and I didn't."

"What are you talking about?"

"My daddy. He's not really a millionaire, but he knows how to move money around, other people's money especially. So he bought up a bunch of stuff, a lot of it on margin, and filled I don't know how many cargo pods on the *Cascade.* Seeds, lots of seeds and bulbs and cuttings, genetics and spices, meat stocks and grow tanks, tools of all kinds, fabbers and rare earths, I don't know what all, even a lot of specialty foods and drinks. He figured having all that stuff on Hella, we'd be rich."

Jeremy nodded. "I've seen the manifest. Everybody has. All of that stuff becomes the property of the whole colony."

"No, you don't understand. Daddy had no intention of letting the colony have it. He was prepared to leave it in orbit unless the Council gave him special treatment. Madam Coordinator refused. That's when he started negotiating with Councilor Layton—"

"Oh," said Jeremy.

"There were a lot of private messages and finally Councilor Layton told Daddy not to worry. Daddy got very happy about something. When I asked him, he said that Councilor Layton was going to handle the political problem. I didn't realize what he meant. I should have known, shouldn't I? If I'd said something then, maybe somebody could have done something, but I don't want anybody to think that I was part of it, because I'm not, I wasn't—"

Jeremy stopped her then. "Nobody was thinking that."

She wiped her nose and looked to him. "How do you know that?"

"Isn't it obvious? HARLIE trusted you."

"Oh." But she didn't stop sniffling.

"Does anybody else know about those private messages?"

"I don't think so."

Jeremy fell silent, thinking.

I looked across to Charles. "HARLIE's going to leak them. Isn't he?"

"Probably. If he can find them."

But J'mee wasn't finished. "Jeremy—when we deliver this video, when it gets broadcast and everybody knows what happened, won't they see that Daddy was part of it too. What'll happen to him?"

Charles and Jeremy and I all looked at each other. None of us knew what to say. We wanted to tell her everything would be all right—but she'd just confessed that her dad was part of Coordinator Layton's conspiracy.

Finally, Jeremy said, "Did your father know what Councilor Layton was planning?"

J'mee shrugged and shook her head. "I don't know. I don't think so."

"If he didn't know, then he's not an actual accomplice. He might . . . I don't know. I'm not a lawyer. There are a lot of ways this could come down, J'mee. It all depends on what he knew and when he knew it. And what he'll do when he finds out the truth. That's why we have to show him the video. If your dad is as smart as you say—"

"My dad knows all the smartest ways to be stupid," said J'mee. She folded her arms, as if that was the end of the conversation.

I cleared my throat, my way of saying that I had something to say. "Well, maybe you can convince him to be a little smarter than that?"

J'mee sniffled one last time. She lowered her mask so she could wipe her nose on her sleeve. "I don't want to show him the video. I don't want to show anyone the video. I'm afraid of what'll happen." And then, looking around at us, she said, "But—we have to, don't we?"

"It's the right thing to do," said Charles. He reached over and held her hand.

J'mee nodded slowly, then pushed herself up to her feet. "All right, let's go."

We still had a long way to go. Commander Khuri had been right. The tunnel was long, so long that we started wondering if we were going the right way, but Jeremy said that some of the lava tubes were fifty klicks straight downhill, and this one was nowhere near the longest.

At one point, I started giggling. Jeremy asked me what was so funny. I said, "The noise is off. Even if I wanted to turn it on again, I couldn't." Then I had to explain to him about the implant and the noise and why I'd gone to Doctor Rhee.

"Why did you do that, Kyle?"

"I wanted to find out who I really am. And I wanted to know . . . I wanted to know who you really care about."

"Oh," he said. "Well, here's your answer. I knew there was something different about you at X-Station. I didn't know what it was. Now I do. I like it. I like you this way. Are you going to turn the chip back on?"

"Maybe. Eventually. But if it doesn't work right, I'll turn it off and leave it off. Is that okay with you?"

"Of course it is." He patted my shoulder and aimed the light forward. "Better be careful now. It's getting steep." He called back. "How are you doing, Charles?"

"I've had better days." Then he added, "I'm coming. I'm coping."

J'mee called, "He's doing the counting and breathing exercise. He's fine."

When we finally reached the bottom of the tunnel, it branched. We went through several narrow caverns—some of them looked like they'd been carved, others looked like fractures in the lava, places where the weight of the different layers had broken apart, leaving narrow chasms and sometimes even wide corridors. There were boards bridging the worst of the cracks—and in one place a rope bridge went across the widest. As tired as we were, we picked our way slowly and cautiously. My feet hurt—and both my legs, and my good arm too.

Finally, the passage came to a tunnel that had been carved, the walls were too even and scored with regular patterns, the evidence of a digging-bot. "This tunnel was made," I said. "Didn't the seismic monitors reveal the digging?"

Jeremy laughed. "How do you hide a noise, Kyle?"

"Hide it under a louder noise?"

"Right. Whenever Winterland digs a tunnel or remodels a cavern, somewhere an X-Station tunnel is being dug as well."

"Oh. That makes sense." I thought for a moment. "Can I ask? How many people are living at X-Station?"

"You can ask," Jeremy said. "I can't answer. I don't know. That's one of the biggest secrets. Not even all the exiles know. The whole thing is supposed to be a safety valve for the colony. It's a long story."

"You can tell me later."

"No, I can't." He looked to me. "Seriously, Kyle. I can't. I don't know very much. Only what I need to know. And that's almost nothing. We're not supposed to talk about it. And you're better off not knowing—because you can't reveal what you don't know."

"Oh," I said. "I guess that makes sense too."

We stopped talking for a while and concentrated on the trek. Every so often, the corridor branched. Mostly we took the right branch, but not every time. I had long since lost all sense of direction. Jeremy didn't have a map, but he had a list of specific directions. Up, down, left, right. As long as we followed them exactly, we'd get where we were supposed to go. There were no signs anywhere, no identifying marks, nothing that would help an unwelcome explorer find their way. I was glad we didn't find anyone's bones. That would have been bad. It gave me an uncomfortable feeling, just thinking about it.

And then finally, after what seemed like forever, we stopped for what Jeremy said would be our last rest. Here, he collected all but one of our flashlights, our air-masks and canteens, and whatever food we still hadn't eaten—anything that would have been evidence that we'd been to X-Station. We didn't talk much. I think we were all too tired to say anything.

Jeremy sat down next to me, put his arm around me and pulled me close. I didn't mind, not even when he rumpled my hair and kissed my cheek. He whispered, "Hey, kiddo. It's gonna be fine."

"I know."

He grunted. I wasn't sure what that meant.

"Jeremy? Are you gonna be okay? Will you be able to find your way back?"

"I'm not going back the same way. No need to. From here, I'll go back to the farm. Not the big one, one of the little ones that not very many people know about. One of the test beds. I'll stay there until it's safe. Once you get that video out, as soon as the storm breaks, the weather truck will start pinging its arrival. That should get a big crowd down to the docks. I'll probably see you there."

"Promise?"

"I promise." It was okay, we didn't need to stinky promise.

"All right." I took a deep breath. "I'm ready to go. Charles? J'mee?"

"We're ready. Anytime."

"HARLIE? You ready?"

The monkey was safe in my backpack. It chirped a single beep of readiness, then it went silent again.

"Okay, let's roll." I don't know why we say, "Let's roll." I mean, it's the right thing to say in a Rollagon. But it makes no sense at all when we're walking. People don't have wheels. But we say it anyway.

It wasn't far to the end of the corridor. Here was a steep vertical tube with a ladder carved into the side. At the bottom was an access to a ventilation tube. Jeremy didn't come with us. "This is it, kids. Make it count." He levered Charles and J'mee down the tube, kissed me one last time, and pushed me after them.

At the bottom, the ventilation tube was narrow and we had to crawl. It was windy here—at some distant far end, this channel opened to the outside, catching the relentless winds coming in off Hella's stormy ocean, but this deep in the ventilation system, we were safe. The air had been scrubbed and filtered and slowed down.

It was all explained in one of the videos I made about Winterland. The incoming air was irradiated at least a dozen times and passed through multiple air-turbines too. By the time it arrived at the settlement levels it was only a mild breeze—except during a super-storm. That's when multiple sets of internal louvres had to shift their pitch, blocking the worst of the assault, bringing the speed of the wind in the vents down to a manageable velocity.

Usually we only got five or six super-storms in winter, but sometimes it was hard to tell, because sometimes the storms were so big and lasted so long and kept hitting us one after the other that sometimes it felt like it was just one big super-storm that lasted all winter long. Nobody knew for sure if this storm would break or last for months. The weather software couldn't keep up with Hella's atmosphere. It would be hard for even a heavy-duty weather truck to travel the few kilometers around the cinder cone to get from X-Station to Winterland Station. But Captain Skyler said they would do it—as soon as the video went public.

There were multiple branches here, but Jeremy had given us very precise instructions. But even if he hadn't, the interiors here were clearly labeled and identified. There were even maps showing airflow and exits and where each vent came out. And warnings not to go up the several lava tubes that connected, they hadn't been fully explored.

Captain Skyler had picked out the safest exit for us. It was the one where we would be least likely to be seen or caught. It was a vent that served one of the cargo corridors, not the big one, not even the second deeper one, but the one that was used for overflow, when a whole bunch of trucks all came in at the same time.

If the last convoy had gotten out of Summerland in time, those trucks would have been parked here and crews would have been already servicing them, getting them ready for the spring migration. There was always a lot of work to do. I'd helped with the cleaning two years in a row—all the Class 1's did, that was almost everybody under the age of three. The Class Zeros were still in diapers. Hella Rule Number One: If you're old enough to work, you work. If you want calories, you gotta spend calories.

But there was no one here now and only a few work lights remained on. Just enough to keep people from banging into things. It was a large empty space, dark and gloomy.

A thick screen blocked the vent, but it could be unlatched from the inside. We wouldn't have to kick it out or shout for help either. It came out high on the wall just above the catwalk and that was a little problem, especially for Charles and J'mee. They were still thinking in terms of Earth gravity. But eventually, they had no choice. J'mee backed out of the tube, and she and Charles held each other's wrists. He lowered her as far as he could and when he let go she only had to drop another two meters to the catwalk. I couldn't do the math in my head without the noise, but we figured it couldn't be much worse than a two-meter fall on Earth and the catwalk wasn't rigid, it might have enough give to soften the impact.

When she was ready, she let go. She fell and stumbled, and she cried out too, but more from the shock of landing than from any pain. "I'm fine," she said. "I'm fine."

Then it was Charles' turn. I could only hold onto him with one arm, but J'mee stood up beneath him to catch him and help break his fall. Charles said it would be okay, because J'mee was stronger than both of us. He was right. She caught him and even though he came down clumsy, neither one of them fell.

Finally, it was my turn. I had no one to lower me, and my left arm was in a cast, so that complicated things too. I had a slightly higher drop—but J'mee and Charles were both there to catch me. It was awkward, but nobody fell down and nobody got hurt. We all looked at each other and laughed, I don't know why, we just felt silly.

"Okay," said Charles. "We gotta get serious. J'mee?"

She nodded. "Give me a minute. I have to—" She wiped her nose and sniffed. "We had to leave our dog behind. I miss her so much. Daddy wouldn't let me bring her, he said—he said a lot of things—" Her voice broke. "It still hurts. I want—I want my dog, and—" Then she said, "Okay, I'm crying now, let's go."

We hurried along the catwalk, to another one that crossed the top of the cavern, and then down the ladder-tube. By the time we got to the bottom of the cavern, J'mee was sobbing loudly. "I didn't want to leave her. She didn't understand. She was barking and whining and jumping at the gate. I wouldn't let go. Daddy had to drag me to the car. I didn't want to go to the moon, I didn't want to go anywhere. I didn't want to come to Hella—I just want to go home."

She was very convincing. I believed her.

We didn't know if the reception chambers would be empty. There was a small caf here too and a row of offices, but we bypassed them by going through the tool and equipment bays. If there were no trucks here, there would be no service teams, and the tool bays would be deserted too. Only a few silent bots waited along the walls.

J'mee stifled a sob and looked around. "Where are we?"

I pulled her close as if I was comforting her, the same way Jamie used to comfort me. I pointed ahead. "We're almost there. It's just past the apartments. These are reserved for the service teams, so they should be empty. Just the other side is Broadway."

I didn't want to tell them that we were passing under live surveillance cameras. I was afraid they'd look up. We needed to hurry, so I said, "Don't cry, J'mee. We're almost there. See? Look?"

That was our agreed-upon signal for her to cry louder. As loud as she could. She started howling then. "Don't let it get me! Don't let it get me! I want to go home!"

Charles understood as well. "Come on," he said. "Come on!"

We had to look tired and dirty and hungry, and we didn't have to pretend. We were already tired and dirty and hungry. We hurried past the empty apartments, down past the decorative gardens, and into the passage that led to Broadway. There were people there, and they saw us; they turned and shouted. Several came running toward us. But we had to get to Broadway. We needed to attract a crowd, a big crowd—so we ran from them as if they were monsters from the caves.

"Don't let them get me! Don't let the monsters get me!" J'mee was shrieking now, almost incoherently. She charged ahead in a mad panic, with Charles and I doing our best to catch up to her, but she was faster than either of us.

Hella gravity is normal to me, but people born on Earth have trouble adjusting, they don't have the muscle memory. They have to learn how to walk a whole new way, they have to learn how to run differently too. J'mee must have been practicing. With every step she threw herself forward, scrambling and bouncing like a terrified rabbit, always looking like she was about to stumble, but always catching herself each time. She hurtled through the gathering crowd like a bowling ball, even knocking aside a couple of people who tried to catch her.

And the noise she made—she wasn't trying to make words anymore.

She just screamed and shrieked and waved her arms for everyone to get out of her way. She was warding off the invisible creatures—

"Booger-jacks!" I shouted. "There are booger-jacks in the caves! The booger-jacks are after us! Don't let them get us!" Charles started shouting too. Some of the people chasing us stopped and looked back the way we came.

And then, finally, we were running up Broadway and there was a real crowd here, too many to push aside, they caught up with us, they surrounded us, and we collapsed into their arms, out of breath and too exhausted to speak. J'mee fell into someone's arms, still sobbing. Charles went down onto his knees. Someone grabbed me into a restraining hug, I couldn't see who. I just kept repeating the same words, over and over, "Booger-jacks in the caverns, in the tubes, we heard them, they chased us, we couldn't find our way out, the booger-jacks are real, don't let them get us!"

We must have been very convincing. I think we even believed it ourselves. Everything turned into a blur of faces and noises and confusing questions. Someone shoved a water bottle at me, I drank thirstily. I kept looking around, "Where's Charles, where's J'mee? Where's my mother! I want to go home!" And always, "Don't let them get us!"

I recognized one of the truck drivers. "Who's after you, Kyle—?"

"Booger-jacks! In the caves! They chased us! We got lost!" I could hear J'mee crying. Charles was protesting something. And now, other voices started making themselves heard—authoritative voices. "They're incoherent."

"They're in shock. Get them to Med-Bay—"

"No. These are pilgrimage kids. Take them to the executive Med-Bay—"

"Someone call Doctor Rhee."

"What happened to them—?"

"We don't know—"

"They've been lost for three days—"

"Isn't that the little brain-bot?"

"Shut up! He can hear you!"

Someone tossed me over his shoulder. Other people lifted J'mee and Charles. We were carried somewhere at a run. A crowd of people surrounded us. A couple security guards came running, but the crowd ignored them. People shouted and even more people came running. I couldn't see clearly, everything was bobbing up and down, but I could see enough to know that the crowd around us kept getting larger and louder. Everybody had questions or advice or simply kept repeating what they thought they'd heard.

"What's going on—?"

"There are booger-jacks in the caves!"

"There's no such thing—"

"The kids saw them—"

"They didn't see anything. They're hysterical—"

"They must have seen something—"

"Somebody must have done something to them—"

"Were they kidnapped?"

"We'll find out—"

And a few shouts of, "It's all right! You're safe now! You're safe!"

We weren't, but we were the only ones who knew that.

Executive Med-Bay isn't much different, just a little smaller. There isn't a lot of extra room on the exec levels. Not yet anyway. Coordinator Layton had announced an expansion of the section. He said it would be necessary to increase the administrative staff before the new colonists landed. But the work hadn't started yet. He was still reorganizing things.

But the exec Med-Bay was big enough for us. We took up three of the six med-beds. Nobody else was in the section, just us and Doctor Rhee and one of her nurses. His name was Jolly. He was tall and skinny and hardly ever talked.

After she finished scanning each of us, she shooed him out. "Go to the caf. Get sandwiches and fruit juice. Charge it to Med-Bay." She came over to my bed and parked herself in a convenient chair.

"All right, Kyle," she said. "What's going on?"

I looked across to Charles and J'mee. Should I tell her?

"Don't look at them," she said. "I'm asking you."

"I—I can't tell you. I don't know. I mean—" I stopped.

She took my hand in hers. She turned it face up as if she intended to examine it, but she held my hand so I could clearly see what she was doing. With her index finger, she drew an X across my palm.

"Kyle, whatever it is, you're safe now." She drew another X.

It took me a second.

Oh. Right.

Captain Skyler said that only two people at Winterland knew the truth. It made sense that Doctor Rhee would be one of them. But what if she wasn't?

I looked up at the ceiling, at the walls around us, then back to Doctor Rhee—my way of asking if someone might be listening.

She nodded. Yes, someone might be.

I still wasn't sure. Nobody had told us about Doctor Rhee. Maybe in all the excitement, but no—

Or maybe she wasn't in the right place to help, so we weren't supposed to take the risk—

I couldn't figure it out. Not without the noise. "I don't want to talk to anyone," I said. "Only Captain Boynton."

"Not your mom?"

"Yes, my mom. But Captain Boynton too. Where is he?"

"He's with the searchers. A lot of people have been looking for you.

All three of you." She added, "But everybody knows you're safe now. The searchers are coming back, but it might be a while. Some of them went pretty deep. So I thought you might want to talk to me first." She folded my fingers over and squeezed my hand.

"I don't think there's anything to tell—"

"All right, have it your way. But there will have to be an investigation, probably a big public investigation. It looks like you violated the safeties. You put Charles and J'mee in danger. A lot of people are going to want to know what you did and why. You'd better be prepared for that."

I gulped and nodded. I didn't know if she was serious or saying it for the cameras. I thought I was doing pretty well, but without the noise I had no way of checking. I wanted everybody to know everything, but without the noise, I was on my own.

Doctor Rhee softened her tone. "Kyle, I have to ask you. Does this have anything to do with your—with the procedure?"

I shook my head. "No. Yes. Maybe a little. But not really. I mean—I don't know what I mean." I didn't want the conversation to continue. I was afraid I might say something I shouldn't.

J'mee must have realized what was happening because she started shrieking again. "Where are we?! What's happening?! I want to go home?! Where's my Daddy?! Don't let them get us!"

Doctor Rhee straightened immediately, grabbed something from the supply cabinet and strode right up to J'mee. "Knock it off, kid. I don't want to sedate you, and you don't want a reputation as a hysteric." She held up an injector, and J'mee shut up in mid-shriek.

"I thought so." Doctor Rhee looked around at the three of us. "All right, I get it. I hope you know what you're doing."

At least, I think that's what she intended to say. Before she could finish the sentence, three men came pushing into the room, one of them shouting and shoving Jolly out of the way. He was protesting,

"You can't come in here—" but they ignored him. All of them were big, but the shouting man was the biggest. He was very angry and very loud. "Where's my daughter?! What are you people doing here? Letting children get lost, running around in caves with who knows what kinds of monsters?" J'mee's dad. He glanced around the room as if looking for someone to attack, but when he saw J'mee, he stopped.

He went immediately to her bedside. "Are you all right? What do you mean, disappearing like that? I told you not to hang around with these people! If that little freak-boy touched you in any way—"

"Daddy! He's my friend. Chigger too."

"Is that what they want you to say? Come on, I'll take you home—" He bent to scoop her up—

"No! No! We have to stay together!" She pushed him away.

He whirled on Doctor Rhee. "What the hell is going on here?"

"I think I can explain." She was still holding the sedative injector.

"You'd better," J'mee's dad demanded. He glanced at the injector in her hand. "What's that for?"

"It's for you if you don't stop yelling. This child is in shock, and I'm not releasing her. She doesn't leave until I say so." She pointed to the two bodyguards. "You two, wait outside. And don't let anyone in." They looked to J'mee's dad. He nodded and they left. After the door closed behind them, Doctor Rhee pointed to a chair. "You'd better sit down." After he did she handed the sedative injector to Jolly. "J'mee, do you want to tell your father what's going on?"

J'mee nodded reluctantly. She sat up straighter. "Daddy—? Will you let me tell you the whole story? Do you promise not to interrupt? Stinky promise?"

"What's a stinky promise?"

She showed him. He made a face. "That's silly."

"Daddy, this is very important."

"Fine. Stinky promise."

J'mee took a breath. "Daddy, I know that you and Mister Layton have been making plans—"

"Coordinator Layton," he corrected.

"You promised not to interrupt—"

"Fine. Go on."

"He's not the Coordinator. I mean, he shouldn't be. I know that you've been making plans with him, but, well—I don't think you should. you shouldn't have anything at all to do with him."

"Sweetheart, I know you mean well, but there's a lot you don't understand. This is grownup business—"

"So is this, Daddy. And stop interrupting. Mister Layton crashed the lifter. I mean, he arranged it. He wanted to kill Captain Skyler and Madam Coordinator and everyone, so he could become Coordinator—"

"J'mee, you're too smart to believe those silly stories—"

"Daddy, shut up! Please!"

He started to rise. "J'mee, I'm your father. Or have you forgotten? Hanging around with these—these menials?! You will not talk to me like that. We'll finish this conversation only after you remember your manners." He made as if to leave—

"Daddy! They're still alive! They weren't on the lifter. And there's evidence that proves that Layton did it. His whole family—almost. Marley confessed! There's a video!"

For a moment, he hesitated.

"Daddy, they're alive. I saw them."

"Where?" he demanded.

"I can't tell you. I mean, I won't tell you where they are. Not until the video is broadcast."

"Sweetheart, listen to me. Videos can be faked. Whatever these people are trying to do—"

"Daddy, everybody's going to know what happened. If you knew about the crash, and you don't say something first—"

"That's not going to happen! Whoever you saw, whatever they said, it's a lie. You're too young to understand. There's too much at stake. There are selfish people everywhere who want to stop us from having a good life here—"

"Daddy! No! You're not listening!"

"I've heard all I need to. You're hysterical, and I'm taking you out of here—" He bent to pick her up. She tried to push him away—

Doctor Rhee pushed him back. She stepped between them, holding her hand out sideways. Jolly slapped the injector into her hand and she held it up right in front of the big man's eyes, really close. "Step back, sir! She's not going anywhere with you. She's my patient. She's under my supervision. She's not leaving here until I discharge her." Before he could speak, she added one more thing, "And you really do not want to piss me off."

Whoever J'mee's dad had been on Earth, he wasn't used to people getting in his face, not like this. But nobody argued with Doctor Rhee. Or any member of the med-staff. It wasn't healthy.

He didn't back down. "I can have you suspended—"

"I doubt it, but do you really want to go without health maintenance?" She met his angry stare with polite calm. "While your body is still trying to adjust to this planet?"

That stopped him. He stepped back.

"You haven't heard the last of this."

"Neither have you. I suggest you think long and hard before you do anything stupid. Your daughter is trying to save you from being held as an accomplice to a criminal conspiracy."

"You believe her? Or are you part of it too?"

"The question is whether or not *you* believe her. She's your daughter."

J'mee's dad didn't answer. He glowered at Doctor Rhee, decided he had nothing else to say, and stormed out of the Med-Bay.

Doctor Rhee turned around and looked at us. "Well, this is going to be interesting. You three stay here. Jolly, watch them. I have some calls to make." She handed him the sedative injector and stepped into the next room, but she left the door open so she could peer out at us from time to time. I don't know if we were supposed to hear what she was saying. Probably. Or she would have closed the door. We looked at each other in silence and listened hard.

"Yes, they're here. They're safe. But I don't know for how long. How soon can you get here? Isn't there anyone? Yes, I know it's a secured level, but—all right, see what you can do. I'll think of something."

After a bit, she came out and looked at us. "Well, it's about to get interesting around here. Now, let's see if I understand this. The lifter was sabotaged. Layton ordered it. But they're alive anyway. And Marley confessed. And there's a video to prove it. Is that all?"

"Um—" We looked to each other. We didn't want to say anything about HARLIE. "Um, pretty much. Yes."

"Do you have the video?"

Charles started to answer. "We—uh, kinda."

"We're supposed to give it to Captain Boynton," I said.

"That's going to be a problem."

"Huh?"

Doctor Rhee didn't look happy. "Coordinator Layton has assigned him a pair of bodyguards. They're not to leave his side."

"But he doesn't need—oh."

"Uh-huh. That's right. Anything you want to tell him, you might as well tell Layton at the same time."

"So it's up to us, isn't it?"

Charles nodded. "Yep."

We all looked at each other. None of us said anything for a minute.

"So, I guess we'll have to—"

Before anyone could finish a sentence, the door whooshed open. This time it was the two big men who'd come in with J'mee's dad.

They both looked angry and one of them held a stun-club and pointed it at Doctor Rhee. "Get out of the way."

Doctor Rhee looked to Jolly, shrugged, and they both stepped back.

The one without the club turned to J'mee. "Where's the video? The video you told your dad about?"

She folded her arms and shook her head.

He turned to Charles, then me. "Which one of you has it?"

The other one waved his club and said, "Don't bother. Just search them."

It didn't take long, but they were thorough. They found all but three of the decoy chips that Captain Skyler had given us. They tossed them onto a table, with all of our other belongings too. Including the monkey. It flopped on the table, lifeless.

"Is that it?" asked the one.

"Doesn't matter. Take it all."

I shouted. "Please, sir—not my monkey! Please—"

The man with the club grabbed the monkey and held it up by one arm, as if it might be dangerous. He frowned at it suspiciously.

"It was a present," I said. "It's all I have."

Doctor Rhee spoke up. "Jack! That's his binky. It's his emotional support."

Jack shook his head. "Julie, I have my orders."

"Yes, we all have orders. Mine is to protect the health of every human being on this planet. And that includes their mental health. Look at the damn thing—it's broken. But it's important to the boy. You can see that for yourself." And then she lowered her voice even more. "Jack, you know Kyle. You know his family. And you know his situation—his condition. You know what he's been through."

Jack hesitated.

Doctor Rhee stepped forward, intense now. "Jack, you have to know what this means to him. You have a kid of your own."

"Aw, come on, Julie—don't go there."

"If you take that toy, you know what's going to happen—it'll end up shoved into some closet somewhere. Nobody will remember where. And he'll never get it back. And he'll have a whole new set of betrayals to deal with. It's hard enough for him already. Why do you want to make it harder?"

"I'm not a monster, Julie—"

"Then stop acting like one." And then she stepped back and looked at both of the men. "I gotta ask you this. This isn't about the monkey anymore. It's about you. You know what's going on. Do you really want to make any more enemies—more than you already have?"

"Oh, the hell with it, already!" Jack threw the monkey at me. It bounced off the bed and onto the floor. "Keep the damn thing." He scooped up all the decoy chips and shoved them into a carry bag. He looked to Doctor Rhee. "You're the last one who should be talking about enemies, Julie. Things are going to be a lot different around here."

And then he left. Both of them left.

Doctor Rhee came over to me, picked up the monkey from the floor and pushed it into my arms. "I hope that was worth it," she said.

I looked to Charles and J'mee. "We have to do this ourselves, don't we?" They both nodded their agreement.

Doctor Rhee said, "Whatever it is you're thinking of doing—"

"I'm not thinking of anything," said J'mee. "We've lost. Game over. I quit." She pushed herself up. "I'm going home. Charles, Kyle, are you coming?"

"Huh? What?"

"Come on!" she said. "I'm hungry. I'm tired. I want to sleep in my own bed tonight. They took all the chips. Nobody's going to believe us. So I don't care if the things in the caves eat them all. I'm done."

"J'mee—?" Charles looked upset. I didn't understand either.

"I'm done. We're done. Like the song says, kiss today goodbye and point me toward tomorrow."

Oh. Right. Kiss today goodbye and point me toward tomorrow. That was our agreed-on code. Follow my lead. Play along.

Doctor Rhee stared at us, J'mee to Charles to me. "All right. Fine. But I'm going to walk you home." She explained, "I want to make sure you get there safely. We don't need any more excitement. Jolly, hold the fort. If anyone asks where I am, tell them you don't know."

It wasn't far from the executive Med-Bay. J'mee's dad had a suite close to the Council rooms. Doctor Rhee pretended to be leading us there. We passed a few people in the corridor, but aside from a couple of curious stares, no one tried to stop us. J'mee waved to Troy at reception, Doctor Rhee reassured him that we were all under her supervision, and he buzzed us through.

As soon as we entered the suite, I stopped to stare. These rooms were spacious. Charles and J'mee took it for granted, maybe that's how big rooms were on Earth, but the only things small on Hella are the living spaces. Most apartments at Winterland are cozy, which is a polite word for tight. There was enough room here for six apartments. It wasn't fair.

J'mee must have seen me frowning. She said, "Coordinator Layton cleared this space for us. I think they had to move some offices. Wait here. I want to make sure we're alone." She left us for a moment while she searched through all the other rooms. *Other* rooms! This was a lot to think about. I went over to the window and stared out at the distant cinder cones. One of the farthest ones was smoking, not badly though.

When J'mee came back, she said, "It's safe. We can talk. Daddy has the place swept for bugs sometimes two or three times a day. He doesn't trust anybody. Not about business."

We stopped talking because Doctor Rhee was on the phone. "Sandwiches for four. No, make that five. And lemonade. No, not that crap—they need some real protein. Send them to the executive Med-Bay. Jolly will know where to bring them. Yes, that's right. Thank you."

She turned to us. "First things first. You're going to rest, clean up, get some real food into you, and then you're going to tell me everything. Or maybe we should start with that."

"We need to get to the HARLIE box," said J'mee. "This is closer."

Charles said, "It's around the corner, down the hall and—"

Doctor Rhee finished the sentence. "—and right behind the security desk. There's the problem. How do you get security to buzz you through? Have you figured that part out?"

"We were hoping that Captain Boynton could get us in. Or even J'mee's dad." Charles said that.

"Yes, well—" Doctor Rhee stopped there. She didn't know how to finish the sentence. "Maybe. I dunno." She shook her head.

"You have an idea?"

"No. Not really. Why the HARLIE box?"

"It's the easiest way to get the video onto the grid so everyone can see it."

"Hm. Can I see this video?"

"Better not," said Charles. "If we play it anywhere, it could be tapped, and Mr. Layton will know we still have it and what's on it and—right now, it's still safe because he thinks he has all the copies. As long as he doesn't know, we have a chance."

"All right," she said. "I have to trust you. You have to trust me. I guess that's fair." Doctor Rhee turned to me. "Kyle, I have to ask. As your doctor. How are you doing?"

That made Charles and J'mee look up. Charles said, "Huh? Is there something wrong with you?"

Doctor Rhee looked to me. "You didn't tell them?"

"I didn't tell anyone. There was a lot of stuff happening all at once. There wasn't time. When I finally had a chance to think about it, I decided to wait and see if anyone noticed a difference."

"And?"

"Well, Jeremy said he did, but that was only after I told him. I didn't tell anyone else."

Charles spoke up then. "Kyle? What didn't you tell us?"

"I turned my chip off. For a while."

"Oh," he said. "That's cool. Are you okay without it?"

"I think so. I'm feeling things different. More personal maybe, but not like selfish. Maybe it's that nuance thing. I dunno. I do miss being able to know stuff just by thinking. But—it's okay. I don't miss the noise. I feel . . . nicer. Like there's more me."

"Are you ever going to want it back on?" asked J'mee.

"I don't know. Maybe. But only if it isn't so noisy. It's a little harder making decisions without it. I have to ask myself what's right and wrong. There's no one else to ask. But at least they're my choices, aren't they? Not something the implant says."

Doctor Rhee said, "You might make more mistakes without the implant."

"But they'll be my mistakes, won't they? Not someone else's."

She didn't look happy. "That's one way of looking at it, I guess."

"Making my own mistakes—isn't that what responsibility is all about?"

"I will not argue with you, Kyle. You are not a dummy. And right now, I'm think that maybe you just proved something. Remember that thing we were talking about? That the implant might have caused some parts of your brain to change. Maybe develop some new abilities? I think that might have happened."

"Wow," said Charles. J'mee too.

"But—" said Doctor Rhee. "I also think it's because of the way you used the implant. What you studied, what you learned, what you practiced."

Jolly arrived then with a big tray of food, and we fell to it eagerly, stuffing our faces with fried egg sandwiches—adult-sized sandwiches with bacon and cheddar cheese on fresh wheat buns, and strawberry lemonade to wash it all down. Charles made grunting noises like a pig, and we all laughed.

"Did you have any trouble getting in?" Doctor Rhee asked.

Jolly shook his head. "Nah. Just another tray."

"Yeah, a sandwich can go anywhere—" She stopped in mid-bite.

We all stopped. We all realized it at the same time.

Sandwiches. Can go anywhere. Because people are always working.

"What?" said Jolly. "Something wrong?"

"Uh, no. We're good." Doctor Rhee's voice went funny. "You know what—I came up here in a hurry. I forgot to grab a kit. And um, these kids are still kinda hyped up, so I'm gonna want to check them over again. Will you grab my kit from the Med-Bay? And um . . . make sure the sedative-injector is loaded, will you do that? Thank you, Jol."

"Sure, Doc." And he was gone.

As soon as the door whooshed shut behind him, we all looked at each other.

Doctor Rhee said, "Wait. Finish eating first—"

Of course, we didn't wait. We all started talking at once, mostly with our mouths full. It wasn't the greatest plan, it was silly and probably wouldn't work, but it was just silly enough that nobody would suspect what we were really up to.

The best part was that it didn't take much planning or preparation—all we had to do was show up. We only needed one thing. Well, maybe two. Jolly brought up Doctor Rhee's medical kit. She said she felt naked without it. I thought that was a weird thing to say, and I explained. "But we're all naked, always. All of us, all the time—under our clothes, I mean." Charles and J'mee stared at me for a minute, then they both burst out laughing. Maybe I was missing something. Nuance? Without the noise, I couldn't check every sentence.

When Jolly returned with the med-kit, he looked puzzled, but we couldn't tell him what we were up to. The fewer people who knew, the better—especially if we were caught. We didn't want to get anyone else in trouble. Doctor Rhee told Jolly that she needed to be sure that we weren't still suffering from shock. The three of us were still so turmoiled we might have trouble sleeping. Maybe even nightmares. Jolly seemed to accept that and she told him to turn in for the day.

The second thing—actually, the first—required a call down to the caf. Doctor Rhee called. They said it couldn't be ready for at least an hour, so we used the time to shower, and this time it didn't matter that we were all naked—"naked *without* our clothes," Charles joked. We started rehearsing our separate parts even before we dried off. Finally, it was time to dress.

We have lots of holidays at Winterland. Summerland too. Everything's a party. There's a big one for the equinox, another for the solstice, one for the start of a migration, another for the arrival. We do Thanksgiving, New Year's, and Memorial Day. Then there are the anniversaries. Arrival Day is an important one, but Acknowledgment Week is the biggest. So the executive apartments always have an assortment of costumes and makeup and masks. We burrowed through the closets to see what we could find. There was plenty.

J'mee wore an exo-skeleton costume. It made her as tall as Doctor Rhee and she looked like a Power Warrior.

Charles chose a carnosaur costume. He had a huge headpiece and a big floppy tail, red-brown scales and floppy feathers. We could see his grin inside the carnosaur jaws. He looked like he'd been swallowed whole.

Doctor Rhee put on a rainbow wizard hat and a rainbow coverall. She took a few things from her medical kit and stashed them somewhere under her robe.

And I dressed as a ground-monkey. HARLIE was the baby-monkey on my back.

As soon as the cake arrived, we were ready. Doctor Rhee stuck some sparklers in it and we headed for the security desk, all singing. "Today is your birthday! So put on your pants! We're having a party! We're all gonna dance!"

We hopped up and down around the security desk, making as much noise as possible. Doctor Rhee plopped the cake down on the desk in front of the reception guard. "Okay, Nance—let us in!"

Behind the desk, Nancy Varga blinked in confusion, looking from one to the next, trying to sort us out. "Nobody told me about a birthday—"

"It's J'mee's birthday," I said. "It's not on the calendar yet."

Charles added, "Her dad promised her!"

Doctor Rhee said, "In all the excitement, he must have forgotten. Come on, Nance. This is important—"

"I don't know," she said. "I should check—" She reached for a button.

"You'll spoil the surprise!" I shouted.

She hesitated. She looked uncertain. "Coordinator Layton has been very specific. I really can't—"

That was as far as she got.

"Okay. Plan B," said Doctor Rhee. She reached over and pressed the sedative injector to Nancy Varga's neck.

"Hunh? What did you—" And then her eyes rolled up, and she sank back in her chair.

Doctor Rhee grabbed Nancy's hand and pressed her index finger to a green button on the desktop panel. The security doors whooshed open. "You have ten minutes. Go!"

Doctor Rhee pushed us forward. Charles grabbed the cake. And he almost dropped it! A man walked carelessly around the corner, J'mee bumped hard into him. He was one of the aides who'd come down from the *Cascade* with Captain Boynton. He was a big man. He almost knocked her over.

"Michael Brown!" J'mee looked up at him and smiled. "Unca Mike!"

He blinked—and then he recognized her. "J'mee, you know better. Nobody's allowed in here."

She grabbed his arm. "I need your help, Michael."

"Huh? What the hell—?"

"Michael, I need to—Charles needs to get a message up to the ship. To his mom. He needs to let her know he's all right. The network isn't connecting, but we can do it through the HARLIE box, can't we?"

"You mean the transceiver?"

"Yes. The big orange box."

Michael Brown scratched his head, puzzled. "Um. They moved it."

"Where?"

"I don't know. They didn't tell me. Coordinator Layton said it was necessary. Something about protecting it from troublemakers. Everything is locked away."

Get out.

That was the noise—except it wasn't noise. The noise was gone. I said, "Well, um—okay. I guess if we can't, we can't. We'll go now—" Charles and J'mee stared at me, confused.

Michael blinked as if he was just recognizing me. "Oh, you're Kyle, right. The kid with all the videos. Charles, why are you carrying a cake? J'mee, what the hell is going on here?"

"It's too long to explain. We need—"

Get out.

There it was again. "We need to go." I said it aloud. "Now."

"J'mee, what is going on?"

"Um, nothing." J'mee frowned at me, but she gave Charles a push. "We just—it's all right. We'll go." We left him shaking his head in confusion. "Kids—"

Back outside, Doctor Rhee was checking Nancy Varga's pulse. She looked up as the door whooshed shut behind us. "That was fast—"

"They moved the transceiver," Charles said.

"We can't get in," said J'mee.

Under the desk. Let me look.

I didn't question the noise. I pulled the monkey from my back and rolled under the security desk—

There. Hold me up.

I lifted the monkey up to the underside of the security desk.

"A little to the left, please. Now up. Higher. That's good. Thank you, Kyle." The monkey extended a part of its anatomy and plugged himself into the socket. I didn't know if I should be embarrassed or curious. HARLIE must have guessed what I was thinking, because he said, "Relax, Kyle. It could have been worse. Think about it."

Oh. Right.

After that, the navel connection didn't seem so strange anymore.

"Kyle?" That was Charles. "You'd better come out. Now." Something about the way he said it—the monkey disengaged itself, and we slid out from under the desk.

Drop me.

The monkey went limp in my hands. I left it on the floor and rolled out from under the security desk. When I stood up, there were two guards in black pointing guns at us.

Jolly stood behind them.

He was speaking to someone on his pad. "Yes! I've got them! I've got them! We're at the security desk, executive level! Yessir, we'll hold them!"

Doctor Rhee was trembling. "Dom! What did you do?"

"I did my job. I have a family. I have to think of them. And there's a reward. An executive apartment. We want to have a baby. And . . . with all your damn rules, we were never going to be able—"

Doctor Rhee shook her head sadly. "I am so sorry. I should have—"

But that's as far as she got. Coordinator Layton marched in, followed by Bruinhilda and three more guards. I recognized some of them, we used to be friends, but I guess not anymore.

I didn't know what happened to the others. I ended up in a half-finished apartment at the far end of the executive wing.

It didn't matter. We had lost.

There hadn't been time to hack the grid. There hadn't been time to upload the video. Nobody would ever know the truth.

There wasn't any furniture in this apartment. There were a few working lights and no heat at all. There was a mattress and a blanket and a bucket. Every so often, one of the guards brought me a tray. A sandwich and lemonade. I guessed they didn't know what to do with me. I wondered where everybody was. J'mee and Charles. Jeremy. Jamie. Mom. Captain Skyler. I didn't know how much time had passed, they didn't cycle the lights for night and day, so I wondered if they'd forgotten about me, but the guard was still bringing me food and once in a while emptying the bucket.

I did cry.

I hadn't done a lot of crying in my life. I'd had tantrums. I'd had raging outbursts. I'd screamed a lot. I remembered some of it. Mom had held me in a restraining hug, more than once. But then they'd put in the chip and all that stopped. But so did the crying.

Now I was crying again—but not like before. This time, I sobbed. I wept. I was alone and unhappy and I even understood why I was crying.

And then maybe it was a long day, maybe it was longer, the guard opened the door and said, "Come with me." I followed silently. She took me to another apartment. She pointed at the door to the bathroom. "Wash yourself. Put on a clean longshirt." She pushed me forward.

I wanted to stay in the shower forever. I didn't think I'd ever get all the dirty feelings off. I washed myself twice, three times, and was starting to wash again when she banged on the door and said, "That's enough. Dry yourself and come with me."

This time, there were two guards and they took me downstairs to the hearing hall, where important meetings were held. Sometimes it doubled as a courtroom. It looked like that today.

Coordinator Layton sat at the high desk and he had the gavel and the bell and he wore a black robe and a hard expression. I didn't see Mom or Lilla-Jack or Charles or J'mee—or anyone else I knew. Only Doctor Rhee. She looked sad.

The hearing must have been going on for a while. Coordinator Layton looked up as I was escorted in. "Sit down," he ordered me.

I looked around. There weren't a lot of people here. None of them had friendly faces.

"Where's my mom?"

"Sit down."

"Not until you tell me. Where's my mom?!"

Coordinator Layton took a breath. "Your mother is under arrest."

"Huh? No! Why?"

"Because she's part of the conspiracy. Now, sit down!"

I saw Doctor Rhee on the opposite side of the room. She made a quick sit-down gesture, so I sat.

Coordinator Layton was sitting on a high dais. Now he looked around at everybody else, all the people he'd appointed since taking over. "I think we can settle this matter quickly. Doctor Rhee has confirmed that turning off Kyle Martin's implant has left him susceptible to audio-visual hallucinations and delusions."

He cleared his throat and put on his official voice. "It is the opinion of this hearing that while he was under the influence of his . . . his condition, his syndrome, and without the moderating influence of his implant, and consumed with grief for his older brother, Kyle Martin was able to convince his friends from the *Cascade*, especially Charles Dingillian, that his brother and others had survived the crash of the lifter, and they went looking for him in the lava tubes, where they were lost for several days. Even worse, when they returned, young Mister Martin was even able to convince Doctor Rhee that there was substance to his delusion."

He looked at me. "Kyle Martin, the purpose of this hearing is to determine your future here on Hella. I speak for all of us, not just the people here in the room, but everyone on Hella—we have great affection for you. We have great regard for the work you have done. But . . ." He took a breath before continuing. "But you have created an uproar. You have disturbed the stability of the colony. You have done great damage. Do you understand?"

Don't argue. Don't say anything.

Oh. That was interesting.

I stayed silent.

Coordinator Layton glared at me from the high desk. "Kyle Martin, do you understand what I am saying? Everything that has happened since your chip was turned off has been a hallucination. None of it was real."

I looked to Doctor Rhee. She hadn't looked at me since I was brought into the room. She didn't look at me now.

For a moment—

Wait. What?

It never happened?

No. It was real. I was there. I saw Jamie. And Captain Skyler. And Madam Coordinator. And X-Station. And Commander Khuri.

A delusion? A hallucination?

Even the voice?

Had HARLIE planted the whole thing in my head?

No. That didn't make sense. But it did.

The only people who could confirm it weren't here. I said, "Where are Charles and J'mee?"

"They are secluded. They are legally juveniles and cannot testify in this hearing."

"But they—"

"They are the victims of your hallucination, Kyle Martin. This hearing isn't about your delusions. It's about what needs to happen next."

"Doctor Rhee? Tell them. Please—?"

"Kyle—" There was something weird about the way she said it. "Everything that happened. It's all in your head. Isn't it?"

At first I—oh, wait. She was right. It was in my head. Everything I know is in my head. What's real and what isn't real. It's all inside me.

Even the voice.

I had to think about that. I had to figure this out.

By myself.

No noise.

Just me and nuance.

Finally, I looked to Mister Layton. "I understand what you are saying."

"We cannot allow you to have any more of these hallucinations. It would create a danger to this colony. No more hallucinations. No more delusions. But—" he paused for effect "—Doctor Rhee says that we cannot turn your chip back on without your permission. It's—" He looked annoyed. "It's about patient consent. And because you are old enough for a Passage Ceremony, you are entitled to make the decision yourself. But this time, the implant will have to be programmed with much stronger behavioral restrictions than before. Will you consent to that?"

"What's the alternative?"

"That hasn't been decided. Doctor Rhee argued for this option first."

"May I ask Doctor Rhee a question?"

"You may."

"Doctor Rhee, is that true? That I was hallucinating?"

She stared straight into my eyes. "Kyle, listen to me. Listen carefully. Listen hard. What you experienced was real to you, wasn't it? It's very important that you understand that. The question—the real question is this. Was it real for anyone else? Can you tell the difference? Only you can answer that."

Yes. Nuance. Fascinating.

I closed my eyes. I pretended I was thinking. I listened to the silence in my head. There was only me in here, no one else. But if I could still hear HARLIE, then maybe I wasn't alone. How was he doing that? I had to think about this. I counted to myself. When I reached ten, I counted again.

"Kyle Martin, are you listening—?" That was Mister Layton.

When I opened my eyes, I turned to face him. I knew what to say. "I only want to do good for Hella colony. If that means I have to have my implant turned on, then please turn it on."

Layton looked to Doctor Rhee. "How soon can you arrange that?"

"I can do it from here," she said. "May I have my tablet?"

An aide passed her the unit. She took it and thumbed it to life. "Kyle, this shouldn't hurt. But you might feel a little funny—"

She tapped.

The noise came back in a roar, a torrent of information, images and sounds and smells and tastes. A cascade, an avalanche, a tsunami, an overload, a supernova of bright whiteness, it was all too much! I screamed and passed out—

—— and woke up in Med-Bay.

Jeremy was holding my hand.

The screen behind him glowed with the video we had made. Captain Skyler. Madam Coordinator. And Marley Layton explaining how she had hacked the lifter.

"Welcome back, kiddo. How are you feeling?"

I pointed at the screen. "It *was* in my head, wasn't it?"

"Yep, that's right." Jeremy squeezed my hand. "HARLIE knew there was a chance you'd get caught. So he stashed a copy in your implant. Just in case. All it needed was for you to agree to turn the chip back on. It uploaded to the grid automatically. And it'll keep replicating until Layton resigns or whatever. It's been playing forever. I guess everyone has seen it by now."

"Jeremy, how long was I out—?"

"A day and a half. Doctor Rhee had you locked away in intensive care. With a dozen guards at the door."

"Guards?"

"Don't worry. They're from the *Cascade.* Remember that meeting in your apartment? Where we figured out the lifter had been sabotaged? Captain Boynton shared that information with the colonists on the *Cascade.* They took a vote. They authorized him to serve a warrant. Three pods of rangers came down to serve as marshals. The pods came in under the horizon. Without any guidance from Winterland. And HARLIE hid their tracking. The rangers were waiting behind on the other side of the mountain until they were needed. But then Layton put Boynton under house arrest. So the rangers never got the signal. Not until the video went live."

"So there's going to be a trial?"

"I don't know." He fell silent. He looked unhappy. "No one knows where Layton is right now. Or Bruinhilda. Or the rest of them. We think they went into the caves. But one of the trucks is missing, so maybe they're heading outland. We'll find them."

"Wow." I looked around. "Hey. Where's my mom?"

"She's down at the docks right now. But she's been sitting by your bedside for a day and a half. She only left because Captain Skyler is bringing Madam Coordinator and all the others home. She wants to be there for Jamie and Emily-Faith. And Captain Skyler, of course. Captain Boynton invoked the Suspension Clause and the High Court put everything on hold until Madam Coordinator arrives. There's gonna be an emergency session. But the court will probably reappoint her. A lot of people are going to ask a lot of questions. Nobody is sure how to answer some of them yet. Because there are some things nobody wants to talk about, but I think we're going to have to. It's going to get interesting. A lot of things are going to be different. You woke up just in time."

I sat up. "Hey—"

"What?"

I put my arms around Jeremy and hugged him tight. "I'm sorry," I said.

He looked at me. "Huh? For what?"

"I had an insight. I mean, I think it's an insight. You tell me. They're still your family. And I think maybe you still might feel bad for them."

Jeremy said, "Yes. That was an insight. Thank you, Kyle. And yes, I do feel something. I feel sad. My dad is a very smart man. He could have been a great man if he hadn't been so . . . so stupid. So, yes. I feel sorry for him. And even for Bruinhilda. She wanted more than anyone could give her. But they got what they chose—" He pulled me back into the hug. "And I'm going to get what I choose."

It took a few days for everything to get sorted out.

Some of the rangers from the *Cascade* were also medics, so they wouldn't let us leave until we had all been scanned and cleared. That was a nuisance, but necessary. I didn't know what they were checking for, but medics don't scare me anymore.

The weather truck arrived—there were pictures on all the walls. They told a story about how the storm had knocked a lot of branches down and they were stuck in the purple forest until they could fab the necessary tools for clearing the way, but some of us knew better. That didn't explain why they hadn't logged in, they just said they couldn't get through, maybe it was the storm? I guessed Commander Khuri had given them the speech too. But Madam Coordinator whispered to Jeremy and Jamie and me that X-Station was going to disappear for a while anyway, and the official report would probably be sealed for a long time.

There were a lot of reunions. A lot of people were crying, Jeremy said they were crying for joy. I remember Mom hugging Jamie for a long time. Then she hugged me, which was all right with me, this time anyway. Then she went back to hugging Jamie. Somewhere in there, she also hugged Captain Skyler and kissed him too. Like I said, there was a lot of crying.

Madam Coordinator told us not to worry about the Laytons or any of their people. They were going to be exiled to Misery Point. If they worked, we'd send them supplies. If they didn't work, we wouldn't. She said it was the best the Council could come up with.

J'mee's dad was very upset that Mr. Layton was no longer a Coordinator, or even a Councilor. Her dad had been negotiating some sort of special arrangement for his supplies and equipment, and now he'd lost whatever advantage he'd thought his wealth had given him. There was no evidence to suggest that he was part of the Laytons' plot, but just the same it didn't turn out well for him. There was enough stink of collusion that he had to donate almost his entire seedbank to the colony to start looking like a hero again. But he was allowed to keep his flower seeds. J'mee said that would probably be enough for him to rebuild his fortune. It would take a while, and we'd have to allocate farm space, but people really like fresh flowers. And on Hella, they get *big.*

Madam Coordinator won the special election. Lilla-Jack and Mom both stood for seats on the Council as well, and both of them won. There was no more talk of Genetic Protection or any other part of Mr. Layton's plan.

In the spring, the *Cascade* began dropping pods as fast as we could open up new apartments and dorms. At least a hundred of the new colonists went to work expanding the farms so there would be enough food for everyone. Some of them also went to work fabbing new fabbers and new bots so we could continue the expansion of Winterland. Later, we'd transfer some of the bots up to Summerland for that expansion. A lot of the newcomers were impatient to see the leviathans in person.

Jamie and Emily-Faith moved in together. That was nice.

Mom started showing the first hint of a baby-bump. So she and Captain Skyler had a big beautiful wedding.

With chocolate cake.

And I moved in with Jeremy.

We decided to keep things the way they were. For now anyway. We didn't have to decide anything until we wanted to decide it.

It was an easy decision to make. Because the noise isn't noise anymore. It's just a much quieter part of me. Useful when I need it. Silent when I don't.

So I guess this is what happiness feels like. I'm still learning, but I could get used to it.

And the monkey—? We never found him. We searched. We checked the monitors. We scanned the entire station. It was like he never existed.

Except for one thing—I didn't tell anybody about it—but late one night, while I was lying quiet and happy next to Jeremy, waiting to fall asleep, I thought I heard a voice.

You did good, Kyle.

Maybe I imagined it, but I'm pretty sure I didn't.

APPENDIX

A Note on Time

There are 36 hours in a Hella-day, 36 days in a Hella-month, and 18 months (plus 3 days) in a Hella-year. So each Hella-year has 651 days.

651 days, at 36 hours each, comes to 23,436 hours per Hella-year.

An Earth-year, of course, has 24 hours in a day, and 365.25 days in a year. That comes to 8,766 hours per Earth-year.

As hours, at least, are the same on Hella and Earth, we can get the Hella-to-Earth-Year conversion with 23,436/8,766 = ~2.6735. Each Hella-year is approximately 2⅔ Earth-years.

See the chart for some example conversions.

HELLA-YEARS	CONVERTED TO EARTH-YEARS	NOTES
1	2.67	
2	5.35	
3	8.02	
4	10.69	
5	13.37	~Kyle's age (almost)
6	16.04	~Marley's age
10	26.74	
15	40.10	
20	53.47	
30	80.21	
40	106.94	~Hella colony's age
50	133.68	
70	187.15	
100	267.35